My Wife

ELLIE HALL

ABOUT THIS BOOK

He's a new Mr. Mom. She's a jilted bride. When her role as the nanny develops into a marriage of convenience, will playing house become less of a game?

Liam

I don't know what I'm doing. In fact, I have no idea where this kid came from. I mean, I know *that* part, but when he showed up on my doorstep, not only did I have to put everything on hold, but my hockey coach threw me into the sin bin. It might not be entirely undeserved.

Jess

I'm a certified walking, talking romance wreck, then I meet the guy who I think is my prince. On our wedding day, he leaves me at the altar. This means I'm headed back home to my small town and into Granny Dolly's meddling arms. At least there will be cookies.

Liam

I'm drowning in potty training, team commitments, and legal documents. I'm not sure how much longer I can keep my newfound father status secret.

Jess

I get a job helping the Big Bad Wolf. Yet, somehow, I don't get bit. Except by his son, who's ninety-nine percent adorable and one percent feral. Like his grumpy dad.

Liam

I was all about that loner life, but when my money-grubbing ex attempts to ruin me, I propose a marriage of convenience to my assistant. She's practically part of the furniture, almost living here rent-free. Turns out I don't mind. Kind of into it. Into her.

Jess

I need a favor that comes in the size and shape of my boss, so when he suggests we get married, I have to remind myself that it's not real. Nor are my feelings for him. Probably. Maybe a little. Like crumb-sized.

Between lingering looks, arguments over the toothpaste cap, and tingly moments, will this grumpy sunshine pair let love bloom?

<u>My Wife is the PERFECT fit if you love</u>:
- •Grumpy sunshine duos
- •Single dad
- • Slow-burn romance
- •Beauty & the Beast vibes
- •Small town romcom
- •Found family

•Closed-door content: no cheating, no swears, just sweet & swoony kisses

This is a clean, sweet, closed-door hockey romcom with lots of sweet kisses and a happily ever after. Lace up your skates and get ready to laugh, swoon, and have all the swoopy heart flutters!

READER NOTE

Dear Reader,

Welcome to Hockey Town, where the ice is slick and the love is thick! You may have already visited Cobbiton if you read any of the Nebraska Knights Holiday Hockey Romance books. But if you're new, slide into this closed door, sweet, clean hockey romantic comedy series.

Cobbiton is like your favorite cozy sweater with its charming Main Street, lots of community spirit with annual events, including the Christmas Market, 4th of July Cornament, and the Happy Hockey Days festival.

Here you'll meet a cast of quirky characters and hear all the local gossip. Between the pages, you'll experience hockey with heart, flirty skating, found family, fake dating turned real, grumpy x sunshine, second chances, and more.

There's also the recently constructed Ice Palace, a world-class arena, Once Upon a Romance bookstore, the Milk Mustache cookie truck, Busy Bee Bakery, Juniper's Hair Salon, and Spaglietti's, everyone's favorite pizza joint.

I enjoy leaving "Easter Eggs," also known as cross-world

references, fun details, and surprise cameos in my stories. Be on the hunt for characters, products, places, bands, businesses, and more from my other books. I love to hear when you spot them!

You might also notice references to the Ice Breakers from *Love on Thin Ice*, a multi-author series that includes my book *Love at First Skate*.

What's more, my author friend Gigi Blume and I teamed up and you'll spot mentions of Liam and the Knights in her book *Cross Check Christmas* in the Toronto Titans Hockey Romance series.

All the books in both of my hockey romance series (plural) stand alone but are better together for a richer reading experience.

I hope you enjoy these pucktastic page-turners and have all the swoony heart flutters.

Happy reading! ♥ Ellie

P.S. Get a free copy of *The Secret Book Boyfriend*, Gracie & Vohn's grumpy-sunshine romcom when you sign up for my weekly newsletter. It's my gift to you! She owns a book store and he's the Knights' assistant coach. You'll also have access to my bonus content library with loads of extras, including deleted scenes, missing chapters, extra epilogues, playlists, coloring pages, and lots more.

Visit elliehall.com to sign up.

1

LIAM

IF I WERE the type of guy who kept a journal, I wouldn't be able to write today's entry because my arm is asleep and hurts worse than stepping on a Lego brick—a new frontier of agony that I recently experienced.

In this house, enter at your own risk. Lesson learned. It's shoes on all the time now.

Having slept on the floor for the thirteenth night in a row, I shouldn't be surprised if I develop a full-body cramp or find a kid's toy lodged somewhere indecent. Can't afford that. Not today. After two weeks in the proverbial penalty box, I'm back on the ice.

I should be more excited. Truth is, I'm exhausted. I roll onto my back, trying to shake out the numbness in my arm which feels like I'm being stabbed with a thousand cold, tiny needles.

January in Nebraska is no joke and I'm wondering if the heating system in my new place is busted.

Last month, I moved into The Old Mill to be closer to the Ice Palace rather than commuting from Omaha. It's a factory building in Cobbiton converted into an indoor shopping space on the lower floors, offices and studios for artisans on the middle level, and four massive lofts on the upper level.

I shiver and the hairs on the back of my neck lift. I sense someone staring at me. Well, not just anyone. Risking a glance, I look up at the bed across the room. Yup. He's already awake, as usual, looking at me with wide blue-gray eyes.

I'm not keen on acknowledging that they're the exact color of mine, but the resemblance is undeniable. But that's where it ends. Whereas I'm almost six and a half feet tall, he's pint-sized.

"Morning, kid."

He blinks at me.

"We made it through another night," I mutter.

Thumb in his mouth, he watches me as I sit up and give my arm a hard shake.

He seems to shrink into his covers but still watches my every move.

Going to be real. It's unsettling.

The kid doesn't speak but has full-on meltdowns if I leave the room at bedtime. After a few sleepless nights, I tried everything. Standing in the doorway until he dozed off—turns out the floor squeaks. Sat in a chair inside the room—my footsteps must've tipped him off even though I tried to be stealthy.

Totally exhausted one night, I fell asleep slouched against the wall. It inadvertently worked like a charm, and the kid finally calmed down and slept.

I'm going to figure out a solution and it's not getting an air mattress. I'm a grown man with a king-sized bed in the master bedroom and I intend to sleep in it.

Seriously, I will.

First, we need to get our bearings. The best way I know to do that is on the ice, which will finally again happen today.

However, this may present a new problem. I've been keeping my newfound fatherhood situation on the hush.

Arm still aching with pins and needles, I continue to flap it, elbow jutted out.

The kid's lips widen around his thumb and it falls out as the corners of his lips lift ever so slightly. I've yet to see him smile. Then again, I've been told I have a resting grump face.

The puck doesn't fall far from the stick ... or something.

On my feet now, I flap my arm, desperate for it to wake up. I'm no use running defense with only one functional limb.

The kid gets to his feet and mimics me but flaps both arms. I know next to nothing about children except that I once was one long, long ago, in a lifetime far, far away.

Is he mocking me?

In a swift motion, I scowl and flap my arm more forcefully than I would to one of the guys in the locker room.

The kid's face falls and his eyes widen with alarm.

Wrong move, Ellis.

Maybe doing the chicken dance was fun for him. I'll do just about anything to keep him from crying.

"No, no, no. We'll flap, flap all morning. This rooster will make us breakfast and get ready." As he watches me flap my arms once again, his expression clears and he copies me.

I release my breath, relieved that we're not going to re-experience the first few days of him living here. It was traumatizing —for both of us.

The truth is I don't know what I'm doing. In fact, I don't know where this child came from. I mean, I know *that* part, but when he showed up on my doorstep, I had no idea what to do.

Still haven't figured it out.

I've been trying to remain normal, which means keeping the surprise addition to my household from my team, coach, family, and everyone except my lawyer until we get our footing.

Or our *strutting* like a pair of poultry, as the case may be, this morning.

I make eggs and steak for breakfast. Meal of men and champions ... not chickens.

Finally, out of a two-week penalty box, I'll need strength and fortitude.

My brother Hendrix says I'm chasing an elusive hockey high. That it's never enough. No stat is good enough. No award. No accolade.

My answer: I'll let him know when I get there. I'm so close. Or I was.

He wouldn't understand, but I have my reasons for going as hard as I do.

A heavy sigh escapes from deep in my chest.

I take the eggs off the skillet and pull the steak from the grill, serving both of us.

Some of the other guys on the team have home chefs or meal delivery. They say I should too. I don't keep a suggestion box nor did I send out a survey. How I do things is fine.

Bringing more people into my life leads to more complications.

More debt to pay.

At first, the kid just picked at his food. In contrast, I have a big appetite in the morning, and like everything else, he's started copying me.

Except for the crying. I don't do that. Ever.

After cleaning up, I say, "Kid, brush your teeth and get ready to visit Mrs. Kirby."

He looks at me blankly.

"Remember her? She's the one with the dog."

He stares at me in reply.

I show him to the bathroom and then rush to mine because recent experience has proven that if I don't shower and get ready fast, I'll find the contents of the foaming hand soap pump bottle in the toilet—wouldn't put it back in the container even if I could. Or the hallway wall redecorated with marker—yeah, the permanent kind. Yesterday, I turned my back for two seconds—okay, it was more like two minutes—and then noticed it was quiet. Too quiet. A trail of what could've been mistaken for raccoon footprints dipped in shaving cream led me to where he'd coated the window with the stuff and was drawing circles in it. Guess he couldn't keep his finger off the dispense button once he got it working.

Gone are the days of taking luxuriously long showers before and after practice. My thoughts scramble because I can't let myself think about how my game schedule is going to work with the kid.

With the bathroom door cracked open, after I shut off the water, something slams.

Wrapping a towel around my waist, I hurry to the hall, only to find the kid where I left him, standing in the bathroom, his hands by his sides, nothing out of place. Quickly assessing the rest of the loft, I figure I must've been mistaken.

I seriously need to sleep better. Now I'm hearing things.

This also means he didn't brush his teeth or get ready like I asked. When do children learn these skills?

Pressing my lips together, I race back to my room, throw on some clothes, run a comb through my hair, and grab my toothbrush.

For what seems like the hundredth time, I show him how to put on the paste and then what to do once it's in his mouth.

He came potty trained, so I figured he'd know how to do this too. Then again, he also came with a pet hermit crab and a ratty plastic bag of clothing, so go figure.

When I start brushing my teeth, he's still frozen. I repeat the directions, showing him, but he doesn't budge. Looks like it's going to be one of those days. So far, we're seventeen out of twenty-two. At this rate, I'm not going to win the Father of the Year award.

Letting out a huff, I take the toothbrush and clean his teeth for him, saying, "You're going to have to learn how to do this yourself at some point. Even chickens know how to brush their teeth."

He remains impassive ... I can't read this kid, not like my brother, who I know like a book. He'd challenge me and say something like, *Chickens don't have teeth, genius.*

Who am I fooling? I know next to nothing about barnyard animals or fatherhood.

Get it together, Ellis.

After an agonizing ten minutes of morning preparation, we're out the door and downstairs. I knock on the glass door to Mrs. Kirby's Sewing & Alterations studio. Her Maltese yaps.

To the kid, I say, "Listen, don't paint his fur with lipstick again. Mind your manners. Be good. Got it?"

He just looks from me to the door to me again.

I'm like seventy-five percent sure I can trust Mrs. Kirby, an older widow, not to blab about my situation. She thinks I'm a handyman and not a professional hockey player because I once fixed a shelf for her.

She opens the door and says, "You're five minutes late."

Also, she's what my mother would call persnickety, but stuff like that doesn't penetrate my ironclad exterior.

My response: a grunt.

But she's right, which means if I even hit one traffic light, I'm going to be late to practice after being in the sin bin for two weeks. Let's just say there was an incident.

I say, "I'll be back by four."

"And not a minute after. I have to get home to make Elizabeth her supper."

The Maltese yaps as if that's the magic word.

Mrs. Kirby passes me a piece of paper. "This is the bill to reimburse me for Elizabeth's grooming. Darlene said it was a lot of work getting the lipstick out of her fur."

I pull out my wallet and pass her the cash.

Mrs. Kirby keeps her hand out and I realize she wants payment for babysitting up front.

I slap a large bill into her palm. "I'll give you the rest when I pick him up."

"At four," she repeats.

"At four," I confirm.

Patting the kid on the head, I make my getaway. I rush down the hall, take the stairs, which will be quicker than the elevator, and race through the parking garage.

For the next few hours, I have my life back.

2

JESS

TECHNICALLY, I can't claim that I've been left at the altar. I haven't made it that far. Yet.

While I wait in the dressing room, dubbed the "Bridal Suite" for today's purposes in one of Los Angeles's old Art Déco theaters, I tell myself Rexlan is stuck in traffic. That he's having a wardrobe malfunction. It could be that he forgot to feed the dog. Not that he has one. Perhaps he was pet-sitting and failed to mention it to me.

Once, I suggested we get a puppy. From the other room, his mother shouted a resounding no because of the skinks—specifically the lance skin, a legless kind. They're a type of lizard that looks like a snake. She has them in abundance. At first, I thought it was a bit eccentric. This is LA, after all, but it's a bit odd how she's built her life around lizards.

"Where are you, Rexlan?" I whisper.

In the last month or so, he's neglected to tell me about several late-night meetings, work trips, and important appointments to further the reach of the Skink Society—his mother's pet project turned six-figure online venture. Could he have forgotten our wedding day?

The guy is busy and has his assistant in a tizzy. Every time I've seen Cassleigh lately, her cheeks flame red like Rexlan has been making her work so hard she can scarcely catch her breath.

That's how I feel now. My chest tightens because he has to know this is our big day. The one we've planned for. Well, the one his mother orchestrated, but still.

Where is he?

Standing behind a pair of wooden doors inlaid with etched glass while the guests eagerly await our appearance, I nervously bounce on my toes.

A grandfather clock ticks loudly, punishing me with worry as the seconds pass. A cold sweat prickles against the itchy crinoline inside my wedding gown—or that could be the special blue collie webbed lizard skin pouch filled with crystals that Sorsha Coogan, Rexlan's mother, sewed inside so I'd have something old, new, borrowed, and blue—technically, the thread was the new thing.

If you ask me, her belief in the omnipotence of skinks is a big load of nonsense. But people buy it every day. I've spent the last three months packaging and mailing orders for her website, among other things.

This family wants me to be part of theirs, so how can I say no? After all, this is everything I've ever wanted.

Maybe except for the wedding cake. I would've gone with personal-size Bundts in a variety of flavors for everyone.

Also, I didn't get a say about the guest list.

This wedding gown wasn't my choice either.

According to Sorsha, it's a trumpet fit, which I read does not complement my figure, but my *momster*-in-law to-be knows best. It's more like a tube on the top, giving way to a wide skirt.

In the back is a bustle and a long train. I look like a bloated, upside-down goose. I set out to be an actress but didn't have this in mind.

I dab my forehead with a tissue as the women in my bridal party mutedly whisper among themselves.

"Do you have your phone?" asks Amy, one of the bridesmaids.

Pamberlie, Rexlan's sister and the maid of honor, just moved back to Los Angeles from Phoenix a few days after Christmas last month. She waves her hand dismissively. "Don't make a fuss. He'll be here. Probably."

He, being my fiancé, also said he'd be home from a business trip to Singapore on my birthday, but flight delays left him stranded. Not that I hold that against him. But it didn't escape my notice that when unforeseen circumstances attempt to keep him from his important meetings, he finds a way. Or, rather, Cassleigh does.

Speaking of, I'm surprised she's not here. Despite Sorsha insisting Cassleigh not join us, Rexlan placed her at a top table, claiming she's the one who keeps him afloat.

I want to think that's my role.

The MOG, the mother of the groom, waves her phone. "Rexlan is not answering my calls. He always picks up for me. You two looked like you argued last night." The line between her eyebrows is already an inch deep.

I look around as if she could be speaking to anyone but me. My mouth opens and closes. "Argued? No."

"There was tension during the rehearsal dinner," she accuses.

"He wanted to leave early. Said he had a few things to finish up for the Skink Society." I assumed it was because we'd be gone for ten days on our honeymoon.

"He's turning into his father."

I hope not. The man is on wife number six.

"Where's Rex's assistant? She always knows where he is," Pamberlie says.

The wedding planner appears and pumps her hands in a slow-down motion. "Everyone relax. This happens all the time."

"It does?" I read at least twenty-five hundred square feet worth of wedding magazines along with the equivalent in blog articles and it seems rare for a groom to be late.

"He probably has a good reason. A great one. No one would pass up their wedding day, especially to their one true love." The wedding planner's smile is one part consolation and one part pity. Or perhaps I'm too much in my head.

"I assumed he'd pick someone taller," Pamberlie says, towering over me. She's a former model with a slender build that is a perfect contrast to my curvy one.

An uneasy feeling winds its way through me like the slithering of a snake. Deep down, it was Sorsha who pushed us into this marriage because she wanted her son to quit playing video games, fooling around with some girl from high school, and grow up.

Apparently, I impressed her with my organizational skills, self-motivation, and how I was a maverick when it came to maintaining a website and online store for her, ahem, 'Business.'

The truth is, everything I know about technology, I learned from video tutorials.

Another ten minutes pass. The wisps of hair that stylishly hang from my updo stick to my neck. I desperately need to reapply deodorant and have a sudden craving for a piece of chocolate.

Okay, that's a lie. I want a vat of it. But that's not going to help me now.

At the cake tasting, Sorsha shamed me for licking the frosting off my finger. Later, I overheard her telling the wedding planner that we were having a vanilla wedding. No chocolate allowed.

I suppose that's fitting for me because, after everything that happened before I met Rexlan, I'd made a vanilla life for myself. It was simple, quiet, and some would say boring. But I've had enough excitement to last a lifetime.

Then Prince Rexlan came along. He's not actually royalty, but he swept me off my feet ... and maybe got cold feet. I pray that's not the case.

"Do you think he has the time or day wrong?" says Rory, another one of the bridesmaids—all chosen from among Sorsha's Skink Society—where we all help with customer service, packaging orders, and answering emails. Not to mention, I have a high rate of confidence it's a lizard-worshipping cult.

I'm afraid when we return from the honeymoon, Sorsha is going to try to induct me into it.

"Typical Rexlan. He was late for graduation because he was hooking up with Amy in the library—probably the only time he set foot in there," Pamberlie says.

Amy rolls her eyes but avoids looking at me. "That's not true. We'd meet there to study biology all the time." Her cheeks turn red.

Pamberlie huffs. "Where are all the groomsmen? Their one job was to get Rex here on time."

The wedding planner interjects, "Actually, for a successful wedding, groomsmen have a variety of responsibilities, ranging from—"

Sorsha shoots me the stink eye—skink eye?—as if the timeline going off the rails is my fault.

I could really use a family of my own right now, a hug even, someone to assure me that everything is going to be okay. I kind of thought the Coogans were my magic family goose. The uneasiness in my stomach that's built up for the last few months suggests I've been living in a delusion. But it's too late to go back now, right?

Several people talk at once, then abruptly go quiet when my fiancé's voice filters through the room. Relief rushes through me. Rexlan is outside and probably has a reasonable explanation for his tardiness.

"Yay! It's officially our wedding day. For a second there, I was afraid he wasn't going to show up." The shakiness in my voice ebbs with each word as he continues to talk.

His voice is coming from a cell phone. In the background of the video call are the sounds of laughter, talking, loud music, and ... that can't be right.

I frown and the flutters in my stomach nosedive into a stony pit filled with spikes and electric eels. Dramatic, but true.

Sorsha lifts her phone to eye level and barks, "Rexlan Levi Coogan, where are you?"

Only, he doesn't answer and instead says, "Babe, I'm going to make you the happiest wife on the planet. Show me the rock, Mrs. Coogan. Show the world!"

I look around, confused, because everyone in this room has commented on the dainty emerald engagement ring Sorsha gave Rexlan for me to have. The others must be confused too because they murmur and whisper, but I can't quite make out the distinct words over the fuzziness in my ears. I have a fleeting thought about my grandmother, who is Deaf.

We're not blood relatives, but she adopted me when I was in high school. The fact that I didn't tell her or my best friend Cara about this wedding makes me feel like I'm going to break out with a rash of shame.

"How can I be Mrs. Coogan, if we're not yet married?" I glance at Sorsha. "Unless he means you."

She lowers her phone, but not before I glimpse Rexlan, Cassleigh, and the unmistakable flash of a slot machine against the backdrop of Las Vegas.

"Let's go back to the room and start our honeymoon," Rexlan says from the phone.

A couple of the women gasp, Amy loudest of all.

Pamberlie's eyes flash and her expression turns murderous.

Amy says, "Is he standing her up?"

Reality barrels my way like a meteor on a collision course with Earth, sucking all the air from the room. "Can I talk to him?"

"Obviously, he's occupied at the moment, Jess," Pamberlie hisses.

Unsteady, my body freezes over and my teeth start chattering. My pulse thunders. I look around for a place to sit down, but the bridal party surrounds me.

Rory asks, "Was that Cassleigh with Rexlan?"

Amy says, "Why are they in Vegas and not here?"

She must not have been at the top of her academic class.

The shiny, sparkly wedding day world splinters and shatters around me as my eyes brim with tears of embarrassment.

"Rexlan, my fiancé, just eloped with Cassleigh in Las Vegas." I realize I've said this out loud in an eerily calm voice.

The wedding planner says, "We need to take action. Evasive or decisive, your call."

I'm about to ask her to please make a brief but clear announcement to the guests when Sorsha interrupts. "This is beyond humiliating. I'll never live this down." I want to comfort her, but have several feet of satin, lace, and other fancy fabrics along with a mountain of what very much feels like animosity between us.

Then to me, she adds, "I always said you were flaky."

Well then.

In the recounts of awful mothers of the bride or groom in the wedding articles I read, mom-zilla types would often deflect and place blame.

Turning my attention to the wedding planner, who has been the consummate professional, even when Sorsha requested nineteen change orders. I kept track because I'd sneak a foil-wrapped Dove chocolate into the wedding planner's purse each time.

Sorsha's accusatory gaze is trained on me. "You are such an embarrassment. I knew we shouldn't have gone through with this. I never wanted my son to marry you, anyway."

Ouch. I wince.

Pamberlie's eyes narrow. "Mother, I distinctly recall you saying that Jess is better than Cassleigh because the day Rex brought her home after band practice in high school, she was grossed out by the skinks."

Sorsha says, "I forbid it! Rexlan can not be with that little brat."

"Too late," Pamberlie says.

Not only did I just lose my fiancé, this means I've also lost my job. There's no way I can run the Skink Society shop and website now.

Pamberlie continues, "My brother is such a loser. I can't believe you didn't see right through him. All the late nights, the trips, and when he dipped out of the elaborate three-month anniversary plans you made because he supposedly just had to go to a modern art gallery opening. Rex wouldn't know art from his elbow." She shakes her head as if royally disappointed in my naïveté.

But there's a difference between wanting to deny reality and facing the aftermath if I confront it.

"Rexlan and Cassleigh sound lovely together," Rory says with a little flourish at the end of the new Mrs. Coogan's name like *-leigh* which rhymes with *day*. As in, this was supposed to be my wedding day.

"I thought it was Cass-lee," Amy says, pronouncing the last part the way Rexlan's assistant does.

"Does it matter?" Pamberlie asks.

"She's your new sister-in-law!" Amy says with a cheer.

Everyone else has the decency to remain quiet.

The sadness that threatened to consume me turns hard. I'm not angry, more like resolved.

To leave.

Now.

I thank the bridal party and the wedding planner.

She asks, "What would you like me to tell the guests?"

"Please express my gratitude for their time and my regrets. You can let them know Rexlan got married today ... to another woman. They can donate their gifts to a charity of their choice."

Sorsha turns on her and says, "Not so fast. I pay, so you do what I say."

The wedding planner goes still, but before she receives instruction, Sorsha says to me, "You ruined everything, Jess. I knew you were just trying to strike it big with our family's empire."

Eyes bulging, I shake my head.

Pamberlie crows a laugh. "That's rich, coming from you, Mother, living off the child support for Rex and me and sour grapes."

She hisses, "That's Liz-Fizz, an all-natural lizard elixir, not *grape juice*."

Through a crack in the door, I eye the cake, standing alone in an adjacent room and awaiting the reception. As a hobby baker, I asked if I could handle the cake. Of course, Sorsha said no. But still, cake is cake.

Biting the inside of my lip, I calculate how quickly I'll be able to cross the floor in these shoes and make it to the door.

Ignoring her daughter, Sorsha sneers and to me, she says, "You'll pay for this."

Whatever fabric glue, stitching, and hair spray hold me together threatens to dissolve, but I won't let these people see me cry. No one ever has.

Still in my gown and with my purse over my shoulder, I rush toward the wedding cake, pick it up, and blaze through the doors, gulping the fresh and balmy air when it suddenly starts to rain.

3
LIAM

I GUN it all the way to the Ice Palace, the Nebraska Knights practice facility and arena across town as if I'm trying to outrun my new normal—sleeping on the floor, waking up with a kid staring at me, and doing the chicken dance at the break of dawn.

Being a father.

The thought squeezes my brain and my chest.

Having blazed through every scenario in my mind about how this happened, and why Pam, who hardly qualifies as my ex, thought it was a good idea *not* to tell me that we had a kid, I repeatedly find myself at a dead end. She's taken herself out of the picture, so it's not like I can give him back.

I've considered detouring and finding someone else to take care of him. His nose is constantly running—he refuses to learn how to blow it. There's the sleeping issue. Plus, he refuses to talk.

I'm not totally stone-hearted and imagine he's had a tough time. But what am I going to do? I can't turn my back on him.

However, I can't square the circle that is my hockey career and this new responsibility that I didn't know existed.

To say I'm in a belabored state of shock is an understatement.

I've already broken a sweat by the time I reach the locker room, drop my gear, and get to the gym. I find my name on the roster posted on the wall. Today I'm in Group C, highlighting my recent demotion.

"Hey, look who is back," crows Grimaldi, third-string wing.

Great, I'm with the benders and bench warmers.

Grady claps me on the back as he exits the weight room with Group B.

I've played for two other teams in my career and every coach, assistant coach, trainer, and everyone in between has a different way of doing things. Coach Tom Badaszek is the most hardcore of them all, which is why it shouldn't surprise me to find him in the gym.

But it does.

I'd expect him to be in the rink with Group A right now.

Grimaldi says, "So how was the time-out chair?"

I grunt.

"Was the naughty step really that bad?"

I tighten the laces on my trainers and get in line for the equipment rotation.

Crouched, I sense a figure looming over me. If Grimaldi is trying to assert himself in the pecking order—seriously, what is it with the chicken stuff today?—he has another thing coming.

When I glance up, Badaszek gives me a nod. Rising to my feet, I stand several solid inches taller than him and am not easily intimidated, except by arguably one of the greatest coaches that has ever lived—and fatherhood. That has me running like a chicken with its head cut off.

Giving my head a little shake, I dismiss those foolish thoughts and lengthen my spine. "Morning, sir."

He nods mildly. "During your hiatus, did you get everything sorted out?"

"Everything?" I ask dumbly.

His tone is firm when he replies, "Yes. Everything."

I blink a few times, much like the kid looking at me wide-eyed this morning. I got nothing sorted out.

The recent stress, impairing my judgment, may have been what got me temporarily put in a time-out.

Wait. Badaszek can't know about the kid, can he?

"Sir, nothing like what happened during the game against the Titans will happen again."

His gaze penetrates me for one long moment as if he's measuring the truth in my words.

I can assure him that my laughter was a one-time-only event. Nothing in my life is remotely funny right now—wasn't then either, but I may have had a hysterical break from reality for thirty seconds that resulted in me laughing at the coach in front of the entire team.

Not my finest hour, never mind the fact that I never laugh at anything. Ever.

Badaszek says, "You signed up for this knowing full well how things work."

"Yes, sir, of course."

Unlike some teams, the Nebraska Knights are not party boys. We're men built for a gladiator sport and are expected to show up for practice and games prepared not just to give one hundred percent. No, Badaszek requires two hundred percent. I bring three hundred.

That's not to say we don't have fun, but you won't find any of our guys "playing the field." Puck bunnies aren't welcome.

The general debauchery sometimes found among high-paid athletes is not tolerated.

Or else.

I won't lie and say I haven't had a few flirtations in the past —the kid being a prime example of that. However, I can promise I won't be having that kind of fun in the future. The results of Pam's burning me, means I don't want or plan on having so much as a fling or a relationship. The end.

"Glad that we're on the same page," Badaszek says and walks to the front of the room, where he addresses the team in an uncharacteristically cheerful voice.

As he scans Group C, he pauses on me, making me feel jumpy inside—a rarity. If I were to describe myself in a few words, it would be "Rock Solid." If someone asked my brother Hendrix, he'd call me the golden boy. Ingrid, our sister, would say I'm Mr. Muddy Boots and to skate faster. As if.

Usually, nothing rattles me.

But I've been shaken—like a snow globe—on this chilly winter day and I can't figure out which way is up. Right now, I feel like I'm sliding down a slippery chute like in the popular board game. Would the kid like that? Is he old enough to play or would he chew on the pieces?

Too bad he didn't come with a manual. My mother would know these things, but then she'd also have to know she's a grandmother and that makes me feel like the ice is cracking beneath my feet.

Badaszek demands my attention when he continues, "Glad you all joined us today. As you know, I'm in the business of making not just a good team, but a great one. Exceptional. Stanley Cup winners."

The guys cheer.

"Someone in your life gave you the, 'You'll never make it to the NHL' talk, or maybe it was a voice in your head casting doubt. Yet here you are. In five, ten, fifteen years, when you're retired, don't be stuck with coulda, shoulda, woulda's. Be like a hockey puck. Hard, fast, and dangerous if you hit someone in the face."

His gaze flits toward me again, the enforcer, my brute strength unleashed during extenuating circumstances like a game against the Storm, who're known for unnecessary roughness.

"Whether pressure is coming from people in your life or you're putting it on yourself, remember you have nothing to lose, except for a few teeth ... and everything to gain if you give your all."

Grimaldi elbows me. "And a time out."

Badaszek's eyes narrow. "After a brief leave of absence, that I trust gave Ellis some time to reset and realign his priorities, I'm pleased to announce that he's our new captain."

I don't know the technicalities of how sound travels or how the ear works, for that matter, but like when in the shower this morning, I must be hearing things.

Grimaldi grumbles, "If that's the case, I'm going to get the whistle more often and start wearing my time in the penalty box with a badge of honor."

Assistant Coach Vohn Brandt all but growls at him in warning.

"Congratulations, Ellis," Coach says, confirming what I heard.

All eyes are on me, some approving, others filled with the same question I have.

Why?

I fight the urge to sit on the floor and put my head between my legs and breathe into a paper bag. Instead, I tell them to do their job and walk to the front of the room. Maybe I strut. I can't be sure. Never mind my arm, my entire body feels numb.

Coach extends his hand for me to shake. His grip is firm. Mine is too. But my grasp on reality feels slippery.

"Sir, this means a lot, but I couldn't possibly be team captain." I try not to glance around the room at the third-string players. Wouldn't he announce this to the whole team, or at the very least, have me practice with the A-list? Or pick someone from that group?

Then I realize. This is a joke. On me.

Appointing me team captain after I laughed in Coach Badaszek's face during the Titans game is ludicrous.

He's using me as an example, showing the players whose egos might be bloated enough to think they can get away with mischief that they will be remanded to hockey joke jail.

I can't see my expression, but I'm not the slightest bit amused. Except for that one lapse in judgment, I've been nothing but an asset to this organization. I work hard and show up early—until recently.

Meanwhile, my phone has been vibrating in my pocket. I worry that it's Mrs. Kirby, meaning I probably won't get away with staying late. She told me to be back at four and not a second later.

Vohn, who rivals me in surliness—at least that's what I've been told—asks, "Done?"

Badaszek rubs his hands together. "No, we're just getting started."

"I mean with Ellis. I need to go over the code of conduct and expectations with our new captain. Cara has some papers for him to sign, too." Vohn barely disguises the roll of his eyes.

I never knew being captain was so formal, but this can't be real.

Clearing my throat, I say, "Sir, with all due respect, I sincerely apologize for what happened during the game, but I cannot—"

Badaszek gives a short nod. "Yes, I read your letter."

A few of the guys snicker.

Yeah, I wrote the coach a letter of apology. When the incident happened, I was running on less than two hours of sleep and handfuls of Goldfish Crackers and Gummy Bears—I'm convinced they're both kid-crack. Not that I admitted any of that to him. More like I took responsibility for being a disrespectful idiot.

"I cannot accept this position."

He claps me on the back, hard. Either that or an earthquake struck Nebraska and jostled me. "Time to man up. Step into a leadership role."

My mouth opens and closes as my coach scrutinizes me, practically dares me with his eyes.

He leans in and says, "We're a team. No one wins alone. Focus, prepare, and expect the best from yourself and the guys." He pauses before adding, "The key is knowing when to press and when to ask for *help*."

In my dictionary, *help* is a dirty word.

Then again, I'm not sure I've heard right because the guys are clapping, realizing now that this isn't a joke. They congratulate me as I make my way to the door to join Vohn.

Yesterday, I was an underdog. Now I'm the top dog.

It hardly seems fair.

This also means that Redd must've turned in the "C." He has a few rugrats and I think his wife is pregnant again, so being captain was probably too much with his schedule.

The reality that it's going to be impossible for me stops me in my tracks. Vohn notices I'm not beside him and stops. "Is there a problem?"

Yes. No. Both.

I grunt, which is admittedly, my response to most things.

Keeping pace with Brandt through the hall, he's quiet, but that's no surprise.

Outside Coach Badaszek's office door, he says, "If you're wondering whether you deserve this, you don't."

"I'm well aware."

So why did Coach give me this honor and responsibility?

For the second time in about three weeks, I've been blindsided. First, when a toddler that I didn't know existed appeared in the lobby of the Old Mill building with a note taped to his shirt from his mother—my ancient history ex.

Now this.

Vohn tips his head, indicating I enter the office where Cara Arsenault, one of Badaszek's triplet daughters and his assistant, will get my paperwork squared away.

"I'm missing training," I say, trying to delay this.

"You missed two weeks of training."

"I hit the gym." Sort of. I mostly had the kid sit on my back while I did push-ups. Bringing him to the building's new workout room was too risky.

"Why did you walk me to the office like a child?" I ask, genuinely curious.

He snorts. "Because I refused to believe Badaszek named you captain until I saw it with my own eyes."

Ignoring what sounds like a rude comment, I nod in agreement. Vohn and I are more alike than not, shooting from the hip.

"If you think someone else would do a better job ..."

"Still so cocky even after getting benched." He shakes his head and starts to walk away.

But that's not how I meant it. More like he should nominate someone else. Anyone but me. I can't handle this right now. Not that I'd ever admit it.

Entering Cara's office, I expect to catch a whiff of failure, because that's what this feels like, or more accurately, failing upward. Instead, a candle burns with a label that reads *Egg Nog on Ice by Candlegram*. Must've been a holdover from Christmas.

I practically stumble. It's eleven months away, but does Santa visit the kid? Do I have to wrap gifts? Put up a tree? I brush my hand across my forehead.

"Good morning, Captain," Cara says, saluting me with a cheerful smile.

I grunt.

"That kind of day, huh?" she says, reading me.

More like that kind of month.

She types on the computer and then passes me a digital tablet with the Knights logo on top. "A few quick forms for you to sign, confirming your commitment as team captain."

My phone beeps in my pocket again. I skim the first form and add my signature with the stylus. The screen freezes on the next one and while Cara wrestles with technology, my phone continues to beep.

Even though this is a more formal process than I thought, I take a peek at my device, praying the kid didn't set the building on fire or shave Elizabeth—the Maltese. Who names their dog that? Then again, the kid's birth certificate was a surprise.

The messages are a bunch of Monday morning meme nonsense from my sibling group chat, a reminder for my haircut appointment, and nine missed calls from Mrs. Kirby. I tell myself that she's just reminding me to be on time. But sweat beads on my upper lip.

"Are you okay?" Cara asks.

I nod longer than is customary as if trying to convince myself that I'm all right. My phone, still in my hand, vibrates.

"Do you need to get that?" she asks.

I shake my head, also longer than necessary as if trying to

convince myself that my reply to Cara's question is true. *Yes, I'm okay.* Debatable.

"Being the Knights team captain comes with a lot of extra responsibilities. Dadaszek must really respect and admire your leadership skills," she says offhandedly all the while presenting me with the last digital form to sign.

Meanwhile, my phone buzzes like an alarm clock. Maybe I need to wake up from a bad dream. But it's just Mrs. Kirby, reminding me not to be late.

4

JESS

I FEEL like a wet paper bag. Soaked in my wedding gown, I race to the hotel across the street from the theater where we'd planned to spend the night before leaving tomorrow for our honeymoon.

Three-quarters of the way there, I have to stop because I get a cramp in my side.

The shred sessions Sorsha insisted I offer up to the skinks in homage so I fit into my dress—there was a lot of Bundt baking in the lead-up to the wedding day—did not prepare me for this kind of workout.

The relentless sobbing also causes me to suck wind. While at the cross signal, a garbage truck takes the turn a bit too fast and splashes the hem of my gown with filthy puddle water—I think there's an empty food-to-go container and an ookey baby wipe floating in it.

Instead of going inside the swanky hotel, freshening up, and hiding under the bed like a normal person, I get behind the wheel of my Nissan that came off the factory floor the same year I was born.

Before I realize it, I'm on the freeway, heading northeast.

I thought today was the first day of the rest of my life.

Rexlan wasn't late. He was eloping.

Sorsha's final comment echoes in my ears.

You'll pay for this.

I wasn't using the Coogan family to strike it big.

When I was looking for a room to sublet in Los Angeles, Sorsha welcomed me. Sure, I thought it was odd that she only wore green and her entire house was outfitted in the same color with a reptile motif, but the rent was right and she offered me a job managing her website.

Considering I was an unemployed, aspiring actress, how could I say no?

Some people follow experts and others believe in the healing power of teas and tinctures. Sorsha purports that skinks are the solution to all of life's ills and the Skink Society holds secrets to success, health, and wealth.

With her encouragement, and lizard love potions (which I merely pretended to consume) Rexlan and I clicked ... maybe ... when we were together ... under her watch.

Looking back, I should've seen the warning signs. When his "friend" from high school moved back to town, he was away a lot. Sorsha was not enthusiastic, but supposedly he was gaining traction and signing big deals for her to host conventions and give talks all over the world.

Turns out he was with Cassleigh.

I'm such a fool.

The ruined wedding cake rides in the passenger seat. I gather a clump and stuff it into my mouth as my thoughts flail, much like my life, much like the red windsock tube man outside a car dealership gusting in the wind with a sign that says *Zero Percent Financing.*

I feel like a big zero. So far, the scoreboard of my life has me down points and the opposition in the lead.

Today, I went from the highest of highs to plunging into the pits of despair.

Driving in silence, I don't stop until the little red low gas indicator light dings when I'm still outside Las Vegas. That means I've been driving for about four hours since leaving Los Angeles, primarily on autopilot. That also means I could stop, track down Rexlan, and give him a piece of my mind—but not a piece of the remaining and slightly lumpen, soggy wedding cake. No, instead he deserves a knuckle sandwich, but even that might be too good for him and I tell myself not to waste another thought on the jerk.

Running on fumes and—okay, fine—some very nasty fantasies of Rexlan accidentally falling out of a window (into the hotel pool), I don't want to make his new wife a widow, but maybe he can experience that terrible swooping in his stomach as his world speeds by. Or losing every last cent at a casino or waking up outside a twenty-four-hour club (I've heard the sidewalks can get mighty gross).

I tap the dashboard. "Come on, Shy Eye Good Guy. We can do it."

I'm heading back to the small town I declared home after years in and out of the homes of foster care families until I landed at a little house on Silver Queen Street and my life changed forever.

On the upside, I'll soon be in Grandma Dolly's meddling arms. At least there will be cookies.

After getting gas, I head toward the rest stop building. I can't help but feel people staring at me. A little girl's lips quiver and she whispers to her mom about the scary lady. It's getting late and I've taken a personal safety class. I prepare to attack if anyone comes at the pair as they get into their car.

After going to the bathroom, I gird myself as a terrifying woman emerges from the stall. Her hair is plastered to her head like a wet cat. Makeup streaks down her cheeks, reminding me of a sad clown, and her beauty pageant gown droops like a tulip in desperate need of water and sunlight.

Oh, wait. That's me.

My hands slap my cheeks. I'm the scary lady!

I tug on the paper towel from the automatic dispenser, but the machine doesn't refresh them quickly enough. I need a bath, now. My look is horror movie bride and it's not pretty.

Rubbing the rough paper against my face until my cheeks are pink, I manage to remove much of the waterproof makeup. Using my fingers, I try to add body to my limp and damp hair while smoothing it at the same time, resulting in my looking like a windblown ball of yarn.

Head down, I hurry outside and get behind the wheel of the Nissan. I drop my forehead against it.

What. Am. I. Going. To. Do?

In a fit of embarrassment and uncertainty, I started driving out of LA. But now what? My whole life is back in Los Angeles. At least I have my purse, which contains chocolate. Three pieces, which will not be enough no matter if I return the way I came or press on.

Even though I look like a zombie bride—at the next rest stop, I grab a variety of chocolates, reminding me of Granny Dolly's cure for everything.

Chocolate chip cookies.

It will be nice to visit her, especially since she couldn't come to the wedding that wasn't ... because I didn't invite her. I realize now that perhaps I was lured a little farther down the Skink Society path than I realized. But for once, it was so nice to be wanted, to feel like I belonged somewhere, even if it was a thinly glazed lie.

My responsibilities back in Los Angeles are minimal, namely the houseplants I can't seem to keep alive. Maybe this means marriage, motherhood, and family life aren't in the cards for me.

Wilting, I hang my head.

After a canceled wedding, I'd expect my phone to beep with messages and ring with calls from people checking on me and offering support, or to get the juicy gossip. However, it remains painfully silent, highlighting the life I had with Rexlan and his family was more in my mind than rooted in reality.

Likely, I'm part of a social media post about a jilted bride. I don't dare check.

After also getting a large coffee, I resolve to continue north to Nebraska. When I cross the Colorado border, a sane person not dressed in their wedding gown would book a hotel room, but I've been battling insomnia for months. My mind wanders down a rabbit trail as the beams of headlights pass in the other direction.

My sleeping issue started shortly after Sorsha insisted Rexlan and I get married. During the next hours, I try to connect the dots, analyzing situations and circumstances that should've been red flags, warning me that the long hours he spent with Cassleigh were suspicious.

But the painful truth is that my relationship with Rexlan and the idea that I was part of his family was one big stamp of approval.

The girl who'd been abandoned was adored.

The girl who was guarded could trust.

The girl who came from nothing had a future.

Or so I thought.

The prolonged silence and darkness presses against me from all sides. I tune the radio until I land on a Taylor Swift breakup song which is oh-so perfect. I sing along until it turns to static. Unable to find another station, I switch to the AM frequency. It isn't lost on me that it's past midnight, technically a.m. now as I barrel north.

A late night, er, early morning talk show comes on and the DJ invites listeners to call in to discuss their love life woes. Before the commercial break, I catch the back half of a guy concerned that his girlfriend won't introduce him to her BFFs. Sounds familiar. When DJ Melody comes back on the air, I learn the show is called Love Lines After Dark. Dawn still feels far away, so I tell my phone to dial the number.

DJ Melody's cool, soothing voice welcomes me to the live call. "Give us the report on your relationship and we'll see if we can dial it in."

I blurt, "I'm a jilted bride on the run."

Belatedly realizing that might sound like I committed a crime of passion, in barebones detail, I relay what happened.

DJ Melody says, "That's how it ended. Go back and tell us how it started."

As I cruise along the empty ribbon of road, I retrace my steps back to the beginning when Rexlan kissed me after a particularly intense fight scene on his video game followed by his character getting cozy with the woman he rescued from a belligerent bear.

DJ Melody chuckles softly, sweetly. "We've all been there. Well, not *there*, but when physical feelings get the best of us, reason goes out the door."

"His mother encouraged it ... I think it was because she didn't like the woman who turned out to be his real girlfriend." I don't say Cassleigh's name, but from what I've gleaned, she didn't buy into the whole skink thing. I didn't either, but I do have a habit of looking on the bright side, smiling, and nodding politely.

"Do you think Sorsha was the type never to find fault with her son?"

I snort a laugh through my nose. "You got that right. I take it you've heard stories like this before."

"Every night. So now what? What's next for our jilted bride?"

"I guess I'm going home to pretend this didn't happen."

"That seems like it will be hard to do."

I say, "Not really. My grandmother makes really good cookies."

She chuckles. "I mean the forgetting part."

A long sigh escapes because she's probably right, but in the last hours, I've gone from feeling panicked to dazed, but now something like a wave of relief washes over me.

DJ Melody says, "I only know part of the story and it's still fresh, but in case we never speak again, I'd like to suggest something. Take it, stash it somewhere in your mind, and it'll be there waiting for you when you're ready."

Even though she can't see me, I lean in, eagerly wondering what she's going to say.

"In time, allow yourself to forgive your ex-fiancé, Sorsha, and everyone who hurt you, maybe even going all the way back to when things happened that made you cling to a need to feel wanted."

The advice is like pouring alcohol on a wound. It stings for a moment, but I know it's for the best and will ultimately help me.

"And don't discount love in your future. I don't think your ex was the one. Perhaps you came close to jumping into things with him before you were ready and this was a wake-up. A rude one, but still. Maybe you came across a prince when really what you deserve is a king."

We end the call, but DJ Melody's words stick with me for the remainder of the drive. I did think Rexlan was my prince charming, which would make me a princess—something I could only dream of as a child before I realized that the world is made up of rakes and rogues, bounders and cads, more than real royalty.

Will I find a king? Doubtful, but I lift my chin and keep on keepin' on.

5

JESS

HELLO, *Hockey Town.*

As I roll into Cobbiton, the small town where Grandma Dolly lives, I pass the massive Ice Palace sports complex. It's the home arena for the Knights, the Nebraska hockey team. While I'm here, I'll definitely be taking a break from all manner of men, whether they wear a crown or a helmet.

I have nothing against the sport, in fact, Grandma Dolly is a super fan, but I left here telling myself when I returned, I'd be a new and improved version of myself, having succeeded at life. Employed, married, and with a happily ever after at the ready.

The plan was not to be a wedding day reject. Rather, I wanted to make it on my own.

No sooner do I turn onto Main Street, than I need to use the ladies' room. Actually, it's more of an emergency and I can hardly appreciate how the pale pastel sky paints Cobbiton with watercolor brush strokes. I've always loved the early morning before most people are awake—these days I see it more than is healthy, being up most of the night since normal sleep habits are a rarity.

Just like everyone in this quirky town, the main street, intersecting 4th, has its own unique character. We have Once Upon a Romance, a bookstore; Spaglietti's which has the best meatballs; the Buy & Bargain, my favorite thrift store ever; and what looks like a new hair salon.

Unless you're Mrs. Gormely, the town gossip, the friendly chatter of the townsfolk fills the air, except right now. Only the bakery is open on this cold winter morning. Fresh bread, pastries, and pies hide behind its steamy window.

I never let myself get too comfortable anywhere because I inevitably have to leave. However, I have nowhere left to go. Cobbiton is my safety net and unfortunately, it has holes in it.

I park on the street and hoist my wedding gown a few inches so it doesn't drag on the frozen ground.

Inside the Busy Bee Bakery, the sign on the bathroom door says, *For Paying Customers Only*. I've been running on caffeine and fumes, so I may as well get another coffee and maybe at least a couple of Nina's famous Danish kringle pastries with honey and pecans—I'll surprise Grandma Dolly with an assortment of baked goods.

The buttery scent and the coffee-infused air give me a second wind. Or perhaps I'm on my third ... or fourth wind? I've lost count.

It kind of feels good to be home. Yet, I'm not ready to face the public if I run into anyone who asks why I'm wearing a wedding gown and makeup that's over twenty-four hours old. I plaster on my 'Everything is fine face,' trying not to stand out too much, and get in line behind a tall man and a toddler.

Nina, who owns the bakery, is the friendliest person on the planet, but that also means she chats up all the customers, asking about their lives and the day ahead.

That's all to say, the line tends to move slowly.

I have to pee so badly I can feel it in my eyeballs. Short of leaping over the counter and retrieving the key—which might prove difficult in this gown, never mind the fact that I couldn't clear a hurdle on a good day—jumping the line is the only thing that will keep me from having an accident.

Desperate, I tap the man ahead of me on the shoulder and say, "Excuse me."

He doesn't turn, keeping his massive back toward me. Shoulder to shoulder, he's practically a yard wide, built of solid muscle that tapers to a trim waist and a very firm, um, backside. I can't help but notice since I'm practically eye level with it.

I'm short. He's tall, so perhaps he didn't hear me all the way up there. Also, his son is antsy, so he's probably trying to keep him occupied.

Always look on the bright side!

Clearing my throat again, I say, "Pardon me, sir, I'm just wondering if—"

His head snaps in my direction.

I shrink back from the imposing big cat.

He has a scar on his lip, wears a snarl, and all but bares his teeth.

I shiver and not only because I really, really have to pee.

He slowly looks me up and down with what can only be described as a joy-starved gaze.

"Hi. Um, if it's okay I'd like to please scoot ahead of you to ask Nina for the bathroom key and then come back and grab some things. But you can order while I'm gone. I mean, as planned since you're in line waiting too." I realize I'm rambling, but the flow of words won't stop like I'm negotiating a hostage situation and know if I go quiet, I'll lose his attention and the robbery will continue.

I add, "It's an emergency. I'm desperate."

He grunts in reply. As he faces forward again, he mumbles to himself, "You and me both."

The little boy with him has a serious case of the wiggles. If I wouldn't look conspicuous and like a lunatic since I'm still wearing a wedding dress, I'd join him and do the potty dance.

He grips the child's hand in his big one. There are still two people ahead of them, and the sweet little fussy fella sags as the man's deep, rumbling voice echoes in my mind.

You and me both.

He has trim, dark blond hair but sports some stubble. His nails are clean, but he has calloused hands. The overall picture is that he's tidy but has a certain kind of wildness that might solely be because of his size. Kind of like a domesticated wooly mammoth.

The snapshot I took of his face included a wide brow, stormy blue-gray eyes, a strong nose, and full lips.

It's like women across the world were surveyed to compile the perfect man and this is what they produced.

Or maybe that's just me.

I tell myself to stop drooling. Is that a symptom of having to use the bathroom?

Anyway, he's probably married. There's no ring on his finger, but do they make them that big? An ironic laugh comes from my throat. I'm the one in the wedding dress.

Peering around his side, I wonder if I could just tiptoe by unnoticed.

Casting me a grimace as if concerned that I'm a weirdo, he picks up the little boy.

Never mind. Time to come up with another plan.

My heart makes a cartoonish throb at the sweet sight of a huge, overgrown man with a little guy in his arms. However, that doesn't change the fact that I really, really need to use the facilities. My, "Awww" turns into a soft whimper.

I'm not sure how much longer I can last.

To get his attention, I pat his very firm arm.

He glances at me as if remembering that there's an annoying little fly nearby.

Time to break out the glitter guns.

I say, "It's already a lovely day, isn't it? Perfect for a walk in the park. A picnic perhaps. What are your plans after you so kindly let me grab that bathroom key real quick?"

He grunts and doesn't look my way.

What does a woman in a wedding dress have to do to get his attention?

Ah! I realize the problem.

Hopping at his side, mostly so I don't lose my bladder in the middle of the bakery, but also so he can't ignore me, I say, "Sir, I understand how hard Mondays are before coffee, but I assure you that I'll only take a second to grab that key ... I just need to go potty." I say the last part at a whisper.

Frowning at me, he says, "I don't need coffee."

I chuckle. "Tea or whatever—"

"I don't need anything." His voice is a low, thundery rumble.

"Okay, well, maybe, um, you feel like doing a good deed and will just let me place my order super-fast, grab the key to the ladies' room, and then you'll never have to see me again."

"Stick to that last part."

I huff. "Rude."

Mercifully, Nina rings up the last customer between Mr. Meanie and his precious place in line when his son starts to have a tantrum. Trust me, amigo, I want to cry too.

His arms flail and his little fingers move in a vaguely familiar way. The corner of my lip lifts and using my hands, I send him a little ray of sunshine and a rainbow from a signing song I learned when I'd go to ASL storytime with Grandma Dolly.

The child goes still and looks at me with the same blue-gray eyes as his father.

I do a few more child-friendly signs, thankful I can help even if his dad is a great big growly bear.

As if suddenly realizing the little boy is no longer a writhing, upset mess, he turns toward me, gaze hard. It lingers for a long moment. Something trips inside, sending a swizzly feeling through me.

Or maybe that's just because I still have to pee.

6

LIAM

MERCIFULLY, the kid is quiet when I place my order at the bakery counter, but he fools with my baseball hat—my feeble attempt at an incognito disguise.

We wouldn't have come to this place here in town if I weren't desperate ... and soon to be running late, but I can't risk being recognized, especially not with the kid.

I didn't think this through entirely. I blame the lack of sleep.

He removes my hat. As I take it back, he tosses it over my shoulder toward the woman who had the audacity to ask to cut ahead of us.

Wearing that ridiculous gown, she bends over, picks it up, and regards the letter K in blue stitching.

I motion for her to give it back, but the person at the register asks for payment. I give her my card when I realize the kid is quiet, apparently entertained by the sideshow behind us.

Now, she's wearing my favorite baseball hat. I should be grateful for whatever sorcery she's working, but she can't just cut ahead because she's small and cute ... or wearing my Knights cap.

I frown. No, she's not cute. More like she wandered off a horror movie set in a wedding gown. Yes, she is short. Like just barely over five feet tall.

After I pay, I carefully balance the kid and our items in my hands. Badaszek could have us try to juggle hot coffee, fresh muffins, and a writhing child as a cross-training exercise.

Forget it. He cannot find out that I have a kid. Or does he already know? I go back and forth in my mind long enough for the child to start fidgeting and inadvertently kick me in the groin.

Yeah, I've got a real balancing act going on.

The groan I try to conceal as I do my best not to double over could put me in the contending for Cobbiton's Biggest Weirdo with the woman behind me in line, waving her hands nonsensically at the kid.

I'll have to talk to him about stranger danger.

As I pour and mix creamer one-handed, my grip on the kid loosens. He wiggles. I set him down to attach the cover to the cup and he rushes across the bakery toward the hallway.

How do parents do this?

A growl rises in my throat. We've been here too long and I'm afraid I'm going to be recognized. I'm drowning in toddler training, team commitments, and legal documents. I'm not sure how much longer I can keep my newfound father status secret.

Grabbing our grub, I hurry after the kid, calling for him to stop and wait, but he doesn't listen. Never does.

The hallway contains two bathrooms and an exit. I try to anticipate his moves as I would an opponent on the ice. If I deke left, what will he do?

He regards me for a long moment and then his chin starts to tremble.

Oh no. Not here. Can't deal with the crying kid in public.

I say, "I got us some breakfast. It's time to go."

Eyes wide like a scared animal, he looks around.

I shift my weight, realizing I'll have to put the coffee down if I want to pick him up safely. Gazing up at the ceiling, I silently ask, *Why is this my life?*

The hum of a hand dryer comes from behind one of the bathroom doors followed by a hoot of surprised laughter.

The door flies open and the woman in the wedding gown practically blows into my arms.

In a voice that's too perky pre-coffee, she says, "Whoa, Nelly with a side of jelly. That thing is powerful. Nearly knocked me over."

I grunt because she nearly did the same to me. The brief contact we have makes me feel like I'm crawling out of my skin.

She straightens and smooths her hand down her dress. "Excuse me. Sorry. But boy, do I feel better."

My expression wrinkles as I recall her asking to cut the line so she could, and I quote, "Go potty."

"Looks like I wasn't the only one." She waves her hands at the kid.

He shakes his head.

Maybe his mother already had the stranger danger conversation with him. Perhaps this entire episode is him sensing this woman is a menace and trying to lead us to safety.

Way to go, Little Man.

I turn to leave and say, "Come on, let's get out of here."

Not hearing the patter of little feet behind me, I go still. The kid remains glued to the spot.

"We have to leave," I say, hoping that a group of Knights fans isn't out there waiting for me.

To be clear, I'm not one of the team hot shots with puck bunnies chasing after me. Not that I care. A long time ago, I decided that I don't like people. Makes it easier to keep my distance. Relationships of any sort get complicated. Lead to trouble. Easier to avoid them altogether.

I have a sorely neglected social media account, there are several created by fans, and rumors of a hashtag, but I cannot be bothered. Not when I have the Cup to win, a kid to take care of, and now a team to captain.

Picking up on my stream of consciousness, I say, "And I'm going to be late for my meeting. Let's go."

The kid shakes his head.

"Do you have to use the bathroom?" I ask.

He stares at me blankly.

The woman waves her hands again. Why is she still here?

"If you'll excuse us," I say, breezing past her to scoop up my son and rush out the back door—no sense in risking being noticed.

No sooner do I reach him than he starts crying again.

"I'll get you a cookie if you stop," I say.

"You shouldn't bribe children. It doesn't set healthy boundaries." Even as she reprimands me, her tone is unflinchingly perky.

I whip my head in her direction. "This is none of your business."

Hands bouncing around in the air, she says, "Someone is wearing cranky pants this morning."

The kid goes quiet and then starts shaking.

What is going on? Is she actually a witch bride and has put a hex on him? Not that I believe in that nonsense, but—I tip my head to the side.

It's my turn to blink.

I think the kid is laughing.

Grinning, the Wicked Witch of the West disguised as Glenda after a long night in a saloon waves her hands again.

The corners of his lips twitch as if trying to lift into a smile and then he makes a hand gesture.

My jaw clenches because I have no idea what I'm witnessing. "What are you doing to my son?"

Brown eyes sparkling, her grin doesn't falter. "Talking to him, obviously." Her tone has a real *duh* quality to it.

"Using some kind of sorcery?"

Through gritted teeth, she says, "I really hope you're joking."

The kid moves his hands around and starts laughing. There's no mistaking it. My chest gets warm and does a weird, melty thing. Maybe I'm allergic to honey. They put it in the coffee here instead of sugar.

Giving my head a shake, it's time to leave. "Come on, kid. Let's go."

He remains still except for his hands.

Meanwhile, the short woman with curves and a dimple in one cheek beams. She looks to be about my age, mid-twenties. Her lips are peachy and plump with a little line through the lower one. Not that I'm paying attention.

Through jovial laughter, she says, "He asked if I'm a princess."

"He did not."

She moves her hands. "Uh, yeah. He did. Even asked where my crown is." She sighs.

"All right. Enough of—"

"He told me he's a king, so what would that make you?" she asks with a laugh as if this is all some big joke.

Then my thoughts sharpen. "What did you say?"

She yawns. "I should get going too. It's been a long drive."

I look from her to the kid who moves his hands in a distinct way.

"What were you saying about a king?" I ask, my tone sharp.

Her eyes brighten. "Ah, I know. You'd be a knight. Is that what the K on your hat stands for?"

I lengthen my spine.

Her jaw lowers. "Are you on the hockey team? My grandmother is a huge fan. Oh my goodness. Could you sign something for me? A napkin? The gown?" While she speaks her hands move simultaneously.

It's one thing to use your hands while talking to emphasize a point, but this is something else. Then it clicks.

"Wait, did you say *sign*?"

She nods.

I point to the kid and then to her. "Are you two signing?"

"Obviously. Also, you can't give a tiny guy a cookie for breakfast." Notably, she doesn't wave her hands around.

"No one asked you."

"No one consulted me about the last twenty-four hours, yet here I am." Blocking our exit from the hallway, she leans her head against the wall as if about to take a nap.

I'll have to mention to the bakery owner or law enforcement that there's a deranged reprobate disguised as a witch bride loose in Cobbiton.

My phone beeps and I grumble. I'm late because of the kid and now this lady.

"Could you please move?" I gesture to her gown that takes up half the hallway.

She seems to surface from her dip into La La Land and says, "Gosh. Yes. Of course. I am so sorry. Forgot where I was for a moment. I should go."

"Finally, you speak some reason."

With a huff, she plants her hands on her hips. "I'm reasonable. You're the one who's on the verge of an adult temper tantrum."

"Am not."

"You so are. Maybe *you* need a cookie. Some sweetness in your life to counteract all the sourness. Strictly speaking, it's not a good morning habit." She drops her voice to a whisper, "Sometimes, for a treat, I'll have a little bite of cake. I have one in the passenger seat of the car. It kept me going the whole ride here. And coffee. Some chocolate. Maybe I'm eating my feelings. But here, take this. I consider it an act of service." She reaches into her purse and produces a wax bakery bag, then holds it out for me to take.

I grimace. "I don't want your dirty cookie."

"Go ahead. It's not poisoned or anything. I just got it from Nina. The baker. She bakes the bread, but gets these delivered fresh daily from the Milk Mustache." She says each word slowly like she's speaking to, well, a toddler.

"I have no idea what you're talking about."

"Sheesh. I'm just trying to be nice."

Over my shoulder, I call, "We have to leave."

Finally, the kid moves, but instead of coming over to me, he rushes toward the woman and wraps his arms around the skirt of her tattered gown.

"Don't touch him," I growl at her.

She holds up her hands and then waves them around again.

There he goes with the chin trembling, but this time his eyes start to fill up with liquid.

"Your hands are full. How about I just carry him to your car?"

"I don't think that's a good idea." I'm about ready to stomp my foot. No, never mind. I'm not going to give her the pleasure of thinking I was going to have a fit.

She crouches down and signs to him. Must be something his mother taught him instead of the normal childhood stuff like listening.

His little shoulders relax a little, but when she stands, he grips her like a koala climbing a eucalyptus tree.

"Okay, fine. We'll do this your way. You can carry him to the car, but if you do anything strange or suspicious, I will tackle you. Got that?"

Her cheeks turn the slightest shade of pink, but maybe that's because she's picking up the kid and restricted by that monstrosity of a dress.

Watching her every move, she weaves through the tables, bumping a few with the bustle of her gown. I don't know a ton about girly stuff, so I'm grateful I got stuck with a son rather than a daughter.

I grunt.

"What was that, Mr. Meanie?" she says over her shoulder.

At the same time, someone calls, "Hey, Liam, are you going to be a chump or a champ the rest of this season?"

Ignoring the heckler, I keep my head down, so close to escaping this place without being recognized. I've been avoiding local spots, but the line at the drive-through at my usual place was too long. I'm late anyway.

The guy says, "Let's just hope you can keep it together." The words are a challenge.

I glance from the guy wearing a Knights sweatshirt to the woman and my kid. Her eyes darken and her lips pucker as if offended on my behalf.

Or there's more she wants to pile on with the accusation of me having an adult tantrum and calling me Mr. Meanie.

Expertly balancing my son on her hip, she moves her hand, and the little kid offers a half smile. Maybe she's telling him he can have the cookie after all. I briefly consider it myself before giving my head a shake, that's stupid. I haven't had cookies or cake in years. She must've cast some kind of sweet spell over us.

Thankfully, we make it out the door without anyone else

recognizing me. It's early on a sleepy Monday morning which is why I thought it would be safe to quickly pop into the bakery.

Laughter and giggles drift from nearby and someone says, "There he is!"

Another teenager adds, "My brother is going to be pumped. He thinks number forty-five is the best."

Acting on instinct, I grab the woman's arm and hustle her and the kid toward my truck. Then I realize I've miscalculated.

My mind reels with stories from other guys about crazed fans. That's what this must be. She's the ringleader, sent word to her coven, and now they're in pursuit.

But she has my kid.

The witch bride says, "They just want your autograph and I want one too. Well, not me. Could you personalize it *To Grandma Dolly. I'm your number one fan?*"

We stop by my truck. "Shouldn't it be the other way around?"

She guffaws. "No, I am definitely not your number one fan. No offense, but you could be less rude. You wouldn't want someone to think that you're a stinker."

I'm about to defend myself, when, still holding the kid, she makes a motion with her hands. He laughs again.

I squint but don't have time for her games. She could be using sign language, but why would she do that and how would the kid understand? "Did you just tell him, that I'm—?"

He mimics the motion she just made and giggles before burying his head in her wild mop of brown hair that's half up and half down.

They both laugh like they have a little secret.

I say, "We've got to go."

"Or you could stay and sign autographs and take photos like a normal sports star. Obviously, they adore you."

"I'm late."

"Yeah me, too. Late for my appointment with life." A flash of sadness spills over her features, but it's quickly replaced with a sunny grin that somehow makes the clouds above disappear for a moment.

The snapping of cameras on phones and the squawking of the fans fade as I meet her brown eyes.

"Today is a new day. Carpe diem!" Her hand forms a light fist and she sweeps her arm in front of her chest, pumping the air slightly.

The strange thought that the world is a dim place without her smile beams into my mind. Perhaps I need that cookie after all.

I blink and the world comes back into focus. What am I thinking? I don't need anything or anyone.

7
JESS

GRANDMA DOLLY WILL BE DISAPPOINTED I met one
of the Knights players but didn't get his autograph or a selfie.
Instead, I got a snarl and a whole lot of attitude.

Having him write that he's her fan would've been a hoot.
But the guy has no sense of humor. Didn't smile once. Not even
at his precious baby.

It's too early in the day to be so surly if you ask me.

As I get in my car, he peels away in his big truck, leaving
me in the dust.

Not that I was expecting him to stick around. Not at all, but
that old lonesome feeling of seeing the backs of people leaving
returns, stinging a dark place inside that my own personal positivity hasn't quite reached.

It always has. Probably always will.

I'm determined to defy the odds with my unfailing and
unflinching optimistic attitude. It never lets me down.

Grandma Dolly calls me her ray of light. Maybe I won't
mention my encounter with Mr. Meanie. However, I will make
it my mission to get the cantankerous hockey player's auto-

graph. I snap my fingers. That's thinking too small. I'll get all of them to sign a team photo. Oh, she'll love that!

I take a long sip of my coffee. My body buzzes as if not sure whether it wants to fall into a deep sleep or seize the day.

Either way, I'm still in this gown so if I fell asleep like a fairytale princess, I wouldn't object to a prince waking me up with a kiss. I chuckle.

The little sweetheart from the bakery said his name was King. Pretty clever if he was playing pretend, but I'm guessing that's not his actual name. He seemed to understand more ASL than he could sign—not bad for a little guy.

I'd rather hang out with him than his father. What does he have to be crabby about? He has an adorable son, admiring fans, and a hockey career.

I pat the steering wheel. "Also a nice truck that won't break down if you look at it funny. Thanks for getting us here. One more leg of this trip. Onward to Grandma Dolly's," I say with gusto.

I sip the coffee on the short drive through town. It's sweet and creamy, just the way I like it.

Despite the circumstances that prompted my flight from Los Angeles and the fact that I'm running on empty, I prefer to drive on the sunny side of the street—to look for the upside in every situation.

For instance, I appreciate how Cobbiton tries for cheerful in the winter rather than sticking out the drab during these long, cloudy winter months.

Lights glow warmly from within the Once Upon a Romance bookstore. The Lunchbox sandwich shop and deli have colorful banners hanging from the eaves of the building. Spaglietti's hasn't yet taken down their Christmas decorations, which I appreciate because the Coogans don't celebrate in favor of Skinkmas. Even the Buy & Bargain thrift store has a wreath with red winter berries on the front door. Outside the new toy store is an array of tree stumps, of varying heights, surrounded by snow. Atop each one sits a woodland stuffed animal toy like they're having a party.

I bet the little boy would love that. His dad could stand to have some fun. Or smile. Or have cake. He probably doesn't let himself eat sweets. I'd like to see him try to resist my Bundts. Ha! One bite and he'd be grinning from ear to ear.

As I near Silver Queen Street, I pass the Old Mill building that was converted to shops, artisan spaces, and offices. Lanterns and evergreen swag line the pathway that leads to the main entrance strung with pinecone bunting and golden bows. The lime-washed white pops like a snowy castle against the black wrought iron trim, fixtures, and natural wood accents.

Yes, it's good to be back ... for now. It won't be for long because I have plans. Big ones! And the likes of Sorsha, Rexlan, and Pamberlie aren't going to stop me.

No sooner am I parked does Grandma Dolly rush out the door, arms wide, and fingers flying.

It takes everything in me not to collapse into her embrace— even though she's pleasantly plump, I'd risk knocking us both over, given my attire.

She squeezes me tight and then grips my upper arms, holding me at a distance and looking me over. It's the same quizzical expression I've been receiving at every stop between here and Los Angeles.

I sign that it's a long story.

It's only been a year since I was last home, but the modest cottage is as cozy as I remember with a warm fire crackling in the wood stove. Grandma Dolly's reading chair is as lived in as ever and more framed photos cover the wall. A big bookshelf lines another and is stuffed with novels that tell stories of travels without leaving home and trinkets containing memories made in faraway places. From the adjacent kitchen, the aroma of cinnamon and vanilla tells me Grandma Dolly is ready for the day with freshly baked cookies.

A worn wooden dining table, surrounded by mismatched chairs, stands ready for gatherings and laughter shared over treats and yummy meals alike.

I take a seat and she pours us each a coffee. Settling in, she asks me to explain what I'm doing here in a wedding gown. There is no denying the maternal concern pinching her features ... or the rocky crags of guilt in my gut.

I take a moment to admire her sparkly strands, her kind eyes, and the way I'll always feel at home with her before delving into the dismal reality that I'm a jilted bride.

After I tell her the sordid tale, she sweeps me into another hug. My shoulders relax and my eyes fill, but I cast the tears away. Not even this woman who has carried my world on her back has seen me cry.

She signs, "You're wearing your 'Everything is fine' face."

I shrug.

"This is a huge deal. It's a shock."

"I'm coping. Had a lot of time to think on the drive here."

"I wish you'd have called. I'd have bought you a plane ticket."

I drop back into the seat and hold my head in my hands for a long moment. She pats my arm.

Then I sign, "I don't know what I was thinking. I guess I got swept into Rexlan's world. The first red flag should've been that his mother was limiting the guest list ... or prioritizing the lizards before that." I could go on.

Grandma Dolly doesn't hide the hurt on her face.

"I'm so sorry." I want to deny the shame I feel about going along with Sorsha's plans because I felt wanted, but I let it hit me in the gut. "None of my friends were invited either. Sorsha was so convincing. Since I had a small guest list, she said it would be unbalanced. Easier to just go ahead with the three hundred people she wanted to invite."

Grandma Dolly tips her shoulder and signs, "I suppose since she was paying for it ..."

Sorsha's words that I'll be paying for this echo in my mind.

"That's no excuse. I got sucked into their world and—" Sparing her the backstory involving the lizard cult because I don't want her to be more concerned than she is, I rattle on about how nice they were, thoughtful and attentive.

How could I have been so naïve?

"I thought I'd left the past behind here in Nebraska, but all those years of rejection resulted in me going along with the Coogans because I thought they genuinely liked me."

Grandma Dolly signs, "Sounds like you got love bombed."

"I temporarily had a potato for a brain."

She cracks a smile.

I apologize because I now clearly see how wrong it all was. I tell my grandmother that I don't plan on getting married anytime soon, but next time, she'll be the guest of honor.

She offers to make me eggs and toast, but I take another cookie. I know I've been forgiven even if I don't deserve it.

We chat some more and then she brings me to my old room, now her crafting space.

I'd like to say I fall into bed and get some much-needed rest. Instead, my mind churns, flashing with images of the video call Rexlan accidentally made to his mother while eloping. My thoughts flash forward through the cake binge drive here and skid to a stop in front of the big brute of a man and his sweet little son at the bakery.

Or maybe I am sleeping and this is my body telling me I need to use the bathroom. Pee dreams are the worst.

I get up and find the sun low in the sky. Checking the

clock, I must've been out for over six hours—a record as of late. I'm lucky if I get in two hours of solid sleep at a time before I wake up as wired as if I'd just downed a double shot of espresso.

Next to a plate of shortbread cookies, Grandma Dolly left me a note saying she'll be gone for the afternoon for an appointment and errands, but she'll be home in time to watch the Knights game.

Some things never change and I'm grateful for that.

Tonight, we'll both curl up on the couch with a bowl of cookie snack mix between us. It's Grandma Dolly's special blend of cookie crumbles, pretzels, raisins, M&Ms, and the usual cereal bites. It's a sweet and salty treat that can't be beat.

She'll tell me about this year's lineup for the team. Mr. Meanie bursts into my mind. There's no denying how rude he was. He wasn't a gentleman, he was a *rough*man. A big brute and I hope he wishes he'd let the poor woman in the wedding dress use the bathroom this morning.

I start toward the refrigerator but am stuck. My gown snags on a drawer handle. Yes, I'm still wearing it. May as well get my money's worth—not that I paid for it. Also, I need help getting it off. Sorsha said there are ties under the zipper to "Keep all the fluff tucked in." That's a direct quote.

Letting out a breath through my nose, I decide to wear this thing until it's in shreds. After my second cookie, I change my mind. Actually, no, I want to forget this day, er, yesterday ever happened.

Los Angeles was an aspirational move. I had grand plans of living a stellar starlet life. Still do. I'm not sure what that will look like or where it'll be, but I'll only stay in Cobbiton temporarily. I don't want to impose on Grandma Dolly's generosity or have anyone find out that the *diem carped* me more than I *carped* it.

@THEPUCKPOST

Number forty-five @TheRealLiamEllis for the Nebraska Knights hasn't been spotted since Christmas Eve. Rumors circulate that he was sidelined for naughty behavior. Maybe Santa didn't check his list twice.

The defenseman generates buzz on and off the ice. Especially when matched up against Henri Valjean—the two have unspoken beef and lay on the lumber, resulting in a long list of penalties.

Last year, in an explosive post, the Titans D accused Ellis of busting his shoulder. After an investigation, officials deny this, citing a preexisting injury. Critics suggested Ellis has an anger management problem. Diehards suggest Valjean purposefully antagonizes him. However, the damage to his reputation was done.

These antics resulted in him being named The Beast as well as heated debates among fans, some praising him for his tenacity and others criticizing him for his sudden scarcity.

Most recently, sources speculate that he came unhinged during the Christmas Eve game, laughed his coach out of the locker room, and was subsequently sent on a two-week vacation. So we've heard.

While we don't see a record of a fine imposed against the goon, maybe he slipped someone a big bill and they called it good.

All we know is the Knights will face the Titans again, including Hendrix Ellis, Liam's brother who wasn't available for comment.

Is Liam in the permanent penalty box or did a distraction result in a temporary hiatus, putting this member of hockey royalty on the rocks?

♥💬💌 5,196 Likes

@WriterOnTheStorm: Ellis is a showman. He will do anything, including knocking around Valjean, for attention.

@DollyPuckton: Watch your mouth, young man.

@HockeyAddict764: The speculation is exhausting. Just tell us facts, including when he'll be back.

@JimJimmyJames: Maybe The Beast needs a hug.

@DollyPuckton: I'll be the first in line. Yeehaw!

>Read more

8
JESS

I CALL MY FRIEND CARA—WE met my senior year in high school when I moved here and have stayed in touch.

Sort of.

I didn't exactly mention the whole wedding thing when Sorsha said I couldn't invite anyone from my side "of the family," not that I have one.

Cara is still at work and tells me to meet her at the Ice Palace.

It's not until I'm in the parking lot do I realize I might encounter the sourpuss from the bakery. Plastering on a smile, I tell myself, if I do, it'll give me a chance to get that signed photo for Grandma Dolly. See? I'm always turning lemons into lemonade and wedding gowns into everyday wear.

As I step through the automatic glass doors, I smooth my skirt and get more than a few curious looks. I parade into the relatively quiet arena in the calm before the storm. My grandmother said they're playing Carolina tonight.

Hopefully, Mr. Meanie is busy sharpening his skates. I have no interest in being around someone so rude, so why does a fluffy marshmallow of excitement drop out from under me and give way to a void of disappointment?

There's no arguing against the fact that he was attractive in a big, imposing, swoop-in-and-save-the-day kind of way. But I am not looking for romance or a relationship. I'm barely out of one. Besides, he's probably married.

However, when I take an honest look at things between Rexlan and me, we were running on my optimism and Sorsha's insistence that we get hitched. She just didn't want him to marry Cassleigh.

He was probably with me because he was too scared to defy his mom and I'm too nice to say no to.

Before I can talk myself out of a frown, someone shrieks from down the hall. I look around, alarmed. Cara rushes toward me, calling my name then abruptly going quiet as she looks me over from head to toe, wearing an expression that goes from shock to curiosity. "What are you wearing? I need a story time and I need it now."

Ushering me into an austere office, I tell Cara almost everything, including some of the details I skipped when relaying events to Grandma Dolly. It's not that I want to keep anything from her, but she'll worry, which will prompt her to bake more cookies, and then I'll never fit into a wedding dress again.

What can I say? They're hard to resist.

Cara exclaims, "So he left you at the altar? Want to hatch a revenge plot?"

"Yes, but no. You know me. I'm just hoping for a plot twist. Like I'll wake up and none of this ever happened."

"Can we talk about the red flags?"

"Where to start? There were so many. I was in a fog."

"Or drugged. Did they drug you? Tell me he drugged you so I can be mad at them on your behalf and not at you since you didn't mention YOU WERE GETTING MARRIED."

"You're talking in all caps."

"I KNOW."

"I'm a terrible friend. But his mother was overbearing and when she said the guest list was full, I didn't want to impose."

"I think you should start imposing in *your* own life, especially when it comes to *your* future, *your* own marriage."

"During the rehearsal dinner, when we were practicing our vows, he said his assistant's name. Cass."

Cara's eyes widen.

"Also, last month, his buddy did warn me."

"I want all the gory details. Actually, we need backup. The girl squad. I'll text you the date and time. At the Fish Bowl."

"I thought you hated that place."

"Technically, it's where Pierre and I first met. He was wearing an ugly Christmas sweater." She lets out a blissful little sigh. "But I want to know where on earth you picked up a guy who'd walk out on your wedding day?"

I grouse, "Should I even be surprised?"

Apparently, not hearing me, Cara says, "You're wearing your 'Everything is fine' face."

"I'm coping."

"Or in shock."

"What else am I going to do? Wallow in my misery?"

She pounds her fists on her thighs. "Revenge, revenge, revenge."

"The fact that he'll have to deal with Sorsha is probably bad enough."

"But you said she was making excuses for him."

I gaze at my hands. "So was I."

Cara taps the air with her forefinger. "I know, we'll get revenge by showing him what he's missing."

My brow wrinkles. "Like a rebound relationship?"

"I mean more like we'll show him that you're thriving without him."

I shift from foot to foot. "How about we get me out of this gown first?" Then I can forget that Rexlan Coogan ever existed. That's the plan and I'm sticking to it.

"Did you bring a change of clothes?"

I clap my hand to my forehead. "No. I rushed out of the house, desperate to get this thing off—do you have any idea how hard it is to use the bathroom with a bustle?"

"A trumpet-style gown with a bustle." She makes a cringing face.

"And lots and lots of tulle or is this organza?" I ask.

"It's strangely shaggy and layered like a lizard molting." Cara flits her hand across the fabric.

"How did I let a woman who worshipped lizards talk me into this?"

"Because I wasn't there."

"I'm a wreck."

She holds up a hand. "That's not thriving-Jess-post-jilted bride language. The solution is simple. I'll go grab some Knights spirit wear."

Leaving me alone in the office with only hints that someone as sweet as Cara occupies the space with its dark wood paneling, deep red wallpaper, and heavy frames filled with hockey awards, I can't help but wonder why I always feel like I'm coming in last despite my best efforts.

Can a gal get a win?

Moreover, why didn't I let myself see how wrong things had gone with Rexlan before I'd showed up at the end of the aisle under his mother's marching orders?

Cara pops back into the office and waves a hoodie and leggings with the Knights logo. "Grandma Dolly will insist you wear this every day from now on." She guards the door and helps me out of the gown while I quickly change. We keep a running dialog.

I say, "She's very excited about the game against the Carolina Storm tonight. Congrats, by the way, on the new job."

"It only took me three college degrees to realize that what I wanted to do didn't require any of them."

I sigh. "I'm still not sure what I want to do."

"Open a bakery. Your Bundts are the best. Did you see the new Old Mill building? They have spaces available."

I nod. "I do need a job."

Cara taps the air like a Christmas light blinked on—it's her favorite holiday and she still has red and green candy in the bowl on her desk. "That's it. You could be Ellis's assistant."

"An assistant like you? I'm hardly hockey-qualified. The only things I know about the sport are only translatable through sign language."

"I mean the personal assistant to one of our players. My father put him on ice for a couple of weeks." She returns to her seat behind the desk.

I sit back down in the leather chair. "If he's a hockey player, isn't that his preferred habitat?"

"I mean he got in trouble. Technically, Dadaszek took him *off* the ice for some R&R. Something is up with number forty-five. I think my father knows, but hasn't mentioned it to anyone. Yet he just named him captain. Baffling. The man has his mysterious ways."

"Hmm. I'm always up for helping people, but does he want an assistant?"

"What Ellis needs and what he wants are likely two vastly different things. Half the time these guys are so single-minded about the game, they let their personal lives fall by the wayside. Their health, relationships, and other responsibilities suffer because of it."

The idea of helping someone in need has always uplifted and inspired me. I spent the better part of my life on the receiving end of charitable people who went out of their way to help. However, back then, I was hidden so far in my shell that I never revealed how much their kindness meant to me.

There was the Nelson family who always sent me to kindergarten with a homemade lunch. Then Mr. and Mrs. Jaronisky who brought me to church. Oh, and the Reids. Even though their daughter hardly talked to me at school, she is the sole reason I survived freshman year ... and algebra.

Everything changed when I came to Cobbiton. Grandma Dolly worked a miracle and helped me see all the good in the world. She drew me out of my self-imposed silence and fear one cookie at a time. Then I met Cara and I found my BFF forever—except during that little blip in Los Angeles when I dropped out of everyone's lives and nearly got sucked into Sorsha's lizard cult.

Cara says, "He could benefit from someone as uplifting as you."

I arch an eyebrow. "Is there something I should know?"

"Professional athletes have a lot on their plates. Pierre dwells in Pierreville, but he's an anomaly. They're under so much pressure to perform, it can get the better of them. I think Ellis is struggling with that a bit. Plus, he comes from a legendary hockey family, so I imagine not only does he compete with the other teams in the league, but also has to vie to keep up with his brother and his dad's legacy."

"That sounds like a lot for anyone to manage emotionally."

"Manage? Ha. More like push it deep down into the dark and then let it explode out of him on the ice."

"What do you mean?"

"He's a defenseman and our team thug. Need to put the fear of pucks and sticks and blades into someone? Ellis is our man. Suffice it to say, he has had some past anger management issues. Actually, it's primarily between him and one other player. Henri Valjean."

Cara gets a call and answers professionally and confidently. So much has changed in three hundred and sixty-five days, yet I feel like instead of taking any steps forward, I'm back where I started.

I've gleaned that Mr. Badaszek runs the show on the ice and Cara now takes care of everything off of it. She was a perpetual student for years, earning multiple degrees, but she's found her calling. It gives me hope that someday I will too ... even though I don't know exactly what that is.

When she hangs up, I say, "Are you authorized to hire me? I don't want you to get in trouble for giving your bestie a job. I might be able to apply at the diner again."

Cara kicks her feet onto the desk and pretends to smoke a stogie. "I call the shots 'round these parts, pardner."

We both giggle.

She drops her legs and adjusts her swivel chair. "Back to Ellis. The thing is, as far as I know, he's single so it's not like he has anyone to confide in or to have a life with off the ice. I imagine things can build up, you know?"

"How sad." How familiar.

"Yes and no. I think it's circumstantial."

"Is he hideous?"

"Have you seen the team roster? Obviously, I'm biased because Pierre is a dreamboat."

I recall Badaszek's disdain for The Frenchman, now known as Cara's husband, who was previously highly sought after by female hockey fans.

"My dad is super strict about casual hookups because they can cause drama and interfere with the players' focus. He wants marriageable men. Suffice it to say, Ellis is as handsome as they come. Last season, there was a contest on social to see who could reel him in. The entries targeting him were wild and wacky. I don't think he looked at a single one."

"So who won?"

"Nobody. He doesn't date. There's no female main character in his life. No love interest," she says with a wistful shake of her head.

"I get the picture."

"Sorry, I've been preparing for Gracie's book club meeting at Once Upon a Romance next week. But Ellis is unapproachable. They call him The Beast. He's married to the game."

Thinking about the broad-shouldered and well-built guy at the bakery, I murmur, "Seems like this place is infested with beasts."

She continues, "I think right now, some of his responsibilities are demanding his attention, so he needs a helping hand. I'll run it by my father, but he won't say no, aware as he is of the power of a good assistant."

"Cara, I don't want to impose." Or be a charity case. I have a lifetime of experience with that already.

"You could be his assistant or we have an opening in locker room sanitation." She taps her chin.

"Clean the locker room?"

She waggles her eyebrows as if in any world cleaning up after stinky athletes would be appealing.

"I'll take my chances as an assistant, even though I have no idea what to do."

"Just think of it as a lot of adulting. Making appointments, grocery shopping, doing life, but with a professional athlete so there will also be public appearances, engagements—"

Given my recent attire, I blanch. "Like marriage?"

She chuckles. "No. He's not the type. More like product endorsement shoots and luncheons—he begrudgingly does team events and community outreach. Not exactly the poster child for the Knights. There'd likely be a lot of scheduling ... and coaxing."

Actually, I'm good at that. I'm serious about organization and have an obsession with planners, stickers, and pens. I live and die by my bullet journal to keep everything from my daily tasks to my big goals and dreams to be an actress structured and productive. I have lists and trackers for everything including how much water I drink each day, my weekly exercise routines, and reading lists. Of course, each has a dedicated sticker and color system for a visual reminder of my achievements. It's a little way to pat myself on the back because it's not like anyone else will, maybe except Grandma Dolly, though she's more inclined to give enthusiastic jazz hands and cookie prizes.

I never thought of it before, but it's almost like I was made for a job like this.

"Speaking of being an assistant, I have to get back to work. Big game later."

"Grandma Dolly and I will be watching, in our matching Knights merch, under a Knights branded fleece blanket."

"Is she still making those?"

"Every year for Christmas, at least four people get cozy with the giant heads of the players plastered on the fabric." I'd hate to doze off and have Mr. Meanie's mug staring at me.

"We should hire her to supply the merchandise booth. I bet fans would love them, especially since it's chilly in the rink."

"She'd be thrilled, but let's take it one step at a time and see if I survive being a personal assistant first."

Cara bounces on her toes. "It's going to be great." Then she goes still.

"What?"

"Well, be warned, he can be a bit moody."

The gown rustles as I gather it in my arms. "Moldy?"

"Broody."

"Like a chicken? I have no fear!"

Her smile is delayed, but when it comes, she says, "Yeah. You've got this."

With the tattered gown in my arms, I reach in for a one-armed hug. "Thank you for getting me out of this dress and not being mad that I didn't invite you to the wedding that wasn't."

Her lips tip to one side. "At the next one, I insist on being your maid of honor."

We exchange a laugh, but as I leave, gown in hand, I have my doubts that there will be a next time.

Lost both in thought and the maze of hallways in the depths of the Ice Palace, I get turned around trying to retrace my steps back to the lobby when my foot catches in the mess of fabric I'm carrying. I should just throw this thing out. Or burn it. Though, it seems like it's going to cushion my fall as the floor gets closer.

Then I abruptly stop as a strong hand grips my arm.

"Watch where you're going," a low voice rumbles.

I straighten and meet a pair of fierce blue-gray eyes.

Sweaty from head to toe, the guy from the bakery chews on his mouth guard.

My positivity battery is running low, but I muster a bright smile. "Hello again and thank you. I hope you've had a wonderful day since we last saw each other this morning."

He scowls. "What are you doing here?"

"I was just leaving." No need to prolong this encounter or give him any personal information; you can never be too careful. It's not that I'm scared of him, more like I won't have a sweaty six-and-a-half-foot giant raining on my welcome home parade.

He points to the gown in my hands. "Why were you wearing that?"

"Are you the fun police?"

His eyebrows lift a micrometer, but he schools his expression.

"No, seriously, are you? It's been a while since I've been in Cobbiton, do they have a new community ordinance?"

Rude and crude, he snorts before carrying on down the hallway.

It isn't until after he turns the corner that a reply comes to mind. I'm always a minute slow, a day late, and a dollar short.

Sticking out my tongue at Mr. Meanie's back, I low-key snarl, "I wore it because I wanted to." Well, not this particular dress because as Cara noted, it's not especially flattering. Sorsha insisted. I let her. If I'm brutally honest, she pushed me into the whole thing ... even after I moved to Los Angeles and declared that my life choices were mine after nearly a lifetime of moving around in the foster care system—only to allow Sorsha to take charge.

I push those dismal thoughts away because today, er, tomorrow is a new day. Hopefully, the sun will come out, and I can begin again.

New (old) town! New job! Nothing can stop me now!

When I get back to Grandma Dolly's, I flip the page in my bullet journal, and using my favorite assortment of colorful pens, I put my plans to paper ... though my big dreams page remains a scribbled mess of ideas and inspiration. The Hollywood one didn't quite work out as expected. Maybe I'll get lucky like Cara and get my big break.

There's nothing like hope ... and Grandma Dolly's cookies to keep me going.

9

LIAM

TONIGHT WE'RE on home ice at the Palace, matched up against the Carolina Storm.

Our forward and Duffton from the opposing team start strong, fast-paced with the puck coasting across the ice with perfect passes and assists. He scores a greasy goal on Robo in the office for Beau during the first period. Into the second, the Storm lags and loses steam, relying on brute force rather than strategy and skill.

I'm big and fast but my secret weapon is learning the strengths and weaknesses of all the other players on my team to compensate and on the others to dominate. Once you know where the kinks in the chain are, it's easy to slide in and strengthen them or break them.

Eight minutes on the clock, Jack gets us our first goal against his old team. Another ten pass and it looks like Cole from Carolina is going to score, but Beau blocks it with a great butterfly save. We take possession and I keep the Storm running scared, giving Hayden a chance to score, gaining us a one-point lead.

Predictably, the fans go wild and then get just as upset when the Storm snag another goal on Robo at the top of the third. They chant "Beast" and wear Beast costume accessories like wigs and horns and head masks or face paint along with their Knights jerseys.

I wish they wouldn't.

Time to turn up the volume. Jack takes charge, not letting the puck out of his sight until Mikey is open for an assist.

Ramirez from the Storm tries to block me from getting into position, but I'm unstoppable and pull away to keep the opposition's forwards from pickpocketing.

We get another goal, taking the lead once more until the clock runs out, the buzzer sounds, and the Knights win the day.

As we take a victory lap, I notice on the jumbo screens overhead, the words "#1 Fan Dolly ♥ the Knights" scroll by.

The witch bride's comment from this morning comes to mind, but it must be a coincidence. Then again, I did run into her in the hallway earlier. Hopefully, the saying that things happen in threes isn't true, because I definitely don't want a triple play with that crazy woman.

I'm peopled out.

For years, I longed to be captain and promised myself if I ever got the role, I'd continue to be the first to arrive and the last to leave. However, I have to dash to deal with Mrs. Kirby and then with the kid.

Pierre whacks me with a towel. "Where are you in a rush to? Hot date?" He's also one of our defensemen and Badaszek's son-in-law. How the guy dubbed The Frenchman—and not because he's from the country—managed to date, no less marry the coach's daughter, and make it out alive is something we're all still trying to figure out.

Hayden wolf whistles. "Liam, on a date? That'll be the day."

I toss them a dirty look and shake my head. The game has gone way late. Mrs. Kirby is going to sic her mini Maltese on me.

Most people work forty-hour weeks, but this gig is all day and well into the night. On the flip side, we get offseason downtime. Unless you're me. I train year-round.

"Nice blocking, Cap," says Redd, right winger and former captain.

I cock my head and say, "Listen, I didn't ask for this."

He claps a meaty hand on my back. "No, but you're the best man for the job. I was glad to pass the torch. Family life is keeping me loaded with commitments. A guy only has so much bandwidth."

Nerves ball up in my stomach. "You don't say."

"Just wait. Someday you'll have a family and understand. Enjoy being single now. But the fun really starts when you meet someone special, settle down, and start creating a team of your own." He winks.

I vaguely recall him not having a kid one day and then being a dad the next. Er, maybe stepdad? Could be that he got custody of his sister. I know these guys nearly as well as I know my own brother. Or I thought I did. Maybe not.

"Happens every time. You sign with the Knights, you're also committing to marriage," Pierre adds.

Bouchelle says, "I'm the new guy, but Badaszek has a knack for playing matchmaker."

"I what?" comes a loud, booming voice from the hall.

We all shuffle around as if we're teens caught with our hands in the cookie jar.

Commencing the debrief, Coach says, "The Carolina Storm have had an inconsistent few months."

"Could be because we poached their MVP," quips Grady, another defenseman.

I have no doubt Badaszek heard him but he ignores the comment. "Sometimes they come in and crush it and others it's a gimme game without much effort on our part. Tonight, they were firing on all cylinders—"

My thoughts drift to how I am not and that largely has to do with my living situation. The kid was the happiest I'd seen him after we ran into the wedding witch at the bakery. But as the day wore on, he fell into sullen silence, not that he ever makes much more than a peep—seems Pam ascribed to a "Children should be seen and not heard" policy. Not going to lie, I love to hear my nieces and nephews laughing.

The coach praises our stick handling and formation when running offense. He makes a few suggestions for improvements to limit opportunities for the opposition to score. Possibly for the first time in my career, I'm not focused. I glean that at the next few practices, we'll be drilling back-checking, interceptions, and interrupting plays.

"Oh, and Captain," he calls.

I surface from my thoughts and ask, "Yeah? I mean, yes, sir?"

His forehead furrows for a moment and then he says, "Good goon work."

The guys chuckle. It's well known that although my hockey skills have improved over the years, I'm most known for my ability to—how do I put this nicely, in a way that the witch bride wouldn't find rude?—intimidate the other team.

Realizing that was my cue from Badaszek to give my first "Recaptain" what we call the post-game recap talk by the team captain. Sometimes it's meant to review aspects the coach didn't discuss, offer a pep talk, show tough love, or hand out kudos like candy.

Seated on the bench, elbows on my knees, and shoulders bunched up toward my ears, I clap my hands together as if that'll snap me to attention. It's time for me to say a few words —not my strong suit.

I clear my throat. "Ambition isn't how a team wins. It isn't an action or path to a trophy. It's not enough to *want* to win. Everyone wants to score. Get to the Finals. To win the cup. Differentiating ourselves isn't about reinventing the wheel. It isn't even about working harder."

"What's the secret sauce?" Pierre asks.

Grimaldi says, "As if Ellis would tell."

Grady says, "His last name is on the Stanley three times. He knows something about winning."

"My father and brother both have their names on it and I do once, but it's not because of any one thing I did or because I have a secret. There is no secret." The words are harsh but true and I aim them directly at Grimaldi.

A round of groans issues from the group and ripples through me. If I were in their seats, I'd groan too. Although I'm known for being grumpy, they deserve better.

"Of course he'd say that," Grimaldi pipes in.

Resolve building, I channel my father and his many pep talks and say, "How we rise to the top is by giving our all at each practice, each game. When you want to stay out, go home and sleep. When you're tempted to have another hot dog, have a steak instead."

"That's what I'm talking about," Redd says with a nod of approval.

"So it's about discipline?" someone says from the back of the locker room.

"And grit, fortitude ... and playing like a team and not a one-man clown show." Once again, I direct this at Grimaldi.

I leave off the part about offensive and defensive IQ because this doesn't need to turn into a TED Talk. There will be time for that later. We're all beat and I've nearly reached the end of my word count limit for tonight.

"Let's go," I say, concluding.

"*Let's go* like you're hyping us up or *let's go* like we're done here and it's time to leave?" asks Pierre, the smart aleck.

I level him with a death stare. The guys don't respect me as captain yet. Not that I blame them. I don't suppose Badaszek is going to reveal this is a joke or change his mind.

I have to prove myself and I will. I always do.

As I exit, Vohn, the assistant coach pulls me aside. "Well done, but next time try not to look like you're going to murder the rest of the team if they don't listen to you."

"Says the guy who never smiles," Pierre says, having overheard.

Beau, loading up his bag, grunts.

The three of us aren't much for sparkle hands and team spirit cheering circles. However, the witch bride with her wide smile could be part of a cheerleading squad with her unwavering grin and enthusiasm. Just thinking about it makes me tired ... and it's very unlikely that I'll even be able to sleep in my own bed.

Also, why does the woman from the bakery keep popping into my head?

When I get outside, I try to take a deep breath of fresh air, but the winter chill is like icicles in my lungs.

I toss my gear into the back of my truck when another image from this morning surfaces in my mind. I have what feels like mental vertigo. Like I didn't realize I was standing on the edge of a cliff and tip over the side. My thoughts are in freefall.

The woman at the bakery was doing *sign language* to the kid. He was signing back.

Could he not be able to speak or hear?

My thoughts bob and weave. The possibility that my son

can't hear makes me feel like I have a bison sitting on my windpipe. If I overlooked this very important fact, I'm not fit to be a father. Then again, his mother could've had the decency to mention it in her scrawled note before she left him in the lobby of the Old Mill, where I now live.

My lawyer is still trying to obtain his medical records and her whereabouts, among other things.

Sitting in my parked vehicle, my fist pounds the steering wheel. My muscles seize as I remind myself to take a steadying breath. There's no sense in breaking something, least of all my hand. Kind of need it if I'm going to provide for the kid.

I don't know how to do this. How to be a father. How to move past denial that he is my son.

Instead, I drive.

Elizabeth, Mrs. Kirby's Maltese, yaps when I knock lightly on the door. The older woman looks peeved. "You're ruining her beauty sleep. You do realize she's a candidate for the dog show this November."

"I had no idea." I don't care that I sound snarky as I retrieve the kid from where he's curled up on an upholstered chair.

He hardly rustles. Is that because he doesn't hear the dog barking or us talking? I'm about to ask her if the kid talks while she's watching him, but she's soothing Elizabeth.

"I suggest you find that child a mother," Mrs. Kirby says as I exit.

"Yeah. Thanks. Great advice."

Nothing about this situation is sustainable. I'm going to have to find a nanny or childcare or something.

Back at the loft, after I tuck the kid in, I down a liter of water. I'd ignored my texts all day and check them now, reading several from family and friends, including some on the siblings thread, congratulating us on the win—though Hendrix tells me to tighten up my offside awareness.

I have other issues to focus on, namely that I haven't yet told my family about the new addition to my life.

There's no world in which I should be trusted with taking care of anyone, no less an ankle-biter, but I don't know what else to do. It's almost been a month and now it's gotten to the point where I don't have a good answer when they inevitably ask why I didn't tell them that they're grandparents. Mom and Dad are the last people on the planet I want to upset—or to remind that I'm the loser son, even though, on paper, I appear to be a hands-down winner.

Ingrid will punish me psychologically and Hendrix will take it out on me next time we're on the ice. It's a tight spot all around and I'm not used to doing anything other than powering through, steamrolling on a pair of blades if I have to.

Before I plug in my phone to charge, I notice a red dot indicating a message for me waiting on the official Knights team app. I slouch against the counter, feeling unusually tired. I don't know why Badaszek thought I'd be cut out for captain. Then again, it's something I've always wanted and have worked hard for.

The waiting message is from the coach's secretary and daughter. I skim it, then reread it.

> Cara Arsenault: Once again, on behalf of the Knights Organization, congratulations on being named Team Captain. This demonstrates your motivation, commitment, integrity, and positivity. As such, we're delighted to inform you that we've hired an assistant to help you manage your personal and professional tasks. Think of it as a perk that comes with your additional responsibilities. 😊 Jessica Fuller is a consummate managerial maven, self-motivated, and mega-cheerful person.

The sarcasm isn't lost on me. I've had about enough for one day. Plus, I don't need help. My comment this morning about not needing coffee echoes in my mind.

I rub my eyes, rereading the message. At this rate, I'll have to drink espresso just to remain upright.

Me: No.

Cara Arsenault: Too late.

Does she mean it's too late to reply or this assistant nonsense is already in motion? Not only do I not need help, I don't want it. Not from Cara's well-intentioned placement of a lethally cheerful person in my life. Not from anyone.

Tomorrow, I'll decline the offer and turn the assistant away if I have to. Right now, it's time for me to sack out on the floor and hopefully dream about my life when I slept in a bed like an adult and my sole focus was hockey.

10
LIAM

I'M on the phone with my mother, running late, and the kid refuses to keep his shoes tied. No sooner do I have them laced up than he pulls one end and they come apart. At least we made progress with pants and socks.

Did I spawn a nudist? I don't want to know. However, I do want to ask my mother what she did when my brother or sister gave her trouble—she's always quick to tell me that I was perfect, but this situation is not.

Yet I'm not ready to tell my family about the kid.

Mom muses, "I don't know whether it was the Roberts or the Robertsons, but one of them hit our car with their golf cart after they left game night. No one will own up to it."

"Are you asking for my services?" I say in an even tone.

My mother laughs. "No, you keep your gloves to yourself. It's just now we have a rental. All they had available for the next few weeks was a Mini Cooper. Can you picture your father driving one of those?"

Ordinarily, my mom would have my full attention, but I'm tying the kid's shoes again and looking for my trainers.

Until he showed up in the lobby, my life was orderly, straightforward, and crumb-free.

I make one more sweep of the closet—the kid rearranged it the other day while I was on the phone with my manager, trying to keep track of dates and responsibilities. When I came back, he had his hands and feet in my size fifteens, lumbering around like some kind of safari animal.

"Do you think you'll be able to make it home for Dad's birthday? Your brother and sister will be there."

"Yeah. Uh, I think so. Let me check the calendar."

"My big boy, always so busy."

From the other room, comes a crash followed by a wail.

"Mom, I have to go. I'll—"

"Is everything all right? Is that someone crying?" Never misses a trick, that one. Not when Grannie Bell and Aunt Goldie were taking care of my siblings and me when they took their twentieth-anniversary cruise, and certainly not when we decided to trap Santa when we were even younger. In the first instance, we took the runabout boat onto the lake and accidentally ran aground. Mom knew something was up when everyone's shoes were still soggy a week later. She also caught our fishing net snare on the top of the chimney before it caught fire. Must be where the kid gets his propensity to climb.

"Yes. No. It's fine. I've got it."

Do I though?

Just then, the app for the building dings, meaning there's a guest downstairs waiting to be let up. I'm not expecting anyone and doubt it's a fan—the doormen and welcome desk attendants are good at spotting them and turning them away.

"Mark your calendar for the birthday. Oh, and we'll be at your next game in LA. Wouldn't miss that. Hendrix said the locker room there smells like the water at an amusement park ride. Is that true?"

"Oddly specific, but I haven't noticed."

The kid's cry continues and my phone beeps again, indicating the waiting visitor.

Needing to calm the chaos, I say, "Gotta go. We'll talk soon."

"Oh, all right. I'll say goodbye. I miss you, son. I love you and your father does too."

I don't hear her hang up before I rush down the hall to find the kid half-buried in books and stacks of boxes askew next to the built-in shelves. Still haven't unpacked.

"What were you doing? Never mind. Don't answer that." I move some of the books, making sure there aren't any broken limbs or bruises.

The kid is still crying and my phone is still beeping. To make the noise pollution stop, I click to accept the visitor and then go to the kitchen and grab a cookie.

My mother sends them and I usually leave them for the crew at the Ice Palace. As tempting as my mother's cookies are, I won't keep in top form by indulging. My diet and fitness regimen are strict and right now, I should be at the gym.

"Are you all right?" I ask, holding the cookie up for the kid to take.

He slows to a sniffle.

"You can have this, but you can't climb on the furniture or up the walls."

Not that I have much in here, since I moved in December. Just then, someone knocks on the door.

Gritting my teeth, I say, "Don't do that again. Do you understand?"

He hesitates and then takes the cookie while I risk leaving him alone long enough to see why someone is at my house this early.

Over my shoulder, I say, "Clean this up and then feed your

crab. We have to go soon." Or ten minutes ago. But if the crab starves to death, I'll be hearing more crying. I'll also be cleaning up the books later instead of taking an ice bath because the kid is not going to listen to me.

The reason that may be the case and how I've possibly overlooked it for nearly a month makes me cringe inside. I should make him a doctor's appointment. I am so under-equipped for this—I can't even manage to get us out of the house on time.

When I get to the door, I spot my sneakers under the kid's coat. He's supposed to hang it up. My aggravation grows when a light knock comes again.

I tear it open and bellow, "What?"

A woman in a fitted dark green jacket over denim jeans stands outside the door. She wears ankle boots and dangly gold earrings. Her hair is freshly styled and her face is familiar. She greets me with a confident posture and a grin that's full of playful flare.

Then I meet a pair of brown eyes splashed with amber. They sparkle and her smile deepens, revealing a dimple on her cheek. "Good morning. I'm Jessica Fuller, your new personal assistant, at your service."

"What are you doing here, Witch?"

Her smile vanishes and the sparkle in her eyes dims. "What did you call me?"

"You're the wedding witch from the bakery."

She rocks back on her heels and lets out an exhale. "Oh, that was just Monday. No big deal. I'm back in the saddle, as they say." Her voice is far too chipper for this early hour.

My eyes slide across her, but she doesn't flinch.

"Let's pretend the wedding dress thing didn't happen. I was going to show up today dressed like a 1960s secretary. But the overall look was less *Mad Men* and more Old Mona—

Grandma Dolly took a typist class in junior college. She still had her interview outfit. Oh, and Ella, Jack's wife, has a maid uniform from her days working as a housekeeper at his resort that I could wear. Such a Cinderella story." She sighs.

I hardly follow what she's saying and am about to interject that she can leave now, but by some force of nature, she continues to speak.

"Back to Grandma Dolly's wardrobe. She's filled out a lot in recent years. The woman doesn't throw anything away though. If I land a role, even a job as a 1970s disco queen, she's got me covered."

I envision a fitted gold jumpsuit and for some reason, seeing this woman in that is strangely intriguing.

I ask, "What are you doing here?"

She smiles with her full, peachy lips and then says, "As mentioned, I'm your new assistant."

"No." I slam the door.

I expect to hear her walking away. Instead, the loft is quiet. Too quiet. I tell myself the kid is just busy eating his cookie. He's not tearing apart the furniture nor did he choke on an M&M. Wait. He's not allergic, is he? I dash into the other room and find him holding the cookie and just staring at it.

Brushing my hand down my face, I say, "We've got to go."

He doesn't move. I need to sweat until the tightness in my chest and the rest of my muscles goes away, my thoughts still, and my life is like it was before.

Simple. Orderly. Focused.

With a grunt, I point at the kid and then the door. He slowly gets up and walks across the room toward the door. At least he hasn't tried to make a break for it yet.

Oh good. Now I have a new thing to worry about.

The missing sneakers are on my feet and I open the door.

Jessica Fuller, I think she said her name was, is still standing there.

"Excuse me, Mr. Ellis, I'm here from the Knights as your new assistant."

"No."

"Yes."

"No."

"Yes. Are we playing some kind of repeating game? Is this like telephone—you know, like kids play in grade school?"

Before I can answer, she bounces on her toes and starts waving her arms wildly at the kid.

He brightens and then makes a motion with his hands.

Not this again.

I take the kid's little, sticky hand in mine. "There will be none of that. Leave," I order the witch bride.

She bounces along beside me as I take long strides down the hall. Probably too long for the kid because he stumbles.

"I'll come with you. Just tell me what you need help with and I'll do it. Within reason. Like, I won't pluck your back hairs, not that I'm suggesting you have any. Nor will I lie, cheat, or steal." She goes abruptly quiet, then says, "He can't leave without shoes."

"What do you mean?"

She points to the kid's feet.

I tip my head toward the ceiling and let out what probably sounds like a growl.

His hand slides out of mine.

Her eyes widen.

I say, "Come on, let's get your shoes."

I expect defiance or at least noncompliance.

However, she makes a gesture with her hands. I watch carefully, cautious, perplexed. She repeats the motion with two fists facing down and then taps them side by side. To my surprise, the kid hurries down the hall.

We return the way we came and she follows, keeping close so that I can't shut the door behind me quickly enough to keep her out.

Spinning in a slow circle, she exclaims, "Wow. What a lovely loft you have. So much open space and light ..." Then she whispers almost to herself, "And so little furniture. Oh, but—"

The kid digs around in the rubble of my books for his shoes.

"What happened here?"

"A kid happened."

She makes a sort of tickling, scratching motion at her sides while saying, "Was someone playing little monkey? That's not safe."

The corner of the kid's lip twitches. He holds up the cookie, which was on the floor well beyond the five-second rule, and passes it to her.

Once more, while moving around her hands, she says, "Thank you for the cookie. Is this why you were climbing on the shelves?"

I respond, "No, I gave it to him so he would stop crying."

Her brow furrows and in a low voice, sans hand motions, she says, "You can't use food that way. It's not healthy for a variety of reasons."

I incline my head. "I'll handle my household, thank you very much."

"Speaking of, how can I help today?" she asks with that peachy smile.

"By leaving."

Her face falls. "Cara said you need help."

The kid toddles over and stands next to her as if confirming that fact.

"I don't need help."

"At least let me put your books on the shelves."

She crouches down at the same time as I start to gather the books.

We bump into each other and my left hand grazes hers.

A whoosh rushes through me that I promptly dismiss ... or try to, but it sizzles there, on my skin, like an ice burn.

"I said I can do this."

"Okay, well, do you have any appointments you need to be made, um, errands run, emails answered? I can manage your schedule, set up meetings, answer calls, and of course any other household tasks. Do you have a dog to walk? Do you need an oil change? I do. Not me, I mean my car."

I scowl as I shove *The Art of War* back on the shelf. I reread it every year. As captain, I should get each of the guys on the team a copy and require them to write an essay.

"The stoics. I wouldn't have expected anything less. No self-help guidebooks. Ooh, The Bible. That's my favorite one. Best read ever. Ten out of ten recommend."

"Do you ever stop talking?" I mutter.

She makes a gesture at the kid who is now eating the cookie. I pray we don't pay for that later with him barfing. The floor was clean until he came along.

The kid smiles slightly in response.

I ask, "What did you do?"

She winks at me.

That little motion of her brown eye lifts her dimple and sends another whoosh through me. I push the couch across the room so the kid can't use it to climb again.

"Rearranging things? Sparse décor. I can help decorate."

"I don't have much." I prefer to keep things minimal because stuff requires attention, cleaning, and maintenance. Just like people. Can't let anything distract me from hockey.

"We have that in common," she says under her breath.

"Recently moved in. Haven't unpacked," I say.

"I can help." Man, is she persistent.

"I said I don't want your help."

She taps the air with her finger. "Technically, you said you don't *want* help. Not my help specifically. Since we don't know each other yet, you don't know how very helpful I can be. I'm the most helpful helper that has ever helped."

"So you're a *professional* personal assistant?"

Pink dusts her round cheeks. "Um, no. Not exactly. But I did help run a six-figure home business, before taxes."

"I don't want to know what that means. You can leave now. Don't come back." The words are harsh but final.

She nods slowly and starts toward the door. The kid hurries after her, nearly tripping over his own feet.

My gaze follows her and despite the sway to her stride and unfailing smile, onboarding another person into my life is too much at the moment. Simple is better and leaves less room for mistakes to be made.

Pausing with her hand on the doorknob, she says, "If you change your mind, please let Cara know. I'm really good at cleaning, organizing, and a variety of other things, including but not limited to making sure your socks match."

The woman exits. She's one big bomb of happiness that I just can't handle.

Her gaze drops to my ankles.

The space between my eyebrows pinches and I look down. Sure enough, one of my socks has stripes and the other is solid.

11

JESS

AS I PLOD down the hallway of the renovated Old Mill building, the words, *You are such a failure*, echo in my head.

So far, in life, I've managed to survive, but I have numerous *Almost but not quites* on my personal scoreboard.

I almost had a family, but never knew my father and my mother cared more about the men in her life than about me.

I almost finished college but was rejected for the non-renewal of my loans.

I almost got acting jobs, but they always hired someone else.

I almost got married, but my fiancé walked out on me.

A long sigh escapes as a sad little cry comes from behind the door. I'm certain Mr. Meanie took the little boy's cookie away. The monster—for giving it to him at seven a.m. in the first place and then probably tossing it in the trash.

The guy himself could really, really use a cookie.

There's a children's picture book called *If You Give a Mouse a Cookie*, but I wonder what would happen if you gave a grump one ... or a cake.

I could bake one and find out.

Now there's the cringe of having to tell Grandma Dolly and Cara that things didn't work out with Mr. Ellis. The former will wonder why I at least didn't get his autograph and the latter will hook me up with the locker room custodian position. However, that'll mean I'll still have to see that neanderthal on the daily.

When I reach the elevator, I give a wry smile because his socks didn't match. I shouldn't have pointed it out. He seems like the kind of person who cares about that kind of thing, doesn't have a single fingerprint on his vehicle's windows, and never wears wrinkled clothing.

He's an uptight monkey butt—yeah, juvenile, but true.

Who's calling my name? My full name.

I turn around.

He stands in the doorway, and says, "Jessica."

The little boy tears toward me, arms wide open. I scoop him up and he clings to me like a little marsupial baby.

I wonder where his mother is, but a twinge in my chest makes me worry she is like mine or perhaps she's a gorgeous and highly successful lady boss who usually takes care of the household, is a powerful CEO, and manages to make a healthy dinner every night, but she's away on business and her troglodyte husband is playing Mr. Mom.

Yep. This guy would only date, no less marry, a woman with unfairly long legs. Hairless too. I bet she never gets spider stubble.

Liam Ellis grips the doorframe overhead. I'm not sure whether he's holding up the building with those massive biceps or needs someone to lean on.

"Yes?" I ask, not sure if the child just wanted to say goodbye or if I'm keeping this job I so desperately need. On second thought, cleaning locker room toilets wouldn't be the worst.

The little love muffin nestles into my neck like he never plans to let go. I don't sense abuse here—those are red flags I'd see a mile away. My guess is Mr. Meanie does not have the dad thing figured out.

His expression is stony. "I didn't think it would be that easy to get rid of you."

"Yeah, well, I know when I'm not wanted." Which is all the time.

His eyes darken. "You said the team sent you?"

A little burst of hope flares. "I'm good with social media. I'm sure you have an account. I could show it some TLC."

He tips his head to the side and turns back into the house, leaving the door hanging open.

I take this to mean I got the job. I pump my arm in the air and mouth, *Yes!*

Liam stalks like a big cat through the grand foyer of the loft. Of course, a guy like him would live on the top floor. I'd expect nothing less even though I don't know much about his type— the growly, grouchy kind.

The little boy doesn't let go of my hand.

"I could take him to the children's museum in Omaha, out for a wholesome lunch, and teach him how to put on his shoes. He's still a bit young to learn how to tie them."

Or I could run. My instincts urge me to make a hasty retreat.

The child signs that he wants to show me one of his toys and I reply that I'll be right there. First, I have to talk to his dad.

But he takes my hand and toddles down the hall into what I presume is his bedroom—or the guest room. With a glance over my shoulder, I catch Liam watching me carefully.

The queen-sized bed is unmade and the décor is decidedly not child-friendly with slippery refinished floors, a brick wall, and a stack of teetering moving boxes.

By the door is a heap of blankets and a pillow like he lets a hobo sleep in here with the little boy.

I don't want to pry because none of this is my business. I'm here to help with professional tasks, but I cannot figure out what's going on. Okay, and as a child prodigy at adapting to new situations, I'm unduly curious.

This place is huge, so they could be having renovations and the father and son are staying in here while workers are remodeling their rooms. Or the kid is only here temporarily, or—I don't know what, but it's echoey and chilly. Kind of lonesome too.

The little boy and I sign while he shows me his few toys. His vocabulary is fairly limited, but he tells me that he's three, so it's not unusual. He has a little army man, a truck, Legos—which may or may not be age-appropriate considering they're a choking hazard—and a pet crab.

We decide to build the crab a house with Legos. Inspired, he decides to make a whole town for the crab. I tell him I'm going to talk to his dad for a few minutes and make him promise no monkeying around.

The corner of his mouth lifts slightly. I glimpse a picture of myself in him—unsure what was happening in my life, but not counting on anything good.

I find Liam in the living room tidying up his books. For someone who was on his way out the door, he seems to be dawdling, like he's avoiding something.

When he glances over his shoulder at me, fire blazes through my veins, whether because the man is incorrigible or for another reason—if that's the case, I'd like to mark myself as not available. I'm definitely not interested in long, lingering looks or catching the eye of anyone, least of all a tall, fit, and handsome guy like Mr. Meanie. No way do I have a sudden and keen interest in strong, defined shoulders.

"You haven't run away yet." His voice is a low rumble.

"Why would I do that?"

He grunts and pours himself a cup of coffee. To his credit, it smells good and not like burned hair mixed with vinegar—Sorsha had a knack for scalding it even when using an instant plastic K-cup.

I watch Liam carefully, disturbingly intrigued by the contrast between how obnoxious he is and the gracefully powerful way he moves. It sends a swizzly feeling through me. One I will ignore now and forevermore.

He doesn't offer me a coffee and I could use a large right now.

"Jessica, let me make one thing clear—"

"Jess," I correct.

"I didn't ask for help, Jessica."

My smile wavers. "Of course not."

"I don't want help."

"But Cara—"

"Arsenault is not the boss of me," he counters like a fifth-grader.

"But your coach—"

"Just named me captain and with that comes new responsibilities." He seems to relent slightly.

"It does seem like you have your hands full."

"My hands are fine and that's none of your concern." He sets the mug down on the counter with unnecessary force.

I jump, startled. However, I've dealt with people like him and worse, so I rally, lengthening my spine and pressing my shoulders back. After all, I can't very well take him *that* seriously when his socks don't match.

Or did he change them? His feet are hidden behind the kitchen island. "As you said, you don't want help. I understand, but as I see it, I can provide you with something you need."

He chortles, er, chokes?

I take the opportunity to take a few steps in his direction with the express purpose of getting a clear view of his feet.

He asks, "Or do you need the job?"

I open and close my mouth. "You've got me there. Yes, I need the job."

Liam huffs. "And you've never been a personal assistant before, so what exactly qualifies you—?"

If I were a gazelle, there'd be no outrunning him across the wild savannah now. I swallow thickly. The truth is, I've mismanaged my life from start to finish. Even though I try to be well organized and present myself as having it all together, somehow, before I get to the ribbon marking the end of the race, I always fall short and fail.

If I were a team of one and the opposition were life, they'd be up by ten points at least.

I'm not surprised he didn't offer me any coffee, but the fact that he gave his son a cookie from the homemade assortment on the counter, provides me with a response.

I ask, "You're new at this, aren't you?"

My vague, yet pointed, question makes him pause for a fraction of a second. He takes a truculent sip of coffee.

"How old is he?"

"Three."

"When is his birthday?" I ask, hoping he got to blow out three candles.

A full second passes, then another. I glimpse a crack in The Beast's veneer.

"Jessica, that's none of your concern."

My chest clenches. I should retreat, but having had countless birthdays of mine missed or forgotten, I press in. "What's his full name?"

Hesitating, he clears his throat. "King Liam Ellis."

A smile plays on my lips because I was not expecting that response in my game of *How Well Do You Know Your Son?*

"So, he wasn't kidding when he told me his name is King."

Liam rubs the back of his neck and turns away briefly before having second thoughts. The swizzle returns and not because he's pleasant to look at in his commanding, confident way. I'm certain there are soft eyes and a smile hidden behind his tough exterior.

Leave it to me to always try to find the diamond in the rough, make treasure out of trash, or repurpose leftovers. Grandma Dolly says it's because I'm more used to people turning away from me than not. That I need to see my value and accept my self-worth.

Liam is the kind of guy who faces things head-on and whose sole focus is the biggest and best of everything, especially when it comes to hockey, not that I'm paying attention. Much.

So far, the only area in which it seems he falls short is fatherhood. He could stand to attend a how-to class or a convention. Do those exist for new parents? All I know is that I've always wanted to be a mom and he seems like he'd rather be on the ice.

"There are going to be a few rules."

"So I got the job." Not waiting for his response, I wiggle my fingers, wave my hands in the air, and spin in a circle. "Yay. Thank you. You won't regret this."

"I'm sure I will."

"So what are the rules?" I ask, leaning in.

"No personal questions." He holds up his thumb, starting to count them off.

I tilt my head. "Come again? But I'm your *personal* assistant. It's literally in the title."

"I didn't ask for a PA."

I stop short of rolling my eyes. "What are the rest of your rules, Mr. Ellis?"

A normal person would insist I call him by his first name. Liam does not. He'd also call me by my preferred name, Jess. Also, Liam does not. Perhaps I should've withheld my excitement until we're on sure footing. Taking a deep breath, I give it a five-minute break.

He says, "You may not go in my personal space."

"Gladly."

His lip lifts slightly, spotlighting the scar. "You may not go on my phone."

"Wouldn't dream of it."

"You won't discuss my private matters with friends, family, or anyone."

"My lips are sealed." I half expect a non-disclosure agreement to appear out of thin air.

He's holding up all five of his very large fingers, covered in callouses. "Under no circumstances will you wear my jersey."

I frown. "What on earth would possess me to do that?"

"You're the witch bride, you tell me. Maybe some kind of voodoo." His eyebrow arches.

I wrinkle my nose, not wanting to think about my ill-conceived early morning arrival in town still wearing my wedding gown. "I am nothing of the sort. My garment was a result of a poor decision."

"Do you make many of those?" His smile is tighter than a violin string, which plays sadly in the background of my mind because, just like everything else in my life, this isn't going to last.

"We shall see, won't we?"

"Also, don't smile so often. It's too much. You're aggressively positive and optimistic." He squints as if fighting the glare.

Like a reflex, a grin rises onto my lips as I eye the cookies because I could go for one. Thankfully, Grandma Dolly will have some waiting with milk when I get home. She'd flash the sign for a flower—her way of reminding me to keep my chin up like a buttercup. Resolve rushes at me like a lioness roaring back at the king of the jungle.

My wedding was my last failure. I'm going to be the best personal assistant in the state and show this meanie what I'm made of—determination, enthusiasm, and Bundt cake.

While Grandma Dolly makes great cookies, on my first birthday we spent together, she made a Bundt cake just for me. It was the first time I'd gotten one on my birthday. She topped it with sixteen candles, which managed to stand up long enough for me to make a wish for my own family someday and then blow them out. We were dying with laughter. It's one of my best memories. And I've been obsessed with Bundts ever since. They're just so adorable and versatile.

Liam drags his gaze over me. I'm not sure whether my cheeks flush because of the intensity in his eyes or because I'm afraid I have poppy seeds in my teeth. Plagued by insomnia in the wee hours, I tested out a lemon poppyseed Bundt cake recipe and had a bite for breakfast.

After draining his coffee cup, Liam says, "We will communicate by text only."

"That sounds like rule number six."

"It's part of our operating agreement. I'll have my lawyer draft it, but I want to set the foundation now so you know what to expect."

"And what's that?"

"A purely professional relationship for a limited amount of time. I suggest you start looking for another job, so you can have it lined up, Jessica."

"I don't think that'll be necessary." Because for once, I'm going to succeed.

Watch out world and the beasts that inhabit it, Jess Fuller isn't going anywhere! Well, except eventually for brighter pastures because the winter in Nebraska is no joke. I don't really want to stick around Cobbiton for longer than a few months. Six at most. But Liam doesn't need to know that. I'll make him think he's stuck with me forever.

Maybe I am a witch bride because the notion of tormenting him with my *too much smile* makes me cackle inside.

He grunts.

I flash a pageant-worthy grin his way because I can't resist fighting grump with a blast of sunshine. Call me crazy, but I'm determined to wake a glimmer of joy inside the sleeping giant.

12

JESS

STILL IN LIAM'S kitchen and pleased he relented, giving me the job on a trial basis, I stand poised with my bullet journal and gel pen at the ready.

I ask, "Mr. Ellis, please tell me a bit about yourself, your lifestyle, preferences, allergies, or anything that would be helpful in my assisting you."

He stares at his empty mug.

Tough nut to crack. "For example, how do you take your coffee?"

His nostrils flare. "Black."

Like the coal in his chest. I wrinkle my nose because I shouldn't be thinking about his chest and how the fabric of his shirt strains against the well-defined muscles hidden underneath. He's a dad but does not have a dad bod like Rexlan does.

"Let's keep things to a need-to-know basis."

I jot this down. "How about some vital statistics?"

"Why would you need those?"

"Um, you're fit, so you must have a workout routine. Do

you use protein powder? Track your macros? Micros? I can go grocery shopping for you."

"I'm missing training as we speak."

I gesture toward the door. "Well, by all means, go ahead."

"I know my way to the door." But he doesn't move.

"I'm not keeping you here."

His eyebrows lift. "And leave the kid with you? Not a chance."

"He wouldn't topple boxes on my watch." Not that I'm volunteering to be the nanny.

"I don't know you. Don't trust you. Don't particularly like you."

Ouch. The little clouds I keep underfoot disperse and threaten to block the sun installed overhead. I peel a holographic star sticker from the sheet in the little pocket of my journal, write the word *patience,* and then apply the sticker to today's box on my calendar.

However, he doesn't seem to like anyone, except maybe his son. However, deep down under Liam's grizzly bear exterior, I sense a teddy bear, begging for freedom.

Liam busies himself with washing the coffee mug. I'm accustomed to the deep chasm of disconnection, of being unwanted, but being told outright is something that's only occurred a few times. I look through my collection of stickers for a heart. Fresh out.

I close my eyes for a beat, blinking back liquid. When I open them, Liam stares at me. I've backed down, shrunk, and made myself invisible so many times I've lost count. It's gotten me nowhere.

Mr. Meanie will not win my day.

I press my shoulders back, and say, "I see. You don't have to like me for my role as your personal assistant to be beneficial to you and your household."

Before I can say more, his son rushes from his room, struggling to keep his Lego creations intact.

I flash some quick signs of excitement, relaying how much I want to see what he made with his toys.

Liam remains at a distance, watching us with dark, glassy eyes. My money is on him making sure I don't pocket a Lego. In reality, he's the bandit, making off with the smiles, laughter, and happiness of the innocent. Or it could be that he's not the master of his domain. Just someone who found himself at an unexpected destination.

Relatable.

The next thirty minutes pass in a rush before the little boy yawns, possibly having a sugar crash from the cookie and in need of a nap. I ask him to show me his favorite picture book and we look at the images of people playing different sports. I sign each one and he fixates on the one with a guy in hockey gear. I sign *Dad* and he remains quiet as if he's not entirely sure about Liam's role.

He must get a second wind because he starts climbing around, a real wriggle worm. He alternately pats my cheeks and sucks his thumb. I can tell he's tired and isn't used to a routine.

As I carry him over to his bed, he chomps down on my shoulder hard with his little teeth. I yelp. He launches out of my grasp and onto the mattress. Eyes wide with fear, he stares up at me. I want to be upset as I rub my shoulder. His eyes fill with tears.

"That hurt me."

He repeatedly signs that he wants a hug.

I think about what Grandma Dolly would do and explain that we don't bite. I sign that it hurt and we don't hurt each other. We can hold hands and hug. But we don't bite.

He stares at me as if starved for attention like he feels some unnamable pain inside. I do my best to relay what an apology is and show him the sign for sorry.

I accept his apology and make sure he knows that he's forgiven.

His lip wobbles as he figures out the motion for *sorry*.

After a few more minutes, his eyes dip and he dozes off. I slip out of the room and follow a grunting sound where I find Liam doing pushups. He's already broken a sweat as his muscles flex and strain.

"Your son is really sweet, uh, except he bit me."

Grunt.

"What do you know about DHH?"

Double grunt.

"Does he have extreme hearing loss or moderate?"

I expect Liam to continue to ignore me, but he pops onto his feet with cat-like reflexes and says, "Your position is restricted to personal assistant duties."

I press my lips together to keep from saying, *In that case, your position is restricted to dad duties.* "What's first?"

"I'll text you a list along with expectations later today."

Rules, an operating agreement, expectations, and a purely professional relationship for a limited amount of time. Got it.

He narrows his eyes as if expecting me to say something sassy.

So I do. "And making sure your socks match."

They do now.

He squints at me.

"Ding, ding, ding. We have a winner. Liam Ellis is capable of dressing himself. Two black athletic socks for the win."

I don't even get the hint of humor in response.

"Since this is your rodeo, I'll let you take the lead. Should I be self-directed and find some things to do? Will you bark orders? Do you want me to stand at attention in the corner until my services are needed?"

"I didn't sign up for this, Jessica."

"Clearly."

But I'm not sure whether he's talking about having an assistant or something else ... parenthood?

Flipping over to do situps, he grinds out, "You can show yourself out the door."

I watch for a moment, mesmerized by his ability to push through a full sit-up, not a crunch or the assisted kind with someone holding down his feet. He presses on. And I will too, no matter how disagreeable he is. My sunshine was hard won and no one, least of all Liam Ellis, is going to take it away.

"I'll be going then."

"Good," he says, straining now, having moved on to pull-ups, using a bar mounted in the doorway.

"Great," I say, once more captivated by this man doing his workout.

It's not the show of brute strength—okay, a little bit because not even the most skilled Renaissance sculptor could create such muscular perfection from marble. He's burly but not beefy. I'm transfixed by that and how he's so cold when he has a cute and healthy son, a beautiful home, and a successful career.

Somewhere over the rainbow and down the yellow brick road, my version of that exists. I have to hope. I have to believe.

But it's not here.

When I reach the door, the patter of little feet stops me in my tracks and two pudgy little arms wrap around my legs.

I sign that it's time for me to go. The little boy's chin quivers. I want to assure him we'll see each other again, but know all too well the pain of broken promises, so I remind him not to climb the walls, to keep making such cool things with his Legos, and to practice signing to his crab.

Liam appears, sweaty and broody ... and unfairly attractive. Giving my head a shake, I sign, *Goodbye, King Liam Ellis.*

His father asks, "What did you say?"

I sign and speak, repeating my farewell then dropping my hands, I add, "Isn't it a bit audacious to name your kid King?"

"It wasn't my choice," he says with disdain.

"I figured you'd want to wear the crown and be called Hockey King or something."

He takes a few steps, edging me toward the door. "Around here, I do. Don't forget it."

"I'm at your service, your royal hiney-ness." I know it's childish, but I can't help it. I'll do anything to get this guy to crack a smile.

His lips don't even twitch.

"The name King Liam Ellis, almost, but not quite, makes your son a junior."

He blinks slowly as if bored by my observation.

"I'm wondering if I can call him KJ, short for King Junior. It's more kid-friendly."

"Call the kid whatever you want, Jessica."

"It's Jess."

He slides his hand down his face as if exhausted. "Okay, Jessica."

"Jess," I repeat.

He holds the door open for me.

"Wait, um, also, maybe don't call him the kid. You could call him KJ too. It's kind of adorable."

"I'll call him whatever I want."

"Right, but KJ is fun and sweet, right? And while you're at it, you can call me Jess," I say with a friendly little bop of my head.

"See you tomorrow, Jessica." He closes the door some more.

I wedge my body between it and the frame. It's a risky

move since I'm dealing with this rascal. "Sounds great, but please call me Jess and your son KJ."

"I don't know why this matters."

"Because," I say, intending for it to be a complete sentence.

He crosses his arms in front of his chest and slowly asks, "Because why?"

"Because you're not the king, lord, president, or prime minister of me."

"But I am your boss."

"True, but behind every boss is a great assistant." I beam a smile.

"Goodbye, Jessica."

"It's Jess." I bunch up my lips. "You're arguing with me just to argue, huh?" It's like a sport with the guy.

"I could say the same about you."

"No, I'm just looking at the sparkly, rainbow-filled bright side."

"No glitter is allowed in this house."

"Is that another rule?"

"You're the witch bride. You probably cut off locks of guys' hair and use them in anti-love potions."

"That's disturbing and not at all true. Yes, I was a bride-to-be. No, I'm not a witch."

"A real ray of sunshine," he says glibly.

Keeping chipper is what gets me through. "Do you prefer cloudy days?" I lived in those for nearly my whole life and don't want to go back. Can't.

I tell myself to see the good in Liam beyond the lonely man who built up walls to protect himself from something. But what? From the outside, this guy has it all—a great career, a family, and a nice home—after he decorates. Well, almost. Where is his wife, his queen?

His gaze floats over mine, sending a chill that quickly

warms over when I glimpse a teeny tiny tease of a twinkle in his eyes. It's there, hiding.

I say, "I just know we're going to be friends."

He scoffs. "Don't need those either."

My heart pinches. That's rainy-day thinking. "Sure you do. Everyone does."

He leans in, close enough that I can see the fine freckles across his nose and the depth in his blue-gray eyes. My breath catches in my throat.

Liam's voice is a low rumble when he says, "I don't want this."

"Then what do you want?" I risk asking because what else is there to say to that?

"I want my old life back."

"Seems too late for that and sometimes our old lives are overrated."

"Mine wasn't. It was perfect."

"Alone, up here in your tower?"

His throat bobs on a swallow.

"I get it. You were free to do what you wanted whenever you wanted." I'm well out of line, leapfrogged right over it, but his smug, stoic expression draws the bold truth out of me.

He snorts. "No, I was free to focus on hockey and not have all this other stuff to deal with."

"What? Family life? Seems like a pretty good deal to me." That familiar ache in my chest returns. He has no idea what he's taking for granted.

13
JESS

I'M PRACTICALLY out of breath by the time I get to my car. If I were to sum up the last few hours in one word, it would be *horrible*. Terrible. No good. Very bad.

That's a lot of words but I'm not known for brevity, especially when I'm flustered.

Liam Ellis is a brat. He has no idea how blessed he is. I fire off a text to Cara, telling her as much but then I delete it and will myself to be more positive and try again.

> Me: Who knew a guy they call The Beast could be so extraordinary? A delight. A gem of a human being.

> Cara: Are we talking about the same person or are you having some sort of post-jilted-bride break with reality?

> Me: Both?

> Cara: Meet at the Fish Bowl.

O'Neely's Fish Bowl is a local eatery by day and a hockey pub by night. It's ground zero for all things hockey outside of the Ice Palace. Stan, the hockey super fan, owns it. I knew his niece, Heidi, in high school and wonder what she's been up to.

Even though it's been a while since I've stopped in, unless something has changed, every available surface is covered in hockey memorabilia. Stan's photo is in the dictionary next to the phrase *puck head*.

I text a reply and agree to go, but only because Cara is buying me a double order of loaded potato skin pub pucks even though she doesn't know it yet.

While still in Los Angeles, I went on a hunt to find something comparable at the local restaurants, but nothing tops the crispy little twice-baked potato boats served at the Fish Bowl. They're cooked, then split in half, and then hollowed out. The potato gets mashed with butter and cream. Then it goes back into the potato skin and is topped with cheese until it's both melty and crispy. Before serving, they drown it in bacon, sour cream, chives, and if you're feeling wild, jalapeños.

I'm feeling wild.

At the door, Leah greets me with a, "You're back," squeal and a big hug.

Half the restaurant turns to see which of their favorite hockey stars arrived, but it's just little ole me. The girl who showed up in Cobbiton her senior year and refused to talk until Grandma Dolly drew me from my shell with sign language and cookies like you would a cat with a can of tuna.

Leah, a local who also went to Clarkson High, and a hockey super fan who works here stops at at our table. "How long has it been? Don't say a year. That's too long."

"It's been a year and one failed engagement later," I lament.

My usual megawatt, high-voltage energy flickers until I remember how much this town gave to me. Then why did I leave? Because I wanted to boast that I made it in the big wide world when I hadn't been able to before. It was a leaving-the-nest kind of challenge and possibly stoked by pride.

Leah shows me to Cara's table in the back. She sits with a few women I recognize and others I don't. She's sipping on a soda through a straw and introduces me to Brandt, Reddford, Savage, and Hammer.

I know some of the women, but say, "First names, please."

Cara gives her head a shake. "Oh, right. Sorry. I forgot to close my work tabs. This is Gracie, Whit, Delaney, and Margo. She's a wedding planner."

I cast Cara a dark smile. "It's so nice to meet you all. I'm just going to borrow Cara for a minute." I lead her to the corner near the dartboard.

She eyes it warily.

"How could you do this? Why would you think I'd work for him?"

She pats the air with her hands for me to calm down. "You seem upset. I take it things didn't go well."

"He's a living, breathing beast." I give her a quick recap.

"You left out one important thing. Objectively speaking, he's handsome."

"Cara! In no world is that what I'm thinking about right now. The wedding gown is still warm!"

"But you didn't love Rexlan."

I frown but don't disagree. "How would you know?"

"Because you didn't even like him. If you truly did, you would've introduced us. And that's why I've forgiven you for not telling me about the wedding."

I tilt my head from side to side, realizing there's really some truth to the whole hindsight is twenty-twenty saying. "Yes. No. But that's not the point." I wave my arms, flustered. "Liam outright said that he doesn't like me."

Cara's mouth forms a perfect *O*, but before she can say more, the servers bustle by with trays of food and we return to the table, complete with potato pucks.

"Look! I ordered your favorite!" Cara exclaims. "Peace offering?"

"This conversation isn't over."

Gracie, who seems like she was born with a ray of sunshine beaming over her and didn't have to cultivate it, says, "I hear you're Liam's new assistant."

My answer is a grunt and not because he's already rubbing off on me. My mouth is full of buttery, bacony, potato goodness.

Delaney says, "The guy is a lightning rod for controversy."

"And so handsome in that authority 'stache kind of way." Leah waggles her eyebrows.

I nearly choke on my next big bite. "Do you mean like a mustache?"

"She's still looking for love in all the wrong places," Cara says.

"Says the woman who married a hockey player."

Whit breaks in, "Oh, speaking of, you have to stop by The Milk Mustache truck on Sunday."

I lift my shoulder. "Liam could use a cookie."

Whit shakes her head. "I mean with your grandma. We're working on a whoopie pie together. I cannot get the cookie consistency right."

"I'll help you taste test," Gracie says.

My reply comes belatedly because I was thinking of Liam and the cookies at his house. "Of course."

Delaney tells a story about how Ellis got a penalty for what looked like an open ice hit with the shoulder to a rival player on the Titans named Henri Valjean.

"He injured someone? Is that why he was out for two weeks?" Margo asks.

Cara says, "No. My father had another reason. But an official investigation concluded that Valjean's injury was preexisting and he staged the whole thing."

"Aren't there measures in place to prevent that for preexisting injuries?" Delaney asks.

"I thought Liam was the goon, so that came with the territory," Whit says.

"He doesn't date and he's a thug?" I ask, recalling what Cara said yesterday and what I've gleaned about the guy.

"Just your run-of-the-mill grouch with anger management issues," Gracie says breezily like it's no big deal.

"Is that common?"

Margo elaborates, "The Knights claim several verified grumps: Vohn, the assistant coach, and Gracie's husband; Beau, my guy and the goalie along with Liam. There are a few others to varying degrees. But Beau is relatively misunderstood. He's more of a stoic than a true grump."

I recall the books on Liam's shelves.

"Not Vohn," Gracie says with a smile.

"What do they put in the water here or is it the ice?" I murmur.

The conversation shifts from hockey-playing husbands to non-toxic home décor that's suitable for children. Given my new job and KJ living in what amounts to a nicely appointed bachelor pad, I take notes.

When the ladies discuss a shopping trip to Omaha, through gritted teeth, I say to Cara, "I'm seeing multiple red flags flying in the wind."

"Not with Liam. Trust me. But we'll talk later," she says with a smile.

I devour the loaded potato skin pub pucks and everyone slowly filters out, leaving Cara and me at the big table amidst the dinner desolation.

Looking around to make sure Mrs. Gormely, the town gossip, isn't within earshot, I tell Cara about my first two encounters with Liam Ellis. "I didn't realize he was the same guy from the bakery until today."

"I'm surprised you didn't recognize him since Grandma Dolly is obsessed."

"When have I ever paid attention to hockey?"

"Let's see, April before we graduated high school you had a crush on Lane Sheridan."

"That was fleeting and there's no way I'd even entertain a flirtation with a married man fifteen years my senior. Speaking of, where is Liam's wife?"

Cara frowns. "What do you mean? He's very, very single."

"They divorced?" I ask, probing.

"He'd have to have been married first. I told you, the guy doesn't date."

"Then he must have flings."

Cara practically snorts soda out of her nose. "To do that, he'd have to go out. No, Ellis is married to hockey."

"But what about—?"

Cara waves her hand dismissively, but I don't think she knows about KJ, otherwise, she'd mention it or would've suggested I work as a nanny rather than an assistant since it's more in my wheelhouse, having studied early childhood education before dropping out of college.

After crushing a piece of ice between her teeth, Cara says, "Here's the Ellis family dossier. Liam's father is Rainer Ellis, a German hockey player who was big in Europe and then transferred to Canada in the nineteen nineties."

"Oh, so he has a family legacy thing going on."

"Big time. There, Rainer met Belinda Bell, a showstopper, according to the old-timers in the league. She was turning heads and he won her hand. When he retired, they settled down in her hometown of Brookking Sound to raise a family. The eldest you know who, plus Ingrid and Hendrix of the Toronto Titans."

"So his brother plays in the NHL too?"

"Right forward. They're super competitive. Both of them are very physical players."

I recall Liam working out in the middle of the day like his life depended on it.

"Liam played for Saskatchewan and then the Warriors, I think, before joining the Knights with a no-trade clause. With the kids grown up and out of the house, their parents moved to California. Then there's Grannie Bell and Aunt Goldie. They're really sweet with a side of sass. I've met them a couple of times at games. They're all super supportive."

"So no major family drama? No mommy or daddy issues?"

"Nope. They're solid."

I scratch my temple, unsure why he has daddy issues, well, as a father. It seemed like he could hardly be in the same room as his child without having a crisis.

"I'm sorry things didn't go well today. There's always tomorrow."

"That's my line." I absently hum a few songs from the play and feature film, *Annie*. No one knows the entirety of my past, not Cara and not even Grandma Dolly, but they both have enough pieces of the puzzle to get the picture. I always counted on tomorrow being better.

I wipe a bead of condensation on my plastic cup of soda. "Yeah, tomorrow. Did I mention he made up all these dumb rules?"

Cara shrugs. "Not surprising. As you know, for reasons unclear, my father made him captain. He tried to lay a bunch of rules on the team. Too much too soon."

I roll my eyes.

Cara gets a glint in hers. "But you could break the ones he made."

"Aren't you the coach's assistant?"

"And daughter."

"So shouldn't you be trying to protect him and the team? Sounds like you're suggesting subterfuge."

Cara laughs. "Friends first, but I wouldn't suggest anything that would compromise his ability to play hockey. Perhaps you could even enhance it."

My eyebrows pinch together. "Doubtful, but what did you have in mind?"

Cara leans in and we conspire about how I could break Mr. Meanie's rules when I realize I already did.

14

LIAM

BEST CASE SCENARIO, my new personal assistant can lighten my load remotely. There's no reason she needs to come to my loft again, leaving behind her cinnamon, spice, and everything nice scent. Her sweet and unrelenting smile isn't welcome in my home. The last thing I want or need is her help, but the last few days haven't gotten easier.

So maybe she can pick up a little of my slack.

At the Ice Palace, Vohn gets us started on agility and tosses me the puck as it were. While I'd like to go hard, if we're going to get to the Finals, we need to start building our mental muscles.

I run us through a few control and accuracy drills and then pair everyone off.

"You're going to pinpoint your opponent's weak spot. Then you're going to exploit it."

Grimaldi rubs his hands together. "With pleasure."

"Wrong idea. The point of this exercise is for all of us to know where we fall short because I guarantee the opposition is evaluating this too."

Despite my excellence on the ice, unfortunately, Jessica has been able to point out my shortcomings without saying a word. She's great with the kid and while I've overachieved at everything I've ever done, I'm not going to qualify for Father of the Year anytime soon.

After a team talk and shower, I check my messages, hoping Mrs. Kirby still has all her teeth. For the first twenty-four hours after Jessica left, the kid seemed to have adjusted. Then things went downhill fast.

He started acting out, was clingy, and refused to eat anything but cookies. After dinner, he cried until I positioned myself on the edge of the bed. I'll admit it's better than sleeping on the floor, but he's like a pygmy donkey and kicked me in the kidneys twice.

Instead of an ALL-CAPS essay from Mrs. Kirby commenting on who she calls "My maladjusted son," the message is from Jessica.

I instantly regret giving her my number and suggesting that we communicate through text only. She severely abuses the use of emojis. A thumbs up is fine to use as necessary, but each message is littered with sparkles and hearts and smiles.

> Jessica: I appreciate your making clear my role as your new personal assistant with your rules. 😙 Here are some of mine:

> Me: That's not how this works.

> Jessica: Here are my rules:

> 1. Please reply promptly to questions I have, particularly for time-sensitive tasks. ⏱

> Me: Fair enough.

> Jessica: 2. Because I will be in your home from time to time, do not touch my private chocolate stash if you find it.

> Me: I will and it's going in the trash.

> Jessica: 3. If travel outside of Cobbiton or Omaha is required, I need at least a day's notice so I have time to wash my hair.

I'm not sure what comes over me, but I want to run my fingers through her hair. Find out if it's as silky as it looks. No, that's not right. What am I thinking? This woman riles me up and brings out the worst in me. I know I'm being rude, confirming her assumptions that I'm a jerk, but I cannot stop myself.

> Jessica: 4. If you know I'm coming over, please save me a cup of coffee.

> Me: I'll make sure it's from the bottom of the pot and full of grounds.

> Jessica: 5. You may not touch my butt.

I wouldn't even consider it. Well, until now. Her backside comes to mind with a nice curve dropping from her waist.

Shaking my head to rid myself of the stupid, yet sudden juicy desire, I consider my reply. I could tell her to keep that thing away from me if she knows what's good for her ... or steer this conversation back in the direction of general normalcy, at least when it comes to Jessica. The woman has quirks for days ... and has been driving me nuts just as long.

Me: Have your previous employers done that last one? If so, sounds like a lawsuit waiting to happen.

Jessica: Oh my goodness.😳 No! I meant butt.

Jessica: Autocorrect! Bundt. You cannot touch my Bundts. They're a kind of cake. I make all sorts but specialize in personal-sized Bundt cakes with classic and unique flavors. It's kind of my thing. The snickerdoodle with cream cheese frosting is everyone's favorite. Mine too.🧁

Me: In that case, I won't touch your Bundts.

Jessica: Small claims court is no joke.

Me: Are those all of your rules?

Jessica: No, there are ninety-five more. I'm just getting warmed up.🔥

Me: This is nonsense. Meet me at the Fish Bowl in an hour.

Jessica: Okay, boss.🫡

Me: Mr. Ellis is fine.

Jessica: Is that so? I think Mr. Ellis is grumpy.

Me: I meant that you can refer to me as Mr. Ellis.

She doesn't respond, leaving me with a strange, vacant feeling that borders on a craving—like when your nutritionist points out that you haven't had chocolate in over twelve months. If Jessica is smart, she'll keep her chocolate out of my house.

When I park outside O'Neely's Fish Bowl, a nearby car honks and I nearly jump out of my skin. I've been to this hotspot for fans to watch games and gloat about how they're the authority on all things hockey dozens of times. I can handle a little attention, but not a lot after today.

I don't often make appearances here, but figure it's best to meet Jessica in a public place rather than at home because if the kid sees her, he's bound to not want to let her go.

As I exit the truck, what I'm feeling is a peculiar kind of anticipation, like I know a candy bar is waiting for me and I can't wait to tear into it.

I grab a booth table and keep my eyes glued to a game from earlier in the season airing on one of the many televisions. It was against the Titans—my brother's team. Coach put me in during the second period because Ted's knee was acting up. I inwardly chuckle, recalling the game because Hendrix and I were so competitive that our skates practically sent up sparks, melting the ice.

Hayden scores a goal, reminding me this was when Valjean faked a shoulder injury. I push the thought from my mind and glance to my right, spotting a brown-eyed beauty all bundled up. Her lips are glossy and smiling. She waves like we're best friends who haven't seen each other in years.

Of course it's Jessica.

If she had a greater sense of self-preservation, she'd have come in here wearing pads and carrying a stick.

Another woman trails behind her, twice her age if not more, eyes alight with what can only be described as hockey fandom lust. When the older woman's gaze lands on me, it slips for one threatening moment. A subtle shiver runs through me as I imagine her in the paint, on offense, charging me like a bulldog on skates.

Jessica waves her hands like the witch bride she is, and says, "Liam, I'd like you to meet Grandma Dolly."

Giving a lackadaisical wave, I say, "Hi."

Jessica continues, "She's Deaf and an expert at reading lips." So only I can see, she whispers, "Don't do your usual mumbling and grunting. It's rude." Then louder and at an upbeat pitch, she adds, "I'll sign to fill in any gaps."

I tuck my chin back, not expecting this level of confidence and command or the list of rules she texted which were more like demands.

I nod politely because my grandmother would slap me upside the head if I didn't defer to my elder. "Nice to meet you, ma'am."

Jessica mutters, "I guess Cara was right and you weren't raised by wolves. Possums maybe."

"Who's rude now?" I snarl back, then more loudly, "Also, why was Arsenault talking about me?"

"She hired me and gave a briefing. Described you as a loner with zero personality and a limited vocabulary," she says as if awarding me with accolades.

I scowl in her direction.

"At least that was the gist."

I cross my arms in front of my chest, accidentally knocking into the table. "Is that so? Then why did you take the job?"

"I couldn't decline because she and I are best friends and because Grandma Dolly is a super fan ... and I was in desperate need of a job."

The woman mouths a few words and signs rapidly.

Jessica translates. "She said *she* thinks you're dumb and ugly."

My jaw drops a fraction of an inch. What transpired in the

last few days to cause Jessica to go from eager assistant with hope in her eyes to hostile enemy with me in her crosshairs?

The older woman flashes a scolding look and elbows her.

Jessica huffs an exhale. "I'm kidding. Grandma Dolly said that *she thinks* you're more handsome in real life than on TV and the poke check penalty at the last game was unfair."

"Thank you very much. It was a great game. I appreciate your support."

Grandma Dolly signs and waggles her eyebrows.

Jessica blinks slowly at her grandmother who mischievously bats her eyelashes. "She says she appreciates your biceps and wouldn't object to a peek at your—" She coughs and kind of clears her throat, sounding like someone gagging on a duck whistle.

"What was that?"

"You know, your—" Jessica spins her finger in the general direction of my abdominal area.

Grandma Dolly rapidly signs.

"Apparently, in certain circles, your abs are quite the popular commodity. They even have their own hashtag."

"They do?" I nearly splutter my tonic water with lime all over the table.

"Don't sound so smug."

Actually, that was the sound of surprise. My sister says I need to work on my delivery because I'd be the last person she'd want to receive news of a diagnosis from or find out about a new addition to the family. She claims that I'm gruff no matter what and lack nuance.

Jessica beams a smile as if well aware she just got under my skin by referring to my, ahem, skin.

"That's, uh, very kind of you, Mrs. Dolly," I say because how else do you reply to a septuagenarian who makes a comment like that?

"It's Grandma Dolly. Everyone in Cobbiton calls her that," Jessica signs.

The server appears wearing an official O'Neely's Fish Bowl t-shirt. She and Jessica exchange a side hug and happy, bouncy, excited cheers.

"Grandma Dolly, you know Leah. Leah, this is Liam Ellis."

"Yeah. I know who he is." Unlike Jessica and her irrigation system of happiness, this woman actually glowers at me.

Leah says something about Heidi and her baby Bunny—I'm pretty sure that's a health code violation in an establishment like this. The three women disappear to a nearby booth as the bubbles in my beverage deflate. Then, returning to the table, they gush about Heidi's cute baby and not a critter that snuck into the restaurant.

Leah gives us the formal spiel about how O'Neely's specializes in corn and potato dishes, featuring five special sauces.

She asks, "What can I get for the guy who ruined my fantasy hockey league winning streak because he had to go laugh at the coach and take a leave of absence?"

Awaiting my response to that projectile, Grandma Dolly tilts her head at an appraising angle.

Jessica leans in like I'm about to tell her the secret family cake recipe.

"I'm good." I'm not sure where my appetite is at—my mind is on hockey, but the space between my head and the aforementioned abs fills with static. I can't get a read on it other than I feel whooshy. I'll have to ask the team doc to check my vitals.

Jessica says, "You can't just order water. We'll take a double order of loaded potato skin pub pucks. This makes my second this week." She bounces in her seat like that's a major accomplishment.

Grandma Dolly gives the thumbs up.

"Making up for lost time." Before Leah leaves, Jessica gets a smile and I get another dirty look.

Grandma Dolly and Leah exchange a knowing nod that makes me wonder if they're up to something.

I have a strange feeling that Jessica didn't only bring her grandmother here because she's a super fan. Actually, I'm the one who called this meeting. Did she reverse-bait me? Have I been reeled in by the most unsuspecting and possibly unrelentingly cheerful person on the planet? If so, touché.

I'm ready to get down to business and get out of here. The less time I spend with this woman the more likely I am to retain my common sense. "We need to discuss the rules."

"Be my guest," Jessica says with a flourish of her hand.

"Yours seem to be outside the bounds of the assistant-boss relationship."

"I work best with cream in my coffee."

"You're working remotely, you can get your own coffee."

"I'm more of a people person. Things will work out better between us if we have more face-to-face time."

Grandma Dolly signs.

Jessica translates. "She says you have a very nice face."

I snort. "Is she trying to butter me up?"

"She would like a signed jersey, but I'll have to leave the two of you to settle that since I'm not allowed to touch your jersey."

"I said I didn't want you wearing it."

Surfacing from the malaise of constantly keeping one eye and ear on the kid, I concede that was a little aggressive.

Grandma Dolly signs again.

Jessica's chest rises and falls with a long sigh. "She said she'll make you cookies. Oh, but you don't like cookies, do you?"

"I never said I didn't like them. I just don't eat them."

Jessica rolls her eyes. "In the short time I've known you, I've observed that you have a certain kind of mental toughness, likely required for the rigors of your sport. However, I'm not sure how well it works with day-to-day life."

"I didn't ask for your psychoanalysis."

"I'm mostly making this up as I go along, but I wouldn't be doing my job if I didn't optimize my ability to assist you."

"Do I really need your help?"

Grandma Dolly nods vigorously. Maybe I'm not a fan of her after all. Then again, my grandmother can be brutally honest, too. Usually, she's right.

"Listen, all I want to do is play my best, lead the team to the Finals, win the Stanley. End of story." But there's a hidden chapter and I'm afraid of anyone finding out.

"Which is why I thought it would be beneficial for us to have this meeting."

"But I suggested it."

Jessica smiles primly. She commented that she's making things up as she goes along, however, maybe she's more clever than I thought. Why though? I can't track her angle. Is it to annoy me? To tempt me?

Leah brings the potato skins and places them on Jessica and Grandma Dolly's side of the table, only leaving two plates alongside extra napkins. "If there's anything else I can bring you, please let me know. Enjoy." She wrinkles her nose at me.

Predictably, Jessica smiles at the appetizers. Then she and Grandma Dolly join hands and bow their heads in a silent prayer. Jessica takes a bite and then raves about how delicious the potato skins are.

Grandma Dolly signs and she translates, "You're missing out."

They do look delicious with all that melty cheese. I decline a lot of things in my life, but focus and hard work got me to where I am. It's payment for what I did.

Jessica scoops one of the potato pucks onto a napkin and slides it in front of me, narrating each movement like a hockey commentator. "Fuller is in possession of the puck, she breaks away, rushing toward the goal, and she scores!" At that last word, she lifts her arms and cheers.

At the same time, I reach for my water. In a right-handed-oriented world, she's not used to being around left-handed people. Our hands bump and the tall cups of water teeter then totter as we both scramble to make sure they don't tip.

Nostrils flaring, we manage to keep from having a calamity, but this woman is a hazard. She can't be part of my life, especially not with how having any amount of contact makes me feel off-kilter and all whooshy inside.

"Whoopsie."

She's got that right.

"I was making a special potato skin delivery. You looked sad over there without one."

Call me stubborn, but I'm not going to eat the potato skin. Not even if what she did with the commentary before we almost had a massive spill was kind of cute.

I don't like the way I feel around her. It's like I'm behind the wheel but losing my grip and skidding dangerously toward a ravine bordered by animosity and attraction.

I just can't let myself go over the edge.

But what if it's not entirely up to me?

My foot is on the accelerator, but I have to remain in control.

15

LIAM

MEETING WITH JESSICA and her grandmother at the Fish
Bowl last week concluded with the two of them having a very
candid conversation with me about the kid's potential auditory
thresholds.

I'd bet ten to one that this woman would walk over hot
coals, hang glide, and swim with sharks all on the same day.
She's an unstoppable force of hopefulness and honesty.

And I'm not sure how I feel about my fatherhood status
coming to the surface. On the one hand, I can only keep the
secret for so long. On the other, there will be repercussions.

I'm not a liar, but rather an avoider. I'll stay in my lane over
here where everyone drives at a safe speed and uses their
blinker.

Except when I'm on the ice. I spend a lot of time there
during the following days, doing my level best to forget about
hearing Jessica laugh first thing in the morning when she shows
up with my coffee, drawing the kid out of his shell, and
somehow anticipating various things—my passport renewal
documents from the Canadian embassy, a greeting card and gift

for my manager who just added a baby to the family, and making sure the laundry gets done.

But that's not the worst of it.

When we were at the Fish Bowl, while she ate the potato pucks like they were the greatest thing on earth, she wouldn't back down, suggesting the kid see a specialist for a care plan, an ASL tutor who also happens to be a great baker—Grandma Dolly—and that I start learning a few signs.

I went on defense, telling her to keep her nose out of my business. It's an adorable button nose, but still.

That's where my head is now during a home game against the Reno Rebels.

Her comment to Grandma Dolly that I'm stubborn shushes through my head while I play spin-o-rama, keeping the rubber away from the goal and daring the Rebels' left forward to try to take a shot.

Jessica is the stubborn one, not knowing when to stop pushing, trying to get me to open up, and showering me with her unrelenting smile and sunshine.

Some people like the cold and clouds—I'm among the few.

Lew gets a five-hole on Beau, shooting the puck right between his legs. The fans of the opposing team go wild because now we're tied. Knights *boo* and if we're not careful, they'll throw dried corncobs at us.

Badaszek has us regroup, flashes a sharp side-eye in my direction, and sends Grady onto the ice, leaving me to dust the bench.

Gripping my stick and hanging my head to get it back in this game, Redd cuffs me on the shoulder. "Where you at, bro?"

"I do not negotiate with terrorists and this woman is threatening to blow up my life."

His weight comes down on the bench next to me, inviting me to say more even though we both know I won't. He's here for me, but the problem is obvious. I'm thinking more about the kid and Jessica than I should.

My thoughts gather and scatter, leaving one solution. Make her quit.

Then what?

Forget about it all.

But I can't.

Not when I return to the ice toward the end of the third. Not when we go into overtime. Not when I get a total top-shelf cheddar shot. Not when the arena erupts, chanting "Beast."

However, the usual thrill doesn't rip through me, affirming that all my hard work is paying off, reminding me to keep going … to push harder.

Perhaps Jessica and I aren't that different after all.

After a shower, the guys are regrouping and I clock someone saying, "Ellis has been acting different since he got back."

"No, he was squirrelly before he left," Hayden says, gaze locking on mine.

Just like puck bunnies aren't allowed in here, this is a no-gossip zone, so if someone is going to say something, they need to be able to say it to your face.

"Squirrelly, huh?" I ask.

Well, the kid sure can drive me nuts. When he was going to sleep last night, I found half a cookie under his pillow.

"What do kids like to eat?" I blurt.

It's an out-of-character question for me to ask, however, not an entirely out-of-context inquiry since many of the guys have or are in the early stages of being in the family way.

"Do you mean kids, like baby goats?" Ted squints at me and tells a story about how when he was up in Maple Falls, Washington he met a goat named Edgar.

"Weren't you a kid once?" Grady says.

"No, he came out of the womb bearded and surly," Pierre quips.

I grunt.

"Ask the nutritionist what they eat," Robo says smartly.

I jolt to my feet. Why didn't I think of that? I don't need Jessica's help. I've got this. Wait. Was I considering her help?

Mrs. Kirby gave me a veritable childcare punch card and I only have three remaining days for her to watch the kid.

Then what?

"You're right. He is acting different," Jack adds, peering at me. "Somehow stressed and stirred up at the same time."

"Isn't that the same thing?" I ask casually, tossing my gear in my bag and desperate for this line of conversation to end.

Jack shakes his head. "No, like romantic stirrings."

"What are you talking about?"

Pierre says, "He's full of questions. But we have one."

"We do?" a few of the guys chorus.

Pierre smirks. "What's her name?"

"Whose name?" I ask.

"You know who. The woman waiting for you in the hallway." Now Hayden smirks.

Jessica? I didn't ask her to come tonight. Why would she? "I don't know what you're talking about."

"Lately, you've been texting a lot more. Texting with a scowl on your face." Redd smirks too.

"If I were involved with someone, wouldn't I be smiling?" I counter.

Thankfully, Beau snorts instead of smirks. Glad one of the guys on the team is on my side. "Not you."

Never mind.

I huff a breath because there is no chemistry between Jessica and me. I'm not interested in anything with her other than never seeing her bright eyes, dimpled smile, and plump peachy lips ever again. The best thing about her is watching her leave each day.

"Touching her butt is against the rules."

The guys collectively gasp.

What has gotten into me? It's like all the words the kid refuses to speak dam up behind my mouth and are pouring out. Not that he'd say that, but I did.

And. Everyone. Heard.

They *Ooh* and *Coo*, making smoochy noises.

"I meant, Bundt. She bakes." I bolt.

However, I don't make it out the door before Beau hollers, "We all knew. It was obvious."

Not him too. He's the guy I can rely on to remain mum like me. To put his full focus on the game. Then again, he got fooled into falling in love last year with a wedding planner no less. Probably a witch like Jessica.

Who is indeed waiting for me in the hallway. Her long brown hair is down and looks as smooth as silk with soft waves shifting with her movement. The woman practically hums with good vibes, radiating warmth like a human ray of sunshine.

"What are you doing here?" I ask.

"Well, hello to you, too. Great game by the way. The other team passing the puck between your legs was superb."

I square up with her. "I don't think you understand how hockey works."

She twists her lips to the side. "True, but just think of the opportunity it gives you to up your game. We grow through adversity."

"You sound like a motivational speaker."

"Thanks for coming to my talk. I'm offering a limited-time discount on all platinum packages. Just sign over the contents of your bank account and I'll change your life." She holds out a bag of licorice. "I did that once and ended up almost having to file bankruptcy. Turns out the thirty-day money-back guarantee had a loophole. Then I worked for a woman who ran such a company and almost made the worst decision of my life. Thankfully, her son eloped, so no harm done, really."

I turn my nose up at the self-help suggestion and licorice. "No, thanks."

"You requested it."

"I didn't."

As if ignoring me, she says, "Only people who hate themselves eat black licorice. The red kind is where it's at."

"I don't hate myself."

She shrugs as if that's up for debate. "Also, I thought we were sticking to texting to communicate. I had to update the Knights app to read your message and I have a very limited data plan. Took me half an hour to log into the Wi-Fi here."

The pranks among the Knights are pretty mild, all things considered. I blame them. "That's because I didn't message you. Not through the app and not about the licorice."

As if on cue, my teammates parade out of the locker room, surveying me and then sneaking a peek at Jessica. Grimaldi winks at her.

A primal rage burns inside. If we were football players, I'd drag him out to the turf, but before I can do the hockey version, Pierre says, "We smoked him out. I knew something was up. Someone will have to change his app password."

A growl comes from my throat. Time to make her quit being my assistant.

Jessica's cheeks are on fire as if she discerned what they're implying.

"No," I state.

"No?" she says, voice squeaky.

"Nope," I repeat.

"But—?"

"Not a chance."

I'm not sure if we're having the same conversation, but for my part, I want to make it clear that despite the stunt the guys pulled—impersonating me on the app—I'm not interested in her. Not in the slightest. Not even her butt. Especially that.

"I detest cake," I blurt.

She gapes at me. "Cakes are perfect for all occasions!"

"You can't solve everything with cake."

"Why not?"

"Because life isn't a story with a happy ending."

She crosses her arms in front of her chest. "I know that, Liam. But you could ease up on being such a rude, crude, brooding grump."

"And you're a ray of sunshine."

"You say that like you'd rather stay inside with the curtains closed. By yourself."

"At least I like my own company."

"I find that hard to believe." Her chin quivers.

I have to stop this now. Get her out of here so she doesn't cry ... or want to come back. "But you want to see my abs."

Eyes cartoonish, she gasps. "I do not."

"Admit it." This will drive her over the edge. She'll turn in her resignation any second now.

"My grandmother was the one who was interested."

I arch an eyebrow. "Yet you knew about the hashtag."

A color the exact hue of rose petals dusts her cheeks.

I step closer, narrowing the space between us until she's nearly against the wall. "I didn't ask for this," I say, when what I really mean is it's time for her to find a new job.

Except her peachy, glossy lips ripple like she's trying to resist a smile. Like I don't intimidate her at all. Either that, or she's too positive and bright-eyed for her own good.

My eyes lock on hers for a long beat. Her lashes brush her cheeks, then she looks up at me, unwavering.

I feel like I'm losing my balance. She lengthens her spine, growing closer to me.

It's like we're both on the fritz with the question of a kiss on our lips. Not sure whether we want to shove the other into the abyss or hold on to each other for dear life.

Mouth parting, she swallows before saying, "I don't like the way you smell."

Breaking the moment, whatever that was, I cross my arms in front of my chest and lean against the wall. "And how is that?

"Like aftershave and ice. Cold, cold, ice. Like your heart." With each word, she narrows her eyes and leans closer to me.

My lips pooch a little bit, preparing a retort. "What's wrong with that? Sounds as if you like it."

"No. Nope. Not a chance," she echoes my comment from a few minutes ago.

Operating on too few hours of sleep and coming off an intense game, it's like the past ten years didn't happen. I'm temporarily my old self. Lacking impulse control and without thinking, I lean my head to one side and nuzzle her neck, breathing her in.

She yelps. "What are you doing?" Then, in a softer, distracted, delighted voice, she repeats, "What are you doing?"

"You smell like cinnamon and spice." And everything nice under the sun. Heat travels up my neck. I love her scent.

Pulling away, she's not wearing her 'Everything is fine' face anymore. More like it's in flames with alarm. "I'm guessing you hate it as much as licorice."

In reality, I've been craving cake.

She storms off, jeans tight and hips swinging. I cannot resist admiring her curves.

I run my hand down my face. What's happening to me?

WITH THE SHEET pulled over my head, so I don't disturb the kid, I prepare a task list for Thursday and text it to Jessica.

> Me: Arrange travel for same-day return from the game in Oklahoma on Sunday.

> Jessica: Done. ✓

> Me: Return call to the auto insurance company. They want an annual mileage update.

> Jessica: No problem.

> Me: Pick up my dry cleaning. I want the dark blue suit ready for team photos over the weekend.

> Jessica: Do all athletes wear suits to games?

> Me: I'm pretty sure it's just a hockey thing.

I realize now that as the first month of her being my assistant ends, our messages have become more casual with both of us inserting questions and thoughts.

I tell myself I want to keep it simple. Straightforward and cinnamon spice-free. Probably. I mean, I prefer that flavor profile to licorice.

> Me: Tell the watch brand that I only do hockey product endorsements.

> Jessica: Are you seriously passing up one of those dark and gloomy luxury brand ads commonly seen on subway billboards? You have a perfectly broody look that's just begging for the spotlight and for someone to draw a mustache on your upper lip with a permanent marker. 📵 😬

I do my level best not to laugh. I stopped shaving and grew out my facial hair the day she started working for me. Hopefully, she despises it.

> Me: I already have a beard.

> Jessica: I like it when you shave.

> Me: I didn't ask.

> Jessica: By now you must realize that I offer up my opinion free of charge. 😊

She sure does and it's kind of growing on me. Like the beard. But if she prefers me without it ...

> Jessica: My favorite Liam Ellis look is in the morning before shaving. Like an eight a.m. shadow.

She has a favorite? I'm not sure what to think of that, except it sends a whoosh rushing through me.

I tell myself that I preferred life pre-Jessica Fuller. However, there's a lot to like about her.

She's genuine. Not fake.

Sweet. Not saccharine.

Bubbly. Not bombastic.

Scratch the last. Depending on her caffeine level, she can

come in sparkling like a disco ball or bashing through my walls like a wrecking ball.

On the other side of the bed, the kid turns over, letting out a soft little snore.

I take a deep breath, realizing the last time I felt like I had any oxygen in my lungs was when I was with Jessica earlier. She and the kid were playing a patty-cake kind of game. The other day my trainer even noticed, commenting that my inhales were shallow.

What she said at the Fish Bowl floats into my mind and finally lands with a thud. Yeah, he needs to see a doctor about his hearing. I'm so out of my depth, I don't even know where to begin. But I have to start with what's best for him, which means I can no longer deny there's an issue.

> **Me:** Schedule a time for your grandmother to meet the kid.

> **Jessica:** Seriously? She's going to be thrilled. He's going to adore her and learn so much. This is the best decision you've ever made. I've seen her work miracles. We'll have to celebrate!

Before I talk myself out of it, I send a final message.

> **Me:** In that case, make me a Bundt cake.

> **Jessica:** I thought you'd never ask.☺

I'm about to shut off my phone when it vibrates with another text. But my thread with Jessica left off with her message.

The message is from Pam. The words *I want him back* accompany an image of part of our custody paperwork. The fine print.

A swarm of wasps fills my stomach. My face feels hot.

My phone beeps one more time.

It's another message from Pam demanding payment.

I read the segment of the document that remains blurry from the days when I discovered I had a kid.

And there's a deadline.

THE CORN HUSKER
[PRIVATE GROUP]

A hub for the Cobbiton community to connect, discuss concerns, and share upcoming events. Please read the "About" section for advisement about sharing direct sales marketing, self-promotion, and work-from-home opportunities. Remember, corny compliments are allowed but friendly feuds will be deleted. The rules are here to foster engagement and fun while maintaining positivity. Enjoy connecting with your neighbors!

[Post: Saturday 9:12 pm]

Sophia Snodgrass Schuster:
Was anyone on Main Street on Monday morning last month (1/21)? A scene of epic proportions unfolded. As you may know, Cobbiton has another new resident. Nebraska Knights defenseman Liam Ellis moved into one of the lofts in the Old Mill building. He's been seen at the Busy Bee Bakery a few times, but on this occasion, he was outside by his vehicle with a woman wearing a wedding gown. She was holding a toddler in her arms. Sources say this might be former Cobbiton

resident Jess Fuller. Last we heard she'd moved to Hollywood to pursue acting.

Don't comment below that I should mind my own business. I care about Jess. We had English together at Clarkson when she moved here in high school. She must be going through a tough time and while I don't want to pry, if she needs a friend to reach out, I'll be first in line.

Please private message me with any info.

[Comments]

MarshaSimmons: If this is true, it sounds like she could use a casserole.

BarrySmeltz: Esorlda, an enchanting sorceress is on a quest to find a missing stone that's said to protect her heart and the realm from the Shadow Fixers. Could be that Jess Fuller is too. I wrote a book called *Attack of the Voalcan Army* and it's available now!

JessieDunnO'Conner: If you keep posting about your book, I'm reporting you to admin *BarrySmeltz*!

TaylorTipton: You could talk to Mrs. Gormely *SophiaSnodgrassSchuster*

CaraBadaszekArsenault: Or you could mind your own business!

[Sponsored Content]

Spaglietti's is having a pasta party and you're invited. Join us on Tuesday for an all-you-can-eat special, including a pasta buffet with several sauces. Come hungry and bring your friends! All proceeds go to Cobbiton's Youth Hockey Team. *No doggy bags permitted.

16
JESS

I TOSS my phone to the end of the bed and it glances off my toe.

Ouch. Ouch. Ouch.

I rub my little piggy and blame Liam. He is so out of touch with, well, everything. His emotions, his kid, civility. And yet ... I don't let myself reach the conclusion to the itty-bitty spark of ... never mind. Fresh off the rejection train, I can't let myself go there.

Retrieving my device, I call Cara and launch right into it, stream-of-consciousness style, armed and ready with all my grievances, but where to start?

"The message in the Knights portal said to bring black licorice, so I did."

Laughter sounds in the background.

"Is this a bad time?" I ask.

"No, we were about to turn on a movie, but that sound was Pierre admitting guilt."

Through the phone's speaker, I hear him say, "The plan

was to have you bring a new kind of candy each day just to razz him."

I can almost hear Cara roll her eyes. "Plan thwarted."

Anyway, in the hallway at the Ice Palace, he ran cold, then hot. Practically nestling his head into my hair like he never wanted to leave while at the same time slicing me with eye daggers and the clear message to get lost.

Pierre chimes in again, "Ellis's default setting is cynical, surly, and like he has to control every little thing."

"Exactly!" I proclaim. "It's like he wants me to quit."

At the same time, Pierre and Cara say, "Don't do that. He needs you."

"If that's true, and I highly doubt it, he has the worst way of showing it ever. Though he did ask me to make a cake. Probably so when I add a creamy drizzle to it, he can mash it in my face."

They both snicker.

"His play took a dip before the incident with Badaszek—shortly after Christmas."

"What happened, anyway?"

Cara says, "I think he had a breakdown. He puts so much pressure on himself."

Pierre counters, "More like a crack-up. He'd been way off for a couple of weeks. I'd wondered if an ex had reared her pointy face back into his life."

Cara says, "If so, she was a real witch."

Pierre uses a different but rhyming word and his wife scolds him.

"Hang on, I have to put money in the swear jar. Sorry about that, ladies. Sometimes I forget I'm not in the locker room."

Cara whispers, "Have you seen Liam's abs?"

"No, but Grandma Dolly is eager." Fine, I am too. Well, in real life. If HR knew how much time I've spent scrolling

#MrDarcysAbs, they'd fire me. If they're anything like his biceps and all his -ceps, they're exceptional.

"I heard that," Pierre calls.

Cara says, "Some of the ladies in the office have a pool. I bet on you and want to know whether I'll be adding to my glamorous vintage luggage set."

"You know I'll get you anything you want," Pierre says.

"I want to save up and gloat," Cara teases. Then, in a whisper, she adds, "It's to use when I surprise Pierre on a trip to an actual Ice Palace in Sweden for our anniversary."

He must've ducked out of the room.

"That's so romantic."

"Shh."

"I'm back. Had to grab some snacks."

"You were talking about an ex. I thought Liam didn't date."

Cara says, "He doesn't. We're just speculating. But someone must've broken his heart."

"If he has one."

Pierre says, "This is what you need to know about Liam. He has a love-hate affair with everything in his life, including hockey, but that's mostly because of his temper, running alternately hot and cold."

I'm nodding along. Never have I felt so understood. "Exactly this."

He continues, "It's not so much that he has a chip on his shoulder, he just gets frustrated when things don't operate as they should. Rainer, his dad, is German by birth, so Liam, as an aficionado of the fine engineering of his father's homeland, believes everything, including the team, should operate like a well-oiled machine. But it doesn't always because we're human and have emotions."

"He keeps his tamped down real tight. Except the mean ones."

"Those come out on the ice from time to time which led to players and fans speculating about his absence last month."

"That was an amazing summary," I say.

"We spend a lot of time together," Pierre replies.

"I wonder what he'd say about you," Cara says.

"Maybe you don't want to know," her husband murmurs.

"But I do know that you've helped him a ton. Lately, my dad isn't scowling when he talks about him."

Pierre says, "Of course he is. He scowls at all of us. But that's his way of showing affection."

We all laugh and I reflect on relationships. The ones I've seen that are successful and the ones that are abysmal failures. Pierre and Cara fall into the first category. Every relationship I've had lands in the latter. I'm the not-proud owner of a short list of dating disasters.

Though, when Cara told me about Pierre, I never thought it would work out. She's quiet and reserved. According to Grandma Dolly, Pierre used to be known as the Frenchman and not simply because of his French Canadian heritage. While Cara had never kissed anyone, he had a lot of experience in that department.

Still on the phone, he continues, "Now that Liam is back and named captain, I'm concerned he's struggling but is hiding it well."

"You should talk to him." I'm not sure whether Cara is addressing her husband or me. I didn't expect this to become a three-way call, but so far Pierre has been surprisingly insightful.

However, a realization about a crucial piece of Pierre's story hits me like a cell phone on my toe. They don't know about Liam's son.

"He's not the kind of guy to ask for help, but why?" Cara asks.

Pierre says, "Pride."

At the same time, I say, "Stubbornness."

Cara laughs. "You're both probably right."

"But what am I going to do about it?" I ask vaguely.

My bestie starts to say something, probably along the lines of asking why I think it's my problem to fix.

Pierre interjects, "I'd suggest you tell his assistant to bring him candy to sweeten him up but—"

"She's already baking him a cake. Wait, are you?" Cara asks.

"You could just mash it into *his* face." Pierre chuckles.

Cara asks, "How are things coming with the rule-breaking?"

Pierre practically loses his mind when I start to recap the five rules Liam outlined. "No personal questions and you're not allowed in his personal space?"

"I've dented those."

"Tell me what he keeps on his bedside table," Pierre says.

I answer, "A Bible and a box of tissues."

"What a good boy."

"Did it ever occur to you that maybe he meant his personal space, like—?" Cara starts.

Pierre cuts her off. "If you're referring to Liam's abs—"

I click my tongue. "You guys gave me an idea."

"Tell me it's a twelve-month calendar featuring his abs. We could make a mint," Cara says.

"Does my salary combined with my abs mean nothing to you?" Pierre asks his wife, faux insulted.

"It's not always about the money but the thrill of how it's obtained." I can practically see her scheming.

We burst into laughter.

I say, "I was thinking that I'd get him some moisturizer for his calloused hands, but put self-tanner in it and then—"

Around what sounds like Pierre crunching a mouthful of popcorn, he says, "I see where you're going with this, but he'd never use it."

"My vision for the personal space thing was that you seduce him," Cara suggests.

Pierre and I both gasp and say, "Cara!"

"He hates me. Why would I do that?"

"I highly doubt he hates you."

I pout. "He told me he doesn't like me."

"Yikes," the couple chorus.

"What were the other rules?" Pierre asks.

His wife says, "My rule is for you to save me some popcorn."

The crunching goes quiet.

I continue, "I'm not allowed on his phone and cannot discuss his private matters with friends, family, or anyone."

"Those make sense, but *oops*," Cara says.

"This isn't exactly a private matter because it involves me directly," I say, circumnavigating the rule.

"What was the last one again?" Cara asks.

"Under no circumstances am I to wear his jersey."

Pierre hoots so loud I have to hold the phone away from my ear. When he calms down, he says, "Bro does not hate you. Not at all."

I frown, not following but wondering why I care whether he likes me. I'd hoped we could become friends or at least be civil, but that's not probable.

"I can't believe he included that as one of his rules." Pierre is practically dying with laughter. "We're about to flick on a movie, but I promise Liam opposite hates you."

Then the line goes quiet.

Cara sends a text telling me she's sorry for the abrupt ending to the call but that we'll talk tomorrow.

What's the opposite of hate?

No. No way. He definitely doesn't love me. I don't think that word is in Liam's vocabulary.

His actions, rules, and so many of the things he's said, including but not limited to *Don't like you* and how my smile is too much make it very clear that he's one hundred percent not interested.

Not that I want him to be.

Do I?

My thoughts trip over the moment in the hallway after his game. We were so close I could smell his masculine, soapy scent. His blue-gray eyes were dark like the sky just after the sunset.

I remind myself that I'm more of a sunrise kind of gal, always looking toward the promise of tomorrow.

When my boss doesn't despise me.

17

JESS

I TELL Grandma Dolly the good news about her being able to meet with KJ. She loves kids and always wishes she had some of her own, hence my adoption. She'd fostered for years and we celebrated my "Gotcha Day" party a month before my eighteenth birthday. Technically, she's my adoptive mother, but everyone always called her Grandma Dolly … and she likes spoiling me as only a grandmother can, so there's that.

I sign that I'm going to the grocery store if she wants me to pick up anything.

She signs back, "#MrDarcysAbs."

I tell her that I'm still working on the player autographs and that one is a bit of a heavy lift.

Grandma Dolly replies, "He's the one doing the heavy lifting, doing all those abdominal workouts. I bet leg day, glute day, and arm day are pretty good viewing too."

After the conversation last night with Cara and Pierre, I can't keep the smile off my face.

She asks me what I'm picking up and I tell her that Liam requested I make a Bundt.

My grandmother's eyebrows bounce and she winks at me as I walk out the door.

After a long day filled with errands, including scoping out various childcare centers, meetings with several pediatricians, and picking up Bundt cake materials—it's doubtful Liam owns a tin—I get to the Old Mill building just before dinner time.

KJ hugs my legs and doesn't let go as I lug in the shopping bags. I sign that he helps me unload, telling him the words for each item. When we're done, I boost him onto the counter.

He tells me about Elizabeth, Mrs. Kirby's dog, and how much he loves puppies.

I relay to him that he's going to meet Grandma Dolly soon and that she always has cookies.

Liam appears, sporting my favorite amount of facial hair and gives me a curt nod. His phone beeps, but he ignores it.

So much for the cake. He's not getting any treats. Just fish and fennel for a boring dinner.

KJ climbs on the chair and helps me wash potatoes and set the table.

I use the air fryer for most of the meal and soon call, "Dinner is ready."

Even though this wasn't on today's list of tasks, Liam doesn't seem to question it. He digs right in. KJ stares at his plate as if wondering where the cookies are hiding.

I patiently wait for Liam to come up for air in ... three, two, one.

He asks, "Did you put black licorice in this?"

"No, it's fennel and it's good for you."

"Tastes like licorice."

"Serves you right. You didn't even say a word of thanks."

"I didn't ask you to cook dinner. I thought you brought this from the meal service that Nat, the nutritionist, signed me up for."

"I meant thanks to—" I point toward the ceiling. "It doesn't hurt to count your blessing from time to time."

Chastised, he leans back in his chair and says a quick prayer, shoves his fennel bulb aside, and devours the rest of his fish and potatoes.

"You're not setting a good example," I say.

He glances at the kid who's playing with his food and grunts. Once more, his phone beeps with a message, but he doesn't check it.

"This isn't a cake."

"We don't always get what we want when we want it, Mr. Ellis."

"Are you trying to teach me a lesson?"

I tip my head from side to side. "Sometimes we get something even better. We're going to make the Bundt together!"

He starts to protest.

Shaking my head, unwilling to give him an inroad, I say, "You even get to wear an apron." For Cara and Grandma Dolly's benefit, I'm about to add *shirtless* but hold back. I shouldn't push it.

"I don't know how to bake."

"Or use your napkin or say please, but you can always learn."

After dinner, I make a game out of cleaning up with KJ while Liam answers emails on his phone. He glances up at me a few times as if afraid I'm going to leave him with a mess. He suggested I hire a housekeeper, but I told him he already has me. Plus, I don't mind tidying up or spending time with KJ. I rather enjoy it.

As I put away the dishes, his slitted eyes drift over me, predatorily, like if I so much as leave a fork in the sink, he'll poke me with it.

He'll be doing the dishes after we're done baking. So there.

With KJ working as my assistant, I sign the recipe and how first we make the batter. I ask him if he wants special fillings. He asks for cinnamon and sugar. We'll layer and swirl it so when we cut into the cake, it'll look pretty in addition to being tasty.

KJ seems very concerned that we're not going to be able to eat the Bundt tonight. I tell him about being patient and that good things come to those who wait. He already had a cookie, so he'll get cake tomorrow.

I sign and speak, "I had to wait sixteen years before I ever got a birthday cake and blueberry pancakes. It's a toss-up, but those might be my favorite. Just think, you're only three and get to eat a slice of the Bundt tomorrow."

The math is most certainly lost on him, but the look Liam gives me is part curiosity and part something else I'm not sure how to read.

Not having loving parents of my own, it's been difficult seeing the distance between father and son, however, Liam has started to open up, tickling and wrestling with KJ which makes him laugh to no end. He's been making an effort to learn more about the DHH community. I only know this because I had to send an email for him and noticed he had a few newsletters from groups, including one that focuses on Deaf children and parents who hear.

It might be happening slowly, maybe in fits and starts as Liam's pride battles with his love for his son, but I have faith he'll get there. Maybe sooner rather than later because right now, the two of them have their heads bent together over some spilled flour, big and little, same hair color and shape. Using their fingers, they're drawing shapes. My heart swells at the sight, giving me hope.

KJ wants to mix the batter with his hands, but I tell him,

"I'll get some Play-Doh next time I'm at the store." Then a lightbulb goes off in my mind. "Or we could make some."

I don't remember the sign for it, but I improvise and will ask Grandma Dolly tomorrow. I bet she has a recipe.

After KJ butters the fluted Bundt pan, Liam tells the little boy to get ready for bed. His face bunches up with frustration, but I don't think he's upset that it's nearly time to sleep. More like he knows his father is telling him to do something, but he doesn't understand. I think this has been the problem from the start.

Without thinking twice, I take Liam's hands, which are like giant mitts compared to mine. He flinches at first as if coming too close to a flame, but then relents as I demonstrate the signs for, *It's bedtime*.

Elbowing him, I say, "Also, smile. Try to be expressive."

His lips pull back in a leer.

"What are you doing? You're going to give him nightmares."

Trying not to move his lips, Liam replies, "You told me to smile."

"Sir, that is not a smile." My lips fall. "Actually, I've never seen you smile."

He grunts.

The detail sticks with me until after I say goodnight to KJ, promising cake the following day.

He asks, *For breakfast?*

I laugh. "Not for breakfast. After a wholesome lunch."

The song "Tomorrow" from Annie comes to mind and how when growing up I yearned for the hope the next day would bring and that my lousy situation would change.

KJ doesn't have it that bad, but it could be better. For instance, his dad could smile from time to time.

When I return to the kitchen, locked and loaded with admonishment, I find The Beast wearing an apron.

I squawk a laugh and then cover my mouth. I don't think KJ would hear me shriek, but because he hasn't had proper hearing tests done, in case he does, I don't want to scare him.

"That is a look," I say.

"You're a good cook."

Shocked, I tuck my chin. "You didn't eat the fennel."

"I never said I didn't like it."

I remind myself that he did say he didn't like me.

"Then why didn't you eat it?"

The corner of his lip hitches.

"To annoy me?"

He shrugs.

"You're maladjusted or a twelve-year-old boy who never learned how to interact with girls short of pulling their pigtails."

"No, that would be my brother."

"So you're saying that you're suave with the ladies?"

He snorts a laugh and his phone beeps. He continues to disregard it. The guy has major cell phone control. When I get a message or notification and ignore it, my blood pressure reading goes up incrementally. I can feel it.

He says, "You're also really good with the kid."

I'm used to surly Liam and this version of him makes me perspire. I take my sweater off, leaving my camisole underneath, put my apron back on, and start preparing the icing so it's ready for when the cake cools.

After a minute, I ask, "Is this your way of asking me to babysit?" I practically already do.

He shifts from foot to foot. "Things with Mrs. Kirby didn't work out."

"You mean you scared her away?"

Liam watches me for a long moment and then says, "What if I don't want to wait for tomorrow for cake?"

"It takes a while to bake and then has to cool. Help me with this." I gesture to the bowl of frosting.

He starts beating it with the spoon.

"Don't manhandle it."

"Show me."

When I take the spoon from his hands, ours brush well, kind of *stick* together because we're both sticky. This time, he doesn't pull away. My skin melts against his.

We move awkwardly to the sink and he lets me wash my hands first, then I show him how to make the frosting.

I say, "Looks like you have a hockey team bake sale future."

"I think I'm well past that phase."

"Oh, right. You're in the big leagues. But what about when KJ plays?"

Liam's expression goes blank like I unplugged a computer monitor. I incline my head and lift my eyebrows.

"I never thought of that."

"You mean you're not grooming him to fill your skates? I thought all dads wanted their sons to follow in their path of greatness or something."

"If you haven't noticed, I'm not most dads." He leans against the counter. The man is practically a pillar of stone on a good day, but now he's somehow more still. Strangely quiet.

"You're a good father." I'm about to launch into one of my perky pep talks, but the words fall like pebbles into a pond.

He shakes his head and then starts doing the dishes. Over the stream of water, he says to himself, "I don't know what I'm doing."

"No one does."

"Except you. You're a natural."

"A natural what?"

"Mom, caretaker. You just innately know what to do."

A great fissure of laughter erupts out of me. "That's hilarious."

The space between his eyebrows crimps. "What's so funny?"

"I have no idea what I'm doing either." The reason why shoves against the laughter, but I won't let myself cry, least of all in front of Liam.

"Then you're good at faking it. I bet your mom baked you cookies, read to you, and showed you how to do stuff."

Having come up to temperature, the oven beeps. I slide the Bundt onto the rack, telling myself the burst of heat is what colors my cheeks red and makes my eyes water.

"No, Liam. I didn't have one of those." I set the timer and am about to leave, but I don't trust him to know when the cake is going to be done. Should've thought of that before.

After standing there for an awkward moment, Liam says, "Tell me how you became such a good cook and learned how to bake Bundt cake."

My voice is scratchy when I say, "You haven't even tried it yet and you didn't eat your fennel."

He bites his lip. "I will next time."

"Maybe KJ will too so he can grow up big and strong like his dad."

This comment seems to have a similar effect as the one about his son filling his skates. Liam drops onto the sofa and leans back, hammocking his head and crossing his ankle over his knee as if contemplating a deep thought. "I still want to know how you learned to cook."

I fidget with the tie on my apron. "I thought we didn't talk about personal things."

"Are you implying that you want to know something about me?"

"How'd you learn to be such a jerk?"

His lips part and he gets to his feet. "Oh, that's how you want to play?"

"I didn't mean it. The words just kind of slipped—"

He stalks toward me, eyes heavy.

Flustered, I answer his question, "When I was a kid, there was rarely enough food. My mother left one day and all I had was a half-empty jar of peanut butter. I was five. Never saw her again."

He abruptly goes still.

"At fifteen, I got a job at the All Ears Diner & Fuel Station."

"By the highway?"

"I met Grandma Dolly there."

"Like your grandmother would come in and—?"

"No, that's where we met for the first time."

His expression sharpens as if he senses there's more to the story.

"I knew how to sign because, when I was eleven, the family I lived with had a daughter who was Deaf. I learned fast and it stuck with me, I guess." I rub the back of my leg with the top of my foot because this conversation makes my skin itchy.

"Was the Bundt Dolly's favorite?"

"No, she only ever ordered coffee. But we connected. I'd go to her house and she'd teach me how to bake and cook. Always said a gal needs to know how to feed herself and her family— her husband had passed away earlier that year."

"Funny, my grandmother says that too ... and she's a widow."

I cannot imagine this man having a family other than a pack of wolves, though Pierre commented that he has siblings.

"Now, I mostly read cooking blogs and plan a dream that will never come true—to become an actress."

"How does that relate to food blogs?"

"Baking is a lot like building a road to Hollywood, step by step—even though that was a big, fat, bust."

"What happened to Mrs. Hyper Positivity?"

"Miss."

With a lift of his eyebrow, he seems to register this detail of my singlehood and logs it for later. "When do you have time for this blog reading and daydreaming?"

"When I can't sleep which is almost always."

"But you don't cook much?"

It almost feels like we're having a normal conversation with a side of subtext. "Rexlan preferred pizza rolls and not the homemade ones, which I perfected, I might add."

"Whoever Rexlan is has terrible taste."

"You don't know that." I'm not sure why I'm jumping to my ex's defense.

Liam captures my gaze. "I'd try them and guarantee I'd like them."

I roll my eyes because if nothing else this man is a contrarian.

Eager to change the subject, I say, "Tell me how you became captain."

"Kind of fell backward into it."

"You don't seem like the type to fall, not on the ice or solid ground."

"I've taken a few spills."

The sweet, buttery scent of the Bundt cake filters from the kitchen, filling my nose along with longing and the truth that I'll never be loved or even liked—and the man standing an arm's length away from me is certainly not looking.

Not that I am either, at him, though he is kind of cute in the apron.

"You're still wearing the—" I start to pull it over his head when he grabs my wrist and stares at it for a long moment. I'm about to tug it away when he closes his eyes.

My heart jitters and that swizzly feeling runs through me when Liam's gaze meets mine and holds so long I lose track of what happened before this moment.

The oven timer dings, startling me.

I move to brush past him to check the cake and he drops my wrist.

While I like to believe that I generate my own sunshine and warmth, my skin is suddenly cold.

18

LIAM

JESSICA BARELY REACHES MY SHOULDER, yet she takes up all the room in my loft. All the space in my head lately.

Over the past few weeks, I've noticed new things appear one at a time: a few plush throw pillows on the leather couch, a table and a lamp next to the recliner. A potted plant by the big windows. They miraculously started multiplying. Each day, I find something new.

I can't complain because it's tasteful in a rustic and modern way, probably what I would've picked if I cared.

She does. So much. It's almost too much.

I don't deserve it.

As the cake cools, not wanting the conversation to end, I confess, "About becoming the captain, during the game when I laughed at the coach, I'd been put in the penalty box more times than all games combined in my career."

She lifts her eyebrows.

"Everyone wondered what had gotten into me." I let out a long breath, not having spoken about this to anyone.

"So you were grouchier than usual?"

"More like out of sorts. Off my game. Sleep deprived."

"I know the feeling."

"On Christmas morning, before dawn, the doorman called me downstairs. Said it was important. I thought there had been an attempted break-in. Sometimes fans get too enthusiastic." I look pointedly at Jessica.

"Don't worry about me. I'm not a fan." She winks, popping her dimple.

"Turns out it was my ex. Sort of. Semi-ex if even that. We knew each other for about six hours in total. She basically left the kid on the doorstep with a plastic bag filled with clothes, the crab, and a note. Merry Christmas to me," I say dryly.

Her jaw lowers. "I'll say. KJ is the best Christmas present ever."

I brush my hand down my face, afraid to see what happens when I drop this bomb. "Jessica, I didn't know I had a kid."

Her eyes bulge. "Oh. Then he was a surprise gift. Those are the funnest."

"I called the authorities. Went through all the proper channels."

"He has your eyes." Hers soften.

There's no mistaking that he's my son, except one thing. "I figured he was quiet and acted out because of the trauma of the whole thing, but—"

Jessica signs and speaks, "It's going to be okay."

"You don't know that." I shake my head.

She nods. "If you're referring to him being partially or potentially fully deaf, yes, it's going to be all right. More than all right. He's going to have a great life because he has a great father who is going to help him get the resources he needs to express himself and communicate."

My stomach clenches. "Jessica, you've been in this house for a month now. I'm not a great father."

She pats my arm. "You will be."

I angle my head, daring her to defy me.

Stepping fully into my space, which breaks one of our rules, she says, "You're going to be a great dad because you're a great hockey player and because KJ is a great kid."

"He bit you."

She chuckles. "So did you, yet I'm still here."

"I did not bite you!"

"With your words." She takes out a couple of plates and forks.

For some reason, I like that she knows her way around my kitchen, around me.

"For now, maybe it's better that KJ can't understand you, gives you time to work on your delivery."

"Are you suggesting I learn ASL?"

She signs and mouths, *Yes.*

We take our slices of cake to the living room. I plonk onto the couch and tap my fork against hers. "Thanks for this."

"Oh, so you do have manners. Bravo. Encore."

"Ha ha," I say dryly.

I take a bite of the Bundt and the sweet yet spicy cinnamon flavor hits my tongue with a delightfully light and buttery consistency.

Jessica must be enjoying her piece too because, for a long moment, she's quiet, totally uncharacteristic of her.

"You said you have trouble sleeping?"

"Ever since I left Cobbiton."

"And now that you're back?"

"I'll be leaving again."

My shoulders drop a fraction. "Except for when you're here, the kid insists I stay in the spare bedroom with him. I started on the floor, but now he wants me in the bed, otherwise, he cries."

"He's insecure, afraid, not sure what's going on because your communication is limited."

"My communication?"

"Yes, you're his father. Learn how to interact with him. Sign. Be a little nicer."

I wince, slouching against the couch cushion. "Maybe I was born this way."

"Send my regrets to your mother."

I fight against a smile, for all her sunshine and sparkle, Jessica sure can be feisty.

As if picking up on my amusement, she says, "Do you like when I insult you? And I thought the lizard cult was messed up."

"What?"

Shaking her head, she says, "Never mind."

"I like it when you—" But my thoughts bottleneck. Perhaps I do need to work on my communication skills. My role as team captain comes to mind. I need to show up better for them ... and my family.

In a somewhat playful tone, Jessica says, "Use your words, Liam."

"I like it when you challenge me."

"Ah, so there is something you *like* about me."

I recall telling her the opposite. At the time, I wished it were true. I bite the inside of my lip and abruptly get to my feet, my cheeks heating as I plod through alphabet soup. "Yes, yes there are. Is."

"You mean to say there are things you like about me?"

Jessica brings our dishes to the sink. "The Bundt is outstanding if I do say so myself."

She doesn't see me from behind, but I nod in agreement. It turns out, Jessica *everything* is my favorite.

She dips her finger into the extra frosting left in the bowl and takes a lick.

Once more, I grab her wrist. My grip is gentle, a caress like before, but the repeat contact takes us both by surprise.

"Oh, now you're Mr. Manners and don't want me eating with my fingers?"

I let out a shaky breath.

Out of the corner of my eye, she dips her other finger into the bowl, swipes a glob of the frosting, and boops it onto my nose then streaks away.

I could've stopped it, but did I want to? Making chase, my face dabbed with frosting, I threaten to nuzzle her again. She dashes past the bowl, grabs it, and wearing a mischievous grin, lifts her finger and then takes another lick.

"Hmm. It's delicious and would be a shame if I … dumped it on your head."

"You wouldn't." She couldn't reach, but I play along.

"Hmm. If I got it all over your shirt, you'd have to take it off."

I recall her and Grandma Dolly's comments about my abs.

"I'm still wearing the apron." I run my thumbs along the neck strap.

"Baking is a messy job."

"And if you dump that out, there will be more to clean up." Which means she'll have to stay longer. Something spools inside. There's no denying it. I like it when Jessica is here and it's not only because she's great with the kid and a good cook.

It's her laugh. Her smile. Her smooth curves. The cinnamon, spice, and everything nice scent. The way she clings to positive thinking but calls it straight.

Most of all, the way she makes me feel. But how do I make her feel? She called me a jerk earlier if that says anything. I'm not worthy of a woman like her.

Wiping my face, I grab the baby monitor and say, "I should walk you to your car."

Jessica's shoulders drop and she almost loses her grip on the bowl, then slides on her 'Everything is fine' mask. "Sure. Let me put away the cake real quick so it doesn't dry out."

When we get outside, the night is torn between the winter chill and the pending spring thaw.

Jessica wraps her arms around her chest and stops in front of a compact Nissan that looks like it's ready to be recycled.

Pulling open the driver's side door for Jessica, the handle comes off in my fingers, and the interior light flickers long enough for me to glimpse the scattering of clothing, boxes, and other items strewn in the front and back.

"You have to grip it just so." She takes the rusty metal from me and our hands brush, sending a whoosh of warmth through me once again.

"Did you give a raccoon a ride? Live in here with a bum?" I blurt.

"Just because you're Mr. Perfect with nary a crumb in your vehicle, doesn't mean we all have the time or energy to keep our cars immaculate."

Despite how drawn I feel to her, there's no denying that we're the opposite in so many ways.

I grip the window frame of the door because it repeatedly tries to close on Jessica's legs as she moves to get in.

Before she turns the ignition, she lets out a breath, whether because she's hoping this jalopy will start or for another reason, I'm not sure.

Voice thick, I say, "I want you to quit."

She hops to her feet, eyes alight with concern. "Do you not like the daily agenda I make for you with the colorful felt-tip pens or my sticker system? I can do it another way, or not do one at all. I'm here to help so if—"

Before she works herself into a frenzy, I grip her upper arms and say, "Jessica, I want you to help with the kid. Be the nanny."

Jaw parting, she looks up at me. "Oh. But that's not in my job description."

"You're great with him."

"I visited childcare centers earlier. He needs to socialize."

"What if he bites another kid?" I quell the panic in my voice every time I think about how out of control my life has become. How out of control I feel around Jessica. Like I could pull this woman into my arms. Feel her soft warmth melt against me. Thankfully, the car's dented door remains between us.

"That's why he needs interaction, discipline, and structure. When you started playing hockey, did you just fling the stick and puck around?"

"Probably. I was like two."

"And KJ is three. He'll be fine. Trust me. I was." She gazes at her shoes.

I've gleaned there's a lot to her story hidden behind her perpetual smile and bubbly personality. Gently, I ask, "You were what?"

"I turned out fine and so far, KJ has a lot better of a situation. People who care, for starters."

"Then will you be the nanny?"

"After you just insulted my car?"

"Please, Jessica?"

"Could I wear a Mary Poppins uniform?"

"No."

"But I have a costume for every occasion."

"What about the gold disco queen thing you mentioned?" I can't be sure, but I might be grinning. I forget what it feels like.

"I hardly think that would be suitable for—" She gasps and

her hand flies to her mouth. "That sounds like something approaching a compliment."

"Let's not get carried away."

She winks. "But what if we did?"

My chest rises on a long, steadying breath because this woman makes the ground shift beneath me.

"How about you just go away?" I let out a sigh because I don't really mean it.

She grips the top of her car's door and stares down at it.

My family would tell me I've gone too far. I know this but the more distance I put between myself and people, the less likely I'll make another mistake—I don't mean about having the kid. The thing that happened years earlier.

Having somehow recovered from my comment, Jessica bounces on her toes. "I see that little shine in your eyes. We're not just going to be friends. We're going to be best friends."

I ruined my best friend's life. Took everything from him. Can't ever let anything like that happen again.

"Let's just keep things simple."

She salutes me like I'm a military general. Is she mocking me?

"Is this all some big joke to you?"

Undaunted, she says, "As I said, I have a costume for every occasion." Then in a lower voice, as if musing, she adds, "I'm always playing a role. Even in that wedding gown. Thought if I created the illusion of the perfect life, someone would want me."

I'm not emotionally literate enough to know how to reply, but I see a well of sadness or loneliness that I only recognize because I look at it in the mirror every day. But how could this woman who may as well be the Queen of Sunshine possibly feel sad or lonely?

Uncomfortable, I shift back to my point. "Be the kid's nanny. Sign-on bonus is a new car."

"All my worldly belongings are in this thing. It's my life on wheels. I can't replace it."

"All of your belongings?"

"Just about. When I left California. I left behind everything, including my record player and speakers. One was broken, so the sound was lopsided."

"You're my assistant and paid through the team. As the nanny, I can pay you more."

"I don't want your money."

I want her, but I'm not sure how to say so. "Make an appointment for your car to get detailed."

"Your truck was in last week."

"I said your car."

"I can't afford that."

"Also, schedule a tune-up. Actually, forget it. Just go buy a new one. As I said, sign-on bonus."

"Liam, I can't afford that," she repeats.

"You can't."

"That's what I just said."

"I can."

She gasps. "You're not buying me a car."

"If you don't, I'll pick it out and you run the risk of getting a monster truck."

Jessica's gaze searches mine for a long moment. The interior light of the car flickers, illuminating the flecks of amber in her brown eyes.

She whispers, "What if I like monster trucks?"

I take her wrist in my hand and press my lips to it. A shiver runs through her. Recalling what she said about cooking blogs, I say, "I hope you get some rest tonight."

For once, I will because I'll be dreaming of Jessica, even if the kid kicks me in the ribs.

19
JESS

MY SKIN still tingles from Liam's touch. The way his hand wrapped around my wrist wasn't aggressive or possessive. More like the way he may grip his hockey stick. A caress. As if he had the sudden awareness that not everything in the world is hard, a challenge to tackle.

Even when we're not together, I am constantly aware of his presence. There's no comparison. Rexlan and I coexisted. Liam and I orbit each other and I'm afraid, given the blaze in his gaze earlier, if we're not careful, we might collide.

I find myself looking at cars. I've never considered what kind of car I'd buy given the opportunity. I always just make do. But this is crazy. The man cannot purchase a vehicle for me.

However, logically speaking, if he also wants me to look after KJ, in addition to my regular personal assistant responsibilities, he probably doesn't want me driving his son around in a death trap.

Knowing I need to operate at full capacity if I'll be taking care of the kid, as Liam calls him, I should probably work on my insomnia situation.

I've read all the articles about sleep hygiene, regulating melatonin, blue light hazards, red light therapy, and how to neutralize my stress levels for optimum relaxation.

What do I have to be stressed about? I'm blessed.

If not a little disappointed at being back in Cobbiton.

The original plan was to be so successful, I'd fly Grandma Dolly to Tinseltown to see my name in lights. We'd also go on annual cruises, visit the national parks, and trek to a wool museum in New Zealand. She loves to knit, and do basically anything with her hands from signing to baking, playing piano to winning typing contests online.

Here I am again with nothing to write home about. I'm ashamed of my inability to adult like an adult.

To have dropped out of college.

Left at the altar.

My childhood.

All of these failures stack up, then drop like dominos, threatening to knock me down.

But I get up, dust off, put on a smile, and keep going. That's what I always do because the sun will surely come out tomorrow ... and if not then, eventually.

I scroll social media, searching for the secret key to a good night's sleep—someone has it, so please share!

I wander down a rabbit hole, er, cave about the royal family when my phone beeps with an incoming text.

> Mr. Meanie: I just had another piece of cake.

> Me: Nat is not going to approve. 😬

> Mr. Meanie: I couldn't resist

> Me: That's not setting a good example as team captain.

Mr. Meanie: I'm not above breaking the rules
from time to time.

Me: Grandma Dolly would be disappointed.
She's obsessed with your abs.

Mr. Meanie: I'm not sure whether I should be
flattered or frightened.

Me: What? That you're popular in the sixty-
five-plus age category.

I send him the link to #MrDarcysAbs on social media and wait for him to bang my door down because it seems like the kind of thing he'd hate. But right now, snug and warm in my bed, texting my big bad boss, I feel like he's backed off his dislike of me a little.

Mr. Meanie: I don't want to see some
dude's abs.

Me: You mean YOUR abs. Social media users
claim they're yours. Please do me a solid and
confirm.

Mr. Meanie: If they are mine, where on earth
are they getting the images?

Me: You probably sell photos to fund your
rock-chewing habit.

Mr. Meanie: My what habit? I have nice teeth.

Me: That means you never have anything nice
to say.

Mr. Meanie: I liked the cake.

Me: Are all your teeth original?

Mr. Meanie: Why do you care?

Me: Grandma Dolly sends me daily updates to the hashtag. She probably wants to start one featuring your teeth, your toes, all of it.

Mr. Meanie: You mean YOU didn't sign up for notifications?

Me: That's what you took from my statement? 😐

Mr. Meanie: Admit there's something you like about me.

I go still, my hand stiff around the phone. That does not sound like something Liam would ask. I've been baited! Someone took his phone and this is a phishing scheme or they're trolling me. Could be Rexlan and his basement dwelling, internet-video game mafia.

Me: I, uh, have to go.

Mr. Meanie: To sleep?

No, because now my mind will whir and wonder all night.

Me: If this is really Liam, tell me what we're doing tomorrow.

Mr. Meanie: Getting you a new car.

> Me: Beep! That was the buzzer sound. ☒ No, that's nuts. Plus, you have appointments.

I list them in a separate text and then regret it because now if someone has hacked his phone and is posing as him, they'll know where he'll be and when. Suddenly overheating with worry, I kick off my covers. I have to figure this out. Now.

> Me: Tell me something only I would know.

Mr. Meanie: Wait, do you think this isn't me for some reason?

> Me: Obviously. 😶

Mr. Meanie: I knew about the whole #MrDarcysAbs thing.

> Me: You could've just been playing along.

Mr. Meanie: Why #MrDarcysAbs though?

> Me: Because you're stone cold like Jane Austen's male protagonist.

Mr. Meanie: What's with all the sedimentary references?

> Me: Always bringing it back to your abs, huh? Looking at your impeccably sculpted abdominal muscles would have the opposite effect of making me drowsy.

I just glitched. Why on earth did I text that? Maybe I am tired. I should shut this down now. Go to sleep. The three little dots indicate he's replying. Then they disappear. Reappear.

Whoever was posing at Liam realized I was on to them and ghosted.

I tuck back under the covers when my phone beeps. Instead of a message, an image comes through in our thread.

It's a selfie of Liam, shirt lifted, abs on display. I drool a little and I'm not even asleep yet. But his finger points at the side just below his ribs. I angle my phone and zoom in to see a little freckle that looks like a tiny whale shooting a spume out of its blowhole.

In a word, it's adorable. It also matches many of the abs pics on #MrDarcysAbs. But Liam is anything but adorable. He's a brooding grouser whose blue-gray eyes sometimes look like the sky in the morning and at others, they're deep like the dusk.

And when they land on me, there's something else, a spark there that I don't usually see—it's there in the photo on my phone. A swizzly feeling warms me through.

I won't be getting any sleep tonight.

THE MORNING SUN makes the snowy tops of the trees sparkle. I'm operating on a severe coffee deficit when I meet Mrs. Kirby, the woman who runs a sewing and alteration studio downstairs in the Old Mill building, outside the elevator.

"Doing the walk of shame, eh?" she asks.

Wondering if I misheard, I tap the side of my head like I did the car dashboard earlier when the heat wouldn't come on. It was chilly this morning.

I point to the elevator. "How do you figure that? I'm going upstairs."

Her harrumph reminds me of Liam. Could they be related?

"I'll have you know that I'm Liam's personal assistant." And nanny. He's been at away games and we didn't quite go over the details. Should've when we were messaging the other night instead of discussing his abs.

When we text, the animosity cools and flirtation, I think, takes its place. But why can't he be more friendly in person? Though, the photo of his abs was, ahem, quite friendly.

In the polished reflection of the elevator doors, I catch my blurry image, looking a little windswept and pink-cheeked.

"It used to be so quiet upstairs. Now there's just stomping."

"Dancing." KJ loves impromptu dance parties.

"Yelling."

"Singing." The little boy doesn't mind that I'm perpetually off-key. Of course, he can feel the music and I sign the words. It's a lot of fun.

She sniffs with disapproval. "Parties."

"Family life." In some ways, I guess I have been nannying all along.

Just then, the double glass doors to the building open, and Liam jogs in, shirtless, and with KJ in a special kind of back-pack. The kid bobbles along, an oversized Knights knit hat flopping on top of his blond hair. He grins and waves wildly when he spots me.

I wave back, but my jaw lowers and I blink, honing in on his father's abs. I mean the whale freckle, for identification purposes.

Liam's voice, a low rumble because of course he's not out of breath after running who knows how far with fifty pounds on his back, says, "Good morning, Jessica."

I clear my throat and open my mouth, but words don't come. Instead, I sign my greeting.

We get in the elevator and over my shoulder, to Mrs. Kirby, I say, "It won't happen again."

But I'm not sure whether I'm referring to the noise complaint or me ogling my boss's impressive six-pack.

"What was that all about?" he asks.

I gesture dismissively.

Liam's stare tells me he's not going to cast it back into the lake, so I recap Mrs. Kirby's comments.

Not surprisingly, he grunts.

After knocking some sense into my head by mainlining a pot of coffee, and preparing for the day, Liam emerges from the shower. He wears a pair of well-fitted jeans and a soft t-shirt that looks as if it would feel like butter between my fingers. He smooths his hand through his damp hair without throwing off its effortless style. His lips quirk when my gaze lengthens.

"I knew there was something you liked about me."

"Don't flatter yourself."

"At least you're not in your seventies."

I roll my eyes and then blink a few times.

"Have something in your eye?" he asks.

I must be sleeping. This is a dream. No, a nightmare. Is Liam Ellis flirting? No amount of coffee would make it so I could handle that. Chocolate on the other hand ...

Before KJ and I start a baking project, I give his dad, my boss, the man with the abs of stone, the rundown of his agenda for the upcoming week.

"Schedule in car shopping."

I ignore him and plow ahead. "I still need something signed for Grandma Dolly."

The corner of his lip lifts as if he's contemplating an abs shot.

"Actually, make it a team photo. We could have the starting line sign it and anyone else who's willing."

"That's asking a lot."

"You're the captain, aren't you? Flex those muscles."

My cheeks flame.

His lips quirk.

Silence stretches between us until the kid honks the horn on his little trike, telling us he wants to take a walk.

Liam says, "You're being bossy."

"I think you like it."

The week folds into the following month without a signed photo, a new car, or a consensus on whether Liam Ellis is a secret flirt.

However, we do spend a lot of time together. It can't be helped given how my responsibilities are split between personal assistant tasks and being KJ's nanny.

One afternoon, he and I go downstairs to bring Mrs. Kirby a homemade applesauce Bundt cake with a spiced doughnut flavor sugar topping when we meet Liam at the elevator.

I say and sign, "You're home early."

He scratches his temple, seemingly distracted. "I have a lot going on."

Straightening, I say, "I'm here to lighten your load."

"And bring baked goods to the enemy?"

I sign, "Mrs. Kirby is our neighbor. Practically a friend," I say for KJ's benefit ... and maybe because sometimes this feels like home. At least, I'm here often enough.

"After she said all that nasty stuff to you?"

"I'm leading by example. Teaching KJ that we're gracious, forgiving, and generous."

He grunts. "You're aggressively positive."

"Are you suggesting I want to fight your neighbor?"

"No, you're just so optimistic. You don't have to try so hard."

"Don't I?"

"I'm saying you don't have to give cake to the lady who said hurtful things."

"Mending fences. Plus, you've said that you don't like me and I still made you a cake."

He rubs the back of his neck. "I'm a jerk."

"So you admit it?"

"Don't be mean."

I wink.

Color rises to his cheeks.

I say, "Just honest."

"I bet in school you were a suck-up, the teacher's pet."

I gaze at my shoes. "More like the classroom ghost."

KJ tugs on my hand.

"Don't want to keep him waiting for our visit to see Elizabeth."

"Mrs. Kirby's dog?" Liam asks.

"He loves dogs. We should get one."

"No."

"You don't like dogs? I bet you don't like ice cream either. We'll have to do something about that." Flashing him a wink, we disappear down the hall.

20

LIAM

IN ICE HOCKEY, pivoting is a basic move to quickly and strategically change direction without losing momentum. In other words, the player doesn't have to stop to recalibrate.

But for the first time in my life, I feel like I'm running out of steam. Like I might need to break the boards and leave the rink.

Yesterday, Coach Badaszek had us run pivot drills, which made me feel ten years old. No, five years old. According to family lore, I was practically an infant when Dad strapped skates on me for the first time.

He played for Winnipeg after Germany. Hendrix plays for the Titans, another Canadian home team. I'm the family outlier.

My first memory of skating is when I was four—just a little older than the kid. These drills are juvenile, and I can't stop thinking about them. Why did Coach waste valuable time when we could've been practicing advanced plays?

As captain, I should know the answer to that question.

Instead, my mind plays on a loop, like a record's needle stuck in the groove.

Pivot, pivot, pivot.

Records make me think of Jessica mentioning she left her record collection behind when she left California, was it?

I suddenly need to know. What kinds of records did she listen to? Jazz? Classical? Vintage rock? Joni Mitchell?

I only know that name because my sister went through a brief phase in high school and listened to "Both Sides Now" on repeat.

When I enter the loft, the scent of baked goods wraps me in a hug. It's almost, but not quite, like coming home to Jessica's embrace.

I scrub my hand down my face. What has gotten into me?

Pivot, pivot, pivot.

My entire career, I've been heading in one trajectory: domination. Hall of Fame. Ultimate success with Stanley Cup wins. Yes. Plural. I've wanted to break every record.

Not vinyl records, but hockey stats, figures, and top achievements. I want to see my father beam with pride rather than that look he gave me the night that changed my life—multiple lives. I'll never forget it as long as I live ... because I know he'll never forgive me for taking away someone's opportunity to go big.

Now, here I am, blundering along as captain and generally failing as a father.

I spot a swirly Bundt cake on the counter and am about to help myself to a slice when the door flies open.

The kid toddles in behind Jessica who still holds the cake she'd intended for Mrs. Kirby. They both look rather forlorn. I am too, when it comes to dealing with my downstairs neighbor.

"She wasn't there?" I ask.

Jessica lets out a sigh. "She didn't want it. Said she's allergic."

"To what?"

Jessica shrugs. "Nuts? Kindness?"

"You don't put nuts in your spiced Bundt, do you?"

"I told her that." Jessica sets down the cake and leans against the counter.

Grannie Bell and Aunt Goldie would love her. That's a good thing. No, a great thing. But not for me. I can't let myself travel farther down this road because it'll only take me away from my goal of being a hockey giant.

The kid takes off his shoes and plops down to play with his blocks. Looks like he's building a reproduction of Cobbiton if the town's founders had consumed too much corn cider.

Jessica lifts her gaze to mine, big brown eyes shining. "I meant it as an act of goodwill. Being neighborly."

"Even though she accused you of being a harlot."

Jessica gasps, then tilts her head. "Well, yeah."

"Better than a witch bride."

Her lips crinkle. "Is it?"

I nudge Jessica with my elbow. "Hey, don't let Mrs. Kirby get you down. Who cares what she thinks."

Eyes plaintive, she says, "The rejection stings."

"Mrs. Kirby doesn't trust us after the whole incident with Elizabeth."

"The dog?"

"And lipstick." I eye the kid who has exhibited much better behavior since Jessica entered our lives.

"Oof."

"Shortly after that, our childcare arrangement came to an abrupt and sticky end."

"I don't want to know, but look at you, giving encouraging words."

I snort. "Yeah, if I'd only been so successful at practice yesterday."

Pivot, pivot, pivot.

I wring my hand on the back of my neck. "I've never, not in my entire career, dreaded the idea of going to practice." I cannot believe I just said that out loud.

Jessica looks at me thoughtfully. "Any particular reason?"

"I know I'm not living up to expectations as team captain."

"You could bake the guys a cake."

I groan but reach for the Bundt she brought back.

Jessica says, "Keep your hands where I can see them. I'm bringing that to Grandma Dolly."

"I thought she was away at an ASL conference."

"She got back last night. We have an appointment this afternoon."

"We do?" I mentally scan through the agenda she creates for me each day on colorful paper with bullet points and perfect penmanship. She often decorates them with stickers. I'd planned on hitting the gym in my spare time.

"KJ and I do, but you're coming with. We're going to help you start captaining like a captain."

My brow lowers. "How do you recommend you're going to do that? The kid doesn't know how to tie his shoes. Are you even qualified? You don't know a puck from a biscuit."

"I don't need to. It's time for you to learn a new language."

At that, Jessica, the kid, and I leave the deathtrap on wheels in my parking lot and spend the bulk of the rest of the day with Grandma Dolly, with me in the remedial ASL class, and my nanny and son winning gold stars for achievement.

By the time we conclude, half the Bundt cake is gone—Grandma Dolly recognized that I can be treat motivated—and I know ten new signs. She assured me that if I set a goal to learn a new one each day, or ten, or twenty, soon I'll be fluent.

Not going to lie, the kid lights up when I talk to him with my hands. We have a breakthrough and for that reason, I take everyone out to Spaglietti's for pizza.

When we return to Grandma Dolly's house, she signs that she's turning in for the night and will see us in the morning.

I pump the air. "Success. I understood." Also, I had some context clues. But still. This is progress.

Jessica, the master of my schedule, turns to me with a questioning tilt to her head. "Ready for class number two?"

I check the kid's seatbelt and crank the heat. "I asked Dolly to look after the kid for a few hours. Tomorrow you and I have an appointment. I'll pick you up around ten—after my workout and dry land training."

"See you then, boss." She starts to walk away, hips swinging, but before she reaches the door, I call her back.

"Jessica, how did that help me start captaining like a captain?"

"You're learning a new language, right?"

"The kid has a better vocabulary than me and he's three."

She twists her lips to one side as if reluctant to explain. "Since you didn't figure it out on your own, I'll give you a hint. Sometimes, in life, we get so used to doing things one way, we don't realize there's another. Like a scenic route rather than the most direct path. Or communicating with our hands rather than our mouths."

My eyes lock on hers. That whooshing feeling races through me. My lips part, but no words come out.

Jessica grins as if pleased.

Pivot, pivot, pivot.

Maybe she's right. The way I've been doing things isn't the only way, especially when it comes to the team. Perhaps that's Coach Badaszek's lesson as well. He saw I was in a rut and instead of throwing me a rope, he made it deeper so I could see where I was at for myself.

Perhaps it's time to change.

I sign *Thanks* and then pull away. My thoughts linger on

the woman with the full, peachy lips, expressive eyes, and magnetic smile.

The next morning, since we went in my car to Dolly's and Jessica left her hunk of junk on wheels at my place, it takes me almost five minutes to get the thing started. I wonder if the battery is dead and look in the trunk to see if she has jumper cables. Instead, I find the witch bride wedding gown she wore that first day we met.

Perhaps she has to say an incantation to get the engine to turn over.

The kid asks where we're going and I want to tell him to see Jessica, but realize I don't know how. I give him the one-minute signal and try turning the key again. Thankfully, this time the car starts, but it's sketchy business getting to Silver Queen Street.

I'm at once frustrated by the ordeal and miffed that she tolerates this. The Knights must pay her a decent salary to work as a personal assistant, and now I've added to that for her taking on the role of nanny.

The whole thing is pretty fluid, I realize, because she was already spending a lot of time with the kid. She practically lives in the loft. I don't mind much. The least I can do is provide her with safe and reliable transport.

Also, she'd look hot in a truck. Or a sports car. Even a sedan. A minivan?

I stop abruptly at a pregnant yellow light, wondering where that thought came from. I want to tell the kid we're okay, but the words die on my tongue. He won't understand me, anyway. Can he read lips or will he be able to like Dolly? Can he hear any sound at all?

All at once, the death grip I'd had on my life and the control I tried to assert by focusing on hockey to the exclusion of everything else hits me like a semi. Thankfully, not actually because we're on Dolly's quiet, residential street.

Jessica greets us at the door.

Panic building, I blurt, "We have to get the kid to a specialist. I have to research hearing assistance and find out what we can do for him."

Meanwhile, unaware, he rushes into the cozy house and Dolly's outstretched arms. She signs and he smiles with glee. Relief tries to wash through me but gets stuck somewhere between my head and chest.

As her eyebrows creep toward her hairline, Jessica pumps her hands. "Whoa, whoa, whoa. Slow down."

"What have I been doing? I'm the worst father."

Jessica sandwiches my hand in hers. "You're not the worst father. I hope I didn't overstep, but with Grandma Dolly's help, I've been researching and using the resources we have to get him to the top specialists in the state, along with looking at childcare centers. I was just waiting to ask for your permission."

I stagger back. "You did that?"

Old me would've been mad and felt undermined, but I want to scoop her into my arms and spin her around. I've never felt so—supported. But then the argument comes with its fists lifted. I'm a man, I don't need support. Do I?

I have the sudden and stark realization that I've pushed away any and all help. That could be yet another reason Coach named me captain. He recognized my leadership capacity but knew that I'd only be as good as the team. I let out a long breath.

"Once we understand what we're working with when it comes to KJ's hearing, we'll match him with a place he can go where they can help develop his communication skills while also being around his peers."

"So you don't want to be his nanny anymore?" It almost

sounds like I said, *Mommy*. But I didn't, only Jessica very much seems like one with the way she openly accepts him, nurtures him, loves him.

When she doesn't respond, my nose twitches and my eyes prickle a bit. It's windy today. Maybe she didn't hear me. Throat scratchy and not sure what else to say, I figure we should head over to the car dealership.

"Do you still want to go?" More importantly, I think I realize just how much I want her to stay ... with us.

She replies, "Sure."

Holding the door open, I say a simple "Thanks," I gesture goodbye to the kid and Dolly.

Jessica buttons her coat and pulls on her hat. "I see you brought Shy Eye Good Guy."

"That's the name of your car?"

With a little bounce in her step, she says, "Shy eye because the left headlight doesn't work—I've even had it replaced, but it's perpetually dark. Good Guy because I want to send it positive vibes."

"That's not how vehicles operate, but I can see why it doesn't always want to cooperate."

"I see you fine-tuned your meanness meter this morning."

"I wasn't being mean. Just honest. The kid and I are lucky we made it here alive."

"That's because you drive like a Formula One racer."

"I do not." I accelerate, smoking the tires.

Jessica looks at me with alarm.

"Hey, Shy Eye Good Guy has to live a little before he heads out to pasture."

"Shh. He'll hear you." But she giggles and my heart does a funny little leap.

We cruise down Main Street as we leave Cobbiton and Jessica abruptly says, "Stop. I'm having a funding crisis."

I'm about to explain that I'm buying her the car when she points at the Busy Bee Bakery.

"Ah. You need coffee. Didn't sleep well last night? Browsing social media? Scrolling #MrDarcysAbs, perchance?" I tease.

"Pfft. You wish."

Is it weird that I kind of do?

The on-street parking directly in front of the coffee shop is occupied, so I spin around the block and start to maneuver the Nissan into a parallel parking spot. My hand grips the back of Jessica's headrest as I look over my shoulder.

I become keenly aware of our proximity. Could be because the saggy felt roof lining brushes the top of my head. I slide skillfully into the slot.

"You could just use the camera on the dash." She points to the radio.

This car was built before that kind of technology was a twinkle in a computer programmer's eye. I don't take mine off Miss Sunny Sassy Pants. My arm is practically around her shoulders. I could pull her across the bench seat and into me. Then what?

The look turns into a moment that lengthens between us, twists and changes shape. My breath turns shallow and everything falls out of focus except Jessica. Her gaze warms me, silences my thoughts.

Her cheeks flood with color.

I lick my lips.

She whispers, "I need coffee."

Like a rubber band, the moment snaps and then goes slack.

While we're in line at the bakery, I stretch my arms, wondering if I could get away with lacing one over her shoulders now. What would she do? Collapse under the weight? Toss it off, shrieking that I'm manhandling her? Or sink into it?

Hold up, bro. Why am I thinking about this?

The thought resurfaces while we're waiting to test-drive several vehicles. Jessica insists on getting another Nissan compact.

When she gets the keys, I literally have to shoehorn my way into the backseat. Head hitting the ceiling and neck cramping, the saleswoman on the passenger side raves about the gas economy.

"I love it," Jessica says when we return to the dealership.

"No," I say, stretching again and loosening my neck.

"Okay. I understand. He changed his mind. I can still get some miles out of Shy Eye." She smiles at her car, homely compared to the other shiny vehicles on the lot.

Bypassing the suggestions the saleswoman made for a replacement, I stride over to the luxury section, including Nissan's Infiniti model SUVs.

Pointing, I say, "I was thinking of something more like this."

She tries to argue, but the saleswoman, seeing a better commission, goes all in, convincing her it's one of their top-rated options.

Jessica finally relents and declares, "Well, the blue-gray color of this one does match Liam's eyes."

I roll mine.

While we wait at the finance desk for the loan officer to return from his lunch break, I rock back in the chair and drape my arm over the back of hers.

She doesn't move a muscle.

Perhaps she doesn't notice.

However, we both startle when Larry Hamilton enters the room.

"The one. The only! It's Liam Ellis! It's lovely to meet you as well, Mrs. Ellis." We both try to correct him but the man plows on. "I cannot tell you what a pleasure and honor it is to do business with you today. I'm a big fan. Huge. Go, Knights!"

When I'm finally able to get a word in, I tell Larry, "Despite car shopping seeming very domestic, we're not—"

He's already moved on to trade-in value and percentage points.

Jessica and I are not a couple, but do I want to be?

21

LIAM

I HALF EXPECTED Jessica to shed a tear when she parted ways with Shy Eye Good Guy, or bake a cake to celebrate, but she remained surprisingly cool during the transaction.

We head back to Cobbiton, her in the Infiniti's driver seat, maneuvering carefully like she's handling a baby foal and not a vehicle built with four-wheel drive. Not only is it a safer option during inclement weather, but it could also handle some off-roading.

While she focuses, I can't stop asking myself why I didn't tell Larry the loan guy that Jessica is just my assistant.

But perhaps she's more than that.

I guess.

Maybe.

She clears her throat and says, "I'm going to line up KJ's appointments. There might be a few you'll want to come to, but if you're at work, I can bring Grandma Dolly."

"The kid loves her." Even though I've had a rough start to fatherhood, I can no longer deny my affection for my son. It's been hard to know how to show it without coming off as a total dweeb, not that KJ would care, but still. My memories of my father are good with few exceptions, but he was often gone playing hockey and kind of obsessed with my brother and me making progress in the sport when he was around. It worked out well, but what kind of father do I want to be to the kid?

"I'm guessing they got into plenty of trouble today. But, um, I'm guessing the specialists are going to have some questions about his background."

"We can have my primary care and sports physicians send my history over if necessary. They'll see that I'm quite the specimen."

The corners of Jessica's lips curve in a private smile but then fall as she turns onto Main Street. Maybe she needs more coffee. "It would also be helpful to have information about KJ's mother."

Except for the increasingly chaotic and somewhat threatening texts she's been sending, when I think about that role, Jessica is the only person who fits the profile.

"In addition to health history, there might need to be some documents signed, sometimes custody comes into play," Jessica speaks carefully, almost nervously.

"There's nothing to worry about. I'll give authorization. I have full custody of the kid."

For now.

"Great. Any information, records, and such that you have on file would also be helpful."

I shake my head. "He only came with a note."

The meaning of this batters me like an entire fleet of hockey players armed with sticks and pucks. If only I'd known about the kid, I could've done something sooner to help. "I don't know if he went for regular checkups and had his hearing evaluated, or if it was overlooked entirely."

She shifts as if uncomfortable.

Swallowing back a thick lump in my throat, I say, "Thanks, Jessica."

She nods and then pats the steering wheel as if wanting to change the subject. "Thank you for this. I think I'll name him Bigfoot."

"How about not?"

"That's no fun. Life is about relationships."

"You can't have a relationship with a vehicle."

"Tell that to Shy Eye Good Guy. We made a lot of memories together."

She starts to tell me about them, including how once a duck jumped into the passenger seat like she was a cab driver.

Jessica breezes past my moods like nothing can bring her down. Not that I'm trying to diminish her. But it's impressive how she just keeps on smiling. Must live a charmed life.

For the next few days, I have one boot on the ground and the other on the ice until we travel to Pennsylvania for a game against the Generals. They're a decent team and I need to keep my head in the game.

The front line is relentless, reminding me of Jessica. Beau refuses to let the puck in the net. Our defense is tight with speed and agility. 'Bama and Hayden each get goals. The Generals do too and the game is tied at the close so we go into a sudden-death overtime with three on three.

Pierre gets the job done.

Unfortunately, our flight back is delayed due to a band of storms dipping down from Canada. I take the opportunity to call my parents who gloat about having moved from Brookking Sound northwest of Toronto to sunny San Diego, at least during the winter months.

They're both on speakerphone, encouraging me to visit. Little do they know *me* is now a *we*. A trio, if I add my assistant and nanny, Jessica.

I brush my hand down my face, wishing I were at home with them in Nebraska. However, with the chill in the air, I wouldn't say no to a family trip out west.

So why haven't I told Mom and Dad that I'm a father?

My mother asks, "When is your next game in Los Angeles?"

"We'll come up," Dad says.

"My assistant will let you know."

"Oh, Jessica? She's a darling," Mom says.

My jaw smashes into the worn linoleum floor of the airport. "What?"

"She and I swapped recipes."

"When? Where? Why?" This is news to me. I immediately start pacing because of what this could mean.

Mom answers, "She wanted to know when your birthday is."

"But how'd she get your number? She must've gone on my phone. That sneaky little rule breaker." My voice is tight.

"Can you really be mad since she was being thoughtful?"

Mom knows I'm not a big birthday guy.

Fear pierces my gut. "Did she say anything else? Mention any other birthdays?"

My mother laughs. "She wanted to know what kind of cake you like."

Dad says, "Your mother said she has a marvelous Bundt."

With his German accent, it sounds like he says *butt*.

"She does." I clap my hand over my eyes. "I mean the cake."

"Well, of course. I tried her recipe and I think the secret is the temperature of the eggs when combined with the sugar for a silky consistency. If that gal is as genius with baking as she is with managing your life, I'd say she's a keeper."

I stagger like the airport was struck by a meteor, or maybe

that's just me because everything surrounding me remains still. However, I feel like the earth was thrown off its axis.

"She's a very helpful young lady. Keeping you on the edge of your blades," my dad adds with a hint in his tone.

"You can say that again," I mutter.

"I was just reviewing the schedule and it looks like you have a game in Toronto next month. We'll be in Brookking Sound for Grannie Bell's birthday, so we'll see you then for sure."

"I do love watching my boys play together," Dad says.

I've given up on reminding him that we're on opposing teams—Hendrix plays for the Titans. It's less of a *together* situation and more of an *against*.

"And don't be shy about bringing a guest." Mom's tone is light, airy, and suggestive.

My stomach clenches. They can't mean the kid. Jessica wouldn't have mentioned him. She knows the rules. So why did she and my mother exchange cake recipes?

GAMES BOOKEND the week as we countdown to the playoffs which begin at the end of the month.

I'm just coming off the ice after we trounced the Oklahoma Thunder, which, to be fair, isn't hard to do, when I spot a familiar face in the hallway at the Ice Palace.

Cara waves at her best friend as she rushes into Pierre's arms. Even after the exhausting slugfest on the ice, he still manages to lift her up and spin her around.

I warily approach Jessica who holds the kid's hand and wonder what they're doing here.

She beams a smile. "We couldn't wait until you got home."

"There's nothing that couldn't wait." My tone is harsher

than I mean, but if anyone puts two and two together, I don't know what I'll do.

Her expression flattens and then quickly reconfigures to her usual cheerful smile.

The kid hops up and down.

"Go. We can talk later." I don't dare say *home*, lest I give myself away. If anyone finds out this kid is mine, it'll change the game entirely.

However, the kid, my son, signs something that I vaguely translate as pig or bear. Donkey? That would be me. A great big wild beast.

Giving my head a shake, I repeat, "I'll see you later."

Jessica doesn't move for a long beat. Her nostrils flare. If she were the witch from Hansel and Gretel, she'd bake me into a cake. Her mouth opens and then closes as if she's debating giving me a piece of her mind. Then with a shake of her head that's more disappointment than disapproval, she turns on her heel.

It's then I notice that she and the kid are both wearing Knights jerseys. My last name, our last name, is emblazoned across the kid's. On Jessica's back are the letters G-R-I-M-A-L-D-I.

Magma builds inside, threatening to erupt with volcanic ferocity, and from behind, I grip her shoulder and growl, "Take that off."

Startled, she turns around. "What are you talking about?"

"Take off the jersey." I burn holes in the shiny material with my stare.

Jessica tilts her head to the side. "Why? I borrowed it from Grandma Dolly. It was closest to my size. She has one for nearly every player on the team. Figured you'd be happy to see us supporting the Knights." Her tone is innocent, but if she spends another second wearing Grimaldi's last name on her back, I will be very, very guilty.

"Take. It. Off," I repeat.

"I'm only wearing a camisole underneath, Liam. What else should I put on?"

I tear my jersey off and shove it toward her.

"What has gotten into you?" Then, like a lightbulb going off, she seems to understand. Her jaw lowers at my audacity.

My expression sharpens.

The kid must sense the tension because he gets wiggly. The last thing I need is for anyone to notice them, least of all Jessica wearing that jersey ... or the camisole. My pulse is already high and threatens to blow off the roof which would be a shame since this is a new building.

"Put it on."

"Who's being bossy now?" she gripes, struggling to discretely change tops.

"If you're going to wear anyone's jersey. It's mine."

"What about the rules?" she asks as her head pops through the neckline.

My lips press together because she's got me there. I recall ordering her never to wear my jersey. I don't know where my head was then and I have no idea where it is now except incensed that Jessica was in Grimaldi's number.

"Stop with your questions," I bark.

Our gazes meet. A long moment passes between us, stretching, lengthening, morphing.

Fluffing her hair out from the collar, she says, "Or I could ask more. Double down. What has you so peeved when you could be happy to see us? Why are you being irrational? You could explain yourself. How can you be so attractive when you're mad?" Her eyes widen as if surprised at having said the last one out loud.

She shouldn't think I'm attractive, but the heat rising along my neck suggests I liked hearing that. My fist grips the air and tightens.

Her gaze drops to it.

I grit my teeth. I've never wanted anyone so badly in my life.

I want to kiss this woman, but I have to resist.

Her lips part and her eyes dip to my mouth. "Oh," she breathes as if realizing something.

Before either one of us can do anything stupid, I give the kid a high five and turn to leave, then with a grunt, say, "Get out of here."

But I have to stay away from her.

If I don't, I will lose control.

This whole thing was a mistake.

Except, when I'm around Jessica, when I smell her and hear her laugh there is no denying the rushing, sweeping, whooshing feeling like in those seconds as the puck races toward the net. It's anticipation and uncertainty. Excitement and hope. But even better.

I have to out skate it.

22

JESS

LIAM IS OUT LATE which is not at all like him. I imagine him brooding in a dimly lit bar over an amber-colored drink with ice cubes in it.

Fast asleep, KJ is probably dreaming of puppies and playdough. I wish I could say I was halfway there myself—I'll keep the puppies. Could do without the playdough. I've been finding little dried pieces of it everywhere, including in my hair. Instead, I've been stewing on the sofa.

That rascal has no right to tell me what to wear. But that's the least of it. We were there because we had important news to share. The man's priorities are off.

All he thinks about is hockey this, hockey that. All hockey all the time.

I text Cara, wondering if Pierre is like that too. Not that I'm thinking about having anything more than a working relationship with Liam. The janitorial job in the locker room isn't looking so bad. Unless the entire team are clones of number forty-five.

> Me: Ellis had a temper fit in the hallway earlier.

> Cara: I heard. I was going to call.

> Me: Why is he so moody? 😔

> Cara: Well, you were wearing someone else's jersey.

> Me: First, I was showing team spirit. Second, he explicitly told me NOT to wear his jersey.

Then again, I have been intent on breaking his stupid rules.

> Cara: That tells you everything you need to know.

Before I can ask her to elaborate, the key sounds in the lock. I startle as if caught doing something naughty. Gathering my things, I make a beeline for the door.

Liam with his massive frame blocks it and doesn't say a word.

"Pardon me, I'll be *getting out of here*, Mr. Ellis," I say, parroting his dismissal earlier.

He doesn't budge.

I usually give him a rundown of what he missed while gone. Maybe he's waiting to hear it. I remind myself to be professional. "There's a celebration cake on the counter. I hope you eat all of it and get a stomach ache." My tone is normal even though the words are anything but, yet they just spilled out of me.

His eyebrows lift as if surprised to hear me say something that's not sweet.

Lifting my gaze to his and doing my best to straighten to my full height, I punctuate my comment with a sunny smile.

He rubs the back of his neck and winces. "I messed up."

Dropping back slightly with surprise, I nod in agreement. "You did."

"I wasn't ready. No one knows."

"No one knows that hockey's biggest baddie is a dad?"

Liam's expression tightens as if stubbornly trying to fit into a pair of skates he's outgrown. "It's none of their business."

"I don't understand why it's a secret. KJ is great."

He mumbles something that sounds like, "I'm not."

"What about your family?"

"Were you listening?"

I narrow my eyes at him, prepared to explain why we showed up at the arena even though I now regret it. Even though I don't feel like I owe him an explanation. "We received the results of your son's audiology testing today. Got really good news. I couldn't get ahold of you. We told Grandma Dolly, baked a cake, and wanted to surprise you."

"So you showed up at the Ice Palace wearing some loser's jersey."

My jaw tightens. "That was your takeaway?"

He grunts.

"Also, if I'm not mistaken, that loser is on your team and so am I. Er, was. Despite being a captain, you really don't play well with others."

"My job is to lead."

"I don't know how your coach evaluates your performance, but if it were up to me, you'd get maybe one gold star instead of five. The example you're setting for your son could use improvement."

"Good thing you're not my coach."

The comment reminds me that I'm nothing to this man

other than the person who fetches his coffee, makes his appointments, and takes care of the son he may very well be ashamed of.

My nose twitches and my eyes tingle. "I thought it would be nice for you, for us, to be there to tell you that KJ has some hearing ability." I start to tell him the prognosis and the super positive outlook the doctor had for some hearing with assistance in KJ's future. Grandma Dolly was ecstatic. It was, dare I say, music to her ears.

How does Mr. Meanie respond? With a curt nod.

Liquid brims in my eyes. "You don't care, do you?"

Liam's nostrils flare.

Anger burns through all the positive slogans, affirmations, and upbeat quips I arm myself with to combat the ever-present shadow of pain from my own childhood, where no one cared until Grandma Dolly came along.

Squaring up to him, I say, "If it weren't for KJ, I'd quit and write you a strongly worded letter, including but not limited to I hope you're happy with your stupid, solitary existence where the only thing that keeps you company is the ice which will never keep you warm at night."

Liam's chest heaves like he's going to explode.

I stand my ground, unafraid. "You try to be all big and intimidating. When really you're just a miserable, lonely, sad, sad man."

His face hardens and he remains unmoved, a stony pillar of ice, chilling everything around him.

"There's nothing you could do to me that hasn't already been done and yet I am still standing, Liam Ellis. I will stand up for your son and kids like him, like me, until I take my last breath. Kids who were abandoned, unwanted." Each word I speak is a promise.

He blinks a few times as if coming out of a trance or

surfacing from his thoughts—probably replaying the game in his mind. Stupid hockey. "You don't understand."

"Oh, I think I do. You've made how little you care abundantly clear."

He shakes his head, somehow warming the room with the movement. His voice is tight when he says, "No, Jessica. The problem is I care too much."

And just like that, his mood goes from cold to hot. Not hot like *hubba hubba*, #MrDarcysAbs, but overcome with emotion as his eyes glass over. However, just as soon as I notice, he blinks it away.

I lift my chin, not done with this showdown. "If that's the case, you could work on showing it better. Maybe even a smile from time to time. A kind word goes a long way. You could also talk about what's on your mind. Let people in a little. I mean, even a hint could help."

He scrubs his palm along his stubble as if trying to massage out an explanation. "If I mess up ..."

I lift my eyebrows, hoping that by showing interest in what he has to say, I'll coax him into using his words.

"If I make a mistake—" He shakes his head.

"Let me see if I can help you. When you saw us at the arena, the proper response was to gather KJ into your arms, give him a big papa bear hug, and show him how happy you were to see him."

Liam's expression returns to a careful mask, but he's listening, so that's progress.

"Then you'd exclaim your surprise at seeing us there with smiles and a cake. You'd ask about the special occasion."

His grunt sounds slightly more like an invitation to continue like he's taking notes, or maybe that's just the hopeful optimist in me.

"I'd tell you the good news. We'd do an ASL cheer, maybe share a family hug—"

His eyebrow lifts sharply.

My mouth opens and closes but no sound comes out.

Liam's blue-gray stare burns cold into me.

"I mean, you'd hug KJ again because of what this means for his future. Then you'd sign to him about how much you like seeing him in Knights gear and that someday he'll wear a big jersey just like you, but instead of having number forty-five across the back, it'll be his own number."

Liam's eyes darken and his fist clenches the same way it did earlier. "Don't ever wear anyone's jersey again."

I cock a hip. "First, the fun police and now the fashion police? Who do you think you are? Never mind. Don't answer that. I don't want to know." I brush past him and out the door, thankful when I get outside and the cold air dries my eyes.

THE NEXT FEW days are turbulent. Liam isn't so much cranky as he is sullen. Meanwhile, KJ and I tour childcare facilities. The first one emphasizes exploration and is a hit. He especially enjoys the indoor and outdoor climbing areas.

The second one is a "child-led" center and a bit chaotic. Feathers float in the air, tinny music blasts from a small speaker, and I trip over a cardboard tube that I think contains something alive. I imagine Liam would disapprove, which is why I move that one up on the list. Kidding.

The third smells like damp socks and raw onions. KJ clings to my side.

We return home for lunch to find Liam storming around, claiming that he can't find a box.

He thunders, "Have you seen it?"

"What kind of box? A hat box? A box of oatmeal?"

"It's small and velvet."

Oh. That kind of box.

"It was here and now it's not." There is no mistaking the accusation in his eyes.

Jealously rings through me at the idea of someone special in Liam's life. Someone who gets the nice side of him. Then memories flood back. I was always the outsider.

The first person a foster family turned to if something went missing or was unusual. I never belonged, didn't have a family team in my corner. No one to defend me, to look out for me. Color rises to my cheeks. My lips part, but words don't form.

"Have you seen it, Jessica?"

"I'm sorry, no." Presuming I'm right about the contents of a box like that, I'd never have touched it. This also highlights everything I don't know about his personal life. I'm just the help.

I shake my head and hurry KJ to his room for a nap. Phantom guilt follows me even though I didn't do anything wrong. Then again, when it comes to Liam, it's like I can't do anything right either.

He doesn't say another word to me. For five days.

KJ and I visit a few more nursery schools and settle on the first one with him attending two mornings a week until he turns four.

Grandma Dolly and I are sitting in her kitchen with KJ as we all work on a puzzle. I tell her that he's come so far since we first met. I sign that he's so much happier and well-adjusted.

She replies, "That's easy when around you, Sunshine. You spread it everywhere you go."

I snort. "Tell that to his father."

"Ignore him."

It's hard to. But instead, I simply sign, "The man is a brute." A handsome one that I'm irrationally attracted to.

My phone rings. It's Liam. The guy probably sensed I was talking about him and wants to make me as miserable as he is. I answer, feeling like an egg about to crack.

He orders, "Come home. Now."

Clearing my throat and summoning patience, because let's be real, it's starting to wear thin, I use my most pleasant voice. "What's the magic word?"

"Jessica," he warns.

"KJ and I are at Grandma Dolly's finishing a puzzle."

"Don't keep me waiting."

I close my eyes, summoning the dregs of patience. "Be there soon."

Thankfully, my grandmother didn't overhear the conversation, but she must recognize the apprehension in my expression.

She asks, "Do you want me to come?"

I reply, "Thank you, but no. It'll be fine."

I'm done with Liam and his bad moods, demands, and lack of manners. Most of all, I don't want Grandma Dolly to know I've failed, again. It's time for me to part ways with this man. To leave, exit stage left. It breaks my heart to imagine leaving KJ, but the childcare center seems like a great place, and he can still see Grandma Dolly twice a week.

When we get to the elevator in the Old Mill building, Mrs. Kirby approaches with her dog.

"Good morning," I say with a little less sparkle than usual.

She looks me up and down, and the dog immediately proceeds to try to pee on my foot. I yank it away and am careful not to step in the puddle.

Mrs. Kirby says, "Looks like the kid had an accident."

I scoop KJ into my arms. He is dry and great with the bathroom. I tell myself to be kind and rewind to the moment before her dig.

"It's chilly for early April. A great day for baking."

"Don't bother bringing me any of that cake." She makes a face.

"Wouldn't dream of it," I say airily.

When the elevator dings, she bustles past me. I sign to KJ that I'm going to get some towels to clean up the dog's mess when something washes over me.

The woman rejected my cake. Said my kid, er, Liam's kid, peed on the floor and didn't return my friendly greeting. Maybe it doesn't pay to be nice.

By the time I unlock the door, I'm cranky, no I'm *raging*.

That's it. No more Miss Nice Gal.

After KJ settles in for his nap, I march to the new workout room I had installed here in the loft where I find Liam bench-pressing what may very well be several hundred pounds. Shirtless. Abs on display.

Doing my best to minimize the distraction, I say, "What?"

He racks the bar, towels off his face, and slowly rises to standing. "We need to talk."

"I'll say."

He looks me over as if seeing me for the first time, or in a new light. Maybe it's because I didn't bounce in here riding a unicorn and bow before his royal majesty while wearing a radiant smile.

Dripping with sweat, he says, "I have to shower."

That means I'll have to wait. Typical. He disappears into the bathroom.

Oh, this means war. I'm done. It's over. Instead of retreating, I go to the kitchen, take out a carton of heavy cream, and whip it into a frenzy.

"Liam Ellis, you are going down in a blaze of creamy glory." I lick my finger. "It'll be a shame to waste this on him."

No sooner do I have it layered in an aluminum pie tin—I don't want to use ceramic and break his nose or anything—does he stalk toward me. I advance, lift the pie plate, and before he realizes what's happening, I mash it into his face.

I expect him to growl and possibly attack, but he lets out a yell of surprise.

Glaring, he wipes it from his face. "What was that all about? Did one of the guys put you up to this?"

"No, Liam. I'm done. Totally over the moodiness, the crankiness, the grumpiness. Grow up or I'm getting out. For good." I didn't mean for that to come out as an ultimatum but am certain this man wouldn't hear me otherwise.

He swabs his cheek with his finger and then makes a show of licking the whipped cream off of it. "Mmm. Tasty."

I scowl ... and maybe drool a little. It's hard to ignore my body's reaction to this man, to the awareness that he has a soft side that I want to tease out.

The left corner of his lip twitches.

"This isn't funny."

"By definition, you mashing a pie, er, cream, into my face is."

"It wasn't meant to be. The whipped cream was me sending a message."

"That I need to take myself less seriously? Message received. I also wanted to let you know that I found the box I'd been looking for. Grady called while I was on my way home. Said he found it in his hockey skate."

Sobered because that wasn't what I expected to hear, I say, "Oh. Good. I thought that you thought—"

Liam's expression is surprisingly open, light. "That you took it? No way, Jessica. You're the one who finds things. Fixes things. Brightens the day, the night, you are a force of light I've needed in my life. You forgive and—" He goes abruptly quiet because something is happening.

I was not expecting that.

My face feels hot. My nose stings. Jaw tight. Eyes wet. It's then that I come apart. It all comes flooding out of me.

"What's wrong?" he asks, alarmed.

"I'm not crying. I do not cry." I don't know where this comes from, but a lot of salty liquid spills from my eyes.

"Was it something I said?"

"Yes," I whisper through a sniffle. "It's everything you've said and how you've said it."

I have thick skin and don't need praise from someone like Liam. I know who I am—I do bring light—and I guess all these tears needed to get out of the way so I could continue to shine it.

And there was that little thing about forgiving, so when he wraps his arms around me and pulls me to his chest, I don't resist.

Liam Ellis has never had a hug from me before and it's going to change his life.

23

LIAM

I WRAP my arms around Jessica and never has anything felt so good. Not the thrill of winning a game. Not even the Cup. Because winning isn't what it's about. Rather, not losing. Control mostly. If I let it slip, everything will fall to pieces. Again.

Her arms lace around my middle and she holds tight with her cheek pressed to my chest. Her eyes are closed and she squeezes. It's full-contact warmth and sends a whoosh through me.

I expect her to let go, but she doesn't. Through some form of osmosis transfer, like snapshots in a dream, I feel alternately sunny, light, and hopeful.

We remain like this for far longer than a customary hug, but it isn't awkward, more like melts something within me and between us.

Just before we part, I kiss her forehead which is like popping a cork because she's no longer wearing her 'Everything is fine' face or the look of terror I glimpsed right before she mushed the pie into my face.

"I never want to see that again," I say.

She shakes her head. "No, Liam. Your days of barking orders are over—"

My lips dip and my stomach tumbles. Was I barking orders? I feel the need to explain myself. "I wasn't—I was being direct."

"When you talk to me, use a different tone. You're not the hockey captain of my team. Try again. More *sotto voce*. Less aggressive. More tender."

Chastened, I clear my throat. "Usually, you're all smiles, heart wide open, pure sunshine. Whatever came over you was intense."

She lowers onto the sofa and says, "That's not who I want to be."

"Right, you're Miss Sunshine all the time."

She shakes her head. "Not always. I lived under a rain cloud for more than half my life. It took Grandma Dolly baking me a cake for me to see things differently. To trust, mainly myself."

"She's a great baker."

"The only reason I'm still here in your house is because I got a second chance. I'm willing to give you one too, mostly for KJ's sake."

The words slice deep and the knife glints in my eyes, reflecting the truth of how miserable I am sometimes. How everything between Jessica and me balances on the edge of that same knife.

She holds my gaze with a fierce strength I've rarely witnessed, reminding me that while the sun can warm and be a beautiful source of light, it can also burn.

"I wasn't always sunny, as you say. My mother abandoned me. I never knew my father. I was in foster care, group homes, shuffled around, rejected. Mostly because I didn't talk. Didn't trust my voice. Didn't believe anyone would listen. Unfortunately, I was repeatedly proven right. Thankfully, Grandma Dolly didn't need me to speak to 'hear' me. To understand me. Same for you and KJ."

My chest clenches at her story and the truth behind her calling me out for the way I've maintained distance between my son and me. Distance I'm trying to close. However, a door to the past remains open, blocking my way. From the darkness sounds a voice, telling me I'm not good enough for Jessica or KJ.

I rasp, "I'm so sorry."

"You don't need to be. I'm not going to say that I wouldn't be who I am today if it weren't for all my previous experiences. I could do without some of those. However, I know my worth. I learned to trust myself. I would never lie, cheat, or steal. Least of all your velvet box."

I shake my head. "Jessica, I never thought you—"

"If you haven't already learned this lesson, buckle up, big daddy, because you'll need it as KJ's father and it'll serve you well in just about every other interaction you have. Sometimes actions speak louder than words."

My head turns fuzzy and my eyes burn as a memory rushes back. "I know."

I'm about to tell Jessica everything, but the words don't come because my actions nearly took a life. They stole a dream and I've lied about it ever since.

She tilts her head and her face softens. "You do?"

I close my eyes for a long moment and take a breath. "Yes, I do. I'll work on it. Be less closed off."

"Less demanding."

I wince, "I'm being clear. Not leaving room for error or misinterpretation."

"You come off like an egotistical thug living in a high tower who thinks everyone is here to do his bidding. I'm your assistant, not your servant."

It crushes me that she thought that, even for a second. I'm not sure where this sudden glimpse of self-awareness comes from, but the army I built to protect myself from ever making a grave mistake again stands down.

I repeat, "I know."

"Okay, so—?"

"So, I'll play by your rules. Say please and thank you. Use *sotto voce*—speak gently and kindly."

"Good. That's great."

"But I wasn't done. So long as you never wear Grimaldi's jersey again. Anyone else's for that matter."

"I'll follow your rules too and that means not wearing yours either."

My pulse trips as I sit down on the couch. "But what if I want you to?"

"You want me to wear your jersey?"

I lift my shoulder in a bashful shrug because that's as far down that road as I can travel for now.

"Sure," she says, sitting down a measure away.

I bite the inside corner of my lip and blurt, "I blew it at practice earlier."

I tell her about how my tough love approach with the guys didn't go over well. Vohn has ownership over that method. Apparently, they need something else from me, but what? At this point, I don't know how else to be.

Our conversation weaves between a few anecdotes about how Grandma Dolly took her in, hockey, and the kid.

We communicate, connect. It's the most open I've been in a long time, and it's nice. A breath of fresh air as we listen to each other rather than give advice.

She asks, "Why were you put in a semi-permanent penalty box?"

I replay it in my head all the time, never having discussed it with anyone. Not my father or Hendrix, not even the other guys on the team.

"During an intense game, Badaszek brought us back to the locker room to regroup. He got down on the ground and was demonstrating us crowding around the net. It was a funny position and I accidentally laughed."

"So you were suspended? No wonder you've been so ornery. I would be too if I was practically fired for smiling." She tosses me a pointed eyebrow.

I wince. "Coach wasn't intending to be funny. I was running on very little sleep and already on his short list for what was called unnecessary roughness and, uh, a bit of a scandal in the league a few years back." I scratch my temple. "I tend to have a short temper when things don't go my way."

"Maybe you should go to daycare with KJ. Learn how to behave yourself and play with others."

I snort. "The two-week suspension seemed extreme at the time, but I can't help but wonder if Badaszek knew I had some personal matters to tend to and wouldn't request time off."

"Is that when you found out about your son?"

"I was less than two weeks in, playing Mr. Mom. I had to jump right into fatherhood without any idea what I was doing. I think I cracked."

Jessica's hand presses into my arm. "I'm sorry that you had to go through that alone, but why didn't you—?"

"Ask my family for help? Because I—"

"You think you messed up? KJ is not a mistake. He's the greatest blessing in your life."

The words pierce my heart. My eyes well up. I look away.

She's right though. I love that little boy with all my heart, but it also brings with it a risk.

"Sounds like your coach offered you grace."

"And you are too. I don't deserve it." My voice threatens to break.

She takes my hand and laces her fingers through mine.

"I ruin things, Jessica. I'm the mistake," I whisper so softly I'm not sure she hears.

A long beat passes.

"That's not true."

"I still don't know what I'm doing."

"You're doing a great job."

"No, you are."

"We are together."

I shake my head. She's just being her usual nice self. Never has anything bad to say. Then again, she did make it clear that actions speak louder than words and I think there's still some whipped cream by my ear. I'll have to shower again.

I continue, "But none of that explains why he made me captain when I came back."

"Your coach must see the leader in you."

"More like loser," I mutter.

"The potential to be a great father. For some people, it takes time to grow into parenthood. For others, they just never quite get there."

Her hand leaves mine, taking with it warmth and hope. I reach for it, securing my palm around hers.

Gaze gentle, she says, "Liam, don't be so hard on yourself. Especially when the little boy was just left on your doorstep. You had no idea. Most dads have nine months to prepare. Then, they're still not ready. No one is. We learn as we go. Do you think you could try that as a captain and a dad?"

"How did you get so smart? So insightful? Reflective?"

"I was angry at the world for a long time about my situation until I realized no one owes me anything. Each day is a gift. It's up to me whether I receive it or toss it in the trash and light it on fire. Return to sender."

I balk.

She smiles. "Or greet it with a friendly wave and do my best to get through, leaving things better than I found them. I chose to make my life into a little positivity project."

No, she's a masterpiece.

@THEPUCKPOST

We are back, baby! The Knights make a triumphant return after losing their last two games. Do we have @TheRealLiamEllis to thank? His performance has notably improved after a rocky holiday season with some sharp assists and an impressive attack on defense, rendering @GrahamBrown01! more of a ∘∘ at least when it came to the box.

Is The Beast a Grinch? We'll leave that up to you, however, his heart can't be pure ice because rumors are lighting up the hockey-sphere about him having a secret family. Sightings of Ellis with a woman dressed in a wedding gown, carrying a kid circulated earlier this year and more recently they were seen at the arena with the same unidentified woman wearing his jersey.

The real question is has Ellis joined the #KnightsNation marriage and parenting pool, and if so, will he continue to seize the day or will he crack up, er, freeze up?

This is no laughing matter and we want to hear from you!

In other news, we're considering adding a weekly gear review post. Give us a thumbs up if you're interested.

♥💬📨 3,821 Likes

@HockeyAddict764: I thought this was supposed to be unbiased reporting. Sounds like you're a #KnightsNation super fan.

@DollyPuckton: Is that a problem @HockeyAddict764?

@WriterOnTheStorm: Ellis is a showman. He will do anything, including knocking around Valjean, for attention.

@GoldefortheGoal: If you can include discount codes for the gear review, go for it!

@7YHDFFFB: DM to collab

@HockeyAddict764: That's a bot! Don't click the link! Also, Ellis's personal life is his business. Let's hear more about hockey and less about rumors.

>Read more

24

LIAM

WE HAD our rules and Jessica threw them out the window like a bouquet of helium balloons.

Except one.

I left her one of my jerseys and a piece of chocolate. I regret my behavior and that my default setting is to jerk. I want to change that. For her. For KJ. I'm pleased to see she's wearing it at my game against the Mustangs.

She's also here with the little guy, which is a big deal.

I flash them a sign after we score a goal and they both clap and cheer.

I can only imagine the speculation. But perhaps anyone paying attention will think she's a single mom and we're friends.

But the feelings I've developed for Jessica aren't friendly. They're not acrimonious either. More like strong. Bigger than I've ever felt.

She makes my heart pound.

My breath shallow.

The woman grew a smile inside of me so big, that I imagine it's going to break out any minute.

But one of the Mustangs' defensemen drives toward me to make room for his forward to pocket the puck. I deke and pivot, turning the tables at the same time Grady swipes the biscuit. Hayden offers an assist and then slaps the puck to 'Bama who slams it into the net.

Our goal song comes on and the arena chants along.

I skate to the boards and press my hand to the glass just in case the kid doesn't know it's me under this helmet. I was always so proud to see my dad out there, a titan on the ice. Scoring goals and taking names.

My son grins ear to ear and then scrambles out of Jessica's arms and starts to try to scale the glass. Now, we're really making a scene. I'll deal with the fallout later.

Grandma Dolly plies him with a cookie and he returns to sitting.

After the win, the three of them meet me in the hall outside the locker room.

It's like a do-over from before. I'm prepared this time.

It's rare for me to have people waiting—other than occasionally my family.

A thought floats through my mind, this is my family. At least here in Cobbiton.

Grandma Dolly signs, congratulating me on the win. Asks to see my abs. I pretend not to understand.

Jessica speaks and signs, "I promised KJ that he could touch the ice."

Glancing over my shoulder, I'm eager to get out of here to avoid questions but lead them to the rink.

It's time for me to shift priorities, but that doesn't make it easy. It's one thing to know what to do, but an entirely different thing to understand how.

No sooner do we exit the warm room, the child goes bonkers, it's like I let a bull into an arena draped in red. He slides in his little sneakers onto the ice, arms windmilling, but I don't need to catch him before he finds his balance. The Zamboni just resurfaced the ice and he glides.

Grandma Dolly signs, "Looks like a natural."

She's got that right. "Everyone says that about their kid, but wow."

"Takes after his dad," Jessica says and signs.

A little beam of pride shoots through me.

She lifts onto her toes and whispers into my ear, "Remember when I said I don't want hockey to ruin KJ like it has you? I'm sorry."

A defensive retort rises and falls inside, but I don't recall her saying that. It's then I realize she's calmed my inner barbarian by lacing her arm around my waist. I almost don't know what to do other than drape mine over her shoulders. We're like two proud parents, watching the light of our lives find his calling.

Or not. If he wants to be a climber or an insurance adjuster, that's fine too. I don't care ... but the thought dies. I am his father and I do care. A lot. About him. About this woman by my side.

Glancing down at Jessica, I take her hand and lead her onto the ice. We glide together and my palm around hers feels better than holding my stick. A long sigh escapes.

We're more than halfway toward the home net lines before we catch up with the little rascal. Jessica takes his hand and I grab the other. Wearing street shoes, the three of us slide— linked up, it's both graceful and clumsy yet perfect. When we get to the little door where Dolly watches, I urge her to join us.

She shakes her head.

I point to my abs and wink.

She smiles and slides forward, meeting us.

Everyone knows that the sun melts ice, but I feel it shining, in each of my hands, in their smiles and mine grows.

Until we're back in the hallway where we pause because KJ wanted to look at the trophy cases. While I talk to Mikey for a minute, Grimaldi sidles over. Watching him out of the corner of my eye, I dare him to flirt with Jessica. The guy is the one broken link in the Knights chain. I have no idea why Coach keeps him around.

She laughs nervously.

He whispers something to her.

Her expression darkens.

He leans closer.

She turns guarded.

Mikey's voice fades.

I march over, ready to redefine "Stick salute" and shove it where the sun don't shine.

"Let's go," I growl.

Jessica mouths the reminder, *Sotto voce.*

I shake my head. Not with this guy.

"I was just talking to your 'Work wife' about how she could offer me some assistance of the personal kind." He waggles his eyebrows.

"If she's my work wife, then I'm her work husband, meaning she's not available to offer you any assistance of any sort ever."

Grimaldi's expression turns weasel-like. "Don't see a ring."

She glances at her hand.

To her, he says, "Don't worry, baby. I don't sting."

Jessica's smile is tight. "I'm not worried and don't call me baby. Your comment is weird and not at all appealing."

My jaw practically hits the floor. I half expected her to brush him off with sparkle fingers.

Just then, a little pudgy hand fits into mine. I hesitate. Jessica beams a smile, her expression glowing as if Grimaldi doesn't even exist.

I can't say no to whatever grows between us or to my son.

Don't want to.

Not anymore.

"Well, well, well, what do we have here?" Grimaldi asks, breaking into the moment.

Jessica takes my other hand as if to say, *We've got this together*.

Grimaldi adds, "Looks like a happy little family."

Grandma Dolly bustles over and signs, "We have celebration cake waiting at home."

Hate to say it, but Grimaldi is right.

———

THE NEXT WEEK, while the little guy is at "Kinder Care," Jessica and I go to a brunch sponsored by one of the brands that endorses me.

Anytime we're out, people flock to her and she gets excited about kids and babies. She makes friends wherever we go and has a sort of magnetism that people can't resist. It's like a weird symbiosis that leaves everyone but me smiling and laughing.

I tell myself I abhor it, but my occasional smile defies that lie.

Back at the loft, while she's on the phone talking to a woman we met at the luncheon who introduced herself as the Cobbiton Activities Commission coordinator, about Easter events, I get a text. It's one I don't want to read.

> Unknown: Nice family moment at the Ice Palace. Looks like you were the king of the castle. But I could tell everyone Jess is not our little prince's mother.

My stomach twists, but I reply because this message could only be from one person, Pam, my ex. No doubt she saw social media posts, put two and two together, and is now attempting to put me in an uncomfortable position.

> Me: I don't care what you do to tarnish my reputation, but leave her out of this, and above all don't mess with my son.

> Unknown: That depends on what you'll do for me.

Blood rushes in my ears. Without thinking, I take a swing at the wall and shove my desk over before realizing what I'm doing.

Jessica appears in the doorway with a spatula in her hand. "I was just making a cake when I thought I heard—"

"Baked goods don't solve everything."

"Sure they do. I could add some whipped cream. Remember what you said about not taking yourself so seriously." The corner of her lip flickers with a smile.

I hammock my hands on top of my head and pace. Pam must've seen the game. She knows about Jessica. Now I have something at stake which is exactly what I've worked so hard to avoid. It's been better to keep my life simple and not let anyone in.

In a small voice, Jessica says, "I was making it for you to have this afternoon. I have an appointment."

Probably a job interview. I already came so close to losing her. Saved by the pie to the face.

Glancing around at the dented drywall and the mess I made of my desk, I realize I'm not managing my anger.

She starts picking up the scattered papers. "Do you want to talk about it?"

"Stuff triggered me," I say vaguely, a shoddy explanation.

She lets out a dry laugh. "You were triggered, so you smashed your wall?"

"Better than punching someone in the face." What if she's really done with me this time?

She gets to her feet and locks onto my eyes with a ferocity I've never before seen. "It's your job to get over that.

"Harsh."

"Direct," she says, using my words against me ... for me?

I grunt.

"I'm talking about healing. It's not the responsibility of the world to tiptoe around you so we don't upset you, set you off, or *trigger* you. That's on you."

Now, she's being ultra direct. Have I created a monster?

"I'm telling you to get over it."

I ask, "What happened to one of your upbeat, optimism-laced unicorn and sparkles pep talks?"

Jessica plants her hands on her hips. "Life can be a boxer. It's going to knock you down. It's up to you to get back up."

"But I don't know how to come back from this." I flash the texts from my ex which have intensified in recent weeks, including her financial demands and my questions about why she didn't give the kid proper medical care and attention.

Jessica's eyes grow as she reads the messages.

I say, "A Bundt won't fix this."

"Are you suggesting we *don't* try to kill her with kindness?"

"Are you suggesting we resort to murder instead?" Even for me, that's a bridge too far.

Alarmed, Jessica motions with her fingers in a solid *No*

gesture that could be understood by anyone even if they're not fluent in ASL. "I meant to make friends. Everyone—"

"Not Pam," I say, referring to my ex.

"Who?" Jessica's tone lifts in question.

"Pamberlie," I add, using her full name.

Jessica's gaze grows momentarily distant. "Pamberlie Coogan?"

"How'd you know?"

Jessica presses her hand to her forehead. "She was almost my sister-in-law."

25

LIAM

JESSICA and I stare at each other for a long moment as if there were a glitch in a computer program and the screen froze.

"Are we talking about the same person?" I ask.

"It's a unique name," she says.

"And there's no mistaking Coogan."

Filled with disbelief, I crouch down and pick up all the stuff I'd scattered on the floor, feeling ashamed and confused.

Jessica perches on the edge of my desk and studies her hands. "The day we met at the bakery, I wasn't wearing the wedding gown because I thought it was Halloween."

"You mean you weren't testing out a witch bride costume?"

She doesn't look up.

I clear my throat. "I'm sorry for calling you that and for being so rude. I was so caught up in protecting myself, that I wasn't paying attention to all the people I was possibly harming. A coarse word here. A dismissal there. It all adds up. I can only imagine the wreckage."

She doesn't laugh or smile.

An ache that has nothing to do with my workout earlier or

from punching the walls seizes me. The worst thing in my life is when Jessica isn't smiling. This means the best thing in my life is ...

Taking her chin gently in my fingers, I tilt her head to meet my gaze.

"Whatever happened—"

"Despite my hide being as tough as a rhino's and my personality as bubbly as a dolphin and—"

"You're human," I finish, hopefully encouraging Jessica to open up to me. I know what it's like to shoulder burdens alone. Not going to say that I'll suddenly read like an open book, but she has me to lean on. That much I can offer.

She shrugs, folding into herself. "Rexlan and I met on the set of a commercial. I was a cubicle girl. He was the big mean boss, except not to me. In the script, we bonded over antacids. After the wrap, we hung out for a while. His mother showed up. She was very sweet. They took me out for lunch. One thing led to another and soon I was renting a room in their house off Sunset Boulevard, helping maintain her website, packing orders, doing customer service, and denying that I'd gotten sucked into a world that was less sunny and more leechy."

"I thought you said something about their being lizard fanatics."

"They were both charming, Or I was gullible. Living in a new city. I didn't know anyone else. They love-bombed me."

"Sounds dangerous."

"More like a disaster. It all happened slowly then pretty quickly, I became part of their lives along with a bunch of other people. We were one big happy family, which is what I'd always wanted. While Rexlan played video games, I kept him company. While he 'worked,' I helped Sorsha with all sorts of things."

"Don't tell me you baked for him." For some reason, I hate

the idea of her bringing him a cake and him dismissing it because he's pretending to be a commando in Call of Duty. Then again, I haven't appreciated Jessica the way I should either.

"His mother was putting a lot of pressure on him to get married. His parents were divorced, and I learned that when Rexlan tied the knot, the funds his father paid his ex-wife for Rexlan's needs would turn into alimony for her—if the bride-to-be got the father's stamp of approval. According to Sorsha, he was in the movie business and banked a lot of cash in the early 2000s during the reality TV craze."

"There was another clause that would grant Rexlan access to his trust fund, but I don't know the details." She gives a half roll of her eyes.

"Rexlan sounds like a wet handshake."

Jessica's expression creases. "I was just happy someone was paying attention to me."

"You met the father's stamp of approval, but I take it you didn't get married."

"No, he eloped with his secret girlfriend the night before our wedding. I found out at the altar."

I growl, "He what?"

Jessica shrinks further. I sense this is tied to her childhood, into being rejected.

"Whatever you're thinking, stop," I say.

"Is that a command?"

"Rexlan doesn't know what he's missing. You're an amazing woman. Will be an outstanding wife and mother. You are beautiful. Your smile lights up a room. No one can resist it. Not even me, Mr. Meanie himself."

The corner of her lip twitches. She then tells me about the horror show of a wedding day.

"But that's not even the worst of it."

"You sure about that? It sounds pretty bad."

"Sorsha was obsessed with lizards. I figured it was standard mother-in-law quirkiness. She'd created a legit lizard cult called the Skink Society."

I nearly choke on my surprise. "What did you say?"

"A skink is a kind of lizard. She had a website with products and seminars, even a private community for rituals."

"Sounds like a felony waiting to happen."

"I have no doubt they were funneling money through donations, talisman purchases, and their mail-order lizard tonics for healing, restoration, and increased sensation, whatever that means." Jessica presses her hands to her face as if to hide.

"That's possibly the weirdest thing I've ever heard."

So are the strange whooshy feelings I have for her and my constant craving for Bundt cake that just won't quit.

Peeling her fingers free, I say, "I'm not glad you had a pee emergency, but I am glad we met."

Her eyes shine. "Wouldn't we have anyway, since I'm your work wifey?" Her voice is light, almost flirty as she slips out from memories of the past and into the present—into the woman I know and—

It's an astonishing transformation and so are these—what are they called? Oh, right. Feelings.

"Needless to say, I was stood up on my wedding day, lost my job, and my place to live all in the space of an hour. After that, I promised myself that I wouldn't stop smiling or nearly get sucked into a cult again, but I also told myself I'd never, ever date a coworker or boss."

"Did you really?"

She nods and lets out a long, long sigh.

This is a cue for me to break through my self-imposed armor. But I don't. Not yet.

Not before Jessica asks, "What are you going to do about your ex?"

But that's not the question I'm asking. It's more like *What am I going to do about Jessica?*

I DON'T STOP THINKING about my work wifey. My nanny. My peach. My Jessica. But she can never be mine. Said so herself. Anyway, I'm not worthy of a woman like her.

So I flirt with disaster, knowing I'm the only one who will pay the price. It's late, but I send her a text. She might be up reading recipe blogs since she struggles with insomnia. I have the coffee bean bill to prove it. Not that I mind.

> Me: Are you still awake?

> Jessica: Of course I am. Why do you think no one says Carpe Nox as in Seize the Night!?

> Me: That's a very good question.

> Doesn't the moon emoji look like a wheel of cheese? 🌙

> Me: It kinda does.

> Jessica: Want to play truth or dare?

> Me: What are we, 12?

> Jessica: No, then we'd play spin the bottle. 💋💋💋

> Me: Not judging, but you had your first kiss when you were twelve?

Jessica: Technically, no. I went into the closet with Bobby Oatkes. It was dark. I picked up Mrs. Oatkes's shoe. He pressed his lips to the leather sole. We never spoke of it again. 👞 😬 But I was also moved to a new town three weeks later, so …

Me: Clever. Glad he didn't put his dirty lips on yours.

Am I being possessive? Protective? Petty? I don't know, but the idea of anyone's lips on Jessica's makes me want to wipe the smile the guy was sure to have off his undeserving face.

Jessica: How about you? When was your first kiss?

Me: Sounds a lot like we're already playing truth or dare.

Jessica: Just the truth part. I suppose it would be hard to know whether we follow through with dares.

Me: Then truth it is.

Jessica: Okay, tell me something truthful.

My stomach swoops and energy I shouldn't have at this late hour suddenly rushes through me. How much truth can I reveal?

Me: I know you call me Mr. Meanie. Have broken the rules … At first I thought it was childish. Now it's kind of endearing.

Jessica: Says the guy who has adult temper tantrums. I also call you Big Daddy. Just in my head mostly. Is that weird? You're big and a daddy.

Is it odd that I like that she has names for me?

Me: Are there any others?

Jessica: Love Puff.

Me: You do not call me that.

Jessica: I might now. 😂😂😂

Me: Have any secrets?

Jessica: Loads. You?

Me: A few.

Actually, just the one and she can never know. Whatever we have would instantly be over. She'd hate me if she found out.

Jessica: Okay, since you asked and practically had to drag it out of me, I have a deep coffee insecurity.

Me: I didn't ask and I already knew that.

Jessica: Okay, how about this one? I'm a dysfunctional adult.

Me: On the contrary, you're highly functioning, running my life, the kid's, and yours.

Jessica: Turns out it's easier to help others.

Me: Than to help yourself?

She doesn't answer, but I want to help her. Show her how special she is. How important. Smart, beautiful, adored. The desire comes over me with the same forceful drive as I have to win the finals.

Whoa. Time to *pivot, pivot, pivot*. Or not.

Me: Here's one. My brother has major rizz and sometimes I get jealous.

Jessica: Frizz? Why would you be jealous of that?

Me: No, rizz, like confidence, charm. Basically, he's my opposite.

Jessica: Look at you, using slang like a modern man instead of a caveman.

Me: So you knew what it meant. Why'd you ask if I meant frizz?

Jessica: Because maybe I wanted to say that I like how you are.

Me: You constantly call me a grump.

Jessica: I never said I don't like it.

Me: How could you like a grump?

Jessica: Stop being so judgy.

I'm reclined in my bed but feel like I'm falling. Like the world as I knew it dropped out from underneath me. I've let go and I'm in free-fall.

So long as I land with Jessica, I can't say that I mind.

But I cannot entertain anything romantic with my assistant. Certainly can't date the nanny. Plus she was engaged. Probably not ready for a relationship.

However, I fall asleep, wondering what if ...

26
JESS

AS THE WINTER thaws into spring, it's hard not to notice that Liam's blue-gray eyes have been looking more like the sunrise sky in the morning.

But I'm trying not to pay attention because what started as an abiding tolerance of the man, turned into friendliness, morphed into flirting, and is now something I can't quite define.

The more he grows in his relationship with his son, the more I lose my footing. It's like I'm floating. When they hold hands, laugh, play. Forget turning into mush. I dissolve.

I make a buttermilk Bundt cake with caramel icing for Gracie's book club. Everyone devours it, but instead of discussing the small-town romantic comedy with a big-city developer who wants to bulldoze the place before she comes face to face with an attractive contractor who's trying to revitalize it, they talk about their real lives.

Not having much to contribute, I mostly listen, then Meg, whose husband used to play for the Knights but recently retired, asks me, "Your son looks to be around the same age as Milo. Maybe we can schedule a playdate."

"My son?" I stutter.

I glimpse Cara's stricken expression before it disappears, and she asks, "She means the little boy who you nanny."

"Oh, KJ."

"How do you manage being Liam's personal assistant and being a nanny?" Delaney asks.

I sputter. "Um, well, there's a lot of overlap."

"I'm shocked The Beast doesn't terrify him," Whitney says.

"He's a really good dad," I blurt, realizing they didn't officially know about the KJ-Liam connection.

Recently, he's more than made up for his shortcomings early on. They draw lines between the dots in stunned silence.

I try to fill in the space. "I'm just the nanny. Liam's assistant. Basically a work wifey."

"I don't think that's how you use that phrase," Gracie says gently.

Of course, I think about how I almost became Rexlan's wife which would've been the biggest mistake of my life, and how Rex's sister is Liam's ex, which makes Pamberlie KJ's mom. I had no idea she had a kid. I want to hide behind a bookshelf, but this is a romance bookstore so there's no escaping the tangled webs we weave—or in this case the ones other people tie together. They sure could use lessons from Grandma Dolly. She's a talented fiber worker and denier of drama.

Heidi slowly shakes her head and says, "Liam has a kid. He's a father. Darcy is a dad."

As the truth takes shape in their minds, they seem to catch up with this reality, gaining momentum, and everyone contributes to the big reveal that hockey's biggest beast is a dad.

"We voted him least likely to ever request my wedding planning services," Margo says.

The girls start giggling about #MrDarcysAbs.

My cheeks go up in flames, so of course, Cara notices.

While they're seeding the bracket for winning abdominals, she asks, "Is there something you'd like to tell me?"

"Thanks again for the job. You were right. Liam needed help. I've been saving up to move, so I'll probably give my notice soon." The words and my not-even par-cooked plan comes out robotically, sloppily.

Cara's face falls. "Please stay in Cobbiton. I'll miss you too much. Who'll be my cake dealer?" She bounces in her seat. "Please open a cakery. A cake bakery. You can call it Jess-i-cakes! Like Pat-a-Cake, the nursery rhyme!"

"I don't know the first thing about running a bakery. Plus, there's already the Busy Bee."

"That's also a coffee shop."

"Coffee and I come as a package deal."

"If we're not going to talk about cakes, let's discuss crushes," Cara says with an enthusiastic shimmy.

I do a double take because that's not the direction our conversation should go.

All at once, everyone in the room asks variations of, "Do you have a crush on Liam?"

I didn't think my cheeks could get any redder, but they fall right off the color wheel. When I don't respond, everyone squeals.

"I knew it!" Delaney proclaims, hopping to her feet.

"Me too," Whit says, smug.

Gracie says, "I owe Vohn a kiss. That was the bet prize. Not that I'm complaining. He knew something was going on with his defenseman. He was right."

Whit chortles. "Figures one grump would recognize it in another."

Margo shakes her head. "Beau didn't say a word."

"The guy keeps things close to the vest," Cara says.

I start to creep away because it truly is time for me to hide. I may have a thick skin, but the idea of an entire hockey team talking about me having a crush on someone is too much. But how did they know?

I ask Cara, "Did you talk about me to Pierre and then he blabbed?"

"My lips were sealed. Bestie code. But he was one hundred percent sure Liam had a crush ..."

I blink a few times as her words slowly settle. "Liam doesn't have crushes or emotions. He's made of metamorphic rock. You mean that I have a crush on him."

They all shake their heads from side to side.

Cara says, "It's cool if you do, but the bet was about *him* having a crush on *you*."

This time they all nod.

"That can't be. He tolerates me at best. I mean, maybe we're friends." I squeeze my eyes shut. "Possibly flirted once or twice. But—" I don't know why I want him to like me. It's as if ever since I worked my way out of self-imposed solitary confinement, I can't tolerate people not liking me.

I say, "Liam doesn't think of me that way. At all. And has made it abundantly clear."

"Or a-Bundt-antly? Didn't he ask you to make him a cake?" Cara asks with a laugh.

The happy squeals reach the highest of decibels.

When the clamor dies down, I say, "Even if I did have a crush on him or he had one on me, crushes are fleeting. It'll go away." And so will I because I can't handle the disappointment of staying in Cobbiton and having my smile wiped off my face and my heart torn out of my chest. Everyone leaves me. Liam will too.

"Or you both might fall," Whit says.

"Or it could be a rebound," I say, thinking out loud when I should probably keep this to myself.

By way of explanation, Cara says, "Jess is a jilted bride."

Gracie rubs her hands together. "A real-life tale of romance, do tell."

I give them the barebones overview of Rexlan, but of course, they want all the details, which brings us back around to the present day with Liam. But there's only so much I can say right now as I unravel the knots I've tied myself in about my feelings for this man. I keep much of what came before my return to Cobbiton to myself ... for now.

"We have a professional relationship. I'm just confused. Can't possibly have a crush. Even if one of us does, he'll do something dumb or I'll smile too much and—" I slap my hands together. "Blam, it'll be over."

"Newsflash, it could grow stronger." Delaney describes how things went with her and Hayden.

That's when I realize that maybe my feelings for Liam have graduated from a crush to something more. But what? I've never felt this way before. Not about any previous boyfriend, of which I can count on one hand, and certainly not about Rexlan.

But what is it?

Cara squeals. "When you think about him is it like all those warm, cuddly, cozy feelings but enhanced like on the jumbo screen at the arena?"

I stare dumbly at her, wondering if she read my mind or if I'm so far gone I have one of those screens above my head, advertising my feelings, complete with pulsing little love hearts.

Margo adds, "Is he all you can think about?"

Pfft. As if. "He's my boss, so he's often on my mind."

Gracie asks, "Does he stretch a lot?"

"He's an athlete."

"I mean like put his arm across the back of your chair? Lean in the doorframe, surreptitiously flexing?" Gracie lifts and lowers her eyebrows.

Yes, actually, but his muscles are probably tight.

"When your skin brushes his does it feel like it left a mark that you can't ignore?" Leah asks with a sigh.

I swallow. "He's left-handed so we bump each other a lot."

Whit wears a mischievous smile. "Those little tingles inside lead to heart flutters which lead to feeling like you're floating away."

The girls giggle.

My phone beeps, but I ignore it. Another text follows and I check in case it's the guy I want to simultaneously tell myself I'm not thinking about and trying to decide what kind of cake I should bake for him. Maybe that's my measuring tool. Then again, I bake for the likes of Mrs. Kirby.

Instead, it's Rexlan. I ignore the message as the conversation shifts from my so-called crush to the girls discussing the big gala coming up. The Knights are being honored with the Huckle-Strout Award and they all have to attend after a game in Colorado.

Cara describes her formal dress in a sapphire hue with a ruffled skirt that she'll wear with her mother's pearls.

"We have a dog sitter arranged," Margo says.

"It'll be nice to travel. I haven't been to an away game in far too long," Delaney adds.

"Did Liam get you a dress?" Cara asks.

"I already arranged for KJ to stay with Grandma Dolly for the two nights we'll be gone, but I'm only joining Liam in an administrative capacity."

"Then why did he ask Hayden my dress size?" Delaney asks.

"Because he wanted to get punched in the face?" I hazard a guess, thinking of the way Liam reacted when Grimaldi breathed in my direction. Okay, he called me *baby* and said some stupid things too, but Liam probably didn't want me getting distracted.

Delaney smirks. "No, he asked because you and I are about the same height and weight."

I'm not sure how the conversation escalated from the girls asking about KJ to accurately intuiting my crush on Liam, claiming he has one on me, and now masterminding our big takeover of Denver, but here we are.

I can't help but think about the last time I wore a gown and in one big avalanche of words, I tell everyone the details I'd withheld about being a jilted bride ... and the lizard cult.

They look at me in wide-eyed silence.

Seated closest to me, Gracie pats my arm and says, "Darlin', you're safe here."

Cara says, "Where do you find these people?"

I shrug. "I'm just really friendly."

"Or you attract them like stray cats, er, lizards."

Whit, as sharp as a whip, talks about self-worth and boundaries, bad relationships, and the good ones to hang onto.

Cara grips my arm. "That's why we can't let you wander off to another square state."

"What's wrong with Wyoming?" I mentioned the possibility of moving there this summer last time we texted after I saw a social media ad for a dude ranch that was hiring.

"Nothing, but maybe don't be so eager to leave," Cara says.

If I don't make a move first, everyone else is bound to make their exit. This has been true all my life.

Ella says, "I wasn't sure what to think of Cobbiton when I first got here, but even with its quirks, I don't think you'll find any lizard cults."

"Just fans of hockey."

"And corn."

"Plus, you have a great job," Cara chimes.

The goal is to save up and then find the place where I belong with the people I belong to. As the conversation shifts to the Hockey Days event Leah is planning for next year, I guess being back in Cobbiton isn't the worst ... for now.

After I promise to bake a Bundt for the next book club, I head over to the loft. A large white box sits on the table. The tag with the satin ribbon has my name on it.

I open the lid and tears threaten, then fall. My shoulders shake because the last time I wore a gown was to my wedding that wasn't.

A little hand silently slides into mine before I realize Liam and KJ are home. I squeeze his hand and hug him before he scatters to play with his new Legos. He's building an arena— yes, already. The kid is going places. Hockey majors, probably the Hall of Fame.

Liam strides over and concern lashes his features.

"Did someone hurt you?" he asks.

I nod while saying, "No."

The man looks murderous. "Yes? No? Which is it?"

This is the second time I've fallen apart in front of this man, but in this instance, it's not because of the past. Rather, in the very near future, I'm afraid someone is going to get their heart broken and her name starts with the letter J.

My phone beeps and I ignore it in favor of the hug. What-ever Rexlan wants will have to wait. Possibly forever because with sunshine and sparkles on my side, I'm going to see this through until the crush goes away. Or Liam realizes that I'm just a silly girl with stars in her eyes and leaves me, the same as everyone else. Like Gracie's love stories, it will come to an end.

But the kiss he presses to my forehead when my tears stop, tells me I don't want it to.

AFTER MORE THAN a few goodbye hugs with KJ and Grandma Dolly, Liam and I leave for Colorado.

"Did you bring the dress?" he asks when we're already in the air.

"Yes, boss."

His lips form a thin line. "Are you going to wear it?"

"Are you going to use your manners?"

He looks at me blankly as if so pre-programmed to disconnect from the potential for emotion, he has forgotten how to operate like a human.

The girls were wrong. He does not have a crush on me.

"We can try ASL."

"Let's speak first. I'm still learning."

"Okay, it goes like this. If you want a woman to attend an event with you and wear a gown, you have to ask her, politely. Preferably with a little flair."

"Flair?"

"I'm not talking about kissing the top of her hand and getting down on one knee."

With bulging, animated eyes, as if seeing me for the first time, he says, "Oh."

"Have you been evaluated by the team physician? I'm not making this into a joke, but did you take a puck to the head?"

His expression softens. "No, Jessica. I don't want to scare you off. I realize the gown may have been too much too soon, given the witch bride attire in your old car's trunk."

I lean back in the cushy first-class seat, doing my best not to be alternately fascinated, distracted, and terrified since this is my first time flying. Liam said it's no big deal. Yeah. Okay. Same as all these emotions I'm experiencing. No biggie. It's just an ordinary Tuesday. Carry on, folks.

So, it turns out that he's not as out of touch as I thought.

"New rule. Let's communicate. Use our words. Say all the things."

The side of his top lip curls like he's accepting this challenge. As if it's a dare. "All the things."

"Yes, all the things."

"Are you sure?"

"Yes, Liam. I am sure. Hearing you say all the things is far preferable to sitting in silence, wondering, pondering, speculating."

"Be careful what you wish for," he murmurs.

But he doesn't say all the things. Not for the remainder of the flight and not during the luxury SUV ride to the posh hotel. Not when we're alone in the elevator or in the hallway when we reach the end and our respective doors, standing opposite each other.

I sigh.

"Can I come in?" He gestures to the door behind me.

"You want to come into my hotel room?"

"I've stayed here before. The view is spectacular. Looks like I'm on the street side. You get the mountains."

"Yeah, sure." I let him in and he strides right to the balcony.

I follow because he wasn't kidding. The immense snow-capped peaks spilling into lush evergreen hills are breathtaking.

And the moment he lays eyes on those jagged mountains topped with snow, the bandage is ripped off. Liam Ellis does not stop speaking for the next thirty minutes as the sun sets and the stars blink little night lights in the sky. I hear about how he grew up in Brookking Sound, a small coastal town in Canada, playing hockey as a kid, and cycling through two teams before finding his way to Nebraska.

From nearby, paper lanterns glow and then one by one float upward. Liam's arm slides over my shoulders, gripping me snugly to his side. I lean into him. Even though he's practically made of marble, there's a softness to this gesture.

Maybe actions and words speak in harmony.

As more and more lanterns float aloft, amounting to at least a few dozen, I say, "I wanted those at the wedding, but Sorsha said it would disturb the lizard gods since they're nocturnal and all. Then, she added them to her website for a mere ninety-nine dollars a piece to release as an offering to the skinks. She sourced them from China for like ninety-nine cents each."

"I'm so glad you were a jilted bride."

"That's not—" I start to say, but stop myself. "Yeah, me too."

Liam says, "Back home, the town does this on New Year's Eve. It's been ages since I've gone."

"Brookking Sound sounds like a nice place."

"I want you to go there."

"Maybe someday. It's probably not too far from Wyoming."

He chuckles. "It's like the opposite direction going west to east. But I'd like you there with me. At the end of the month. We have a game in Toronto, so we'll be somewhat nearby."

I'm looking into the distance where the glowing orbs seem to meet the stars, but feel warmth on my skin. Liam gazes at me. I turn slightly to face him.

He opens and closes his mouth. If I didn't know better, I'd say his cheeks darken, but it's hard to tell out here.

"Jessica?" Liam asks.

"Yes," I say, but it's more of an answer to the question I sense he's asking.

Then his lips land lightly on mine.

I inhale his soapy scent. Feel the sweep of his stubble on my skin. Absorb his warmth.

It's a brief kiss. Just our mouths brushing. But my heart is pounding. The crush is tumbling, down, down, down like a snowball gaining momentum until it reaches the bottom of the hill. Then, like one of the paper lanterns, it glows, sails into the air, and dances with the stars.

He draws back and the light dims but doesn't go dark.

What just happened? I don't ask. Don't use my words. Neither does he. Maybe because there's no logical explanation.

After Liam leaves to meet with the team to prepare for the game tomorrow, my fingers press to my mouth where I feel the still-present sensation of his lips on mine, like he left a permanent impression.

27
LIAM

I WON'T LET myself think about the kiss, however brief, that Jessica and I shared, and how I memorized the sparkling stars in her eyes. How all I can smell is her cinnamon, spice, and everything nice scent. The way she felt so soft, so close ... until after the post-game team meeting.

The match against the Blizzard came down to a tie, resulting in overtime with Beau in the cage, and I give a recaptain—what we call the team captain's take on the game. That would be me. "Unfortunately, Ronnie Danielson scored on our boy." I clap Beau on the back.

He grunts and looks like he's about to bite my hand off.

"Take it easy cowboy. I need that thing. We can't win 'em all. And they won't either because next game, we'll crush Colorado."

The guys cheer, but it lacks the usual oomph.

It's no secret that Badaszek and Vohn are assessing my every word and every move, wondering if I'm worthy of being a captain. I pick apart where we went wrong and ask my teammates how we could have tightened up the play that resulted in the opposing team breaking away with the puck and charging it down to the goal.

They shout out various technical answers.

"Good, but the way we prevent the other team from scoring on us is to play like a well-oiled machine."

Pierre says, "Here we go. A missive on fine German engineering."

Having been around my father in the locker room from a young age, I tell him off in Dad's native tongue, then say, "We have to approach it systematically, but there is also nuance and a relational aspect."

The guys lean in, probably never having heard me use so many words. Last night when I was telling Jessica about where I grew up, she looked more curious about the fact that I was saying so much than she was about the details.

Could be that she opened a door for me that I'd sealed shut long ago.

At that, I add, "Now, it's time for us to eat cake."

Grimaldi asks, "What exactly are we celebrating? That we lost?"

A ray of sunlight pours into the dim locker room. "No, that we have room to grow. To improve. To be better than we were tonight and show the Blizzard that when we lose, we get back up. We return stronger, tougher, more precise."

Pierre says, "Ah, there he is. I was getting worried for a moment."

I clap my hands together and turn things back over to the coaches.

They shake their heads ... approvingly.

Badaszek says, "Go enjoy the gala. Be on your best behavior."

As we start to filter out, Hayden whispers to Redd, "Looks like he's in love."

The latter holds out his hand and the former slaps a large bill into it. I glare at them but don't argue. They're wrong, so wrong, but I feel like I finally found my footing as captain and I'm not going to mess that up.

I've done enough damage in my life and everyone else's.

Shortly after, when I meet Jessica in the lobby of the hotel to head to the event, I feel like I got punched in the face.

Her hair is in a chignon with strands spiraling around her neck. She wears sparkly earrings and light pink lipstick. The pale blue and white dress Grandma Dolly helped me pick out highlights her curves in such a way that makes me dizzy. Or it could be the sparkle accents.

I don't know where to look without gaping, drooling, wolf-whistling.

Yeow.

Maybe I *was* hit in the head with a puck and don't remember. That could've happened.

Jessica smiles and wiggles her fingers in a shy wave as I approach.

The whoosh rushes through me and I nearly stumble.

"Is this okay? Did I overdo it? You look mortified."

I glance around, hoping Grimaldi didn't hitch a ride to Colorado. Supposedly Badaszek had him stay back for remedial work since his stats have practically dropped from the charts. If he or anyone so much as breathes in her direction the gloves are coming off.

"You look …" I place my hand on Jessica's lower back, ushering her toward the exit. She scuttles, almost at a trot, jabbering about her dress, hair, and makeup.

I stop her on the sidewalk and plant my palms on her shoulders, my thumbs kneading the soft, exposed skin for a moment. I look her up and down, taking her in, wishing this would last forever. "Jessica, you look stunning."

She presses her palm to her chest as if taken aback. "I do?"

I nod. "Yes, you do."

Her fingers trail my cheek. "You didn't shave."

My hand finds hers and I grip it, kissing the top. "I would've but—" I cut myself off because those sound an awful lot like words I'm not ready to say.

She grins. "I like it this way. The perfect amount of stubble."

Well, then.

She's so stunning that when we enter the gala on the white carpet, people do double takes. The press snaps her photo—with me and solo, which is high praise because they must like her ice princess look.

The gala is much like the handful I've been to since joining the league. There are a few speeches and our team is honored with an award, followed by dinner and dancing.

Jessica politely toasts and has only a few polite sips of her champagne, but that's all. Her eyes water from the bubbles. When we take to the dancefloor, her cheeks are flushed and she cuts loose. Smile bright, she kicks it up with the girls until the slow dance when I cut in.

She's soft in my arms. Resting her cheek against my chest, she says, "My head feels funny."

"Maybe we should head back to the room?"

"Yeah. I'm suddenly tired." Her yawn makes me think of a sleepy kitten.

Her burst of energy followed by a crash reminds me of when the kid used to sneak into the cookie jar, get super hyper, and then quickly flame out. At least she's not having a temper tantrum.

I manage to get her back to the hotel, but by the time we're in the elevator, she's a limp noodle so I scoop her into my arms, bridal-carry style and hope she's exhausted enough not to notice. Don't want anyone to get the wrong idea.

In her room, I slip off her high heels as she nestles into the pillows. I check her forehead, but she's a normal temperature. Maybe the insomnia is catching up, or it's altitude sickness from the bubbly—even the little bit she had can affect a person who's not used to this elevation. I set a glass of water next to the bed and look at her for a long moment.

Her lashes brush her cheeks and not a wrinkle forms across her forehead. Her mouth is slack, but she's not frowning. It's a rare moment, not to see her smiling, and I suddenly long for it with an inner tug that almost scares me.

I contemplate kissing her on the cheek. I don't know what I was thinking last night on the balcony. Thankfully, a conversation about the kiss didn't come up and we both casually ignored it. Or maybe it was all in my puck-addled mind.

I'm about to leave when Jessica's arm shoots out and flops onto the bed. Eyes closed and voice muddled, she says, "Sing me a lullaby?"

I could pretend I don't hear, but instead ask, "Huh?"

"Just for a minute."

"Yeah, sure." I sit on the edge of the bed because it would be awkward to stand and sing a lullaby, looming over Jessica. Not that I know anything about lullabies, but I cannot deny this woman.

She grips the edge of my tux jacket and with surprising strength for being half asleep, tugs me toward her.

"Just a quick snuggle."

We're both fully dressed and I wrap my arms around her, little spoon and big spoon. She curls into me, sighs, and soon breathes softly.

I'm sure she's asleep, but she told me to say all the things, so I do. "Don't fall for me. I'm bad. Bad for you. Bad for everyone." I'm the worst.

I must doze off because my thoughts turn to the awful winter night when the car went off the road and it was too late for me to do anything about it.

28
JESS

IT'S OFFICIALLY spring and I have all the windows in the loft open. While KJ naps, I tell myself I'll look for new jobs. That was my plan and I have to stick to it.

Despite getting woozy and sleepy, Denver seemed like a nice enough place. Plus, Colorado is a square state like Nebraska. I open a tab to look for jobs when my finger slips and I wind up at #MrDarcysAbs.

Whoopsie.

I mean, I could just look at them in real life, but don't want to let Grandma Dolly down. She, um, makes sure I stay up to date on these things.

My phone beeps and I jump, afraid I've somehow been caught. But the message is from an unknown number. I skim the text and my stomach knots.

Just then, Liam enters the room, face stormy. "There's something we need to discuss."

I throw my phone like it might explode, yet it already feels like a grenade went off. "What do you mean? I updated the protein powder delivery and canceled that streaming service you weren't using."

He paces and rakes his hand through his hair. "More like I have a problem and you're kind of collateral damage."

"What?" I ask, not liking the way that sounds.

"My lawyer finally got back to me about the screenshot Pam sent."

"Pamberlie?"

Liam nods. "I never knew her full name until I got custody."

"Why wouldn't she have told you she has a kid?"

"Your guess is as good as mine."

"My guess is she wasn't sure it was your kid. Then she looked into possibilities of paternity, and they came up negative, leaving you the remaining option."

Liam's chest expands on a rough inhale. "Yeah. You're probably right. I later found out she'd hooked up with half the team that season."

I wrinkle my nose, but the theory fits with the Pamberlie I'd gotten to know. How she kept the kid from me and the rest of the family is a question I don't have the energy to ponder, but she'd only returned to LA from Phoenix shortly before the wedding, so she was probably tracking down Liam and keeping the kid a secret.

He says, "In the documents, there was some fine print that I'd disregarded because the one time we were together, I told her that I'd never get married. I was like twenty-one. I meant it at the time. I'd only just met her that night ..."

I squirm in my chair, not sure what to think or where this is going.

He stops moving and says, "After she left the kid with me and made it clear she had no intention of taking care of him, the attorneys drafted some documents. The little detail that I missed in my fog of shock was that it stated if I were to remain unmarried at the six-month mark since gaining custody if she wanted the kid back, she could petition the court. That also means she'd be eligible for child support. This was a little way for her to get around some of the laws in her state which prevented me from being required to provide funds since she'd waited so long to disclose paternity."

"Knowing Pamberlie, and I do, along with Sorsha and Rexlan, I'm not sure that's a great idea, but she is KJ's mother." I tap my chin. "I can't help but wonder if this also has something to do with the alimony and trust fund tied to the father."

"If that's the case, sounds to me like extortion."

"That would be quite the court case."

Liam takes a breath so deep the earth rattles. "Pam is just in it for the money. The fine print also indicates that I'd have to sign over seventy-five percent of my salary to her. I don't care about a penny, but I'm not going to let her use the kid for financial gain."

Sorsha's insistence that Rexlan get married so she can collect alimony comes to mind and I elaborate.

Liam crouches down and grips my knees. "Jessica, she left him here with a bag of clothes, a pet hermit crab, and a note. No indication that he'd been assessed for his hearing health. No—" His voice strains.

I swallow back emotion because KJ is such a special boy, I hate the idea of him being neglected and tossed from home to home for a payday.

"I'm the first to admit that I was awful. A bad dad. But—"

"But you figured it out." Nodding I say, "We'll sort this out too."

Hope flares in Liam's eyes and a long pause stretches between us before he paces by the big windows in the loft.

"Let me get this straight. In the custody documents,

Pamberlie temporarily waived parental rights, but the fine print indicates that if you remained unmarried by a certain date, and she wants to return to the child's life, she can."

"Unless I'm married," he repeats, then tells me they met in college the night he found out he was drafted for the NHL. There was a party. It got a little reckless. He hooked up with her. Things escalated. Then he never saw her again. Tried calling and texting. Still has the messages on his phone.

"So she kept KJ a secret from you, but once you claimed him, she's hunting for child support and then some. I never even knew she had a son." Makes me wonder if he was in a similar situation as I was before my mother left.

"If she were a better mother and loved the kid, I'd give her every dime." He flops into a nearby chair.

Liam may be rough and gruff, but I know he's telling the truth. The man says little but goes out of his way to make sure everyone in his life is taken care of.

Thinking back to my college days, I say, "I don't know tons of guys who're ready to get married in college. They're rare like diamonds."

Liam jumps to his feet. "You and me."

"You and me what?" I ask.

"We could get married."

Laughter explodes out of me. "You'll have to forward your application and cover letter to my office."

"Are you saying there is a line of men waiting to marry you? I'm not surprised." He rakes his hand through his hair again.

I hold up a one-minute finger and then use my pointer and pinkie fingers as a pretend telephone. "Hi, is this The Beast's personal assistant? Yes, I'll hold."

Deep wrinkles line his brow. "What are you doing?"

I whisper to him. "Apparently, she's very busy. Mr. Ellis is a demanding man."

He arches an eyebrow.

Going back to my finger phone, I fake listen for a moment and then say, "Excuse me, I'd like to report that your boss seems to have completely come off his hinges, you know, lost the plot." I pause for dramatic effect. "I see. Okay. I'll let him know."

He frowns.

Hanging my invisible finger phone on the phone's base, to Liam, I say, "The Beast's PA also thinks that's hilarious and rescinds all her comments about how you lack a sense of humor."

He waves his first two fingers between us. "I mean you, Jessica. Me. We get married."

I puff out an exasperated breath. "Sure. Yeah. Okay."

"You'll do it?"

"That makes no sense." My eyes are the size of saucers, waiting to hear the punchline of the greatest joke of all time.

He shakes his head slowly. "You're practically part of the furniture, almost living here rent-free."

"When you put it that way, this just gets more and more romantic."

The corner of his mouth lifts. "I don't mind."

"Thanks, Liam." I puff an exhale.

He softens. "I mean, I'm kind of into it. I, um, like you, Jessica."

"Well, that's progress, considering where we started, but I think you're supposed to *love* your wife."

His eyes search mine.

I pump the brakes. "We need to slow down. You just got really big news. Let's think this through."

He takes my hand. I should let go, but I don't.

"I'd planned to leave. Was thinking about Wyoming. A dude ranch. Denver was nice. In fact, I was just about to check out some job openings there. But then I got distracted." My cheeks warm because I was browsing the latest entries to #MrDarcysAbs.

He nods solemnly. "I don't want to hold you back."

"I only intended to be here in Cobbiton long enough to get back on my feet."

"And marriage is furthest from your mind."

"Exactly. Funny though that Pamberlie is back in my life."

"I see no humor in it."

I lift my shoulder. "Maybe we need to bake a cake."

"I don't think there's anything to celebrate."

I grip his upper arms and they're like rocks under my palms, but I give him a little shake to draw him back to my future-is-bright reality. "We're going to come up with a solution."

Liam follows me to the kitchen where I set to work, sifting the flour, mixing the eggs, and setting the cake in the oven to bake.

Just before the oven dings, I get a brain wave. "I've got it."

Liam looks at me expectantly.

"What if we set up our exes?"

"They're related."

"Oh, right."

"Even if they weren't, that's insane."

"And getting married isn't?"

I open the oven only to see the cake fall, sagging in the middle, along with my spirits.

Liam says, "We could try to kill 'em with kindness."

"I'm not killing anyone. Sheesh. Take it easy tiger. Manage your anger and keep the fights on the ice."

"I'm surprised that wasn't your first solution."

"Sadly, I think the Coogan siblings are immune to my aggressive positivity."

"No one is beyond hope and restoration," Liam says softly.

I turn to him, realizing how desperate he must feel to offer a Jess-ism. "You're right."

Everything in me wants to hug him ... and marry him? No, that can't be right. It's not for real. It's just a matter of convenience, more or less the way the nuptials with Rexlan were, for his mother to gain access to alimony, anyway.

THAT NIGHT, I tell Grandma Dolly the whole saga ... of the cake falling.

She signs, "But what's really on your mind?"

I plop heavily into the chair at the kitchen table and tell her about my confusing feelings for Liam.

I leave out the part about Rexlan reaching out to me—he contacted me on behalf of Sorsha, demanding repayment for the wedding. Otherwise, I risk facing the wrath of the lizard gods. Didn't even tell Liam that part because there'd be fists, flames, and an army of angry hockey players on the attack, resulting in blood and possibly jail time.

I also don't mention Liam suggesting we get married until the cookies come out along with some milk.

The longer we sit there, the more empty the cookie plate gets, and the more I divulge, until she knows every single secret.

Grandma Dolly signs, "Just think of all the two-for-one deals you could qualify for. Plus use of the carpool lane, tax advantages, and you'd always have someone to sit with on theme park rides."

I laugh, thankful for her pragmatic approach. "But it would be a marriage of convenience."

She arches an eyebrow. "Signs the girl who just told me about her feelings for a certain Knights hockey defenseman."

I ask about her husband and their wedding. Her eyes turn misty. "You know my real name is Dorothy, but Dell called me Dolly, like the singer, Dolly Parton. Said if that woman could sign like me, she'd be a famous millionaire."

There was definitely a resemblance when my grandmother was younger. I've seen the photos. She was hot stuff!

Her smile is soft and sad. "He loved the way I moved my hands and communicated. The way I styled my hair, my eyes, smile, the cakes." She tips her head back with laughter. "That I never missed a trick."

I sign, "I hope to find love like that someday."

Her lips ripple and she keeps her hands in her lap as if she's holding something back ... I guess not everything needs to be seen or heard to be communicated.

Later that night, while I can't sleep, in my head, I see the graceful motion of my grandmother's fingers and the signs, *What if I already did find love?*

LIAM IS busy with playoffs and we're like two ships passing by day and texting by night. Thankfully, I haven't heard from Rexlan again. But my phone beeps and I check my messages.

> Mr. Meanie: What are you doing next weekend?

> Me: Let me check your schedule. BRB.

> Mr. Meanie: I mean, what are YOU doing?

> Me: Duh. I'll be doing your bidding.

> Mr. Meanie: Haha. I'm wondering if you'd like to take a trip.

> Me: To elope in Vegas? No thanks. Rexlan ruined that for me. 😔

> Mr. Meanie: I was talking about an away game. But now that you mention it, we could get married. Go through with it.

I actually LOL.

> Me: 😄You have a sense of humor and a very nice smile. Hallelujah!

> Mr. Meanie: 💍

For some reason, this detail burrows into my mind and it isn't until the end of the week when we're preparing to head to Toronto, that I realize why.

The man has never used an emoji. Ever.

But I can't shake the feeling that he's not joking.

However, there's no reason for me to marry him other than to protect KJ from being indoctrinated into the criminal Coogan family. What are the chances that Liam and I would both have a connection to the lizard overlords?

The next day, I'm cautious for two reasons. One, Rexlan and his mother repeatedly harass me with messages about how I owe them for the cost of the wedding, plus interest, and promising retribution. The obvious solution is to hire a lawyer. Unfortunately, I can't afford a minute with one, no less the hours it would take to explain the bizarre situation.

The second reason for my concern is I can't shake the message from Liam.

He was joking, right? *Right?!*

KJ is excited for morning playtime at nursery school and I plan for us to make some more play dough. After I drop him off, pick up the ingredients, and swing by the pharmacy to get a muscle-cooling cream that Liam likes, I go to the house to meal prep for the week and am surprised to find him there, barking loudly into the phone from his home office before it goes abruptly quiet.

I resume peeling the sweet potatoes when he crashes into the kitchen, slamming cabinet doors.

"Good morning," I say brightly if only to point out how dismal he's acting.

He grunts.

Slam, pound, slam.

I say, "One of these days you're going to tear those things off the hinges."

He slams one harder.

I turn and tilt my head, lips pursed. "Did the mug cabinet door offend you that badly?"

He scowls.

"I brought you a smoothie." I point to the fridge.

He attempts to slam the door, but it closes softly.

"Why are you so cranky? Does someone already need a nap or—?"

Eyes on me, he leans against the counter and sips the drink.

His gaze trips something inside of me to the point where I may have a moment lapse of sanity because the next thing I know, I'm crossing the tile, planting myself between his legs, and lifting onto my toes.

His eyes widen.

I take the smoothie and set it on the counter.

His gaze turns heavy as if he's in turn shocked and then keenly interested in what's about to happen.

Recalling the kiss he gave me when we were in Colorado, I

press my lips to his. Only this time, instead of the gentle kiss we shared, it's frenzied, like we're up against the clock, clamoring to get in as much kissing as we can before a timer dings. His fingers burrow into my hair and mine press firmly against the solid ridges of muscle on his back. As the kiss deepens, it's a dizzying experience of constant motion, of longing meeting the moment.

When we part, we're both quiet for a long spell until I remember I have to preheat the air fryer for the sweet potatoes.

"What was that all about?" he asks, fooling with the straw in his smoothie.

"I was curious to see if some of my lethal positivity would rub off on you."

"Aggressive positivity," he corrects.

"Pardon *moi*."

"Why would you do that?"

I shrug. "To see if it would stop you from slamming cabinets. Chase you out of the kitchen. Turn your heart of stone into something else."

He grunts.

"Glad it didn't work ... much."

His eyebrows bounce in question.

I let out a long breath, returning to my senses. "Maybe I like the way you are. Who knew I'd want a beast in my life."

"If that's the case, a beast definitely needs a beauty."

"That might be the strangest and sweetest thing anyone has ever said to me, in a rough-around-the-edges way."

However, as I toss the sweet potatoes in the air fryer, I can't help but wonder if he means he also wants me.

29

LIAM

I CANNOT STOP THINKING about Jessica kissing me in the kitchen.

It took me by surprise for numerous reasons, including it made me forget what had me so ticked off that I was taking it out on my cabinet doors.

We're both relatively quiet for the next few days, yet I sense a feeling of electric anticipation anytime we're in the same room together, or when we text at night. It's become a bit of a routine.

She's given me room to breathe and if I've been living in a tunnel, there's finally light at the end.

I can type the things I want to say to her better than I can say them aloud.

Namely, that I want to kiss her again, but she can't know that. I shouldn't be entertaining it. What's wrong with me?

I tell myself it was a mistake.

A wonderful mistake that I'd like to repeat every day.

Technically I could, if Jessica and I entered into a marriage of convenience agreement. But it would be phony. Could I live with that? Could she? Would kissing be included in the contract?

Or perhaps the anticipation I'm sensing is that we're heading to Toronto to play against the Titans, which means Hendrix and I will potentially be going head-to-head.

This also means we're visiting the family.

With the kid.

And Grandma Dolly.

While Jessica puts away laundry, I step into her space and finally say what I should've the other day, "What we did in the kitchen can't happen again."

Her brown eyes scan my face.

For a moment, I'm afraid I might see anger or hurt.

Instead, she says, "Good thing we're not in the kitchen." Then Jessica presses her mouth to mine. If she misheard me, I can't say I mind.

It's instant sweetness, softness, a connection so intense I risk melting. A pulse accelerates and my mind slips onto a single track.

This time, instead of the uncertain territory of our first kiss or the adventure of the second one, the intensity of our mouths moving together falls somewhere in between.

My palm gently cups the back of her head. Her hands grip the spot between my shoulders and neck before sliding upward as mine move down her back. It's like we're finally comfortable with each other.

I'm enjoying this way too much and draw back slightly before changing my mind. She made a good point about the technicalities of my comment and our location.

When we part, I ask, "What was that?"

She says, "It was a practice kiss for our wedding day."

Inside, I jolt. I expected her to say something about glitter and smiles. "So you'll do it?"

She bites her lip. "I happen to need a husband that comes in your size ... if you hire a lawyer for me."

"Everything will be legal."

"Except getting married for reasons of convenience," she says smartly. "The problem is I'm still wearing my jilted bride badge and the Coogan family won't let me forget that I owe them money."

"How do they figure that? It was Rexlan who left you at the altar."

"Sorsha has a complicated concept of the events that transpired."

I tap the air. "Which is why you need a lawyer."

"And a big bad husband who's part beast."

"You want me to intimidate them?"

She shifts from foot to foot. "More like it'll make me feel secure knowing that I have you and the full power of your might and money in my corner."

"And you'll marry me to protect the kid from Pamberlie in exchange?"

"Gladly." Her smile isn't one of unbridled revenge. More like excitement.

"But we can't do that again," I say, gesturing between the two of us.

"Of course not. As I said, it was just a test."

"For what?" The idea of kissing her again makes me dizzy.

"To make sure all the mechanics are working properly. You know, for later like on our wedding day," she speaks nervously, haltingly as if the truth doesn't fill the space between our lips.

So we will be kissing again. Part of me isn't mad about that. Quite the opposite, actually.

The remainder of the week is a continent-trotting whirl-wind with games in Los Angeles, where I see my parents. They insist on going to Toronto too. First, we play the Ottawa

Outlaws before heading to the Blizzard Dome, the Titans arena.

Because of the travel schedule, I won't see Jessica until after the game, which I fully intend for the Knights to win even though my brother has a home advantage.

Three twenty-minute periods of ice time make for a sixty-minute game during which we eat it by giving the Titans openings for three power plays, all of which were successful. I get my seventh goal of the season, resulting in a shootout.

Valjean is all over me, doing his level best to cause trouble. I pour all my focus into the game, putting off telling my parents about the kid until afterward.

When afterward comes with a one-point loss, Hendrix is all too pleased with himself. I remind him that I provided over twenty saves.

This season isn't going as well as in the past, but we're still on track for the Finals.

I can't dash after the game because I'm the captain, but I feel scattered. The recaptain I give is lackluster with me reminding the guys to remain focused when I feel anything but. My head is fuzzy and jumps from thought to thought—the game, the kid, Jessica, the kiss, the game, my family, telling them I'm a dad, the game, repeat.

Before I leave the locker room, Grady claps me on the shoulder. "Hey, you did good. Don't beat yourself up."

I snort.

"I know you're your toughest critic, but the Titans are a top team."

"We can do better."

"And we will, but, uh, maybe you need to, uh, you know—"

I glare at him.

He glances at his feet and then meets my gaze. "Spend some time with your family. Whether they're totally dysfunctional or entirely wonderful, it can help you reset, you know?"

Grady is a formidable man and player. I've gleaned he's had some trials in his life. But I have a newfound respect for him even though I didn't really want to hear what he had to say. I don't intend to be a difficult person to talk to or to be intimidating, but the walls I've built to keep out distractions are high.

Yet Grady faced me head-on.

Meanwhile, I haven't been able to tell my parents that they have a grandson.

"Yeah," I reply to him when what I mean is *thanks.*

He gives me a nod and then leaves.

Taking a deep breath, I ready myself. It's time to be a man.

The Ellises form a human wall in the hallway, all smiles and words of encouragement. Before I can say much more than hello to my sister and her kids, she's off and running with my nieces and nephews who want to get autographs from the other players. Traitors.

Hendrix slides behind me, claps me on the shoulder, and says, "Nice try, bro. Maybe next time."

An unstoppable ball of excitement, the kid barrels toward me, signing with one hand and gripping Jessica's with the other. To anyone who doesn't know he signs, they'd just think he's a squirmy super fan who ran out of patience ... I mean, who'd think I'm a dad?!

Hendrix arches an eyebrow. "Is this safe? Authorized? Does Liam have a permit?"

I roll my eyes.

"Liam is great with kids," my mother says.

It's not entirely false. Even Ingrid would admit I'm a decent uncle. But that's in measured amounts of time on holidays and during family gatherings.

My brother freezes mid-thought. His eyes dart between me

and the child, his mouth opening and closing without sound. "Who do we have here and why didn't I know my big bro is a 'daddy'?" The last word hangs in the air, weighted with shock.

I smile stiffly and deliberately avoid Hendrix's piercing stare. I'm going to get a lot of flack from him and while I deserve every bit of it and probably more, that doesn't mean I'll like it.

He marches toward the kid, who still holds Jessica's hand. They're both wearing my jersey. Sweat beads at my temples when Hendrix's greeting goes unanswered.

Jessica signs to the kid. I recognize *Uncle*. The kid waves and signs his name with adorably chubby fingers.

The silence that follows seems like it'll never end as everything happens in slow motion. My mother's fingers press to her mouth and my father's eyebrows nearly disappear into his hairline. The tension in the room is thick enough to cut with a knife.

It's not because KJ is Deaf. It's because he's mine.

The meaning sinks in even slower now.

Hendrix says, "The little dude has moves. Okay, what's the sign for awesome?"

I swallow thickly because he understood a lot more quickly than I allowed myself to, which makes guilt claw at my insides.

Jessica shows him the sign and Hendrix repeats it flawlessly, indicating to everyone that he's awesome.

In a low voice, so only I can hear, Dad says, "Liam, I see there have been ... developments."

His emphasis on the word makes me wince.

"We met Jess and KJ briefly in the VIP suite, but there was so much going on." Dad is practically a celebrity around here so it's no surprise that he'd be occupied with people chatting along with watching the game, but this is certainly a surprise for them.

I grunt, aware that everyone's eyes are burning holes into me.

Mom, who of course hears everything, steps forward with wide yet soft eyes. "Congratulations!" She means every syllable in the word but likely hurt that I didn't tell her. That I kept this from our family.

"When exactly were you planning to tell us?" Hendrix asks, his voice tight with disbelief.

I don't know. This is one of those moments when I realize that despite my size and age, I can be immature and that brings with it shame.

Ever the one to cut the tension, Hendrix says, "Are you going to introduce us to your fiancée?"

Of course, that's what they'd assume.

Hendrix continues, "I need to know who I'm talking to before I issue a hazmat warning." There's a quirk on his lips, but his eyes remain stunned circles.

"This is Jessica," I mumble, feeling my face burn.

She steps forward gracefully, seemingly unfazed by the family tension crackling around us. "Jess and KJ—short for King Liam Junior. I'm so glad we're getting to spend some time together. I've heard so much about you."

"You have?" All adult Ellises present ask in synchronized shock, voices overlapping with varying degrees of disbelief.

Jessica smiles and shakes her head. "No. Liam doesn't say much, but I'm working on that."

They chorus laughter, of course, charmed by her despite their obvious surprise at the news, and I feel my shoulders start to relax just slightly.

My father catches my eye over Jessica's shoulder, mouthing silently, "We will talk later."

I nod, knowing I have a lot of explaining to do.

But the thing about my family, despite their history on the

ice, is that they're the warmest people on the planet and maybe I knew that even if I avoided coming forth with the truth, they'd accept KJ no matter what.

And maybe their meeting him is the final piece to the puzzle that makes this real.

After an uneventful night in a hotel—where Jessica and I stay in separate rooms—the next day, they offer for us to ride with them to Brookking Sound, but I rent an SUV and we load in for the three-hour trip north.

Having been doing my own thing for a while, I forgot how all-pervasive my family can be. It's not like being smothered with a damp blanket, but navigating this situation—not the roads, I know them well—feels like a trick shot.

When we pull out of the parking lot behind my parents, I say, "Sorry about that with everyone."

"No need to apologize. They were wonderful," Jessica says.

"My wild family?"

"No, you're the wild one, Liam. They're rather tame."

"Stick around, it'll get worse."

"We'll see about that."

Grandma Dolly and KJ ride in the back while I give Jessica a who's who of the Ellis family while she signs to her grandmother.

"My dad was born in Germany and played hockey there before being drafted to Canada in the nineteen nineties. He'll be all too pleased to tell you about the beauty he met shortly after."

"Your mom?"

"Belinda Bell. They moved to Brookking Sound when Dad retired. When the three of us grew up, they then relocated to sunny San Diego—my sister Ingrid followed."

"They seem really sweet together. Cara and Pierre gave me

an abbreviated version of your bio. Though she didn't mention that you're a doting uncle."

"Mom and Dad are all too pleased because Ingrid has three kids and they love being grandparents." I glance over my shoulder at my son. "They're going to spoil him."

Jessica signs and says, "You say that like it's a bad thing. It's literally a grandparent's job."

In the rearview mirror, I see Grandma Dolly agree.

Jessica says, "Tell me about your brother."

"You mean the charmer, the flirt? I'd warn you not to put up with him, but he got a Christmas surprise of his own."

"I take it he found someone special?"

"Oh no. It was an absolute disaster. I thought they were going to bury each other in the snow. But things wrapped up nicely with a bow."

Her laughter fills the truck. "Sounds like a Happy Christmas Ever After."

"Something like that," I grunt, thinking about my boy waiting for me in the Old Mill building when I got back from the festivities with my family.

"You guys played really well. I knew Hendrix was your brother because you both have the same posture when at attention and the same smile ... when you release yours from its bonds."

And there I thought we were nothing alike.

I say, "We've been in skates together since we could walk."

"Has there ever been rivalry?"

"Do you with your siblings?"

She shrugs. "I don't know if I have any."

Her words come with a heavy silence. There is so much I don't know about the woman my parents think is the child's mother, who I'm supposed to be marrying.

Clearing my throat, I say, "He's the right forward. Our positions have different duties, but we challenge each other out there."

"You're both amazing ... and very physical."

I snort. We've been known to accidentally throw elbows on occasion, especially at each other because we know that after the game, we'll snap back into being family. I guess. Unlike other players who manipulate, take advantage, play victim ... Valjean. "If you have a chance, call him Heinrich. He hates it."

"In that case, I should ask, is your real name Liam?"

"You know the answer to that question."

Turns out, she knows a lot about me—what I eat, when I go to sleep, though recently later than usual since we often text at night. How I like my laundry folded—the woman must have nerves of steel to wash my hockey gear. She somehow hides the protein powder the team nutritionist insists I take in a berry smoothie so delicious, that I can't taste it. And she isn't stingy with her smiles even when I don't deserve them.

"I also know that you and your brother live and breathe hockey."

"That's about where our similarities end."

"You're both tall."

"I'm half an inch taller."

"Same nose."

I grunt. "He's a goofball."

"Ah. You're definitely not that."

"Are you saying I don't know how to have fun?"

"Decline to comment."

Maybe I'll have to change that, but we're nearly to Brookking Sound. Home of the Ellis family hockey legacy.

"Did your sister play hockey? Sisters intimidate me," Jessica admits.

"In that case, Ingrid will not disappoint. She's type A. But likable. No nonsense, efficient, brilliant."

"And gorgeous."

"Pregnant too. She has three kids. This will make four."

"This means KJ has cousins around his age."

"Yeah," I answer softly because how will he be able to communicate with them? Then again, he's been doing fine at nursery school according to Jessica.

"Is your sister a stay-at-home mom or—?"

"Somewhere, someone has a bet running about whether she'll leave her job in marketing when the new addition comes along."

"Given your moodiness, I thought you came from a broken family. They're perfect. So why the chip on your shoulder?"

Taken aback, I pause before formulating a response. "It's not a chip. More like the weight of the past."

"What makes you say that?"

I'm afraid she's going to find out soon enough. Brookking Sound isn't the kind of place to keep secrets. "When you said *broken family*, your voice cracked like you're speaking from experience."

"Starting during my third week in kindergarten, I was placed with multiple foster families. Some better than others."

Jessica doesn't say another word. I'm afraid to ask because of what it'll do to her smile.

30

JESS

THIS PART of Canada is in a different time zone, but I can't stop thinking that it's strange o'clock.

In Cobbiton and during the travel I've done with Liam, fans notice him and ask for autographs and selfies. But they don't give me a second glance.

Here, he's a hometown hero and while I'd happily remain invisible, I feel eyes on me, people wondering, and wearing curious looks.

More than that, I'm still processing.

The Ellis family thinks I'm KJ's mom and he didn't correct them.

Grandma Dolly, as expert of a lip reader as she is, didn't seem to notice the mistake. Or, if she did, she didn't comment.

Plus, she's in hockey heaven, having been to more live games these last few months than in all the years she's been a Knights fan.

As we leave the city behind and head north toward Sir William Bay on Lake Huron and then on to Brookking Sound, the landscape changes from big city to countryside with water to one side and rolling green hills to the other.

The islands remind me of turtles and the many boats in the port area represent a different kind of life than in Cornfield, USA, aka Cobbiton.

"This could be a postcard," I say, taking it in.

"It is," Liam says.

When we reach Brookking Sound with its town square and picturesque main street lined with quaint shops and restaurants, I spot Tucker's Coffee across the street from Daisy's Bakery. Phew, my caffeine needs will be met.

Though, I can't shake the feeling I've been here before. "This looks familiar."

Liam grunts as if charming towns like this are a dime a dozen. It's similar to Cobbiton, but with the proximity of the water and the northern location, the air and light are different, silver rather than gold. Liquid rather than amber waves of grain.

"Oh, and it boasts the Rainer Ellis Hall of Fame. We'll have to take a field trip there," Liam says as we pass through a neighborhood.

He turns onto a sunny street bordered by shade trees and onto a sprawling property with a three-story cedar shingle and stone house with loads of windows and multiple chimneys. The wraparound porch hosts rocking chairs, welcoming everyone from the Ellis family to their guests to stop and chat for a while. It's delightful. The various cars we caravanned with are already parked in the driveway.

"This is where you grew up?" I ask.

A nod in reply is all I get from Liam.

Sometimes I just want to shake him ... like a jar of glitter.

"It's the kind of place I would've wanted to live in when I was a kid," I breathe, recalling the numerous apartments and houses I shuffled between. I bet there's a big tree in the back-yard to climb. Maybe a play set. A fort or tree house. Lots of room to wander and dream.

We have a welcome committee waiting for us, including an older woman who looks like she'd join Grandma Dolly for cards and another woman who resembles Liam's mom. They dote on him like he's royalty while Mrs. Ellis pulls me in for a hug. It's my third one. Yes, I'm counting. It's not every day you meet a mother who is so warm and welcoming, rather than "smothering." Yes, I'm thinking about Sorsha.

Belinda ushers me inside. "We're so glad you're here. Let's get you settled in. It looks like my mother and sister have absconded with Liam, Dolly, and KJ. You'll be staying with us. We have a full house with Ingrid and company, plus when she's here, Hendrix and Colette will often spend the night because we're not the only ones who spoil the nieces and nephews."

"Thank you for hosting." My voice sounds small which is how I feel. Not because of anything the Ellises have said or done, but because of who I am and where I came from.

"But of course." Mrs. Ellis goes on to tell me the faucet in the bathroom can be a little fussy because the house is old. No, it's perfect and I am not. I don't feel worthy of this big whirl-wind of a family. They're wonderful. The kinds of people portrayed in movies, but this is real life.

Liam's parents live in San Diego now, but I imagine the interior of the house has remained the same for the last thirty years. It's relatively traditional with timeless décor—a leather couch topped with throw blankets and pillows, several inviting sitting areas, and bookshelves. Custom window treat-ments frame the mutton-bar glass and family photos top the mantle. It smells like lavender, faintly of toast, and just like home.

I love it.

... and I'm staying in Liam's room while he bunks in the TV room.

Crossed hockey sticks cover the blue wallpaper and a photo of his high school team hangs over his bureau. It takes me a moment to find him, but when I do, high school me has an instant crush on high school Liam.

Tucked into the mirror over his dresser are multiple photos of him at games, his graduation tassel, and other memorabilia.

The bedding is deep gray with blue stripes. It might seem weird, but I press the pillow to my face to see if he's always smelled the same—soapy clean and masculine.

Pucks fill a basket on the floor and a balled-up shirt sits on a wooden chair like he left it there during his last visit.

I spin in a circle, wondering how this place and his sweet family produced such a broody man.

After freshening up, I find Liam and his dad downstairs, discussing the game. The mood is slightly more subdued than when Hendrix is in the mix with his more boisterous temperament. Mr. Ellis is somewhere in between, easy to smile but also has a serious side, especially when it comes to the family sport.

Grannie Bell, Aunt Goldie, Grandma Dolly, and a combination of children are on the back porch blowing bubbles on the unseasonably pleasant day. It's a Norman Rockwell painting with the sun a gilded splatter of peachy melon fading into lavender on the horizon backed by a soundtrack of laughter.

My heart could explode.

When I get outside, KJ hugs my legs and asks me to blow bubbles with him. I've never seen him so happy, not even at nursery school. It's as if he inherently knows this is his family.

It probably helps that everyone fusses over him like he's the hockey star and not his dad. Liam seems to prefer it that way.

The woman who could be Mrs. Ellis's twin brings out

refreshments and Grannie Bell asks, "Did you bring the fudge?"

"Do you think these kids need sugar right now?"

They're racing around the yard with the bubbles, seeing if they can make one big enough to jump through. It's a joyous sight.

I glance over my shoulder. Liam is still inside. I wonder if he was the kind of kid to jump into the mix or if he hung back.

I always did until I met Grandma Dolly and realized that I had to create my own fun.

She samples some of Grannie Bell's fudge and passes me the container while pointing out the different flavors. German chocolate, peppermint, butterscotch, and peanut butter.

I opt for a mocha and my eyes all but roll back in my head. "It's so good. You could open a shop in town and sell it."

"Too much competition. Fudge is popular around here."

I speak and sign, "That makes me love Brookking Sound even more. I was telling Liam this place looks familiar."

Grandma Dolly signs and I translate, "Like it was in a movie."

Not skipping a beat, Grannie Bell answers with her hands and voice, "It was the set of *Cookie Cutter Christmas* most recently—coming next holiday season to the big screen nearest you—and several other sweet holiday romance movies before that." She names a few titles.

Grandma Dolly and I clap our hands together because we both watched one of those sweet films on Christmas Eve together while she was in Cobbiton and I was in Los Angeles. We did a video chat, each made snacks and cocoa, and gushed in all the right places.

"Where are my manners? Here I am telling you all about the fudge and I didn't properly introduce myself or my other daughter. I'm Belinda and Marigold's mom. You can call me

Grannie Bell if you have room for another." She smiles warmly at Grandma Dolly.

The younger woman and Belinda's lookalike also signs while she says, "Around these parts, I go by Goldie, but Liam isn't too big to still have to call me *Aunt* Goldie." She pats his arm as he steps in front of the sunset.

To his grandmother, he says, "I didn't know you could sign."

"That's like suggesting I don't know how to read. Of course, I know how to sign," she says, all while signing.

"You should've taught me." He helps himself to a piece of peppermint fudge.

"Your hands were too busy with that hockey stick. Now, where was I?" She regales us with a tale about learning ASL when working as a nurse while stationed on a Royal Canadian Navy ship.

"I didn't know that either," Liam mumbles while dropping down onto the wicker sofa next to me. The sudden warmth distracts me from Grannie Bell's story.

"The young petty officers would always come to me with their maladies." She rolls her eyes. "Headaches, itches, and phantom pains that would miraculously resolve after visiting me in the infirmary. But there were long hours with not much going on. I read the *Art of War* three times, can do sutures blindfolded, and learned how to sign." Grannie Bell also relays that she taught her daughters sign language basics when they were younger and she adds, "Communication is key whether on a flotilla in the middle of the ocean or at home."

Too bad she didn't pass that lesson along to Liam, King of Few Words.

Aunt Goldie playfully nudges her mother's arm. "She didn't mention that she gave those petty officers fudge."

Grannie Bell blushes. "I was their favorite."

"And one of the few females on the ship."

"This was before I met your grandfather."

Just then, Hendrix appears and dips into the now-empty fudge container. "Who ate all the fudge?"

The kids boisterously provide the answer.

Quickly moving on, he holds up his hand for his brother to slap. Do they have a secret handshake? Hendrix bellows, "The Beast. You dominated the game, but too bad you didn't win."

Liam, elbows resting on his knees, grunts.

Hendrix squeezes his shoulder. "How about a little rematch, Ellis family style?" Then to the group at large, he asks, "Who's up for pickleball hockey?"

Collette, a school teacher, says, "The kids could stand to burn off some energy before dinner."

"We'll be the cheerleaders," Grandma Dolly and Grannie Bell sign and speak, respectively.

"And kid corrallers," Aunt Goldie adds.

Ingrid appears and says, "Jess and I are going to stay here and have a sisterly chat."

We are? My stomach tumbles. I sign to KJ, reminding him to use his manners and stay with the grownups.

Ingrid says, "The kids will be fine. There is one grandma and auntie for each."

Liam gets to his feet and Ingrid instantly takes his place.

A wave of nerves shoots through me. Am I going to be given the third degree? Questioned under a bare lightbulb in a cement cell? It's silly, but sisters, whether big or small scare me. Ingrid is just over six months into her pregnancy, her belly is wonderfully round and she's significantly taller than me. It's like Brookking Sound is the land of giants. There must be something in the water up here.

I edge over, giving her some room.

To her brother, Ingrid says, "While you two battle it out on the pickleball court, Jess and I are going to get to know each other."

As if somehow picking up on my apprehension, Liam doesn't move a muscle except the one twitching in his jaw.

Ingrid rolls her eyes. "Don't worry. I'm not going to lead her out onto the dock and push her into the water. It's still freezing." She turns to me. "But do you know how to swim?"

A growl builds inside Liam.

"I'm joking and super pregnant. I'd be lucky if I floated. We're just going to get to know each other."

I cannot fathom what I might say to Liam's sister ... and am afraid of what she might say to me, namely that she sees right through the fabrication his parents so readily bought we didn't officially agree to sell.

31

JESS

INGRID and her husband are why Instagram was invented, highlighting the easy, breezy carefree put together families that give the rest of us mortals agita because we need to wash our hair, put on pants without holes, and use our gym memberships. Her husband is masculine and successful. I gathered that he works in tech. They're a powerhouse, their children are blessings, and twinkling stars float around them as they move effortlessly through life.

At least, that's what it seems like.

While seated with Ingrid and with the rest of the family heading off to play pickleball hockey—whatever that is—Liam's gaze meets mine in a rare moment. It's as if he's silently asking if I'll be okay. I have my security whistle in my purse and am not afraid to use it. I give a subtle nod and he disappears into the dusky evening.

Ingrid turns to me, her ample belly like a beach ball between us. Then, like we're two high school best friends, her voice lowers, and she says, "We are shocked that Liam is with someone. Do you realize that you're the chosen one? He was untouchable."

My eyes must be as big as the rising moon.

"Think Edward and Bella from Twilight. Tell me you know what I'm talking about."

"I've read all the books and watched the movies at least twice each." Okay, dozens of times.

"Phew. You'll fit right in."

"Are you saying Liam is like a vampire?" I ask.

"Depends on what kind of man glitter we're talking about."

Her icebreaker instantly puts me at ease and I laugh. "I'd peg him for a wolf shifter."

She gives her head a shake. "He wasn't always so quiet. Serious, yes, but not so—"

"Gruff, grumpy, grouchy?"

"You know him so well. But how do you stand it?" She taps my knee. "You have a super sunny personality. It confirms the opposites attract theory."

I have about a million questions and am not sure where to start or where the line is between being nosy and coming off like someone who might marry Liam—for convenience. True to form, we didn't get into the details because the guy isn't the most communicative, which apparently is a widely known fact.

Playing it safe, I say, "Which is it? The Beast, Mr. Darcy, Edward Cullen? Jacob?"

"My brother is not known as Mr. Personality, but Mr. Darcy? That's a new one to me," Ingrid says.

I'm thankful for the dim light on the porch because my cheeks turn pink as I tell her about #MrDarcysAbs.

She groans in a decidedly grossed-out way as only a sister could. "How about all the above?"

"Not that I look, much."

"You, of all people, have viewing rights." She exhales and

then sinks back slightly. "Those titles are all lost on him. After everything that happened, he doesn't let himself see anything other than hockey."

"It's his life."

Ingrid frowns. "No, you and KJ are." Her head jerks toward me. "Wait. He told you, right?"

I don't have a chance to answer when Mrs. Ellis pops her head out the door. "We're meeting everyone in town for pizza in about fifteen minutes. Tomorrow, we'll have a big meal here."

It's safe to say there is a long list of things Liam has never told me.

When we were playing text truth or dare, he said he has secrets. Then again, there's a lot he doesn't know about me. But in a way, we're even. Whereas, I know everything there is about his habits from the kind of toothpaste he uses, to his caloric requirements, to how he often loses one sock from the pair, he's in the dark about all that when it comes to me. And his personal life is one big mystery. But if we're going to pull off getting married, he ought to have the basics.

To her mom, Ingrid says, "I promised the kids breakfast at Grannie Bell's in the morning."

"The griddle on Peppertree Lane will be ready and waiting first thing." The screen door closes behind Mrs. Ellis.

Ingrid exhales a sigh of relief. "Where was I?"

I blurt, "The thing that Liam—"

She puffs her cheeks. "I shouldn't be the one to tell you, but he won't. Plus, as a sister, I know no boundaries."

I should laugh, but I sense whatever she's going to say isn't going to be good.

"In high school, he and a couple of friends were at a party. I guess there was some drinking going on. Not Liam. He was too hopeful for hockey back then to fool around with that stuff.

Anyway, his friend, Franklin George, who he went there with, assured him he hadn't been drinking and was good to drive. Marci Valjean—Frank's girlfriend—and another girl named Allison Mitchum got in the back of the car because it was getting late and they had curfews."

Seeing where this is going, my pulse comes short.

"The roads here in the winter are no joke and temps can drop rapidly. If there is any water on the surface, it can freeze fast, leading to black ice. They hit a patch. Franklin was severely injured, forfeiting his future in skates. Allison had her seatbelt on and was relatively okay. Marci didn't make it."

"And Liam has never forgiven himself," I finish.

Ingrid nods. "Understandably, he was different after that but then never snapped back. The official report and investigation confirmed that Franklin was telling the truth. He hadn't been drinking. He just lost control of the vehicle."

"What about Liam? Was he injured?"

"Just a few stitches. He was never like Hendrix, but his personality changed. He retreated, hardly talked to us."

I see so clearly that this is where his need to tightly control everything comes from. It breaks my heart to think he blames himself.

Later that night, it's no surprise that I can't sleep. For one, I'm in Liam's childhood bedroom and it's impossible not to be nosy. I study the framed photo of him and his high school hockey team, wondering which one is Franklin. I imagine Marci and Allison, cheering them on at games. It's all so tragic.

I also can't stop thinking about how I imagined that the man of few words came from one of those families that are posh and snooty, who live in the same house but don't know each other and never eat at the same table.

But I have a strong suspicion Belinda made casseroles and they all gathered around the big farmhouse-style table, said grace, and then talked for hours, debating hockey game outcomes, fishing lures, and when chickens molt—Aunt Goldie is thinking of getting a flock.

That's what transpired earlier at the pizza place while the kids colored on their placemats, played with dough, and then played Uno with a deck of cards Colette had in her purse when our conversation lengthened. All the while Grandma Dolly and Grannie Bell signed a blue streak.

Liam wasn't raised by wolves or possums but by a lovely family. It's the kind of family I always wanted.

When the glowing digital clock clicks to one a.m., I toss off the sheet and gaze out the window at the shining water beyond the sprawling backyard.

How would my life have been different if I had grown up in a place like this? Made memories with cousins instead of trying to remain unseen. It wasn't that I was shy, more like scared if I let anyone know me, they'd reject me. Would I have come out of my shell sooner?

I know better. It somehow would've all fallen apart. The truth is, everyone in my life leaves. Maybe I am a witch bride as Liam said. Or at least, I unintentionally curse things. Ruin them. If he and I really were together, he wouldn't have the bandwidth for hockey and I'd tank his career.

Nope. It's better for me to be invisible.

The old house creaks and groans, but it doesn't feel haunted. Not like the place I lived in for six months while in sixth grade. That place was spooky.

At my back, I feel a gust of warmth, and then a pair of big, rough hands drop onto my shoulders. I'm about to scream bloody murder when a soapy masculine scent reaches my nose and Liam's breath tickles the loose hairs on my neck.

He whispers, "It's just me."

Without thinking, I press my hand onto the top of his. It's

to steady myself so I don't pitch over with fright. Also, for a guy who spends so much time on a frozen rink, he's surprisingly warm.

He says, "I figured you'd be awake."

"I figured you'd want your bed. I'll take the couch in the TV room."

"I've slept on it many times, having fallen asleep watching old games."

He twines my fingers through his and then sits down on the bed. Wearing just a T-shirt and shorts, the moonlight catches the Brookking Sound Hockey logo.

"You were hot stuff in high school," I say before realizing that was a mistake, given what his sister told me.

He snorts. "That was a long time ago."

Yet, he's carried the wounds with him all these years. I wonder if it's hard for him to be here.

"Ingrid told me." My voice is so low, I'm afraid he didn't hear.

Liam tugs me down to sit on his lap and wraps his arms around me. Ordinarily, at his touch, I get all swizzly inside, and I do, but not as much as normal. And not because I'm any less attracted to #MrDarcysAbs. But right now, it feels like he needs a hug and this is the closest he can come to admitting that.

I lace my arms around his neck.

Our gazes meet for a long moment. Sadness and pain fill his eyes.

"Do you want to talk about it?" I fully expect him to say no, but let the invitation hang.

Instead, he nuzzles into my neck. The brush of his eyelashes on my skin tells me he closed his eyes.

"You always smell so good," he whispers.

"Compared to being around a bunch of sweaty athletes, I should hope so."

"No, it's you. I used to think this house smelled like home ..." He doesn't finish the sentence and I can't help but wonder if he means I smell like home.

"Your family has a special place here." I hesitate, then add, "I think I'm falling for them."

He tips us back on the bed and then adjusts so he's spooning me.

"I think it's love," I add, hoping to get a laugh when I realize that might also sound like I mean that I've fallen for him. That I'm in love with him.

He doesn't reply.

Then I jolt, rolling over so I'm facing him. "Will they be upset that we're in here together? Not that anything funny is going on." He didn't even acknowledge that I said I'd fallen in love with his family. "It would not fly with Grandma Dolly."

He looks at me blankly. Thoughtfully? I can't tell unless he's one of those people who sleep with their eyes open. I had a foster brother once who did and it freaked me out until I realized I could tell if he was just staring or sleeping by the sound of his breath.

Liam's is steady, but not the deep kind that comes before a snore.

Unlike him, I use my words, I say, "They think I'm KJ's mom."

"You may as well be."

"Explain."

He fiddles with a piece of my hair.

Swizzles. Incoming. My cheeks get warm and my entire body goes limp. Yeah. I could definitely be falling for him. Good thing I'm lying down. But I have to remind myself that this isn't real. Nor are my feelings for him. Probably. Maybe a little. Like cake crumb-sized.

"Are you going to correct them or are we going to *lie* to your family?" I hiss.

He yawns and lifts then lowers his massive shoulder, blocking my view of the clock.

"I cannot live with lying to these people. They're too good. Too nice. I am not a liar, Liam Ellis."

"But what if it were the truth?" He rolls onto his back and takes my hand again.

The swizzles double.

I huff and am about to launch into all the reasons that's not the case when I realize he promptly fell asleep. I yawn, feeling drowsy myself, then whisper, "They're too good for me."

32

JESS

IN THE MORNING, I wake up alone. Liam must've snuck back down to the TV room, yet his comments remain with me in his bedroom and transform into questions I cannot answer.

I may as well be KJ's mom?

What if it were the truth?

Yeah, there must be something in the air or water here or both, making him delusional—me too for entertaining, even for a minute, that these people would accept me.

I scoot to the bathroom to get ready. From downstairs comes a lot of activity along with the aroma of coffee. Ingrid's voice filters to me about the promise of blueberry pancakes and seeing KJ again.

He and Grandma Dolly stayed with Grannie Bell and Aunt Goldie on Peppertree Lane, which is where we're going for breakfast.

Even though I just woke up and that sounds wonderful, it's like I already need a moment to catch my breath.

While I brush my teeth, someone knocks on the door. This place is huge, and there are more bathrooms, but maybe it's a kid with an emergency. In the homes where I stayed as a child, it was inevitable that someone would interrupt to use the toilet.

I slide the door open a few inches, looking down at a pair of bare feet. Big ones. Size fifteens. Toothbrush in my mouth, I can only imagine my current look—fit for neither man nor beast.

However, Liam's expression is the gravest I've ever seen it, sending a shockwave of anxiety through me.

"Is KJ okay?"

He nods. "Got a full report this morning. Happy as a clam." His tone is low, dry.

"Are you all right?" I ask, considering what I learned from Ingrid and how returning to certain places can dredge up emotions.

"We have a problem."

I knew better than to let myself fall asleep beside Liam. "But you snuck out of the room before anyone woke up."

He shakes his head. "Not that."

I wave my free hand, nervous with anticipation. "Please explain."

"They're planning the wedding while we're still here in Canada."

"Who? What?" I ask, while white foam from the toothpaste drools from the corner of my mouth.

From the foot of the stairs, Mrs. Ellis calls, "Liam, Jess, honey, we're heading over to Peppertree Lane. You'd better hurry up if you want pancakes."

"I do. I really do." Realizing how that sounds in the context of the bomb Liam just dropped I say, "I mean, breakfast."

Lifting his voice, Liam replies to his mom, "We'll be right behind you."

He shuffles me into the bathroom and leans against the counter while I rinse my mouth and face. His gaze never leaves me. In this small space, it's a small space and hard to ignore him, sending a blaze across my cheeks.

"How do you know this?"

"The grandmothers got it in their heads that we're going to get married here, now."

"Even Grandma Dolly?" In the mirror, I pale. She knows it's all a sham, so why would she encourage it?

"She's already having the kid practice how to carry the pillow with the rings on it using a pair of chocolate-covered pretzels."

I cover my laughter with my hand and because I'm in shock. Then my palm slides up to my forehead and I pace the three steps in part of the bathroom not taken up by Liam.

He lassoes me in his arms.

Whoa. Swizzles.

His eyes pin me in place.

I swallow.

He says, "Naturally, my mother was concerned about the short notice. Aunt Goldie was worried your family wouldn't be able to make it in time."

"I don't have any other family."

"That's what Grandma Dolly told them. What you said last night about mine ..." He lets out a long breath. "I want them to be yours."

"Until we tell them we're splitting up." Because that has to happen eventually with a fake marriage. My thoughts race with what it will do to KJ. Who will he live with? Liam may be a brute, but his family will see that he married a monster to agree to something so wrong and lie.

Liam says, "Listen, I know that this is a lot. But I'm willing to sign on until KJ is grown."

"That's like fifteen years." And sounds like a business deal. Which this is.

Him: custody.

Me: legal assistance.

"I'm loyal, Jessica. It's hockey and family. That's it. There won't be anything else in my life."

"You mean *anyone* else? You don't know that. You could meet someone tomorrow and fall in love."

"I won't." His tone is firm, final.

"You can't be sure."

"I can."

Silence stretches between us.

Liam adds, "If between now and the kid's eighteenth birthday, you find someone else, you can leave me. I won't hold it against you."

"But your son might." My shoulders drop. I won't find someone else either. Somehow I know that with absolute certainty. There's no sense in me even looking for love. I'm a romance and relationship wrecker. I walked away from one almost-marriage because my lot in life is loneliness, but maybe not alone ...

I spin in a small circle as if winding myself up like an old mechanical toy. I may as well try a fake one and see how I fare.

Liam asks, "Can we do this?"

I hold up a finger. "They need to know that I'm not KJ's biological mother."

"Ingrid figured it out. They were discussing it last night. My parents are so embarrassed. My mom wants to apologize to you."

"No, I'm the one who is humiliated. I let them think—"

His expression hardens. "You are the mother the kid needs. End of story. You're his mom."

My chin wobbles because I love that little boy as much as I love Grandma Dolly. Maybe more.

"So you'll fix the issue with the Coogans?" I ask, bringing us back to the nuts and bolts of the matter.

"Money is powerful and so are legal documents, so yes. It will all go away."

"And we'll go on with our lives. But I was going to move to Colorado." I gasp.

"I can't leave Cobbiton."

"I know. I understand. I just thought—" I force away the building sadness of my failures, stacking one on top of the next. It's easier for me to pretend they don't exist when I can report back from a faraway place.

But that means I've been lying to myself ... and everyone else. I let out a long exhale because I don't want to hurt anyone or lose their trust, but a marriage of convenience would be the biggest lie of all.

I think of Cara and how badly I want her to be at the wedding if we're really going through with it. I promise myself I'll tell her the truth. Grandma Dolly must not have understood when I told her about the marriage of convenience.

"Does anyone know?" I ask.

"About our arrangement?" He shakes his head.

"Can I have one lifeline? One person to tell?"

Liam's throat bobs on a swallow. "I don't think it's a good idea."

"I owe it to my best friend."

Liam's eyes bulge. "Cara? My coach's daughter?"

"She's good at keeping secrets." Probably. Maybe. I have no idea because I've never needed to ask her to keep one.

"It's a terrible idea." But he doesn't say no.

"What about us being best friends?" I ask with a happy little bounce.

He grunts.

"Can we have a secret handshake?"

The corner of his lip twitches. "Can I touch your Bundt?"

I tip my head back in laughter.

Liam moves close, smoothing my hair behind my shoulder. My eyes lift to his. His gaze lands on my lips. He leans in until we're a breath apart and asks, "Can I do this?

"For practice?"

Instead of answering, he presses his lips to mine. For practice, I'm sure.

We end up practicing a lot—missing out on pancakes, sneaking away to closets, taking long walks in the woods. We kiss so much that I lose track of time until three days go by and I'm in Mrs. Ellis's master bedroom with sweeping views of the water and a well-appointed dressing room, getting ready to say *I do.*

The driveway is full. The dress is on. The smiles are wide.

Is this really happening?

Belinda, Aunt Goldie, Grannie Bell, Grandma Dolly, Ingrid, and a slew of hockey friends somehow orchestrated what's shaping up to be a beautiful day.

From what I've seen, the scenery combined with the décor is nothing short of enchanting. Towering pines, wide oaks strung with fairy lights, and paper birch border what Belinda now calls the wedding barn, previously known as the ice hockey hang-out where we'll have the reception. Artfully arranged wheelbarrows, tin planters, and hanging baskets of wildflowers add splashes of color. At the water's edge is a small platform under an arch composed of evergreen swag, flowers, and ribbon which is where we'll say our vows.

Rows of chairs backed with sprays of cedar, white roses, anemones, and peachy ranunculus and dahlias, wrapped with bows, matching my bouquet, fill in as a live string band plays and birds sing.

High over the lake, sunshine bathes the scene in soft light

and everything glows. I have an upside down and inside out déjà vu feeling ... I have been in this situation before, dressed in a wedding gown, about to get married. But not like this.

With friends, family, and neighbors bustling around, coming and going, everyone comments on how lovely and happy I look. It could be that I'm not under the threat of a lizard cult curse. But I should be a ball of nerves, because the more I think about how we're fooling everyone, the deeper the guilt goes.

It's phony and I need to tell someone that's not Cara. She was so excited to be my maid of honor, I don't want to burst her bubble.

Biting my lip, I excuse myself to the laundry room where I stashed my bag. I dial a number I jotted down in my bullet journal when I stopped at a gas station somewhere between California and Nebraska.

An enthusiastic recorded radio voice says, "Hi, you've reached KLUT, Central Utah's number-one station for daytime hits and nighttime chats. If you know the extension you'd like to reach, please dial it now. If not, please listen carefully as our options on the dial do change, but be sure not to turn yours and tune in to KLUT day and night."

I listen for DJ Melody in the directory and then press the numbers. I hear another recording this time of her inviting callers to leave love notes or call back during her Love Lines After Dark hour. Even with the time difference, I can't delay what's about to happen. But I need someone to know.

Drawing a deep breath, I decide to leave an anonymous message, "Hi, Melody. I heard your show right after I was left at the altar. I'm about to get married again. Not to the same guy. But not exactly for love. More like, well, *like*. I like him. A lot. Okay, maybe more than like. But we have a business arrangement. Kind of. I mean, I think. We've kissed. He's my boss.

Saying this out loud, so scattered and vague, makes it sound crazy and maybe it is. I guess I just needed someone to know. I'm sure you've heard some wild stories, but thanks for listening." I click my phone off, conflicted.

I don't feel relieved nor did I receive a clear sign that I should call off the wedding.

I gaze out the window. Liam, in a tux, stands below with his brother and dad. I'm in the land of giants—tall people, big personalities. Lots of love in this family.

Maybe I don't belong. But perhaps I could.

Catching me alone by the window as I survey the scene unfolding below, Cara asks, "Are you okay?"

Letting out a breath, I answer, "I was his assistant, then nanny, and now I'll be his wife. If he shows up."

"Uh, Jess. We're looking at him. Waiting. For you." She takes my hands and squeezes, knowing what happened with Rexlan and likely that I'm feeling as delicate as the lace on my gown.

"But what if he decides he prefers his assistant?" I realize how ridiculous that sounds because I am his assistant.

She laughs as if I'm joking. More like tangled up with the lie we're telling and the quiet little truth inside along with my ex's family's threats, which is part of the reason Liam and I are going through with this whole thing.

"What if Rexlan crashes the wedding?"

Cara squawks a laugh. "My father, half the Knights team, and countless hockey legends are out there ready on defense. Plus, Liam wouldn't let him. Have you seen the way he looks at you?"

Like he can't figure out how this happened? How he ended up with someone like me? How he wants to run for his life?

Grandma Dolly interrupts and signs that KJ wants to see me really quickly.

I wander into the hall and wearing a wild grin, he rushes toward me and then stops short. Because of the gown, he can't hug my legs. At risk of popping a seem, I crouch down because I sure could use a hug right now.

But before I'm able to wrap my arms around him, he signs, "You look so pretty, Mommy."

My heart leaps and the truth within rises up with sequins and a smile.

I wish this were real. Is it?

The bridal party gathers at the foot of the stairs, the ladies do last-minute touchups, and holding hands, Grannie Bell leads a prayer. My breathing comes quick and the words are little more than a hum in my ears.

I'm sipping air through a straw.

Smiling but not hearing anything being said.

God, if you're there, lead my feet where you want them to go. Please lead me to love.

When we get outside, Liam is at the altar, waiting for me. Dressed in a dark gray tux and freshly shaved, he looks more handsome than ever. Who knew I had a thing for giant athletes ... with abs.

Some people might think working out that much makes him vain and others might think I'm shallow for admiring them. While both might have some truth, what I realize now is that when Liam does something, he goes all in. He doesn't say he's going to work out and then drop off after a few sessions. When he commits, there's no turning back.

Even though I am surrounded by the swarm of my bridal party, including Ingrid and Colette, his gaze finds mine in the crowd. The swizzles inside get all swizzly.

My pulse thunders and I blink because I don't think I can go through with this.

Then the corner of his lips lifts ever so slightly. He

discreetly mouths and signs the word *wow*. Or he could've been shooing away a fly and said *ow*, but it's enough to keep me from running—not that I could get far in these high heels.

It's probably silly to think this, but perhaps like his dedication to staying fit for hockey, we can provide KJ with a loving home ... which is much more than I ever had and I'm ready to give it my all.

33

LIAM

I'VE BEEN to bigger weddings, but not better ones. So far, my grandmother, aunt, mom, sister, and Dolly have outdone themselves. It's phenomenal what they accomplished in only a few days.

Nothing short of a miracle, which tells me we're doing the right thing even though I repeatedly wonder if that's true.

Keep focused, Ellis.

Turns out Jessica is very distracting.

I don't necessarily have an eye for detail. In fact, my sister commented that the chandeliers and disco balls hanging from the ceiling in the barn are going to be lost on me. I was in there for an hour, helping to set up and didn't notice them. Everyone wants Jessica and me to have fun. After all, it's our wedding day. Right now, all I see is her eyes.

My fiancée, even though I didn't officially ask her to marry me, has let everyone assume I did and the ring is at the jeweler. She's been the life of the party. The star of the show. She and KJ fit in with my family better than I do. They loved them both instantly.

And I love holding her in my arms. My life is ice, hockey, and cold temperatures. She's warm, soft, and not a goal to reach or a prize to win.

She's reliable, thoughtful, and beautiful. I don't even mind her aggressive positivity so much. Life was kind of dim without it.

That's not necessarily romantic, but it's true.

Dad also had a talk with me last night and told me what makes a marriage last. Communication was at the top of his list. He also said the secret to a happy marriage is to make each other laugh.

Not my strong suit.

Little does he know this doesn't need to last long. That notion splinters inside of me like ice cracking beneath my feet.

But maybe it could?

I brush it off, telling myself it's a result of being out of my routine, eating too much of Grannie Bell's fudge, and all the excited energy surrounding me.

The thing is, I've been around all the guys on the team when they got married and at some point, they all got jittery. They may not have said as much, but it came out in practice, at a game, or when Micah showed up at my house in the middle of the night begging me to go to the rink with him. He couldn't sleep and knew I was the only one committed enough to shoot around at that late hour.

Now he has four kids. Worked out for him.

I have just the one kid and Jessica. Can I commit myself to them? Being faithful isn't the issue. More like being a good husband and father.

While the groomsmen gather, the processional music plays, and my sister marches, er, waddles down the aisle, followed by Cara, ahead of my bride to be, what if in a reversal of being a jilted bride, she leaves me at the altar?

I snort. She wouldn't. I'd like to say what we have is special. More like convenient. She needs me. I need her. It's that simple.

But will Pamberlie show up? Rexlan? The image of them tag-teaming and crashing our wedding lands in my mind with a jolt.

My brother-in-law leans in and asks, "You okay?"

Hendrix elbows me. "Bro is fine. Just the normal jitters." He nods knowingly.

Knowingly? Wait. Does he know that this is a fake wedding? Well, it's real insofar as we'll be exchanging vows, but it's just a paper wedding for Jessica's and my respective legal woes.

I keep asking myself if this is a mistake. Given the smiles on my family's faces and the little guy's general exuberance and pride at making it down the aisle with the pretzels—Hendrix hung onto the rings just in case—the answer is a resounding no. But guilt festers in my gut for not telling them the entire story. The truth.

"You look like you're hunting down the forward on an opposing team," Hendrix whispers.

My brother-in-law says, "Try smiling."

Hendrix scoffs. "Liam doesn't smile."

I'm about to tell them to quit talking because I can't hear my thoughts when the music changes.

As if from the mist, from the clouds of heaven, Jessica appears before me shrouded in white, an angel from above.

I suck in a breath.

A witch bride she is not.

The woman is ... the most beautiful creature I have ever seen.

Beside me, Hendrix snickers or sniffles? I can't tell. Is he laughing because for a second there I was smitten or is he as captivated as me by her beauty? Never mind the second one. He has Colette.

And Jessica is mine.

My entire body stiffens at the notion of anyone hurting a hair on her head, batting an eyelash at her, talking to her out of turn. If they do, they'll have to deal with me.

Hendrix stage whispers, "That's more like the Liam we know and fear."

Is he reading my mind? I tell myself that he's likely intuiting the normal stages of a groom's experience.

However, my head hiccups and careens toward the thing that I did let happen to Frank, Marci, and Allison way back when in high school. The fateful night Jessica alluded to.

Before I lose myself in grief, I take control and train my eyes on her.

She approaches slowly, her smile growing because she can't help herself. The woman doesn't know how to be anything but cheerful. Even if she has no interest in actually being my wife, I'll be her husband. I'll protect her. I will honor her.

Walking toward me alone, with no father or family other than Dolly to speak of, when she said she'd fallen for mine, a secret part of me thought maybe she'd fallen for me too. But that's silly. Stupid.

However, when we join hands, a familiar refrain echoes in my head.

Pivot, pivot, pivot.

It makes me wonder if I'm doing the right thing. It's not that I have cold feet or the urge to call this off. More like what if we're doing this for real? What if I've been lying to myself about how much I care about this woman, that the next few words I speak as we exchange rings are true?

Deep down, I know the answer. I've been telling myself a

story to keep Jessica at arms' length, to maintain distance because if I let anyone close, I could ruin everything.

Pivot, pivot, pivot.

When I speak her name as part of our vows, her gaze leaps to mine. Our eye contact doesn't waver as if she's aware of the transformation that's occurring inside but will give me time to meet her as a husband.

I told myself that the first few times we kissed didn't mean anything. She's objectively attractive. Later, I justified it by telling myself we were just testing the waters, practicing. I told myself not to kiss her again. That will only distract me from the game. These last few days, we haven't been able to keep our hands off each other.

Pivot, pivot, pivot.

However, not ten minutes later, when we're pronounced man and wife, for a moment, with her mouth on mine, the connection feels solid like ice, but not cold. Like a win, but this isn't a game. It's real life. And I'm married to Jessica.

I had my rules. She had hers. We both broke them, but what about new rules? Just to be cheeky, I land my hand on the *Bundt* I know is there, buried under the fabric of her gown.

When we part, her cheeks rosy and her eyes shining, she says, "Maybe you do have a playful side after all."

Hand in hand, we march down the aisle. It's surreal as everyone greets us, but also very, very real. We just did something I never expected to—that I told Pamberlie I never would. She banked on that.

Yet here I am, and so far, I kind of like it.

The reception is outdoors with laughter and chatter spilling out of the barn and the big house's porch onto the broad lawn and echoing across the water. I'm pulled in multiple directions but repeatedly land back by Jessica's side. It's like now that we're officially married, an invisible magnet draws us together.

The lights strung overhead sparkle, the toasts made are thoughtful, and the edginess that I often feel when back here at home doesn't show up until Franklin arrives with his cane in hand. Seems like Grannie Bell and my parents invited the whole town.

We exchange a nod and I make introductions.

Somehow, Jessica hasn't run out of energy. She's either been sneaking off to down pots of coffee or this kind of activity and excitement fuels her. Meanwhile, I need a nap.

Despite having a permanent injury from the accident, Franklin could be her long-lost cheerful soulmate. They exchange hugs like they've known each other since high school.

Frank shakes his head. "I didn't expect The Beast to have it in him. Senior year, he got two superlatives. Best hockey jock and we voted him least likely to get married."

I shake my head because the second one isn't true. "He's joking."

"There's always some truth in a joke." Jessica winks.

I swallow thickly because she's kept on script until now. We didn't actually write lines to use when people say the usual cliches at weddings, nor did we come up with a backstory other than the semi-truth. Jessica was my assistant. She had a crush on me. I fell for her. It's a well-used template.

However, what Jessica says next rocks me for some reason.

With a little lilt in her voice, she says, "I'm just that irresistible." She smooths her hand down my lapel. "When Liam saw me, he thought to himself, 'Now, that's the woman I need in my life.' I'm an expert laundry folder, great at meal prep, and have sophisticated logistical skills." A certain sweet smile, the likes of which I've never seen before, blooms on her lips.

"Hard to say no to that," Frank teases.

But Jessica isn't done. "Then he realized it wasn't just that he needed me. He wanted me because not only am I an exceptional assistant, I also listen to what he isn't saying, let in just the right amount of light, and am his biggest fan."

The DJ must've turned down the music and everyone must've fallen silent because my surroundings fade. Her amber eyes meet mine with a kind of intensity that's hard to deny.

She lifts onto her toes. I lower my chin slightly.

Can't lie. I like where this is going.

But then she leans into the crook of my arm and adds, "I also make sure he doesn't leave the house with mismatched socks."

Franklin hoots a laugh.

They've snapped me back to reality which didn't change. Nothing did. "Don't Stop Believin'" by Journey still plays loudly, the kids still race around—hopped up on way too much Bundt cake—and the dancefloor is full.

But maybe something inside of me shifted.

Clearing my throat, I say, "Couldn't have said it better myself."

But it's also true. But does that mean I *want* Jessica?

Franklin's wife appears with a sampler plate of mini Bundt cakes, exclaiming how Grannie Bell insisted they try each one. He kisses her on the cheek and she feeds him a bite. They rub noses and it's the most sickeningly adorable thing I've ever seen. The look in his eyes is pure love. I cannot fathom how he found his way after being so broken, losing so much. All because of me.

The three of them strike up a lively conversation for a few minutes. I can't help but wonder what Jessica thinks about me now that she knows that what happened back in high school is my fault. That I'm the reason Franklin can't walk without assistance. I know what I think and I'll never forgive myself for not insisting that I drive, for ruining Franklin's chance for hockey greatness. He was always better than me ... until he could no longer play. Then there was Marci, his girlfriend. I'll punish myself for that for the rest of my life.

The past accelerates like tires skidding on ice. Anger builds inside. I brace myself for the inevitable crash. I'm done with this party. Done celebrating. I cannot fathom why anyone would want to be here around me. Awful, loathsome me.

Just then, Hendrix announces that Jessica and I missed our first dance. They chant until we hit the dancefloor set up in the middle of the yard. String lights surround it, casting an inviting glow. The only thing keeping me from tearing them down is how disappointed my mother would be along with Grannie Bell, Aunt Goldie, Grandma Dolly, and even Jessica.

I talk myself out of making a scene.

Hendrix hollers, "Be warned, Liam is a terrible dancer."

A few people chuckle.

He's not wrong. I was actively avoiding the dance floor, but the real truth is that I'm a terrible person.

Undaunted, Jessica leads me onto the makeshift parquet floor and we assume the proper position. "Endless Love," by Diana Ross and Lionel Richie comes on.

"Is this our song?" she asks as bubbly as ever.

I shrug.

She searches my eyes and says, "Was it seeing Franklin?"

I know what she means but simply grunt in response.

"We don't have to talk about it, but—"

I prepare to hear her say everything that I've been told a hundred times, *It wasn't my fault. The same thing would've happened if I were driving. It's time to move on.*

But I never will. I can't.

Jessica holds my gaze and says, "That's how you got the scar on your lip, huh?"

I grunt.

"Sometimes bad things that happen cause hidden scars. Ones no one else sees. I'll be here when you're ready."

Then I surprise myself by replying. "To talk to you?"

Her expression is soft. "To listen. I'm your wife. You can tell me anything."

"You'd be the last person who'd forgive me. You were in foster care, right? Didn't the people who were supposed to take care of you—your parents—fail?"

"Yes," she says slowly.

"And you hate them. You'd never forgive them."

She shakes her head, eyes somehow light inside the darkness of this truth. "No, Liam. The opposite. I don't hate them and I do forgive them. I had to."

"They forced you to?"

She laughs. The woman, while having an intense conversation, especially while listening to such a slow and romantic song and surrounded by a crowd, must've cracked.

"Liam, if I didn't find a way to let it go, to forgive them, I would've remained stuck, hidden away in my shell, lost and lonely forever. Forgiving them was a matter of life and death when I realized the only person that was hurting, by holding onto all that pain, was me."

The words break through the hardness in my chest, in my mind, and strike deep.

As if recognizing this, Jessica is quiet until the song ends and everyone is invited to dance with us along to the song, "Walking on Sunshine."

In the last seconds of us being alone, she whispers, "They bought it. But we sold the kiss. How could they not?" She winks and then kisses me square on the lips.

My thoughts scramble and when we part, her wide eyes are on mine. I don't need to hear her voice or see her hands, but there is a message for me.

Forgive.

THE CORN HUSKER
[PRIVATE GROUP]

A hub for the Cobbiton community to connect, discuss concerns, and share upcoming events. Please read the "About" section for advisement about sharing direct sales marketing, self-promotion, and work-from-home opportunities. Remember, corny compliments are allowed but friendly feuds will be deleted. The rules are here to foster engagement and fun while maintaining positivity. Enjoy connecting with your neighbors!

[Post: Monday 8:02 am]
Admin

Monday Minute: Before anyone drives themselves nuts with speculation, I was given permission to announce that Liam Ellis and Jess Fuller are officially married.

Along with their families and friends, they exchanged vows at the family home in Brookking Sound, Ontario in an intimate ceremony by the lake. They are excited to begin their lives together, along with their son KJ. Please respect their privacy, however, if you'd like to contribute to the Cobbiton Youth Hockey Team, they're putting together a program to sponsor children with disabilities in the sport. Hockey gear is expensive, y'all!

We're very happy for the newlyweds and wish them all the best as they continue their lives together!

In other news, the permits for next year's Happy Hockey Days event are nearly signed, sealed, and delivered. We are planning on hosting it on the town green much like our Fourth of July festivities and the Christmas Market.

We need your input: Would you want to see a game of pro players against retired NHL stars or our very own Knights against the high school team? Chime in below!

[Comments]

Dorothy Fuller: I have never been so happy. Liam is a wonderful grandson-in-law and KJ is my joy! Congratulations! #MrDarcysAbs

MarshaSimmons: How exciting!!! I'll take this as a great excuse to make them a casserole. *DorothyFuller* Are there any allergies I should be aware of?

BarrySmeltz: I knew Jess was on a quest to find her king, or should I say her Knight?! Isn't Liam Ellis hockey royalty? I wrote a book called *Attack of the Voalcan Army* and it's available now!

Leah Smith: That's not how it works and if you continue to self-promote your book, I'm going to have to give you a warning, *Barry Smeltz*.

SophiaSnodgrassSchuster: Something doesn't add up. If they just got married, why did I see Jess in a wedding gown months ago?

JessieDunnO'Conner: Sounds like a real Beauty and the Beast story. Get it!? He's The Beast.

TaylorTipton: I hope they have a happily ever after.
CaraBadaszekArsenault: They will.

[Sponsored Content]

Attention artisans, crafters, and small business owners: The newly renovated Old Mill building has studio space for lease. Located at the end of 4th Street, give your dream a place to live in this prime downtown location. Each space boasts natural light, high ceilings, and a warm community of creatives. We have the perfect spot for a coffee shop. Inquire within.

34
LIAM

DAD and a few other hockey greats who found their way to the wild north for the wedding, gather around discussing the upcoming finals.

Hendrix, never one to miss any sports talk, joins us. "The Titans are going to win."

I shake my head because the Cup belongs to the Knights.

He continues, "And when we do, I'm going to Disneyland. Since you won't be riding off into the sunset with the Stanley, where will you take your consolation prize trip?"

Dad asks, "You mean his honeymoon?"

I swallow thickly because everything has happened so fast, and because Jessica and I aren't a real couple, we haven't been planning our dream trip for months.

I blurt, "We're going to Berlin to visit Oma and Opa. I'd like to do it for Christmas like we used to when we were kids, but I think those will be blackout dates for next year's game schedule."

Hendrix staggers backward. "You're taking Jess to meet our other grandparents?"

It's a big deal because even though I love Grannie Bell to death, the family king and queen are Dad's parents.

Hendrix mutters, "Maybe I was wrong."

Does that mean he knows this is all fake? Hendrix is the self-appointed family goof, but he's observant. Must've inherited it from Mom.

Uneasiness slithers through me, but one of the guys shifts to the recent Generals' scorching loss to the Titans and we're back on track.

Dad pulls me aside and says a few words about loyalty and marriage, then gives me a long and searching look.

"Anything else on your mind?" I ask.

"There's been something you've never been able to forget. If it means anything, I don't hold it against you. No one does. I suggest you let it go, son. Leave it in the past." He nods in Franklin's direction.

"Easier said than done," I mutter just as Jessica rushes over to us.

Saved by the belle of the ball. My bride.

Late that night, the family sends us to a nearby hotel.

Lights dim, we both crash onto the bed, still in our formal wear.

"We did it," Jessica says, her voice small.

I find her hand and twine my fingers around hers.

"We did," I say before we both promptly fall asleep.

The next day, Mom, Grannie Bell, Aunt Goldie, and Dolly prepare a big pancake brunch and send off.

Everyone thinks it's disappointing that I have to jet to Pennsylvania for a game so soon after the big day. But I need a minute to think. To recuperate. To process what the ring on my finger means.

KJ and his cousins are obsessed with each other. Despite the communication differences, they figure out how to play which is pretty promising. Mom gets misty a few times, probably emotional over all three of her kids now married or in a serious relationship.

At one point last night, she said, *I knew there was hope for you.*

I grunted because that's how she'd expect me to respond, but it's all a lie. I think. I mean, Jessica did look beautiful. We exchanged vows. There was the kiss. Then dancing wasn't the left-footed disaster I feared it would be.

She and Dad tag-teamed me, and her suggestion to forgive was the real disaster because I can't do it. It's impossible. I'm a horrible human. Nothing will change that. Even if she still accepts me even after what happened in high school, she wouldn't want to be with a guy who can't forgive himself.

As I said, *disaster.*

So is the first period of the game in Pittsburg.

We're put through our paces and tested, first by an offensive cluster, resulting in two penalties and a point against us. Our assists are out of sync and we repeatedly lose the puck. My head is everywhere but on the ice.

During a break, we regroup in the locker room. Everyone is in a foul mood, grumbling, and shooting accusatory glances, casting blame for the lackluster play.

It's not until we get the countdown warning for the start of the next period, that I realize I'm hanging around over a dozen guys who're acting how I usually do.

It's miserable.

Or perhaps Jessica is rubbing off on me.

Gripping my hockey stick like a tour guide with an umbrella, I whistle. "Gather 'round. We have to be out there in two minutes. I don't care what you do during those one hundred and twenty seconds, but when you hit the ice, I want to see you smiling. Force it if you have to— during the next twenty minutes, we have to come back and get ahead. Got it?"

They're all silent except for the rise and fall of inhales and exhales.

I arch an eyebrow and demonstrate what I mean.

Someone screams like they just experienced a jump scare. Another guy slow claps.

"Just showing you how it's done," I say, leading the way to the tunnel.

WHEN I RETURN TO COBBITON, I'm married. A father. Jessica is a mother. And we live together.

A spark of excitement burns along a wick, but when I get to the loft, it's empty. Quiet. Lonely.

My footsteps echo as I go down the hallway to check on the crab. A few of KJ's toys were left out.

I lower onto his bed and adjust the head of his favorite plastic soldier figure.

A lot changed fast in my life. I was alone and sinking, not sure how to handle it. Then Jessica entered the picture, shining light, bringing warmth and companionship. The kind I didn't know I needed, wanted.

When we first met, I said that I didn't need or want anything. I was wrong. I need and want her.

The front door opens and laughter filters down the hall.

Jessica hollers, "Home sweet home."

I meet them in the entryway. Jessica has a bag over her shoulder and a box in her arms. Grandma Dolly also has a bag. I help them unload. Jessica doesn't have more than a car full of belongings. While the assumption was that she'd move in with me now that we're married, we didn't discuss sleeping arrangements.

Once the last box is stacked in the hall, Jessica signs and speaks to Grandma Dolly, "Are you going to be lonely without me?"

The older woman smiles warmly and signs. "I'm getting my craft room back. Plus, I expect to see you Mondays, Wednesdays, and Fridays, at least."

"Don't forget games," I add, having offered her a permanent seat in the VIP suite.

KJ rushes toward us, holding his little soldier man, apparently pleased the head is fixed. He signs, "Thanks, Daddy."

I don't know how he knew I repaired it, but my heart melts.

I'm a father and it's my job to fix things. I'm no handyman by any stretch and wouldn't be able to do much more than hang framed photos and build a bookshelf from a kit, but I'm now the guy KJ and Jessica are going to turn to when things need repairing.

This thought follows me for the rest of the day. I become borderline obsessed with fixing the random things around the house like the leaky faucet, a squeaky door, and the wobbly table leg that Jessica, with her aggressive positivity, says is a reminder that not everything is perfect. She also got a stapler with rainbow staples, but it jammed, so I fix that too even though I still don't understand why someone needs colorful staples. Lastly, I spackle the hole I punched in the wall in the home office, promising myself not to do that again.

After we do KJ's bedtime routine which includes me reading a bonus book since I was gone at the game, Jessica finds me in the kitchen, adjusting the loose hand towel holder.

"What's gotten into you? You're being so domestic."

"I'd been meaning to fix this for a while."

She snaps her fingers. "Put a ring on his finger and just like that, the feral animal is tamed."

I scoff.

She watches me for a long moment and then says, "Thanks for fixing the table leg and my legal situation with the Coogans."

"We're not there yet." I can't fix that in an afternoon.

But Jessica and I are married now and I don't want anything in her life to be broken. Not staplers, not cars, and certainly not relationships.

The screwdriver slides from my grip.

"Are you okay?"

I brush my hand through my hair.

No, I'm not.

Because the biggest thing broken in her life is ... me.

"Uh, I should go to bed. Another game coming up. Training. Sleep," I mumble and disappear into my room.

Our room?

Leaning against the back of the door, I hear the sound of Jessica doing what she calls her good night tidy to the kitchen, her feet padding down the hall, and then the spare bedroom door opening.

Not only am I the worst human. I'm the worst husband. I don't even know if that bed is made. Is there furniture in there? I've only been in the second guest bedroom twice—once when I toured the loft to move in and the second time when KJ arrived and I needed to figure out where he'd sleep.

Turns out, I cannot. I toss and turn, my thoughts alternately hopeful and dismal. It's a dark night until the sound of footfalls pass my door and a dim light appears from the kitchen.

Jessica has insomnia. Of course, she's awake.

I hesitate, not sure what I'll say or do. I'm usually dreaming during these long hours. She should be too, so why isn't she?

35

LIAM

THE SOUND of Jessica settling onto the couch reaches my ears. I have a two-second argument with myself before dragging my tired butt to the living room. "Hey," I whisper slowly.

"Hey," she replies.

"Couldn't sleep?"

"I mentioned I have insomnia, but now that we live together, I hope it doesn't disturb you. I try to be very quiet."

"Is it contagious?"

In the dim light, I can see her face screw up. "No, of course not."

"What causes it?"

Jessica shrugs. "Stress. Hormones. There can be lots of reasons."

"Have you seen a doctor?"

"I've tried all the things. From traditional Western medicine solutions to woo-woo witch doctor quackery. I've come to accept that I'm a person who doesn't sleep. It's a hopeless situation."

"That's the least Jessica-esque thing you've ever said."

Lifting her mug to me, she says, "I'm drinking an herbal chamomile blend, but you've been warned that our coffee bill will always be high. Short of moving to Brookking Sound or that hotel in Colorado—I slept well while we were in both places—I'm sorry to say that you married a night owl."

"Me," I say, more of a statement than a question because I realize the common denominator.

She flashes her hand and the ring shines. "Yes, you, Liam. We got hitched. Remember? Thanks for not standing me up."

"I'd never."

"You're a man of your word. That's admirable."

"Me," I repeat.

More to herself, Jessica says, "One of my foster siblings once sleepwalked and would carry on half a conversation before we realized what was happening. Liam, go back to bed."

"Only if you come with *me*," I say, emphasizing the word.

She splutters her tea. "What? We got married and kissed, but we never discussed—"

Shifting from foot to foot because we're both losing precious winks, I say, "No, to sleep. The three nights you got a full rest were with me—in Colorado, at my parents' house, and on our wedding night."

We were both exhausted and I slept in my tux.

She leans back as if assessing the veracity of my statement. "You're right."

"Come on." I wave my hand.

She follows me down the hallway.

Fluffing the pillow, I pat the bed.

Jessica mutters. "Don't be romantic or anything."

Looking cute wearing a pajama set with little penguins holding hockey sticks, I say, "Nice jammies."

"They were a wedding gift from Colette and Hendrix. You

have a matching pair but look dressed for a workout." She slides onto the bed next to me.

I don't mention I normally sleep in just my underwear, but because I was going to check on her in the living room, I threw on some clothes.

"They're clean."

"I know. I washed them."

"You don't have to do that."

I feel her shoulder lift with a shrug. "I don't mind. I'll earn my keep around here."

"No, seriously. We'll hire a housekeeper."

Jessica is quiet for a long moment. "Maybe at some point, but for now, I'd like to do the laundry."

"The deal was a ring for a ring. I'm going to get KJ a new nanny and find another assistant too."

"No, Liam. You're not." She speaks with such firmness in her voice that I almost don't dare argue.

"You. Don't. Owe. Me. Anything."

She twists and props onto her elbows. "Even though I tell myself every day that this is fake between us, did it occur to you that I've always wanted a family and a home? If that means doing laundry and dishes and all the rest, let me try it out. If I hate it and want help, I'll let you know. But there seems to be something, I don't know, kind of special about knowing that I'm taking care of the people I love—" She rolls over and settles against my chest.

If I didn't feel the movement of her chest rising and falling with breath, I'd think she'd died, practically in my arms.

Yet, we're both very much alive ... and in love?

If she meant that in the way that we're playing house and she's acting the role of a mom and wife, fine. But what if she ...? I don't let myself go there.

I am not lovable.

But Jessica is huggable. Like has happened the other three times we've shared a bed, I hold her close, hoping she can fall asleep.

It's for practical reasons. Mostly. I want her to be fresh tomorrow, especially if she insists on taking care of KJ. Also, I don't want to find pencil shavings in my lunch. Back in grade school, my mother had a lot going on and was helping with homework while preparing meals ... and the little cup holding the wood and graphite must've been tipped into my chicken salad rather than the salt and pepper.

After a few minutes, Jessica says, "You've started calling your son KJ instead of the kid."

"So I did." I can't keep creating the illusion of distance and not using his name, pretending that he's not mine. That Jessica is too even if our situation is still murky.

"Did you notice he stopped sucking his thumb?"

"Yeah."

"Also, he's more than doubled his vocabulary and even mouths some words now like Grandma Dolly. Someday he's going to hear your voice, Liam. I just know it."

My jaw tightens and my eyes tingle. I've realized that people with varying hearing abilities aren't necessarily at a disadvantage like I believed. More that they may face challenges people in a hearing-oriented world don't. But that doesn't mean people with the gift of hearing always listen. Learned that lesson.

Soon, Jessica's breathing turns soft and deep. However, I can't sleep and my thoughts peel away like little curls from a sharpened pencil, drawing me closer and closer to the point. It's then I realize that maybe if I can fix her sleeping problem and if there's a solution to what she deemed hopeless, maybe forgiveness is possible too.

I wake up to a heavy weight on my chest. It pokes my

shoulder and then mushes my lips together. I blink open an eye to see Jessica sprawled out on the other side of the bed in her hockey-player penguin pajamas.

I meet a pair of blue-gray eyes that match mine. KJ wants breakfast, so we go to the kitchen and make a big mess, trying to replicate Grannie Bell's blueberry pancakes. When we take the first one off the griddle, Jessica shuffles in, looking adorably sleepy with floppy hair and heavy eyes.

"Morning, boys. It smells good." She points to the pancakes. "Don't throw out the first one. I'll take it. I've always liked the sacrificial pancake."

"The *what* pancake?" I ask.

Even though Jessica is signing and speaking at the same time, the concept of the first pancake always being a dud, goes over the kid's head. I get it though and our second one comes out much better with nice crisp edges and a perfectly fluffy middle.

Maybe there's some life wisdom there, but then why does Jessica like the first one? Wouldn't she want the best of everything?

I have training followed by practice all day and then fly out for an away game against the Titans.

Coach Badaszek asks to have a word when we're done warming up. "Thanks for inviting me to the wedding. You're a man of few words and I knew there was something you weren't telling me. Figured a laugh or two would help you get your feet under you."

He searches my expression as if expecting me to politely chuckle. That's the normal response, right?

Instead, I ask, "You knew about the kid and that's why you pulled me out for those two weeks?"

"I didn't know the details and was certain that you wouldn't request a leave of absence."

"So, you took the first opportunity to force me out?"

Badaszek claps me on the shoulder. "Sometimes you need to know when to toss out the first pancake."

I frown. "Did you talk to Jessica today?"

"Not since the wedding, why? Everything okay?"

I inhale a long breath. "Yeah. Everything is great and you're right about the pancake. I just learned about that recently. This morning, in fact."

"Personally, I like the first pancake—they can be imperfect, but they still taste good."

If Coach Badaszek and Jessica are both first pancake eaters, what does that make me? A fixer-upper? In their own ways, did they spot the problems in my life and swoop in? I thought I was the fixer, the father. The thought that haunted me last night appears along with a certain word that Jessica and I talked about.

Forgive.

As if sensing the wild river rapids of my thoughts, Coach remains quiet for a long moment.

"But you made me captain too."

He nods. "That was a risk, but I know you, Ellis. You stomp around in those skates at first, but then you glide. Never seen a guy as big as you move with such grace matched with speed, agility, and stamina."

I'm glad at least I get one thing right.

Then, Badaszek points at the ice. "There's still one piece of unfinished business."

He could only be referring to one thing. "Valjean?"

"I don't want any blood on the ice tonight."

"Mine?"

"Or his."

"He's the one who—"

Badaszek cuts me off. "Your father told me the whole story

while we were in Brookking Sound. You're the one keeping the unforgiveness alive. When you let it go, he'll show mercy."

"I don't expect this to turn into a redemption story."

"It probably won't, but he'll move on when you do."

"How do you know?" My voice sounds like it belongs to a little boy rather than a man.

"Because I've been Henri Valjean."

Before I can ask what he means, Vohn calls him from the nearest doorway.

Badaszek starts to move away, then over his shoulder, he says, "You don't get this far by remaining stuck in the past. And I'm not talking about just hockey. Take the lessons with you. Recognize the first pancake when you see it, do what needs to be done, and move on."

Later, at the game, we play a dominant first period, with Savage picking up the puck and passing it to Pierre who dashed down the left side while I kept Valjean off his tail. Redd gets a wrist shot before the buzzer, making for a two-zero score. Second period, we continue the assault, getting two power plays, leaving the Titans trailing. 'Bama is a dynamo and Mikey is slick as ice.

My brother gives his all, getting a nifty wrist shot through bumper-to-bumper traffic at the end of the second, but during the last period, we hold the gap then widen it with strong defense and another score thanks to Grady.

I'd like to say Valjean and I play completely clean. There are some close penalties, but no blood for once. Maybe that was the first pancake. We have a chance to try again. Next game, we'll both leave the past behind.

36
LIAM

AFTER THE GAME IN TORONTO, Jessica texts me and includes a photo of her, the kid, and Dolly all curled up on the couch together under one of the Knights branded fleece blankets the older woman makes. They're cheering me on. Well, except KJ. He's looking down at something with a wild grin on his face. Probably a piece of celebration cake.

The sight of it thaws something inside of me.

"Liam is smiling," Hayden says in a low tone.

"Who died?" Redd asks.

Pierre cuffs my arm. "He's married now. Of course he's smiling."

If only they knew it's fake. Never mind. I am not an admirable man. Jessica was wrong. Coach too. They're wrong about me. I add the sham marriage to my list of shame.

My phone beeps again and I read the message.

> Jessica: Get excited for a new addition to the family when you get back. 😉

Now I frown. That can't be. First of all, I know for certain there aren't any other possible children of mine out there. That's one hundred percent impossible with my wife.

Restless, I take an overnight flight back to Omaha and get in early the next morning. I've been using all my away game travel time to improve my ASL with videos and practicing on the guys.

When I get home, Jessica and Mrs. Kirby stand in front of the Old Mill building. Elizabeth repeatedly jumps at something, but a bush blocks it. When I round the corner, Jessica holds the kid's hand and the other grips a baby carriage.

I break out with a cold sweat.

She spots me immediately. "There he is!"

The kid rushes up to me, arms and hands moving so fast I can't read his signs.

Mrs. Kirby looks me up and down, sniffs, and then scuffles away with Elizabeth who repeatedly looks over her shoulder and whines.

I hoist KJ into my arms and glance at the baby carriage, but the sunshade is down. "I'll admit that I was surprised when this little bundle of joy came along, but there are multiple factors that would need to occur, including but not limited to conception, gestation—" I gesture between Jessica and me.

She tips her head back in laughter.

The kid signs and it's very distinct. Basic. One of the first I retained.

Dog.

"You got a dog?"

Jessica pulls back the top of the carriage, revealing a puppy with big brown eyes and as much energy as the woman who brought him home. Lunging for me, he tries to get out of the dog stroller. Still holding the kid, I scoop him into my arms. The animal proceeds to lick my face and then my son's.

"Jessica, what did you do?"

"I always wanted a dog." She bites her lip. "I may have forgotten to mention that."

"Seems like a pre-marriage conversation and a post-marriage decision to make together."

"In that case, I've also always dreamed of having a house with a picket fence, two point five children—not half a child, but a dog. That would be the point-five part, in case it wasn't clear."

"Let's just start with the dog. They're a lot of work."

"I know but they're also a lot of fun and loyal." She scratches the puppy by the ears.

I counter, "They eat a ton."

"So do you."

"They're messy."

"Let's not talk about how you leave your socks outside the laundry basket."

I grunt.

She takes the dog from my arms and says, "Puppers, meet your dog dad. He was rescued from an inhumane breeding operation and is a Bernese Mountain dog mix."

"So he'll be big?"

"Like his dad."

"But why the stroller?"

"He hasn't had all his shots yet, so he has to stay in the stroller when we go outside until he's up to date."

KJ pets the dog a few times before turning to me and signing something along the lines about how Elizabeth kept trying to kiss him and she has germs.

I want to laugh. That's right, buddy. Girls have cooties at least until you're eighteen.

I sign back. "What's his name?"

KJ tries the letters and Jessica crouches down to spell it with him.

"Ranger?" I ask.

KJ nods and tells me it's the same as his favorite army guy.

"We were just about to take a walk." Jessica holds the kid's hand and points to the stroller.

"I'm not pushing it."

Her response is matter of fact. "Yes, you are."

I huff but give in, hoping I'm not spotted by hockey fans who'll post this absurdity online.

While we're walking and the kid is signing to the dog, Jessica says, "I've been wanting to tell you that Grandma Dolly and I have been talking with the audiologist. There is a procedure that KJ is a candidate for."

"You mean for him to hear? What does that have to do with getting a dog?"

"For you or me, suddenly being able to hear after an injury or something like that would be amazing. But for him, it might be jarring. Grandma Dolly explained that there are ways to make the transition easier, one of which is a companion animal."

I nod, understanding what she means and fully trusting Dolly is in the know as she shares some more details.

Then Jessica links her arm through mine. "I have my comfort blanket so I can sleep. Figured he ought to have a buddy, too."

I snort. Why does the idea of being her buddy, a comfort blanket, make me feel warm all over?

"About that. Now that we're married, we need to have new rules."

"What about scrapping them and just seeing how we do?"

That works for about an hour. While KJ takes his post-lunchtime nap, which has turned more into quiet time, or playtime given the new dog, I review game footage. Jessica tosses a pair of dirty socks at me and they land on my chest.

I instantly gag. "What was that for?"

"You left them outside the basket … again."

Since this has been a regular argument, I open up a new tab on my computer. "I'm ordering us separate laundry baskets."

"That's a ridiculous solution. There's only room for one."

"Now you're taking over my bathroom?"

"I'm going grocery shopping. I'll be back with … some whipped cream."

I almost, but don't quite laugh, knowing exactly what she plans to do with that.

Having had a chance to cool off and by that, I mean get rid of those stinking socks—they are genuinely disgusting after a workout—KJ's quiet time is over and he, the dog, and I play around in the living room.

When Jessica returns, we all help with the grocery bags. Except Ranger. But he finds the biscuit treats she got him.

As Jessica unloads, I notice she takes the items out of the bag, one by one, and sets them on the counter.

I ask, "What are you doing?"

"Putting everything away," she answers innocently.

"You're doing it wrong."

"There's a right way to put away the food and stuff?" She looks at me like I've got a screw loose.

"You take them out of the bag and put them directly where they go. Saves time."

She smiles at the array of boxes, cans, and packages on the counter. "Maybe I like looking at them."

My eyebrows bunch together. "It's inefficient."

As I turn my back to the pantry, I catch her playfully sticking her tongue out at me.

Thankfully, it looks like she forgot the whipped cream.

That night, KJ and the dog go to Dolly's because there is a

Knights team event. Jessica and I are both in the bathroom, getting ready.

She asks, "What should I wear?"

"Clothes."

"The Knights aren't secretly nudists? What a surprise given the presence of ice," she deadpans.

"Sassy Jessica." I marvel. I'm not sure if I like it.

"What was that, Lazy Liam?"

I balk. "Lazy? I'm one of the hardest working players—"

She points to the socks on the floor next to the laundry basket. "The Ellises are not common slobs."

My thoughts snag on her smile and how she's an Ellis now. My missus.

I huff and pinch the edge of the hem as I pick them up and then wave them toward her. She runs out of the room, shrieking.

From the closet, which she's also moved her clothes into, she says, "What are you wearing?"

"Clothes," I repeat.

"Liam Ellis, it takes a lot to get under my skin, but I just want to—" She lets out a soft exhale. "I just want to fit in."

"You do. You will."

When she doesn't answer, sadness rumples her features. My mouth opens and closes because I don't know what I did or said, so I don't dare utter another word.

"What kind of event is it?" she tries again.

"It's game night."

"You have tonight off."

"Board games. Cards. That kind of thing. Redd and Whit are hosting. They have a big wood-fired pizza oven so there will be food too."

Staring at me she says, "Couldn't you have told me that to begin with?" Then she holds up her hand. "Never mind. I'll ask a better question next time. Ask good questions. Get good answers."

She wears a red wrap dress with little white flowers. Her hair cascades over her shoulders silky and shiny. Every time she moves, I get a little drunker on her cinnamon spice scent. Perhaps I shouldn't drive.

On the ride over, Jessica says, "So we're going to have to act like a real couple and not a bickering old ..."

"Couple?" I finish for her.

"Yes. Can you do that?"

"Can you?"

"Yes, darling," she says brightly.

I grunt.

After a beat, she asks, "How long have your parents been married?"

"Thirty-five years."

"Do they have any secrets to a lasting marriage?"

"Actually, my dad did say something about that on our wedding night."

But before Jessica can ask me what it was, we arrive at the farmhouse Redd and Whit fixed up. I tell Jessica about their dairy cows.

"Wait. You said there'd be pizza, but Whit runs the Milk Mustache cookie truck. Does that mean there will also be cookies?" Apparently having answered the question for herself, she squeals and all but bolts out of the car, sprinting to the backyard where the festivities are underway.

The scent of cooking dough and wood smoke along with Redd greets me. I gather with the guys including our host, Hayden, Mikey, Robo, Pierre, and a few others who're playing horseshoes. We talk about hockey, naturally.

From across the backyard, I spot Jessica with some of the

women. Her eyes sparkle, her lips part with laughter, and she looks anything but shy or like she feels out of place.

Jack elbows me, obviously having caught me staring.

I don't instantly look away but slowly drag my gaze back to the guys.

In an exaggeratedly wistful voice, he says, "Ah, young love."

I'm about to argue, and tell him that I'm not young—he and I are roughly the same age—nor am I in love. That's ridiculous. Probably.

37

JESS

THE KNIGHTS' wives, girlfriends, and I are bonding around an outdoor table with the heat lamps on, sipping homemade soda Gracie brought and eating personalized pizzas thanks to Redd's wood fire grill skills. Ted, one of the retired defensemen, is here with his wife Harlow and their family to watch a Finals game. The guys treat him like a celebrity and haven't stopped yakking it up.

Ella says, "Have any of you tried one of those woodland nature sounds alarms?"

"Like to wake up in the morning?" Cara asks.

"Jack insists on using the app on his phone and then repeatedly hits snooze ... for an hour. I die a little each morning."

I'm about to comment that at least she sleeps, when I realize I have been sleeping with thanks to Liam. Something about him being next to me must destress me or soothe whatever has kept me locked in insomnia.

Delaney looks around and then whispers, "Hayden recently started watching sports highlights at top volume. He was there. At. The. Game. Does he need to feel like the commentators are yelling at him when he's at home?"

We all laugh.

Gracie says, "Perhaps he wants you to come watch too, so he can show off and tell you how awesome he was at the game."

"Like a mating call?" Delaney laughs.

Whit steeples her hands. "Redd and I have our show. Watch a new episode every Thursday night when he's home. Then that sneak had to go and watch one without me when he was on the road. He slipped up and spoiled it for me. He should've kept it a secret."

"Would you really prefer that?" Margo winces while eyeing Beau over by the bonfire. She clears her throat. "As someone who may have accidentally skipped ahead to the next episode of a certain show Beau and I watch on Tuesday nights, keeping it to yourself is not the better option."

There's a collective gasp.

"I thought he was watching it at the hotel. Maybe." Margo wrings her hands. "I mean, we were left on a cliffhanger and I couldn't wait two weeks to find out what happened."

This must catch his eye because, like a wall of hockey brawn, they all saunter over while I'm blabbing about how I've been struggling with the way Liam reloads the toilet paper roll. "Open side out, am I right?"

"At least he replaces it," Harlow asserts as Hayden, Robo, Pierre, Jack, Beau, Grady, Mikey, 'Bama, Liam, a few others, and even Vohn surround us.

Redd plants his hand on his hip. "What do we have here? A gripe session?"

"Are the ladies really complaining after we wowed them with pizza and awed them with our handsome firelight silhouettes?" Pierre asks.

A few of the guys groan because the man cannot help but grandstand.

"We weren't complaining, we were comparing," Whit says.

"Sounds like Jess was taking issue with the way our man Ellis loads the toilet paper roll," Jack says with a smile and a wink.

I wave my hand. "Pfft. No, I love the way he sometimes only gets the little springy thing halfway into the holder and then it flies out at me in the middle of the night."

He frowns. "At least I put the toilet seat down."

The guys clap as if that's amateur hour.

I jut my chin. "And I love the way you leave the soaked sponge in the sink."

He shrugs. "So, I forgot to squeeze it out once or twice."

"All the times. Do you realize how many germs sponges can harbor? You set it in the cup on the side to dry." If I had a sponge right now, I'd toss it at him.

"One point to Liam. Two for Jess," Hayden says.

Delaney elbows him. "No taking sides."

"Tell us what you love about your bride, Ellis," Ted asks.

Liam's expression darkens. "Uh, how her hair is all over the sink. All over the house."

"Robot vacuum," Jack says.

"Hey, my hair does not get all over—"

Jack pulls Ella into his side. "I love your hair and I love that it's everywhere." He kisses the top of her head.

"Any other words of undying affection?" Beau asks. "Speak now or forever hold your peace."

He and Margo exchange a knowing glance.

Liam steps closer to me so we're toe to toe. He towers over me and says, "You leave water glass ghosts all over the house. Use a water bottle and stick to it."

I cross my arms in front of my chest. "Maybe you're afraid of ghosts because you leave every light on in the loft."

"It's so no one stumbles."

"Weak argument," Robo says.

I snort a laugh.

Liam adds, "Also, I never said I was complaining. Maybe I like seeing the half-empty glasses on the table, counter, bookshelf, everywhere."

I poke him in the chest. "They're half full, Mr. Meanie."

His lips ripple. Our gazes slide together and spark. Something crackles between us. I almost don't realize I'm doing it until it's happening, but Liam laces his fingers through mine. I squeeze his hand and cast him a smile. His eyes brighten as if to say that he didn't realize what was missing from his life until now.

The space between us shrinks as I gaze at his lips and his heavy eyes drop to mine. As my pulse disappears and my senses heighten, I lose my sense of time and place.

From somewhere nearby, one of the guys says, "Ahh. Married life."

Liam and I seem to snap out of whatever haze we were in.

Robo says, "Figured you two would still be in the honeymoon period. Sounds like you've sped past that."

"Watch out for the seven-year itch," Ted says.

Panic rushes toward me. "Is that like a rash?"

Everyone laughs.

This is going to be harder than I thought. My gaze drifts back to Liam's, afraid of what I'm going to see there. But the corners of his lips curl ever so slightly upward. Maybe he's amused, making fun of me and how I shed and can't keep track of my water glass. Or perhaps these grievances are grave and he's considering kicking me out, exposing our lie.

We have skillet cookies with ice cream for dessert, hang out some more, and then say goodnight with Gracie offering to host the next gathering.

On the ride home, Liam says, "About how you unload the groceries—"

I pout. "Oh, right. You forgot to mention that to everyone."

"No, I wanted to tell you that I realized why you do it that way."

"Oh," I say, not sure where he's going with this.

"Having plenty means more to you than say, someone like me who might take it for granted. You really do look at life with the glass half full. It's a good thing, Jessica. Really good."

This time, I don't argue. I never thought of it quite that way, but he's right.

The streetlights alternately brighten him and then cast him into shadow as he says, "It's going to take us some time to get to know each other and get used to each other."

"I don't mind all that stuff I said."

"I know. In fact, you said you loved it." Liam's lips press together as if he's holding back a smile.

"Ha ha," I say dryly.

Then something else I said that first sleepy night in Brookking Sound slides into my mind. My heart somehow gets in an extra beat.

As we pull into the parking garage, I say, "I'm no longer your employee. I'm your spouse. We have to work together. But I'll clean up my stray hairs."

"And I'll squeeze out the sponge."

"You're a team captain. We can figure out how to work together. I'll still do the regular things, but I draw the line at the socks. They stink. Also, I don't want the puppy chewing them, he'll get bad breath."

He rumbles a laugh. "He already has bad breath."

"He has puppy breath."

I pout, offended on the dog's behalf, but the warmth in his eyes shows so much affection I know he's not truly annoyed.

"The kind only a mother could love. But fair point and noted. From now on they go in the basket. From now on, I'll make the effort. For you and because I don't want holey socks."

"Thank you."

He cuts the ignition and glances over at me. "Thanks for coming tonight."

"Wouldn't have missed it."

"For the record, you fit right in."

"They're really nice women. Plus, Cara is my bestie and she'd fill their lockers with shaving cream if they picked on me."

"You women and the cream—shaving cream, whipped cream ..."

"I'm joking."

"I'm not."

"About what?" I ask.

His lips quirk and the little lines around his eyes smile. "You looked really pretty tonight."

My little love and affection-starved heart eats up those words and they taste even better than cookies or cake.

38

LIAM

AFTER SPENDING time with the men I admire and with the little dude who won my heart, it's time for some changes around here. Big ones. And they start with the truth.

I owe it to my family and the woman I love.

I may have done things backward and been a total toolbag, but that doesn't mean I can't fix it.

After a very long conversation with my parents, disclosing the truth about Jessica and my relationship, I ask about the engagement ring.

My mother is hesitant at first, but finally relents when I use the L-word and the P-word—love and please, respectively—and when Grannie Bell insists that she see it on Jessica's finger next time we visit ... or else.

I can hear her in the background hollering, "I knew she was the one!"

I should hope so, considering we got married. But I also lied about the marriage of convenience. After my confession and apology, I ask Dolly to come over while Jessica is out and tell her the story.

"I know," she signs simply.

Relief followed by confusion rushes through me.

She mouths and signs, "Jessica may have mentioned it. But I could tell it was more than a matter of convenience by the way you looked at each other. It's the same affection Dell had in his eyes."

I assume she's referring to her late husband.

My ASL is rough, but I say and sign, "It's a bit backward, but I'm going to ask her to marry me."

She signs, "We all have our own way of doing things. Now, let's get baking before Jess gets back." Dolly bustles into the kitchen, tying her apron. She signs to KJ and he climbs the stool, armed with a spatula and mixing bowl.

I wanted to do this myself, but also figured I'd screw it up so I called in the big guns.

Dolly signs and mouths, "How'd you get rid of her anyway and when will she be back?"

I speak and sign, "I sent Jessica on a wild goose chase to a local hockey pro shop to source me a *bagatelle*." I have to spell out the last word.

The older woman tilts her head back with laughter. "A doohickey? A thingamabob?"

I nod. There's no such thing as a *bagatelle*, but I needed to occupy her long enough to make a Bundt peace offering ... and a proposal.

Dolly instructs me on how to make the perfect cinnamon spice Bundt cake. KJ helps with the icing.

She signs, "It may not have enough time to cool. But it's the thought that counts."

I nod while my son greases the tin cake pan, being sure to get in all the little nooks and crannies.

She signs, "I'm glad you finally came to your senses."

"Do you think she'll like it?" I reply.

"She'll love it, but she also loves you. Never forget that because I think she's been saving up a lot of love for a long, long time."

Jessica's early life makes me sad, but I intend to make up for it by loving the heck out of her now that she's all mine.

After Dolly instructs me on how the cake is done and how to carefully remove it from the pan, she and KJ hit the road. He gives me a big hug and then dashes out the door with the dog.

At last, it's quiet. Too quiet. I've come to like the activity in our home with Jessica breaking into random dance parties, singing out loud (in an endearingly off-pitch tone), and generally making every day merry even if Mrs. Kirby downstairs complains from time to time.

Taking a deep breath, I finish cleaning up and set everything out on the end of the long wooden table.

Keys jingle in the lock and Jessica enters, smiling. "It smells good in here. So good."

"Smells like you," I say.

"Like cake?"

I nod. "I made you one."

She drops her bags. "You made me a cake?"

"A snickerdoodle Bundt. You said it's your favorite."

As if not quite registering, she says, "I got you the bagatelle, er, a baton, baguette, and a basket. I wasn't really sure what you meant by bagatelle and the guy at the hockey store had no idea and so ..."

I step aside so she can see the cake on the table next to some lit candles and the velvet box.

Her hands tent over her mouth and she steps closer, peering up at me and then back at the table.

I plant my palm on her lower back and say, "Jessica, you may remember that I was looking for this little box. It contains Grannie Bell's engagement ring. She still wears her wedding band, but a little birdie from Brookking Sound may have chirped that originally Hendrix was going to propose to Colette with it. But may have changed his mind to go with something custom and gave it to me for safekeeping."

"I'm glad you found it."

"No, I found you. I didn't know what I wanted or needed. Turned out it was right in front of me. I want and I need you. With this ring, I want to formally ask you to marry me."

"But we're already married."

"I want you to know that I want to be married to you. I want you to have this, to be part of our family ... to be mine."

She gasps and turns to me, arms looping my neck. "Yes. I want to be yours and you'll be mine. Mine all mine."

She pecks my mouth with excited kisses in between happy squeals of joy.

I hardly have the ring seated on her finger when she fully wraps herself around me, hugging me tighter than I imagined while repeating the word, "Yes, yes, always yes."

We settle into the embrace and I feel like the past starts to move into the background while the future opens wide and sunny in front of me.

Jessica leans back and frames my jaw with her hands, studying me for a long moment. "You may have been rough and gruff, but I didn't give up on you. You're honest and handsome and so, so, wonderful because you made me a cake!"

"I had a little bit of help."

I slice it and she takes a bite, eyes closed, looking as happy as I've ever seen her. "This is amazing. Five stars. I'll have to give you a sticker."

"I'd like that and I love your planner, colored pens, and aggressive positivity."

She playfully knocks into me. I nuzzle her with my nose. The cake plate gets set aside. The ring sparkles on her finger as

I press my lips to the top of Jessica's hand before folding her into me for a kiss.

———

THE NEGOTIATIONS with the Coogans are more of a hassle for the attorneys than I anticipated, but I'm now a husband and a dad and it's my duty, my desire, to fix things.

First, to get the crazy lizard cult lady and her daughter out of our lives. Turns out that Rexlan is the least of our problems. He's just afraid his mother's lady lizard squad is going to curse him. I can't necessarily blame the guy for falling for his assistant. I mean, it happens.

Tonight is the final game for the Stanley and I need to get my head in the zone and get off the phone. Never mind that the lawyer practically charges by the minute, but the conversation about concessions could cause a migraine.

KJ rushes into the room with Ranger and I fight everything in me to give them the one-minute finger. I just need to wrap up the call.

Jessica follows the boys, takes the phone from my hand, and says, "Good morning, Attorney Sarbo. It's such a pleasure to hear your voice. It's the sound of confidence, the kind that tells me this man makes things happen, resolves problems, and has the moral fortitude to do the right thing and not bend to the whims of the skink people. Listen, I like lizards as much as the next gal. Truly, I do, but not as much as Sorsha. However, I assure you, there is nothing to worry about. It's all a big fat ploy. The money people pay to appease her scaly deities is a scam. She's an extortionist, a criminal. Do you know she doesn't report the money she collects from her website for taxes? So many people have believed their woes would be cured by using her tinctures and talismans, but the elixirs they'd buy from her storefront were nothing more than vegetable oil mixed with herbs and food dye. Plus, it smells like cat pee. Just saying. Don't even get me started on the amulets. She has little kids in countries without child labor laws fabricating those."

Through the phone, I can hear James Sarbo say, "Why didn't you say so in the first place?"

"That she's a con artist? I thought it was obvious." Then Jessica goes quiet. "Though, to be fair, I didn't realize it at first either and nearly made it to the end of the aisle before finding out that Rexlan cheated, snapping me out of it."

"We have an even bigger case than I thought. Do you know if Pamberlie was involved?"

"Absolutely, but she didn't hide that it was all a sham. She made fun of her mother, but definitely enjoys the financial benefits."

Sounds like they're on their way to getting that solved. I turn my attention to KJ who sits on the floor in his sneakers while trying to tape a long piece of tinfoil to the bottom.

I sign, "What are you doing, buddy?"

He replies, "Making skates like you."

Never mind a honeymoon, okay, I would like to visit my grandparents, but that's mostly because I want them to meet the little dude ... and Jessica. This dad thing is pretty cool. I sign, "Do you want to skate with me tomorrow?"

He nods vigorously.

I tell him we'll get him skates like mine. He waves his arms in the air and then hugs my leg.

Jessica gets off the phone and tilts her head to the side. "What?"

Heat draws along my neck toward my ears. "Nothing."

"You were staring at me. Do you want to make fun of how I was duped by the skink queen?"

"No, actually, you handled that perfectly, professionally. Sarbo and I were at loggerheads."

"Oh. Good. I'm looking forward to washing my hands of that mess."

The kid continues to try to attach the foil to his shoe.

I say, "I have a new skating student during the off-season."

"Would you object to two students?" Jessica asks.

"You don't know how to ice skate?"

"Or swim or ride a bike."

"Seriously?"

Her shoulder lifts toward her ear. "Never really had the chance ... but I also didn't give myself one. Your childhood was the kind I only saw in movies. The kind I longed for."

"It wasn't all peaches and cream, Sugar. The three of us Ellis siblings sure could fight."

"While some of the families I lived with while in the foster care system were amazing, there was always a point when I'd have to move on. They didn't want to keep me." Liquid brims in her eyes. "So I retreated. It wasn't so much that I was shy, more like I couldn't keep bearing the rejection so I made myself small, quiet, barely there."

"I cannot imagine you anything but smiley and outgoing. An aggressive force of positivity and optimism."

"When I was in high school, I didn't speak for five months straight. That's why I was placed with Grandma Dolly. They thought I'd sign."

"What happened when you turned eighteen, were you on your own? By then, you lived with Dolly, right?"

"She called me Mouse at first, drawing me out of my hidey hole crumb by crumb. You know, she made me the first birthday cake I ever had. Put sixteen candles in it and every-thing." Sadness fills Jessica's eyes where there's usually a smile.

"That's why you like to bake cakes so much, huh?"

"I never told her the wish I made when I blew out the candles. But she signed that it must've been a good one because from then on, I never stopped smiling."

"What did you wish for?" I dare ask.

"For me to see all the good in things instead of the bad."

"And an aggressively optimistic woman was born."

She snorts a laugh. "I guess you could say that. I also figured since I missed out on sixteen birthday cakes, it wouldn't hurt if I added an extra wish."

"Which was?" I ask.

"This." Her gaze drifts from the dog, drifts to KJ, and lands on me.

A family.

"But then you left Cobbiton."

"I was already in the habit of not staying in one place long enough to get comfortable. I always kept one foot near the door to make a quick exit. In a new place, in the beginning, no one knew I'd been abandoned. Until they did. Inevitably, someone would sniff it out. It was humiliating."

"Did they confront you? Doesn't seem like anyone's business." My jaw tightens at the idea of bullies making Jessica feel bad.

"A few times, but mostly it was just that I knew that they knew. They'd treat me different in subtle ways, but it became like a pebble in my shoe."

"So you'd walk away."

"By leaving Cobbiton and living somewhere else, no one needed to know about my serial failures ... and I wouldn't be reminded. I could start fresh. It's what I'd always done. New school, new friends. I'd forget about the past a little more each time."

"Those weren't your failures."

"But I thought once I was free from that system, I'd be a success. Being an adult is harder than I thought."

I brush the softest part of my thumb along Jessica's jawline. "What if instead of running away from your problems, you run at them?"

"In full hockey gear?"

I chuckle. "In that case, we definitely have to teach you to skate."

She's quiet for a long beat and then in a small voice, she says, "I was never good enough to love."

That hits me in the heart. Yeah. I have one.

I'm afraid to ask her about now, worried that I might not like the answer. She's a flight risk.

Hooking my finger and planting it under her chin, I bring her gaze to mine. I want to do something nice for her. Something extraordinary. But I don't think a fancy car or jewelry is her love language. Cake can only go so far.

I say, "Jessica, I want to keep you."

She blinks a few times.

I nod.

Then she dives into my arms and I hold her for a long, long time. I want it to be forever.

Just before I leave for the arena to prep for the game, Jessica meets me by the door.

"Will you do something for me, please?" Her expression ripples with uncertainty, hesitancy. I worry it's going to be something that I can't do. Is she going to ask me to smile? I mean, I would for her. I told the guys to do so at the game not long ago and we won. If the woman wants a smile, I'll deliver.

I say, "Anything."

She points to the top shelf in the closet. "Could you grab that basket from up there? I'm sorting through KJ's seasonal gear and can't find a mitten."

"I thought it was going to be more like beat up your ex."

"He has his mother to deal with."

"Was that it?" I edge toward the door.

"Yes. No. While you're on the ice, will you wave to KJ if you have a chance? It would mean a lot that you see him from out there."

"Yeah. Of course."

She bites her lip as if there's more.

The clock is ticking. I never used to be less than two hours early for prep. Sometimes I just sat in the empty arena, playing through the game in my head. "Is there something else?"

"Actually, one more thing. Remember how we talked about forgiveness?"

She draws the line at the socks. This one, I don't step over. "Not now, Jessica."

"Maybe later? I think it'll give you an edge on the ice."

I incline my head, wondering what the heck she knows about hockey.

"Carrying around baggage like that from the past can weigh you down, hold you back."

I nod, understanding what she means but now is not the time to think about what happened in high school to Franklin and Marci. Right now, my mind can't be on anything other than winning for my team ... and my son.

Jessica too.

Cupping her cheeks I kiss her square on the lips and swish out the door.

39

LIAM

THE PRESS of Jessica's peachy lips to mine tries to interrupt the thoughts I've had during the ride to the Ice Palace, skating between how I had no intention of ever settling down. Not because I saw marriage as a set of shackles. More like I refused to be put in a situation where I might hurt someone. Again.

Now, I'm a dad and husband. I scrub my hand down my face but do my best to leave all of these thoughts behind as I head into the arena.

But Jessica's whisper, *forgive* stays with me as I change ... doesn't leave. I shouldn't be thinking about how to do that right now. But she was right. It's like a weight, a restraint.

Get your head on, Ellis.

We have a playoff game against the Titans and while I'd like to say may the best man win, I'm loyal to the Knights, so my brother along with Valjean, and the rest of the Toronto team are going to meet The Beast tonight.

I tape my stick, knocking each of my thoughts out of my head with every turn of the roll.

Ted sits down next to me in the locker room and says, "I've

been trying to decide if I wish I were in your skates. But they wouldn't fit."

"Stuff 'em with socks. Put on my uniform and helmet, no one would know the difference."

He chuckles. "I do miss you guys."

"There's been some drama lately."

He says, "So I've heard. Someone was in hot water with the coach after the laughing incident. But I think there was more to the story."

True. I was exhausted, in shock, and ready to boil over, just didn't expect it to come out as laughter. "Did Badaszek give you the details?"

"No, but I watched the game. Three times. Looks like you got into it with Valjean."

"What else is new? He talks trash about my brother." And I don't mean Franklin even though in hockey, whether in high school or the NHL, we think of each other as family, especially on the Knights, which is probably why Ted is in here talking to me.

"What on earth would Valjean have to say about Hendrix? They're on the same team. I've seen your brother talk plenty of trash to you out there."

"Different rules."

Redd slaps me on the back with his gloves. "Ellis will always go to bat for his bros."

"Wrong sport," Grady and Hayden say at the same time.

Redd pumps his hands. "I'm just saying, let's all keep our cool."

"Yeah. Great idea," I bluster.

Jack says, "He just means don't be so hotheaded."

"Okay, geniuses. How should I go about doing that? Any recommendations when someone is trashing your actual brother?"

Hayden says, "Delaney."

Redd nods his head rhythmically. "Whit."

Pierre waggles his eyebrows. "Cara."

Beau comes the closest I've ever seen him come to a smile. "Margo."

Jack says, "The Puck Princess."

I hold up my hands. "You'll have to translate."

Then, all at once, they declare, almost at a cheer, "Jess."

My face pinches. "All right. I'm the captain, it's time to focus."

Ted says, "What they mean is the women in their lives soften their rough spots."

"So, you want me to be a teddy bear?"

Ted grunts. "I'm The Bear. You're The Beast. We mean more like a relationship can help diffuse some of that pent-up energy."

I narrow my eyes.

Hayden says, "We laugh together."

Redd shrugs. "She rubs my back. I rub her feet."

"How does that help you?"

Beau lifts his hand in the air. "We do the opposite. I'm not sure what kind of sorcery it is, but it works."

I think of the witch bride and then my actual bride, on our wedding day, floating toward me down the aisle. Never was there such a radiant sight.

"We're not telling you to lose your edge," Jack says.

"Keep it as sharp as ever," Hayden, one of our wings, adds. "I need that wall of protection."

"Ted might take my place tonight."

The guys erupt with laughter because it's preposterous and would result in fines, not to mention because I'd get kicked off the team, but also maybe because I made a joke.

Robo says, "Maybe Jess is rubbing off on you after all."

It's call time. Ted claps me on the back and says, "Whatever it is, bro. Let. It. Go."

Badaszek says a team prayer and we hit the ice to a ballyhoo, cheering, and absolute fan chaos. Moments after the puck drops, we light up the arena with a score thanks to Jack. The Titans come back with Owen Jablonski channeling his inner figure skater and somehow whacking a shot off the boards and into the goal with a nifty little spin.

I'll admit, I'm impressed.

Second period, Jack gets another breakaway and another goal on Griffin McGregor, but the Toronto team comes back with a point scored by my very own bro. He does a victory dance and blows a kiss to Colette.

I expect Valjean to have it in for me, however, Pierre is in his crosshairs and Sawyer O'Malley has our defensemen locked.

I tell my fellow defenseman, "I've got your back."

Pierre shrugs. "He's mostly bark." He tips his head to the side as if accepting a challenge. "Some bite too. I can handle it."

We continue in this scoring pattern with the Titans keeping up and we close the second period with them having a point on us. Valjean and I both camp out in the sin bin more times than Coach is going to like.

I watch the game intently, but also study Badaszek, following his gaze, wondering what he sees and what clicks in his brain to make him call certain plays. It's almost like he can perceive things before they happen.

Forget playing 4D chess. The guy plays 4D hockey.

He has a way of pushing us right to the edge and just when we think we'll snap, the strength comes. It comes from training. From preparation. From faith. That he knows what the heck he's doing, but it also comes from God. The man is a believer. Me too. He also believes in me, which means a lot. I didn't think I could pull off being captain. Not with KJ. But being forced into the leadership role somehow made me wake up to the reality of fatherhood and what it requires. Now marriage. It's like I hit a warp zone in a video game and leveled up.

Am I ready for everything that's going to come my way? Not a chance, but I know I have the resources to deal with whatever happens. My coach, my team, my family, and above all the Man Upstairs. Can't let any of them down.

While regrouping in the locker room ahead of the last twenty minutes of the game, Badaszek says, "Men, this business comes with flames and flowers. You're going to get accolades and have haters. You don't fight back with your fists, you fight back by winning."

Then we're back out there.

Midway through the final period, my thoughts stray and so does the puck. Above the roar of the crowd, I hear my name. Jessica is on her feet cheering for me. KJ claps and waves his arms.

Like waking up from a decade-long dream, my focus snaps like a rubber band and I'm back, thundering down the ice, blocking shots, keeping Valjean in check, and leaving an opening for one of the most masterful shots I've ever seen.

In one swift motion, Pierre passes the puck to Mikey. He carries it over the line and then with a flick of the wrist, it lands cleanly with Jack. There's no stopping him and he slaps it into the net as the final buzzer sounds, lighting the lamp.

Seeing my family in the stands cheering, something slips away, empties only to be replaced by something else that fills me in a way I never thought possible. At last, I've forgiven myself.

After the victory lap, I shake Valjean's hand, hopeful the past is behind us.

40

JESS

GRANDMA DOLLY TAKES KJ home so they can have some celebration cake before it gets too late. I make her promise to save me a slice.

While waiting in the hallway after the game, I watch as families, wives, and girlfriends gather around their players. They cheer, clap, and hug.

Even though I'm not a hockey super fan like my grandmother, understanding everything that was going on, Liam, along with the team, was remarkable. The smile he flashed while waving at his son and me was the real win of the night.

As people filter out to go celebrate, I post to @TheReal-LiamEllis so we don't have to deal with it later. I sense a shadow looming over me and look up with a smile, expecting it to be him.

Instead, one of the Toronto players leers at me, crowding my space.

My gaze darts around him, looking for an assist from one of the Knights or a passerby, but everyone is occupied. To distract him, I want to say, *Oh look, a puck!*

His gaze narrows and he creeps closer. Maybe he's just sore that he lost.

Nerves wash through me as I wave hello. "Hi! I'm Jess. Can I help you? Also, you played a bang-up game. If that's a good thing. You knocked it out of the park. Wait. That's baseball. Good job. I don't believe everyone should get a trophy, but maybe a participation award because you look like you—"

"Shut up," he hisses.

Up close, I recognize the guy. Henri Valjean, I take a step back into the painted cement wall. "Excuse me?"

He stabs the air with his stubby finger. "I know who you are. Ellis's wife. Now you're on my list too."

"On your list of people who brighten your day? I really enjoy making lists. Have you ever kept a bullet journal?" I ask brightly, meanwhile, I'm concerned he's making a hit list of people he wants to clobber with his hockey stick.

He snarls, now pointing his finger in my face. "If you know what's good for you—"

If he gets any closer, I'm going to acquaint him with my extra-large coffee. As enthusiastic as I was about watching Liam and the Knights play, all I could think about was snuggling up in number forty-five's arms and I needed something to keep me awake.

Refusing to let my voice shake, I say, "Sir, you're being rude and acting in a threatening way. You don't know who I am. I don't know much about you other than your name, but it would be a lot better for the both of us if you left me alone. Or go have a cookie. Or try smiling," I add, flashing mine with quivering lips.

"I'm looking for Ellis and when I find him, it's game over."

"I suppose you'll have to get in line because I'm waiting for him too. Funny, he and I first met in a line. At a coffee shop. I had to pee really bad. Speaking of, I should probably go find the ladies' room. Nature calls. Tootles!" I wiggle my fingers with a wave.

His harsh expression turns quizzical before he glowers, hissing, "You're not worth it, anyway."

Relief sweeps through me followed by tears brimming in my eyes as we go in opposite directions.

As the really truly mean guy from the Titans stalks off, the Knights player the fans call The Beast approaches, looking surly and sour. His frown deepens when I wipe my eyes.

"Great game. Grandma Dolly took KJ home. I wanted to wait." I gesture over my shoulder to the area where families wait for the players.

Alarm ices over his features. "Jessica, what's going on?"

I shrug. "Nothing. I'm tired."

"You're holding what may as well be the Big Gulp equivalent of a coffee. You're wired."

"I only took a few sips."

His harsh tone softens. "Please, look at me. What's going on?"

"Just a bad apple tried to spoil my excitement over the win."

Liam's gaze narrows toward the hallway. "Do you mean Henri Valjean?"

"That name sounds familiar."

"He's Marci's brother."

"The one who—?" I cut myself off because I don't want to bring up the past. At least not right now.

"Remember you offered to listen if I talked about it later?" he asks, eyes dark.

"Yeah. I mean anytime, but now?"

He nods slowly. "You were right. I'd been shouldering the blame. Carrying it around with me. That's not to say that

Valjean doesn't have a right to be upset, but it happened ten years ago. That doesn't change the outcome, but ..."

The end of the sentence Liam doesn't say is that it truly wasn't his fault. Instead, as he looks up, he utters, "Valjean."

This time Valjean approaches with his hockey stick lifted.

"Oh, wow. It's you again. Fancy meeting you here. Such a great game. The Titans really wowed," I say brightly.

Valjean glowers. "I was looking for him and I told you, if you know what's good for you—"

I twist my hands like I'm presenting a game show prize. "Liam Ellis in the flesh and he is very good for me." I shimmy up to his side.

He scowls at the Titans player.

"Tell your yappy little dog to get out of the way. We're going to finish this once and for all." Valjean lifts his stick.

Liam's fists tighten and his glare deepens.

"Those sound like fighting words. Let's not do anything we'll regret, guys."

Liam's nostrils flare. His chest lifts on an inhale, reminding me of an old-fashioned fire bellows that feeds the flame.

"Tell her to get lost ... or else," Valjean says.

My husband grinds out, "You are talking about *my wife*." Liam's tone is assertive and protective.

Trying to keep things light and upbeat, I say, "I do yip."

Liam says softly, "Jessica, you have a very pleasant voice."

"Oh well, thank you. I'm not really a singer, unless in the car with the windows down. In fact, that helped me get through the long drive to Cobbiton from Los Angeles."

But my rambling is lost as the guys face off.

Valjean spits, "Tell her to zip it or I'm going to shut her up if you don't—"

I watch the hurtful words coming out of Valjean's thin-lipped little mouth and then he disappears. I mean, not really. There's no wizardry involved. More like Liam levels him. No punches are thrown, but he shoves him down, making him sit and shut up.

"I'm done with you lording over my life, making me pay for something that wasn't my fault."

And there it is. He finally said it.

Valjean tries to get to his feet. Liam holds him in place with one hand.

"No, listen to me. I've punished myself for years. Nothing you can do to me will hurt worse than what I've caused myself. I've taken your abuse on the ice, physically and the comments you've made about Hendrix."

By now, a crowd has started to gather, including Liam's brother. "What's going on?"

"Liam is having a therapy session," I whisper.

A few of the other Knights must take notice and clear out the nosy nellies.

Liam frowns. "I'm done. It's over. I'm truly sorry about that night. That you lost your sister."

Hendrix moves to intervene, but I grip his arm, mostly because I need something to hold on to and the brothers are about the same size. Plus, I think Liam needs this moment without interference as well-meaning as it might be.

He continues, "But it doesn't do either one of us any good reliving it."

"You have no idea," Valjean growls.

"You're right. I don't. But I was there. It was icy. Franklin said he was okay to drive. We didn't have any reason not to believe him. Marci made him promise to go slow. He did even though she kept tickling his ear and kissing his neck from the backseat. She wasn't wearing her seatbelt. Then we hit a slick patch. He lost control. I've played it over and over in my mind.

Traded places. Wished that it had been me." Liam's voice strains.

My heart breaks for him, for both of them and for what they went through.

Liam glares at Valjean. "When we got in the car, Franklin told everyone to put on their seatbelts. No exceptions. He specifically reminded Marci. She said *you* never made her when you drove her and picked her up from school."

Valjean's face turns red and then his eyes dissolve with liquid and he presses them shut.

I quickly realize that he's been putting his guilt onto Liam, and Liam has been turning his guilt onto himself. It's too much to ask for them to hug it out, but Liam does extend his hand to help his adversary to his feet.

Hendrix claps Liam's shoulder. "You okay, bro?"

He nods, then turns back to Valjean. "Now, apologize to my wife," Liam says in a tone that suggests the Titans player won't be okay if he doesn't say he's sorry.

Valjean mutters, "Sorry."

The guys nod at each other and Valjean whisks down the hallway.

I call after him, "Thanks and have a great night! Good luck next season. Break a—" I wince. "I mean, don't break anything. That's a theater term."

The guys chuckle. Hendrix gives his brother a bro hug and then I get a bear hug.

"I was wrong about you guys," he whispers before letting me go and leaving us for Colette. Did he see our marriage of convenience for what it was ... and what it is now?

When Liam and I get outside, it's warm, almost summer. I let out a long-held breath.

Liam is quiet on the drive back to the loft.

When we park, I say, "Thanks for sticking up for me."

He stiffens. "Don't ever think you deserve anything less."

"Ironic to have Mr. Meanie telling *meanies* to leave me alone."

"You don't win by being nice."

"Bullies always lose."

"Are you saying I'm a bully?"

"You can be rude."

Liam cuts the engine. "How do you propose I dealt with Valjean? He's been tormenting me and then he brought it to you. Not on my watch."

"You could've called him to talk about it before it—"

"Jessica, I've done everything short of writing the guy a love letter."

"Oh."

"Also, I'm not mean." He pouts.

"No?"

"I'm direct."

"You can be impolite."

"Clear."

"Abrupt."

"It's called using leverage, negotiating."

"At times, you're brutally honest."

"You're brutally friendly and upbeat."

I twist my hand so my palm faces the ceiling. "Why is that a problem?"

"Because sometimes it's forced, not real."

"So you're saying I'm fake?" I fold my arms in front of my chest.

"No, but not always honest."

"Maybe I'll change your name from Mr. Meanie to Mr. Cynical."

"It's like you wander around blindfolded, playing pin the

tail on the donkey when there are people who want to touch your Bundt or—"

I almost laugh, but instead say, "And you're blindfolded carrying a stick, trying to bash a piñata."

He almost smirks because he knows I'm right. "Sometimes it's like being blasted with a firehose of confetti."

"And that's bad?"

He exhales and leans over to face me, eyes serious yet imploring. "I just don't want to see guys like Henri Valjean try to take you down."

"I thought you two made up."

"But he told you to shut up."

"I forgive him. It was in the heat of the moment."

Liam's mouth hardens. "Let me be clear, abrupt, rude, whatever you want to call it. No one talks to my wife with anything short of respect." His tone suddenly softens as if he realizes something. "Including me."

"Oh," is all I can say to that. Glad he came to his senses.

We're both quiet as the engine ticks. We get out of the car but don't go inside. Rather, Liam lingers on the sidewalk. Like the times I'd hear that I was being moved to another home, I'm afraid he's going to tell me it's time for me to leave. My stomach twists with knots as disappointment and fear well up inside.

He scratches his temple. "I don't like the idea of you hurting ... or denying that something hurts."

"I'm not the one who plays defense for a pro hockey team."

"I mean the other kind of hurt. The invisible type you mentioned once."

"Like carrying around guilt for years and years."

"Or shame. Or thinking that you're not lovable. Feeling lonely."

I swallow the lump in my throat. "In that case, Liam, will you talk to me like you love me?"

A long, long beat passes when he says more with his eyes than he's ever said with words. "Yes, but also, how about I show you?" He steps closer.

I lift a shoulder in casual confirmation while my heart slams against my ribs because Liam's blue-gray eyes are on me, saying one thing.

He wants me.

Threading his fingers through mine, he draws me into him and the space between us disappears. Before our mouths meet, he plants his lips on the inside of my wrist, then in that little dip in my collarbone, then he tickles my neck with his breath as he trails kisses from under my jaw to behind my ear, and to my temple.

The little tug inside me grows and my breath turns erratic.

Liam's hands land on my lower back. I tug on his shirt.

My cheek brushes his stubble.

At last, our mouths meet. The kiss heats between us, sending the swizzles from my head to my toes.

Liam gently cups my jaw and I twine my fingers into his hair. There's no denying our physical chemistry. I mean how could there not be, at least for me, given #MrDarcysAbs? However, it goes deeper now. So does the kiss.

We were both loners and while he made himself an island, I got lost in the crowd, surrounding myself with people like the Coogans who didn't really care. I was afraid to be alone. Liam was afraid to let people in. We weren't that different after all.

As we settle into the kiss, maybe we're exactly right for each other.

It took a rude awakening and a return home for me to prioritize quality friendships over trying to prove that I was worthy of them. For Liam, it took losing sleep to see that building quality relationships are less risky than being alone.

And all of that somehow worked, in a clumsy way, to bring

us together. I feel the pounding of Liam's heart, for me. His hands are on me, his mouth. He's mine and I'm his.

At some point, all these thoughts disappear, so do my limbs, skin, bones, gone along with complete awareness. Poof. I melt into my man's arms and I'm a puddle.

I only surface from the bliss that is this kiss when I feel something change with the press of Liam's lips to mine. It's then I realize that he's smiling against my mouth. A big, happy smile. It's the one I didn't even realize I was waiting for.

I whisper, "Me too."

A laugh rumbles through his chest.

Communication is vital, whatever it looks, sounds, or feels like. Turns out, I rather like how Liam *isn't* using his words.

Gripping me close, we make out some more on the sidewalk, in the soft night with the stars twinkling above.

When we part, I say, "With all that talk about confetti, piñatas, and pin the tail on the donkey, it sounds like we need to throw a party."

"What are we celebrating?"

"Us."

"Will there be cake?" he asks.

"Yes, Liam, yes."

"So are we communicating now, finally?" he asks.

"I would say so."

He says, "I have one more thing I'd like you to know."

"That you want me to clean up my hair from the sink and stop leaving water glasses everywhere? I'm working on it."

"No, that I love when you fold my laundry, make the bed, and tidy up the kitchen at the end of the day. I feel taken care of." He clears his throat. "I feel loved ... and—" His hands move and he speaks and signs, "I love you."

The truth of his words and how he shows them to me are brighter than sunshine. They fill me and warm me.

"I've never loved anyone other than Grandma Dolly and KJ. But this is different."

He lifts his eyebrows.

"I love you, too. I love when you wrap your arms around me. When you ask about my day, make me tea, when you fix things."

"Yeah?"

"I really love it when you sign. There are lots of ways to communicate."

"I'm ready to learn all of them."

We kiss again and I feel so very loved.

•

EPILOGUE
LIAM

JESSICA SAYS A SLEEPY, "GOOD MORNING," when I come in from my run. With her insomnia gone, lately, it seems like she's making up for lost time.

KJ is not a professional sleeper in his big boy bed, and when I checked he and Ranger were already awake.

He recently had the first cochlear surgery to enhance his ability to hear alongside speech therapy, and has his own language with Ranger—they're best buddies. He also has loads of friends at nursery school and is perfectly at home with his cousins.

Holding a mug of coffee aloft, I pass it to Jessica as she sits up in bed and kiss her on the forehead.

"Hey, sleeping beauty. I'm going to hit the shower. Big day today."

"I'm shocked KJ isn't in here bouncing on the bed with anticipation."

He was telling Ranger about the party.

She chuckles and we spend the next couple of hours preparing for the gathering. It would've been perfect if we could've done it halfway between Mother's Day and Father's Day, but we're well into summer and didn't want to wait any longer now that we wrapped things up with the Coogan's and Jessica signed the adoption paperwork.

We have a piñata, pin the tail on the donkey, and lots of mini Bundt cakes.

Dolly and my parents are the first to arrive, followed by my siblings, with a slow filtering in of the guys and their families from the team.

KJ and Ranger race around with all the kids and I bring Jessica another coffee but notice she doesn't drink it. Maybe she's less of a caffeine fiend now that she's been sleeping better.

We insisted that guests don't bring gifts, but there is something special that I want to present to Dolly. Along with Redd, Hayden, Pierre, Mikey, Grady, 'Bama, and a few others, I say and sign that there's a surprise for her.

Taken aback, she plants her hand on her chest then signs, "Me?"

Jessica bounces on her toes as I reveal a large, flat, wrapped rectangle.

Her eyes widen as she tears the paper and sees a framed team photo with all of our signatures. On a little plaque along the bottom, it says, *We're your number one fan!* At the end of the season, she gave us each a handmade Knights fleece blanket. This prompted Jessica and me to make good on a promise.

In thanks, Dolly hugs each one of us. As she moves down the line, I realize that she's surreptitiously testing everyone's abs. This gets me laughing and when she reaches me, I get a long hug. When she pulls away, she signs, "You have the best abs." Then she pats me on the cheek before she and Grannie Bell disappear—probably to discuss the abs investigation and nibble on some fudge my grandmother smuggled in from Canada.

Jessica glows among the children, showing them how to play a balloon game. The second she's done, and the chaos begins, I lace my arm around her waist, drawing her out of the fray.

Hendrix sidles over and lifts his drink, hesitating as if conflicted before saying, "My genuine well wishes to the happy couple."

I narrow my eyes.

Jessica, likely not privy to my sense that my brother knew our marriage was originally for convenience, innocently asks, "Whatever do you mean?"

"You're the real deal."

She winks.

He swishes his mouth from side to side. "I'm still considering payback. Soggy skates. Lumpy oatmeal. Missing keys," he says, naming different pranks we've played on each other over the years.

I explain a few to my wife.

Hendrix blurts, "Glue."

My eyebrow arches. "Glue? What do you mean glue?"

He chuckles.

Jessica, as smiley as ever today, wears one that's different from the others I've seen. It's almost, dare I say, mischievous. "Hendrix, I'd be careful. I've lived with a dozen families, meaning I have a deep bag of party tricks to draw from."

The family goofball's eyes widen. "You mean pranks?"

She takes my hand and leads me away from the group. In a low voice, she says, "What are the rules?"

"Remember? We don't have those anymore."

"No, I mean in your family for pranks."

A smile slides across my face. "Jessica, are you a private prankster?"

She shimmies a little.

"What else don't I know about you?"

"That I like when you call me Jessica. Everyone calls me Jess and when you use my full name, I feel like I'm all yours. That it's our special thing."

"You are special." I dust my nose with hers but before we can press our mouths together, we're bombarded with balloons.

THE PARTY WAS a hit and KJ and Ranger are curled up in bed, totally wiped out. Jessica looks a little tired herself and I lead her from the kitchen where she's putting some things away to the living room.

"Sit."

She tilts her head and lifts an eyebrow.

"Please."

She does so and I bring her feet into my lap, rubbing them.

"Oh. I could get used to this. Thank you." She moans a little as I get a good spot on her heel.

Lying on the couch, she says, "I'm glad I no longer live with the fear that everyone is going to leave me. That I need to play a role in order to be loved and that you're not burdened with the belief that you weren't worthy of a relationship and had to focus only on hockey. You can have both. Hockey and me."

Her candor surprises me. "I love you. Always will."

She sits up and asks, "When did you start liking me?"

I think about this for a moment. "The Bundt cake."

"One taste and you were hooked? Good to know."

"No, when your phone auto-corrected to butt cake."

She laughs. "Good to know I got you with humor."

"Actually, it may have been in line at the Busy Bee."

"I'm quite sure you hated me from the start."

I correct, "I hated myself. Not you. Jessica, I loved you the moment I laid eyes on you."

She slides next to me on the couch and rests her head on the little crook between my arm and chest. After a moment, she sniffles. "I never cried in front of people before you, the guy most people would've assumed didn't tolerate tears."

"I don't ... except yours. And KJ's, but I'm glad I could help."

"You helped me too."

"To cry? Says the guy with one feeler."

"Like antennae?"

She giggles.

"I feel lots of things, especially for you."

A long sigh escapes, lifting and lowering my chest.

"I thought we were too different."

I nod. "Optimistic versus cynical."

"Surly versus sunny."

I say, "Maybe some of your infectious enthusiasm and warmth rubbed off on me."

"Maybe we complement each other."

"Just don't start shoving people into Plexiglass."

"I am learning to skate."

I chuckle. "Terror on blades."

"I can't imagine had I married Rexlan. Every day with you is like the first day of the rest of my life."

I squeeze her close.

She says, "Are we going to tell our kids we met because I had to pee?"

A low, rumbling laugh rips through me. Getting to my feet, I help Jessica to hers. "I got you something."

"Me?"

I lead her to a shelf holding a box with a bow. Jessica unwraps it to reveal a record player.

She jumps up and down. "This is so thoughtful. Thank you."

I get a big hug and then she puts on a record. It's an older band, maybe from the fifties or sixties, but I recognize the first song from our wedding.

"Can I have this dance?" I ask.

She beams a smile and we slow dance in the living room. The stars in the sky glint off the glass and dapple the wood floor with shimmers.

When the song changes, Jessica leans back and says, "I got you something too."

Both my eyebrows lift.

She bites her lip, trying to suppress her smile, then she squishes up her face as if barely able to contain herself. "I mean, technically, it's for both of us. KJ too. Like, could be for all of humanity or at least the NHL. You just never know."

Slowly, I say, "Jessica, what is it?"

She takes my hand and presses it against her belly.

"Don't tell me you started an account #MrsDarcysAbs."

She laughs.

My jaw drops. "That's why you haven't been drinking so much coffee. That's why you're glowing."

She nods.

I wrap my arms around her, around the mother to our baby and KJ, around my wife, and whisper, "I love you."

She signs back the same and adds, "And your family."

"Our family." Then, with what's sure to be a twinkle in my eye, I say, "Just wait until Christmas."

HOCKEY ROSTER
TEAMS, CHARACTERS, POSITIONS & MORE

The Nebraska Knights are a fictional NHL team in addition to a team roster that includes:

- The Los Angeles Lions
- Empire State Kings
- Carolina Storm
- Nebraska Knights
- OK Thunder (Oklahoma)
- Wisconsin Warriors
- Denver Blizzard
- Cascades PNW/Washington
- Pittsburg Generals
- Rhode Island Royals
- Reno Rebels
- St. Louis Liberators
- Ottawa Outlaws
- Utah Mustangs
- Toronto Titans
- Boston Breakers

- Miami Swashbucklers
- Texas Rangers

The players and their positions, which rotate across seasons:

- Head Coach: Tommy Badaszek (featured in all books)

- Assistant coach: Vohn Brandt, with Gracie in *My Secret Book Boyfriend*

Centers:

- Miguel Cruz, with Juniper in A *Very Hockey Thanksgiving*

- Jack Bouchelle, with Ella in *His Jersey*

Left Wings:

- Hayden Savage, with Delaney in *Stupid Cupid*
- Carson Crane, with Bailey Porter in *Skating into Fake Dating*

Right Wings:

- James Reddford, with Whitney in *Redd, Whit & Blue*

Defensemen:

- Ted 'The Bear' Powell, with Harlow in *Love at First Skate*

- Pierre Arsenault, with Cara in *The Kiss Class*

- Grady Federer, with Heidi *The Ex Puck Bunny*

- Liam Ellis, with Jessica in *My Wife*

Goalies:

- Beaumont Hammer, with Margo in *Margo and the Good Luck Beau*

- Hudson 'Robo' Roboveitchik, with Leah *Her Goal*

Arena: The Ice Palace, Cobbiton, Nebraska

Colors: Silver, black, and red.

Cheers as shouted by fans and performed by the "Ice Maidens," the Knights' hype team:

"Knights of the Round Rink, conquer, rule, and turn the ice pink."

"We side with Silver!"

"Stronger than steel, hotter than the sun, the Knights don't stop until they get the job done."

Official Social Media: @KnightsNation

A LOVE NOTE FROM ELLIE

With a heart full of gratitude, I want to thank everyone who has visited Hockey Town and is rooting for the Knights!

Additionally, a great big thank you to Wenonah my alpha reader for this story with extra TLC for KJ and Dolly.

Gigi, for being the best critique partner for not falling out of your chair when I mentioned the word count (I think the longest book on record for me!)

Jane your hockey enthusiasm, beta reads, and poetic book summaries are outstanding!

To Paula for calling me out on how many times I used the words "Grump and mutters."

My ARC team, who read early versions with such care and honesty. Your thoughtful feedback and excitement is appreciated.

And to YOU, dear reader, having reached the end. Stories come to life between the writer and reader, and without you, these characters would've remained in my head with Liam putting me in a bad mood and Jess getting on my nerves. Instead, they got their HEA! Thank you for giving them a home in your imagination and for choosing to spend your precious time in their world.

There will definitely be TWO more installments in the Love in Hockey Town series, and they really could be part of the Holiday series except they don't center on a specific holiday.

If you want more hockey romcom and haven't already read the others, check 'em out:

Stupid Cupid

Redd, Whit & Blue

The Kiss Class

Margo & the Faux Good Luck Beau

A Fool for April

The Ex-Puck Bunny

A Very Hockey Thanksgiving

Love at First Skate (Tie-In)

The Secret Book Boyfriend (FREE—see my gift to you in a page or two)

Thanks again for reading and I hope to see you between the pages.

♥Ellie

P.S. If you loved this story, please consider leaving a review. Thank you!

ABOUT THE AUTHOR

Ellie Hall is a USA Today bestselling author. If only that meant she could wear a tiara and get away with it ;) She loves puppies, books, and the ocean. Writing sweet romance with lots of firsts and fizzy feels brings her joy. Oh, and chocolate chip cookies are her fave.
Ellie believes in dreaming big, working hard, and lazy Sunday afternoons spent with her family and dog in gratitude for God's grace.

Let's Connect

Do you love sweet, swoony romance?
Stories with happy endings?
Falling in love?

Please subscribe to my newsletter to receive updates about my latest books, exclusive extras, deals, and other fun and sparkly things, including a FREE eBook, the *The Secret Book Boyfriend*!

Get your free copy here: www.elliehall.com 🩶

Made in United States
North Haven, CT
20 June 2025

69999976R00240

Made in the USA
Middletown, DE
19 December 2024